Riding High

Emma Boling has been heavily involved in the Australian racing industry for many years. She has raced and bred numerous horses and has been fortunate enough to win both Group and Listed races. Emma is a committee member of the Moonee Valley Racing Club and Thoroughbred Breeders Victoria. She was awarded Racing Victoria's Woman of the Year in 2002. *Riding High* is her first novel.

Riding High

Emma Boling

MICHAEL JOSEPH
an imprint of
PENGUIN BOOKS

MICHAEL JOSEPH

Published by the Penguin Group
Penguin Group (Australia)
250 Camberwell Road, Camberwell, Victoria 3124, Australia
(a division of Pearson Australia Group Pty Ltd)
Penguin Group (USA) Inc.
375 Hudson Street, New York, New York 10014, USA
Penguin Group (Canada)
90 Eglinton Avenue East, Suite 700, Toronto, Canada ON M4P 2Y3
(a division of Pearson Penguin Canada Inc.)
Penguin Books Ltd
80 Strand, London WC2R 0RL, England
Penguin Ireland
25 St Stephen's Green, Dublin 2, Ireland
(a division of Penguin Books Ltd)
Penguin Books India Pvt Ltd
11 Community Centre, Panchsheel Park, New Delhi – 110 017, India
Penguin Group (NZ)
67 Apollo Drive, Rosedale, North Shore 0632, New Zealand
(a division of Pearson New Zealand Ltd)
Penguin Books (South Africa) (Pty) Ltd
24 Sturdee Avenue, Rosebank, Johannesburg 2196, South Africa

Penguin Books Ltd, Registered Offices: 80 Strand, London, WC2R 0RL, England

First published by Penguin Group (Australia), 2009

10 9 8 7 6 5 4 3 2 1

Text copyright © Emma Boling 2009

The moral right of the author has been asserted

All rights reserved. Without limiting the rights under copyright reserved above, no part of this publication may be reproduced, stored in or introduced into a retrieval system, or transmitted, in any form or by any means (electronic, mechanical, photocopying, recording or otherwise), without the prior written permission of both the copyright owner and the above publisher of this book.

Cover design by Deborah Billson © Penguin Group (Australia)
Text design by Anne-Marie Reeves © Penguin Group (Australia)
Cover images by Photolibrary
Typeset in Fairfield by Post Pre-Press Group, Brisbane, Queensland
Printed and bound in Australia by McPherson's Printing Group, Maryborough, Victoria

National Library of Australia
Cataloguing-in-Publication data:

Boling, Emma.
Riding high / Emma Boling.
9781921518058 (pbk.)

A823.4

penguin.com.au

To Neville and Mum
And to every horse I've had the pleasure of owning

Prologue

The soft grey of first light crept through a chink in the heavy curtains. Abdul Aniza threw off the bedcovers and slipped his feet into a pair of worn leather boots. He briefly touched the twisted mahogany support of the four-poster bed, never wishing to take such luxury for granted. The smooth, perfectly carved wood reminded him of the hours he had spent as a boy paring away at sticks with his father's knife.

He picked up that same knife, now worn with age, and clasped it in a hand still clammy from the horror of his recurring nightmare. Under the wide desert sky studded with countless stars, the presence of horses kept the dreams at bay, but here in the claustrophobic comfort of his room they crowded the pillow.

Floorboards creaked as Abdul walked down the darkened passageway and stairs, stopping briefly to fling on a heavy coat and cashmere scarf before emerging into the crisp winter morning. He paused to let a vixen slink back into the shadows. He was surprised to see her scavenging so close to the house, as the snow had been mild that year and only a light powdering remained on the grass.

Another occupant of the manor stirred at the sound of Abdul's boots crunching on the gravel path outside. Prince Bahir stretched leisurely and stroked the soft skin of his companion, a raven-haired model, who began to awaken, her thick eyelashes fluttering against alabaster skin. Usually Bahir joined the stud manager on his morning walk around the paddocks, but not today. Not while this beauty lay beside him.

She stirred again, and Bahir drew her warm body into his embrace. 'Good morning, lover,' she whispered. He kissed her forehead and ran his fingers lightly across her perfect breasts to see if she would respond. The model stretched and rolled onto her back, allowing Bahir's hand to explore further under the covers.

Abdul leaned on the post-and-rail fence and watched as bleary-eyed groomsmen led eager yearling colts to the paddock gate, the youngsters twitching in readiness to stretch their muscles over open ground after the warmth of the stables. A piece of paper folded in Abdul's pocket identified each of the horses, but it was there out of habit, not necessity. As stud manager and director of Eclipse Stud's global racing and breeding operations, Abdul knew each horse on the property by sight.

The horses were released into the paddock, and for a moment they sought out the affirmation of the herd, nose to nose in greeting, each colt aware of its position in the paddock hierarchy. Two of the colts jostled around the others, nipping and rearing in an instinctive reminder of dominance, before some hidden signal sent them off at full gallop.

The only chestnut in the pack allowed the dark band of bays to outpace him, daring them to set a challenge worthy of his speed, then dashed past them all while they strained to keep up. Wheeling around, the pack crossed the paddock on a diagonal, manes and tails streaming. The chestnut spun them around once more and they galloped down a slope towards Abdul, rearing in the air to halt forward momentum as they reached the gate.

Snorting and blowing plumes of visible breath into the cold air, the rabble of yearlings with their rough winter coats milled around in front of him like a gang of teenage boys. The chestnut colt broke away and approached, nodding a greeting, as Abdul reached over the fence to stroke his handsome head.

For a moment their noses touched, and then suddenly the colt turned and pushed through the pack, taking off around the paddock once more as the rest tried to keep pace. Even at this age his tremendous length of stride and outstretched neck showed the natural speed and balance of his action. But it was the fire in the eyes that made a true champion. Abdul and Prince Bahir had already named him Bismarck.

1

Royal Ascot, England

Crowds of elegantly dressed people streamed through the gates of Ascot Racecourse as Abdul arrived. Looking dignified in the obligatory morning suit and top hat, Abdul deliberately turned away from the people and walked across to the horse stalls to check on his crew. Today, if fortune favoured, the powerful chestnut Bismarck would end his illustrious racing career just as he had begun it – in a blaze of glory.

The four-year-old had proved his champion status and was ready to enter the next phase of his career. Despite his good temperament, Bismarck was beginning to challenge his handlers and riders with aggressive behaviour typical of a stallion. He would soon retire to Eclipse Stud a multiple Group One race winner and pass on his genetic inheritance to the next generation of foals.

Bismarck pawed at the hard ground when he recognised Abdul striding across the Royal Enclosure garden. Abdul responded briefly to the staff's greetings, then turned his attention to the stallion, who immediately lowered his head and nuzzled him in the chest. Abdul stood for a moment, holding Bismarck's great head in his arms. The spell was broken by trainer John Gallows, who led a bay gelding into the next stall to be saddled up. Bismarck bared his teeth in disapproval and the younger horse flinched and shifted as far away as the stall constraints allowed.

'How is he?' Abdul asked, nodding towards Bismarck.

'A bit toey . . . I think he just wants to get it over and done with and stick his head back in the bucket,' John replied while throwing a saddle cloth over the gelding's back. 'Never get between Bismarck and his feed,' he joked.

Bismarck pricked his ears and snorted quietly as a brass band struck up a rousing march to herald the imminent arrival of Her Majesty, Queen Elizabeth II.

Nothing could stop Darcy Ambrose-Taylor from attending Royal Ascot – not the sun that was beating down and making him shift uncomfortably in his elegant morning suit, not the tyrannical travelling distance between Australia and England, and most certainly not the traffic jam crawling up Ascot High Street. Darcy glanced at the time on the dashboard. Just fifteen minutes to go. He had never missed the first race of this time-honoured carnival held over five glorious days in June, and today would be no exception.

'I'll jump out here, Roger, and walk the rest of the way.' He was already halfway out the door despite the car's slow progress. 'I'll ring at the end of the day. Are you watching in the pub?'

'Wouldn't miss it, sir. There's a group of us these days, meet in the same place each year.' Roger spun around and grabbed something from the back seat. 'I think you'll be wanting this?' He grinned and held the top hat out the open window.

'Lifesaver.' Darcy grinned back and popped the top hat on his head, giving it a tap. 'Let's hope I've still got it at the end of the day,' he called back as he paced quickly towards the main gates, barely 300 metres away.

Darcy threaded his way through the crowds. He was keen on an Australian-bred horse in the first race at big odds and wanted to reach the tote before they jumped. A beautiful woman showing off a curvaceous figure in a green dress smiled at him from under her upswept brim and Darcy automatically slowed his pace to match hers for a moment, before remembering the time and continuing his dash to the Royal Enclosure.

He sidled into place in the tiered grandstand just as the horses jumped, clutching his betting ticket in one hand and binoculars in the other. His horse ran a creditable third, kicking off his betting pool for the day. He looked around for someone to share his good fortune but found himself surrounded by unfamiliar faces, a common occurrence at the major carnivals, where regulars were outnumbered by the day punters.

There would be a chance to find friends in a moment, but now Darcy needed to honour a personal tradition. He walked back through the lofty grandstand galleria, with escalators soaring through the glass voids, and strode out towards the parade ring. The winning horse and placegetters from the first race were entering the parade ring as he passed, and he noticed Abdul Aniza talking to the Eclipse Stable jockey. Darcy made a mental note to find Abdul shortly and get the lowdown on the Eclipse runners for the day.

Darcy passed the pre-parade ring and into the Royal Enclosure exclusive area. He chatted briefly to his old friend James Gregory, the CEO of the uber-wealthy Hong Kong Jockey Club, as they walked across the gardens, but avoided the row of marquees already teeming with guests, where he was sure to find distractions. Darcy finally arrived at the Pimms tent and ordered a large one, served out of necessity in a plastic cup with ice, orange slices and cucumber. He took a long sip and smiled in satisfaction. Pimms at Royal Ascot was like strawberries and cream at Wimbledon, a tradition that could not be overlooked.

Darcy had been coming to Royal Ascot since he turned sixteen, and this was his fifteenth consecutive year. He sought shade under a tree and took another long sip of his Pimms, reflecting that he'd now been attending for almost half his life. Inspired, he pulled out the race form and glanced through for any omen bets, but the best he could do was Habitual in the fourth – it was tenuous to say the least, but he circled the horse anyway.

Darcy was born rich. Both his mother and father came from Australian squattocracy, and his father, Henry, had astutely invested some of the family fortune into gold mines at the beginning of the great seventies resource boom.

Henry Ambrose-Taylor had developed a passion for horse-racing as a young man. By the time Darcy was old enough to keep his father company at the track, the family had a major thoroughbred stud in Victoria and one in England. Many years later, before the gold boom went bust, Henry shrewdly sold most of his mining holdings, banking the kind of fortune that placed a man in the world's richest list, and the family moved to England. Darcy finished his final two years of school there before going on to Oxford to study economics and management. He led an idyllic life at Balliol College, visiting the family farm, Kirtling Park Stud, on weekends and attending the races and yearling sales with his father. Horses were in his blood.

From the shade, Darcy surveyed the scene. The Royal Enclosure was like stepping back in time to a more leisured society: one that didn't feel the need to cram every waking moment with activity, information or communication. Morning suits and top hats were compulsory for men, and women were required to dress elegantly and wear a hat. Darcy always wore the traditional butter-coloured linen waistcoat to the first day of Royal Ascot.

His brief reverie was disturbed by an insistent vibration in his pocket. Darcy sighed, downed the dregs of his Pimms and answered his mobile.

No matter how many times Darcy visited the parade ring, he always felt the privilege tangibly, as if it were a badge blazoned on his chest. Racing in England was an elite sport – very different to the boys at the local pub setting up a cheap syndicate back home in Australia. The Ascot Racecourse was a mirror to England's class structure, but far away south in the egalitarian colony, anyone who desired could own an ear of a racehorse.

The Queen had the second favourite in the King's Stand Stakes, a top-class Group One sprint over 1000 metres, and was already in earnest discussion with her trainer, but glanced up as Darcy passed. He couldn't help notice how readily she broke into smiles in this environment, surrounded by the horses pacing around with their strappers. The Queen was a horse woman through and through.

'There you are, darling! We knew we'd find you sooner or later.' A tall, slender woman in a Chanel suit, her blonde hair gathered in a sleek ponytail under a cloche hat, kissed Darcy on both cheeks. 'Did Charlie ring you?'

'Georgie! Lovely to see you. Yes, Charlie just called,' said Darcy with a broad smile.

They strolled towards one of the horses whose jockey had just been legged up. The owner, Charlie, the eldest son of a prominent Australian racing family, was standing nearby. 'He looks in good order,' Darcy said, appraising the horse.

'So do you, my friend, very swish. You do scrub up well,' Charlie grinned. Georgina took her husband's arm and the three friends walked into the grandstand.

'God, I'm nervous,' she said. 'Do you think we've got a hope?'

'More than a hope, Georgie! I remind you – Choisir, Takeover Target and Miss Andretti, all Aussie sprinters who were successful in this race.' Darcy was keen to lay a bet so peeled off from his friends by the tote windows. The odds were showing 15 to 1. It was clear Charlie's sprinter had been underestimated, but it won convincingly.

After an hour of celebrations Darcy ducked off to the stables to find Abdul. Even from a distance he could see how uncomfortable Abdul was in his restrictive formal attire.

He knew little of Abdul's background, but because of Darcy's close ties with the family of Sheikh Faisal bin Hashim bin Asad al Azim, Abdul's employer, and their shared love of horses, the two men trusted each other implicitly.

Darcy shook Abdul's hand warmly. 'How's your boy going?' he asked as Bismarck shifted closer as if to join the conversation.

'The horse that can beat him will be the winner,' Abdul responded earnestly.

'That confident? Well, I'll have to send some of my best mares when he comes down to the Hunter Valley. He'll certainly suit them physically,' Darcy paused to admire Bismarck's strength, 'but I'd be interested in your opinion on bloodlines that might provide a breeding nick.'

Abdul smiled. He knew some people found him difficult to talk to, but on the right subject he could talk for hours. 'I'm always happy to discuss pedigrees with someone who knows a thing or two themselves.'

Abdul and Darcy were deep in conversation when someone called Darcy's name. Two men were approaching, and for a moment the sunlight in Darcy's eyes made it impossible for him to differentiate one man from the other, as they were so similar – both were tall and of slim build. But as they neared, Prince Bahir's handsome face broke into a broad grin, while his childhood friend Jalal bin Muntasir remained expressionless behind his sunglasses.

The oldest son of Sheikh Faisal clasped Darcy to his chest then held him at arm's length. 'You wouldn't miss this for the world, would you? It's been too long, my friend, but I'm coming down to your corner of the world soon so you cannot escape me!' Bahir's family came from the oil-rich State of Qatar, a peninsula bordered on one side by Saudi Arabia and on all others by the Persian Gulf. Their fortune was built on Qatar's huge oil and natural gas reserves but the family lived in cosmopolitan Dubai.

For Darcy, Bahir was the brother he never had. From the moment they met, at Oxford, he had felt at home with Bahir, despite their different backgrounds. In the years since leaving university, their friendship had only grown stronger, and had come to link their families too.

Darcy held out his hand to Jalal, who shook it without much enthusiasm, then turned back to Bahir. 'Abdul was just telling me he's quite confident about the race. You'll have to expand that trophy room of yours, or build yourself another palace.'

'We're still trying to catch up with the Ambrose-Taylors – how many times have you won this race? Three? If we win today it takes our tally to two – so watch out,' Bahir joked.

Jalal went to inspect Bismarck. He was lucky enough to race the horse in partnership with Bahir; in fact, they'd had a lot of success with their horses. He reached out to stroke the horse's neck but Bismarck was not in the mood and went to bite. But Jalal, a competent horseman, knew when to duck out of a stallion's way, and Bismarck's teeth clattered shut, missing their mark.

'Come, let's walk to the parade ring,' said Bahir, throwing an arm around Darcy's shoulders, and the two friends ambled away with Jalal walking a pace or two behind.

An errant gust of wind blew Darcy's hat onto the lawn, and as he turned to retrieve it he glanced back at the stables. Abdul was patting Bismarck and the horse dropped his head low and pushed against the man. Abdul cupped his hand around the velvet-soft ear and whispered to the horse. Bismarck lifted his head and touched his muzzle to Abdul's face, breathing deeply, then stamped a foot and nickered gently. A shiver went up Darcy's spine as he caught up with Bahir. There was something uncanny about Abdul's connection with horses.

The Group One Queen Anne Stakes was raced over a mile and Bismarck had proved almost unbeatable over this distance during his racing career. Abdul joined the others in the owners' section of the stands, binoculars trained on the field as the horses surged across the turf. The Ascot track had an imposing rise of twenty-two metres from the lowest point, Swinley Bottom, up to the winning post, and it was here that Bismarck made a move, smoothly accelerating away from the pack. Abdul held his breath as the powerful horse put his ears back in determination, lengthened his stride and stretched out. With nostrils flaring to suck in oxygen he put, two, three, four lengths on the field and thundered to the finish line unopposed. Flying past the post Bismarck pricked his ears and turned his head to the grandstand. For a fleeting moment his eyes connected with Abdul's.

2

Sheikh Faisal's Residence, Mayfair, London

The lingering summer twilight did little to diminish the welcoming glow spilling out into the street from the Mayfair mansion, but the brightest light was inside. Afifah, the treasured daughter of Sheikh Faisal, sparkled like a precious jewel as she played hostess to the distinguished guests arriving for post-race cocktails. Afifah was elegant and charming, and her youthful radiance was dazzling. Held in place by a star-shaped diamond clip, her dark glossy hair hung in waves down her back. Her pale coral Grecian-style chiffon dress showed off her lightly tanned skin, and her green eyes were full of laughter as she listened to stories of the day's racing.

'We missed you today, little princess.' Darcy had snuck up behind her with Bahir while she was engrossed in conversation.

'Darcy! I knew you'd be here!' She threw her arms around his neck, but at a scowl from Bahir quickly changed her greeting to a formal kiss on each cheek. She glanced at her father and was relieved to see he hadn't noticed her indiscretion. 'Tell me everything about today. Did Bismarck win well?'

'Why didn't you join us?' Darcy manoeuvered a glass of champagne and two mineral waters from a tray.

'I wanted to keep my powder dry for the last three days. Ladies' Day is the best – the dresses, the hats . . . And I can't keep up with you boys.'

'It might also have something to do with those impossible heels you insist on wearing.' Bahir looked down at Afifah's Christian Louboutin patent-leather strappy sandals with ten-centimetre heels.

The Sheikh scanned the room, smiling politely at his many eager guests. Suddenly his eye was caught by a new arrival. A beautiful blonde with hair swept up into a smooth chignon had entered on the arm of a French diplomat. She was tall and elegant in a clinging Donna Karan jersey dress in cerise. A single black pearl set with diamonds adorned her long neck and highlighted her fine bone structure. The Sheikh was intrigued.

His current mistress gazed across the room to see what had attracted his attention and bristled, but the Sheikh ignored her. Her constant demands wearied his ego. He was determined to introduce himself to the beautiful blonde as soon as possible.

'Pierre, how good of you to join us,' the Sheikh said as he walked across to the new arrivals and shook hands.

'The delight is all mine. May I introduce my friend Yvonne Green,' Pierre answered smoothly.

'I'm enchanted.' The Sheikh took her hand and stroked her fingers lightly in a gesture not missed by Pierre, who suddenly realised the mistake of bringing such a beauty before his host.

Yvonne smiled at the Sheikh but gently slipped her hand out of his. 'It's a great pleasure to meet you at last, Sheikh. And what a wonderful party.' Now in her late thirties, Yvonne knew she had to organise some financial stability before the onset of her forties saw her overlooked in the scramble for younger women. Pierre was a sweetheart, but the Sheikh? Could she dare to reach so high? Yvonne yearned for the security such a man could bring to her life.

The trio moved into the room to speak to a clique of diplomats, and Yvonne positioned herself so the Sheikh could admire her assets from every angle. A quick glance confirmed he was watching. The outgoing mistress suddenly became all too aware of the situation and flounced off in anger, unnoticed by the Sheikh.

Jalal arrived at the party carrying the race trophy triumphantly. Afifah pretended she hadn't seen him, but Jalal caught her hand before she could weave away through the guests. His face was flushed with longing and pride. 'You look so beautiful tonight, Afifah,' he said, staring intently into her eyes. 'This is for you.' He handed her the trophy.

Afifah glanced uncomfortably at Bahir and Darcy, who were still by her side. 'Thank you Jalal, that's very kind of you.' Her smile faded quickly and she handed the trophy to one of the staff. She turned to Bahir. 'I'm so proud of you, brother, another Group One race under your belt. And you too, Jalal, of course.'

Jalal nodded an acknowledgement to Darcy before drawing Bahir into a conversation about the day's racing. Afifah took the opportunity to whisk Darcy away to meet her university friends, leaving Jalal scowling in their wake. Darcy suddenly found himself surrounded by a bevy of beautiful young women.

Darcy was one of the most eligible bachelors on the scene, and all the girls eyed him eagerly. But their conversation, punctuated by girlish shrieks and giggles, was too much for him and he looked around for rescue. He saw Abdul standing in a far corner. Darcy singled out the two prettiest girls for later and headed Abdul's way, and was soon deep in pedigree discussions. Bismarck would be eased into a new role away from the racetrack by standing the Southern Hemisphere season at Eclipse Stud in the Hunter Valley, Australia, and Darcy was keen to earmark a few broodmares for the first-year sire.

Darcy suddenly saw his father greeting the Sheikh, and taking Abdul with him, weaved through the room, which was becoming crowded as more guests made their way past the security guards at the front gate. As always, his stepmother Julia was the epitome of style, in a simple black cocktail dress with a sparkling diamond collar around her slender throat. The Sheikh, his father and Julia were in animated conversation when Darcy arrived.

'There you are, Darcy!' Henry Ambrose-Taylor beamed at his son. 'For the life of me I don't think I've seen you for more than an hour at a stretch this trip. No time for your old father, eh?' Henry was a good deal shorter than his son and his sandy hair was peppered with grey, giving him a distinguished look.

'Welcome, Darcy.' The Sheikh clasped his hand warmly. 'I trust we'll see more of you tomorrow in our private box?'

Darcy smiled. 'I wouldn't miss it for the world.'

'Well, that's just terrific, I have to spend time with my arch rival in order to see my own son,' Henry said, laughing. The two families were very close, but there was always an edge of competition whenever their stable colours clashed in a race.

'Ah, now we two fathers are complete.' The Sheikh smiled at Bahir as he and Jalal approached. 'Here is my son, and my soon-to-be son-in-law.' He put an arm around Bahir and Jalal. 'Up to mischief, I imagine, after your impressive win today?' The two men laughed. 'But no, I see Jalal is mooning over Afifah as always – your patience will soon be rewarded, son.'

Henry suddenly spied Abdul who was standing off a little from the group. 'Abdul – excellent, just the man I need to talk to.' The two men were quickly engrossed in conversation about breeding.

Out of the corner of his eye, the Sheikh noticed Yvonne moving outside alone and excused himself. The broad terrace that looked out over the garden was filling up as people enjoyed the pleasant air of the summer's night. The Sheikh found Yvonne leaning on the balustrade in a quiet recess. 'Perhaps I can get you another glass of champagne?'

'Pierre is bringing me a drink, thank you.'

'Well, it's been a long time since I have properly caught up with my good friend Pierre. Why don't you both join me in my private box at the track on Thursday? Ladies' Day is always so enjoyable.'

'Not to mention the Gold Cup, the feature race of the whole carnival. My money's on the second favourite,' Yvonne said.

'Ah, so you know something about racing?' The Sheikh was even more intrigued.

'My family has been in horses for generations, it's in my genes.' Yvonne suspected the Sheikh enjoyed the chase as much as he did his racing. She couldn't help responding to his flirtation, finding herself far from immune to his charm or wealth. 'Thank you for the invitation. We would love to drop in for a drink on Thursday.'

Pierre appeared with a glass of champagne for Yvonne and the Sheikh excused himself to greet another group of guests. Afifah, talking to the wife of an American horse breeder close by, gave Yvonne a haughty glare.

'Let's go back in, darling, it's getting a little chilly out here,' Yvonne suggested, taking Pierre's arm as they wandered through the French doors.

A little later by the oyster bar Yvonne turned to find Henry Ambrose-Taylor at her elbow. It had been some time since they'd seen each other, but the old wounds ran deep between them. 'What the hell are you doing here?' he whispered furiously in her ear. 'Have you forgotten our agreement? It's worked very well for years. I don't want you here.' His grip on her arm hurt and she shook him free.

'This isn't about you, Henry,' she hissed back. 'I'm here with my partner, thank you very much.' The chef passed her a plate of oysters and Yvonne turned on her heel and walked away, concealing her rage under a false smile.

3
Ladies' Day, Royal Ascot

The women's best outfits for each season were always firmly reserved for Thursday, come rain, hail or shine, and as a consequence, most men approached Ladies' Day at Royal Ascot with great anticipation.

Darcy began his day with champagne in the car park amongst a contingent of Aussies who gathered there each year. Feeling the warming glow of his first glass, he proceeded through the Royal Enclosure gardens at a casual saunter, enjoying the scenery.

By the time he reached the Sheikh's private box on the third level of the grandstand, most of the other guests were already enjoying the hospitality. 'No points for guessing where you've been,' Henry said, laughing as Julia began wiping a kaleidoscope of lipstick colours from Darcy's cheeks.

The box was beautifully positioned right on the finishing line, and was big enough to hold seventy guests for a stand-up buffet. It was decorated in the Eclipse Stable's famous racing colours of purple and green in a diamond pattern, right down to the cocktail napkins. The buffet table had a purple and green diamond on either side of a magnificent ice sculpture of a rearing stallion, which was slowly dripping into oblivion.

Afifah bounded over to Darcy and left an impression of her own pink lipstick on both his cheeks. Her Pucci print dress in pink, mauve, grey and yellow showed off her slim figure to perfection. Teaming her dress with Oscar de la Renta slingbacks in yellow, and a small, structured grey hat decorated with pink and yellow flowers, Afifah was a picture of Ladies' Day elegance. She turned to her two university friends, who were smiling shyly at Darcy.

'I've known Darcy since I was a little girl. He and Bahir were inseparable at Oxford – they both read at Balliol College.'

'Yes, I'm practically your brother, isn't that right, princess?' Darcy put his arm around Afifah and tickled her chin.

'Hardly.' Afifah scowled and pushed him away.

Darcy was surprised by her reaction; they had always been close. He put his arm around her more lovingly. 'Come on now, where's that dazzling smile? Today is not a day for frowns.'

Despite herself, Afifah smiled and hugged him back. At that moment Bahir and Jalal entered the box and she quickly twisted free.

'Darcy, I wasn't sure if we'd see you much up here today with all the distractions downstairs,' Bahir ribbed his friend. Jalal was studying his form guide and barely acknowledged Darcy's presence.

'What did you study at Oxford?' one of Afifah's friends asked.

'If I recall correctly, you did a major in economics and a minor in pub crawls,' Bahir joked.

'It's true. Luckily you and your sobriety got me out of many a scrape.'

'Jalal missed out on Oxford, didn't you, Jalal?' Afifah said innocently. 'He studied back in Dubai instead.'

Her barb caught well. The colour rose to Jalal's face and he quickly excused himself on the pretext of watching the next field of horses parade.

'That wasn't very nice. You know how sensitive he is about that,' Bahir admonished, but Afifah just shrugged.

'Until I'm his wife, I can say whatever I like,' she said defiantly.

Later in the day Pierre and Yvonne appeared in the Sheikh's private box. Yvonne's striking Roberto Cavalli dress was in a chinoise pattern of deep greens and purples, and she wore a pillbox hat adorned with a pheasant feather sweeping in a dramatic arc. Pierre politely made his way straight to his host, who had already noticed Yvonne's entrance. Eye contact was intense, but the conversation between them brief as the Sheikh and Bahir made their way back down to the parade ring to see their runner in the fifth.

Yvonne surveyed her surroundings with appreciation. A waiter arrived with a flourish of champagne and, thus armed, Pierre led Yvonne to an acquaintance who was chatting to Henry Ambrose-Taylor.

Henry and Yvonne pretended not to know each other as they were introduced, but the hostility between them was almost palpable as Julia joined the group. Henry shifted uneasily from one foot to the other as he chatted to Pierre, but watched Yvonne and his wife talking. His anxiety only increased when Julia called Darcy over.

'Darcy, darling, do come and chat to Yvonne, I think she could do with some younger company,' Julia suggested kindly.

'Most certainly, but only if she'll give me a tip for the next race – my own judgement is obviously impaired today and I have a bit of catching up to do,' Darcy said, smiling amiably. They moved towards one of the large tote screens on the far wall of the box, and without hesitation Yvonne declared that number four would be hard to beat. 'Do you select by form, name or jockey?' Darcy asked.

'Well, the horse has won at this track twice, is well off in the weights and bred on both dam and sire line to relish the distance,' Yvonne answered with a little smile. She could feel Henry's eyes boring into her back.

'I see you know something about racing, then! I'll definitely take your tip.' Darcy excused himself and immediately joined the short queue for the tote outside the box.

Henry took his chance while his son was out of sight, his voice low but icy. 'I'm warning you. Stay away from my wife and stay away from my son.'

'It's lovely to see you too, Henry.' Yvonne beamed at him as if he had just paid her a compliment.

Darcy arrived back from placing his bet and led Yvonne out onto the balcony overlooking the racetrack, but the seats were already occupied by the Sheikh's other guests, forcing them to stand at the back. As all Darcy's attention was focused on the drama unfurling on the track, Yvonne was able to scan his profile subtly. He was exceptionally handsome, with his dark blonde hair and aquiline nose. His olive skin must be from his mother's side, she surmised, thinking of Henry's pale skin. There was something in Darcy's expression that made her heart skip a beat. The resemblance was certainly there. And then he swept back a forelock and turned to her in triumph, a gesture so familiar and dear to her.

'Well, *you* must be pleased with yourself, and *I'm* very impressed. An easy win, although as the Sheikh's horse ran second we might just keep it to ourselves,' Darcy added conspiratorially.

Yvonne looked down at the ticket in her hand and quickly back to the results. She had been too preoccupied to follow the race. 'That was my pick of the day, I'm afraid, so don't expect any more pearls of wisdom from me!'

When the Sheikh arrived back with Abdul and Bahir, he made a beeline for Yvonne, and Darcy graciously stepped aside, realising his intention. But it wasn't long before Pierre began working his way through the guests and their forest of hats in every shape and size to reclaim his prize. As he approached, the Sheikh leaned forward to Yvonne. 'Have lunch with me next week?' he whispered.

'I'd be delighted,' she responded as Pierre took her hand in a desperate bid to hold onto something he had already lost. 'Hello, Pierre darling, I thought you'd forgotten all about me,' she said sweetly, but her gaze was directed at their host.

Darcy found himself standing next to Jalal while looking at the tote odds and enquired politely after his father, Salah al Din.

'Unfortunately my father is not in the best of health,' Jalal said. 'It's nothing serious. I think stress has just worn him down.'

'These are troubled times,' Darcy agreed, deliberately avoiding the GFC tag bandied around in the media. 'I imagine your business is somewhat recession-proof, though? I mean, the world still needs to cart its products across the globe,' he added hastily as Jalal gave him a frosty stare.

'Yes, thank you, I'm sure our business will continue to flourish,' he replied stiffly.

'Although your share portfolio has probably taken a battering like the rest of us, eh?' Darcy hadn't meant to rile Jalal and felt the need to suggest they were all hurting.

Jalal paled. 'I'm not sure what you've heard, Darcy, but we certainly have plenty of reserves to ride out the storm. Please excuse me.'

Jalal made his way out onto the balcony where Afifah was sitting with her girlfriends, and Darcy shrugged. It was always a struggle with Jalal. As young boys Bahir and Jalal had been inseparable and Jalal still guarded that friendship with possessive jealousy. Bahir and Darcy's close friendship was a constant thorn in Jalal's side.

Outside, the field for the main race was beginning to enter the parade ring. The Ascot Gold Cup was a Group One race run over 4000 metres, with prize money of around £250 000, and this year promised to be a stoush between the two main Irish trainers and their famous stables.

Afifah and her friends rushed back into the box. 'Darcy, would you please take us down to the parade ring?' Afifah asked, wide-eyed with excitement.

'I'd be delighted.' It was a good excuse to get back down amongst the action, Darcy thought. 'But first you have to tell me honestly: are you really going to see the horses parade, or am I just parading you girls so everyone can admire your beauty?' He led them out towards the escalators, mindful of the envious stares of less fortunate men.

4

Shipper's Arms Hotel, Geelong, Australia

Dr Clea Reynolds stepped through the doors of a local pub and was greeted by the cheers of her colleagues. Clea was well liked, but usually avoided invitations for work drinks. Tonight, however, was an exception. She was dressed casually, and her long, honey-blonde hair was free from its usual practical ponytail, appropriate for her work as a microbiologist at the Australian Animal Infectious Diseases Laboratory. She wore very little make-up but still managed to look as if she'd stepped straight out of the fashion pages.

Her boss, Dr Glen Collings, was leaving the company to head up a private laboratory in England. It had been an unexpected move and everything had happened very quickly. 'I'm glad you could make it,' he said warmly as he poured Clea a glass of wine. She was the best scientist he had ever trained, and he would miss her.

'I'm still not sure why you have to go at all,' Clea lamented.

'You've got such a great future here – you know you'll be running the joint in a few more years. Everyone thinks so.'

Glen shrugged. 'I'm going and that's final. I want you to be happy for me, Clea.' He drew her to one side of the bar. 'Only I have some bad news and I want you to hear it from me first.'

Clea looked up sharply. This could only mean one thing.

'They've decided to advertise my role externally,' Glen continued sadly. 'I've done everything I can to convince them the best candidate is right under their nose. But you know what Human Resources are like.'

Clea's disappointment was evident on her face. 'Are they even going to consider me?'

'Yes, you're still in the running. This is all my fault. If I stayed —'

'But you're not.' Clea felt like she wanted to go home. She was young, but she knew she deserved this promotion and had foolishly assumed she would be the top pick. Now she would have to fight for it against other candidates.

Glen gave her a squeeze. 'Come on, you're the best person for the job, they know that.'

Clea wasn't comforted, but she buried her worries and gave Glen a big hug. She would miss him. Arms linked, they joined the rest of the scientists and lab technicians in farewell drinks, but her heart wasn't fully in it. She had always been ambitious, and now she felt an opportunity slipping through her fingers.

Later that night Glen stepped out of the bar to answer a phone call. He frowned as he listened to his younger brother.

'I told you, everything will be all right. You just focus on convincing your wife and kids to come home.'

'My debts were so huge and I know you're not a rich man – how did you pay them? And how will I repay you? You've saved my life.' His brother was on the verge of tears.

'There's one simple answer to that – you promised me, no more gambling. If I so much as hear one whisper —'

'You won't, I promise. I'm a new man.'

Glen hung up and took a few deep breaths. He hoped to God his risk paid off. He'd compromised himself personally and professionally, but it was that or see his brother go under forever. Sometimes the bonds of blood could drag you to places you never thought you'd go.

Clea stuck her head out of the bar. 'There you are. They've lined up another round, I'm afraid.' She had a flush of colour in her cheeks and her eyes were bright from one drink too many. There would be a few sore heads at the lab tomorrow. 'Are you all right?' she asked, putting an arm around Glen's shoulder.

'Yes, I'll be just fine,' Glen lied, wondering if life would ever be the same again.

5

Kirtling Park Stud, Newmarket, England

The day dawned in a splendour of blue skies. A light breeze fluttered the emerald-green leaves of the trees that flanked the broad driveway of Kirtling Park Stud, linking boughs to form a canopy. Darcy's head still hurt, despite the hearty breakfast of eggs and bacon with a dash of Worcestershire sauce. Five days of carnival horseracing had taken their toll.

Armed with coffee and a newspaper Darcy found a comfortable nook in the conservatory where he could admire the glorious summer day while waiting for the ache to subside.

Two hours later, dressed in a polo shirt, jodhpurs and boots, he walked briskly to the stables. Thankfully, a groomsman appeared to saddle up a quiet hack that doubled as a lead pony when the yearlings were being broken in or prepared for sale.

The placid horse clip-clopped out of the cobblestone courtyard and Darcy found himself relaxing. He spurred the horse into a trot along the driveway, then turned through the trees and cantered across the grassy expanse, enjoying the sense of freedom. The house stood in the midst of a traditional park with gardens verdant in the summer sun. Surrounding this oasis was the working stud, divided into broodmares and foals to the right of the house, stallions, yearlings and racehorses to the left. A training heath with sloping hills was out behind the estate and paddocks. One day Darcy would inherit it all, but the thought wasn't particularly comforting to him. Growing up, he had always yearned for a brother or sister – someone to keep him company rolling down the hills, or climbing the stately trees, or galloping around on horseback, wild and free. But there was no family with which to share his privileged life, save a few elderly aunts and estranged cousins.

Darcy slowed his pace as he neared the divide between the leisure part of the stud and the working areas. There was no need to frighten the foals. Ranging in age from three to five and a half months old, they lay in the late morning sun in groups, their stubby tails flicking in sleep or to ward off insects, while the broodmares grazed unconcerned at a distance. Darcy walked his horse on a long rein beside the fence line until he found a paddock that had stirred into action.

Darcy dismounted, wrapped the reins around a post and unlatched the paddock gate. Two of the foals skipped off to a safe distance, but three were curious enough for a cautious sniff and when Darcy made no sudden spooky movements, they boldly nipped at his shirt and snuffled his outstretched hand. He admired their spindly-legged conformation before running his hand down the soft coat of a richly coloured bay. When the foal didn't shy away, Darcy gave him a rub at the top of his shoulder until the little colt stretched out his neck and began to gently scratch Darcy's arm in reciprocation. Mutual grooming was an instinctive act in a herd animal, used to create harmony and friendship bonds. When the scratching stopped the colt shook himself, as if to come back from the land of daydreams, and followed Darcy to the gate. Checking the details of the paddock occupants on a sheet of paper inside a plastic cover on the gate, Darcy realised these colts were worth a fortune. With their top-class breeding they were each worth upwards of £200 000, depending on how they grew, but would all probably be closer to the £400 000 mark.

On the working side of the stud, a bunch of yearlings were being handled individually in a sand roll to give them confidence before they were brought in for preparation ahead of the October Tattersalls sales. The yearling manager was trying to get them accustomed to a bit instead of a simple head collar. The squeals of distress from both the unfortunate in the sand roll and his mates in the yards were heart-rending. It wasn't due to anything the patient manager was attempting, it was simply separation stress that made the yearlings call out dramatically.

'Yer big sook, come on, they're just over there.' The yearling manager spun the young animal around so he could see his friends. 'You'd think I was sticking pins in you with all this carry-on. Just get this into your big gob and you'll be back with them in no time.'

Darcy leaned through the post and rails to watch the painless procedure. Once the colt was calm and his mates finally quiet, the young horse readily took the bit in his mouth, champing on it as the manager led him in easy circles. In ten minutes he was back in the yard, but going by his enthusiastic reunion with the other yearlings, it was as if he had been gone a week.

'Time the cheeky buggers were mixed up with others, they're getting a bit clingy,' the manager observed as he picked his second victim.

Darcy's final indulgence for the day was a gallop up the heath track before he returned to the stables. He handed over his horse to a groomsman and strolled towards the house, only to find Bahir's silver Aston Martin glinting in the midday sun at the front entrance.

Darcy dashed up the entrance stairs two at a time, only remembering at the last minute to pull off his dirty boots. He was still hopping around on one foot when Bahir opened the door. 'Don't worry, we've only just arrived.'

'Is Jalal here?' Darcy asked, noticing the plural and trying not to sound disappointed.

'No, he had to go on a business trip – not sure when he'll be back. I'm afraid I've lumbered you with the little sister. She insisted and I just couldn't say no.' Afifah pushed past her brother and kissed Darcy on both cheeks.

'Well, I'm delighted to have such a butterfly deigning to spend time with a couple of old moths. And you look so . . .' Darcy searched for the words.

'Sexy?' Afifah asked hopefully.

'No, I was going to say English country, but now you mention it . . .' Afifah was wearing a pair of beige lightweight jodhpurs, high-heeled ankle boots and a cream short-sleeved silk blouse with ruffles down the front. Her long dark hair had been plaited and hung like a thick silken rope down her back. Looking at her objectively, Darcy supposed the overall effect *was* rather sexy, but he had known her since she was a snotty-nosed child, and he still struggled to see her as a sophisticated young woman.

'I'm starving,' Darcy declared diplomatically. 'I know you two don't ever suffer from hangovers, but I've organised something pretty stodgy to settle my stomach. I needed some plain home cooking after all the fancy catering and restaurant dishes.'

Darcy led them to a table set up in the conservatory, and both Bahir and Afifah laughed when the shepherd's pie with peas and gravy arrived.

After lunch Darcy led his guests over to the stallion paddocks. Three of the five stallions there were soon to enter quarantine before flying to Australia, where they faced more quarantine before commencing Southern Hemisphere stud duty in September. These shuttle stallions worked the stud seasons in both the northern and southern spring, serving a minimum of 200 mares per year, and each horse earned between five and ten million dollars annually.

Eclipse Stud and Kirtling Park Stud sent mares to each other's stallions every year, and Bahir was currently working on the Southern Hemisphere list with Abdul. The purpose of this visit was both social and business, allowing the prince to look over the stallions again and use conformation as one of the selection tools for potential matings. Darcy's stud manager joined them, rattling off stallion statistics and answering all Bahir's queries.

Out of her brother's earshot, Afifah turned to Darcy with a shy smile. 'When do you leave for Australia?'

'I'm only here for another few days, then I'm flying back via Italy.'

'Would you take me out for dinner one night?' she asked suddenly, catching Darcy by surprise.

'Of course I would, princess,' he said lightly. 'We'll settle a date with Bahir.'

Afifah's face fell. 'But . . . he doesn't have to come, does he?'

'I think you know the answer to that already,' Darcy said gently, and led her towards the stallions.

6

Eclipse Stud, Newmarket, England

The Eclipse Stable truck emblazoned with green and purple diamonds drove carefully up to the turning circle in front of the stables. Abdul had plenty of time to walk over from his office, and arrived as the doors were opened and latched into place. A stud groomsman jumped into the truck and emerged leading a striking chestnut horse with a wide white blaze and one white stocking, who walked gingerly down the ramp. Even from a distance Abdul could see the horse was lame.

Alexander the Great was being turned out to pasture for a spell from racing. His stellar career had been temporarily cut short by one bad foot. An inherent weakness in his near forehoof had been compounded by the impact of racing, and as a result his racing shoes were routinely flung into the air during a race. The horse eased himself out of contention each time, as the tender hoof hit the ground unprotected. Glue-on shoes didn't last the distance, and bar shoes applied to give the hoof extra support also went flying like missiles into the turf. His one white hoof caused all the problems and eventually the weakness had created a nasty abscess that was still in the process of healing. In a desperate bid to keep him in training, he had remained in the racing stables for a month while his foot healed, swimming every day to keep up his fitness levels.

Alexander was led straight to one of the many spelling paddocks at the stud. Despite his sore foot, he gave a fine display of equine exuberance as he appreciated his relative freedom after the routine and close quarters of the Newmarket racing stables. While he was still surveying his new domain, a second spelling racehorse was led into the paddock in the hope they would buddy up and keep each other company. Being herd animals, horses were always happier with a companion.

After a moment of mutual nostril-blowing the two horses trotted off in unison, tossing their heads and springing up into the air at each other. Alexander stopped in the middle of the paddock and tested out the pasture while his grey paddock buddy galloped one lap with tail held high before bouncing to a stop by his new friend.

Peace had descended once again for Abdul after the mad excitement of the racetrack. Swapping his morning suit for jeans and a work shirt, he was back in his domain. He leaned over the paddock fence in the sunshine until the new arrivals picked their way over for a pat. Alexander had been raised on the stud but it had been a while since man and horse had connected.

Abdul gently blew into the horse's velvety nostrils and they remained together nose to nose for a couple of minutes before the horse put his head down for a scratch, their bond rekindled. Alexander had been a breeding experiment for Abdul, who had imported the dam from the USA sight unseen to try out a nick with one of Eclipse's new stallions.

Sight unseen was often a risk when purchasing horses, but the bay mare that had emerged from the horse truck had taken Abdul's breath away. She was as near perfect a horse as you could hope for, with a lovely feminine head and kind eye, straight, well-proportioned legs, a strong shoulder and powerful hindquarters. Abdul had been quietly very pleased with himself.

The mating nick had worked as Abdul hoped. Alexander the Great showed promise from an early age and was Group One-placed early in his three-year-old season. He marked out full black type for his dam on her pedigree page by winning a Group Two race and a Group One, but his hoof interfered before he could show his true colours. Abdul took a personal interest in his recovery.

A few days later Abdul was deep in the tenth generation of a comparative mating for one of the stud's high-performing mares, when he noticed the stud farrier striding purposefully to the spelling paddocks. A quick check of the stud roster suggested it was an unscheduled visit. Curious, Abdul saved the pedigree and shut down his computer.

The farrier, Andrew McPhee, had been working his wonders with horses' feet and straightening foals' legs for close on thirty years. Consequently, there were very few ailments and abnormalities that he hadn't seen. Abdul knew where he must be heading. Sure enough, he found Andrew in the paddock holding up Alexander's foot and squeezing the hoof with a pair of metal pincers. The horse stood placidly for a while, then flinched in pain.

'His heel's worn away,' Andrew muttered. 'They've just kept nailing the shoe into a thinner and thinner hoof wall until there was no way the shoe could stay on under impact. Look,' he tapped the heel of the suspect hoof and Alexander pulled his foot away. 'He's sore because there's nothing to support him, and this hoof is as brittle as plaster.'

'What do you recommend?' Abdul asked.

'Patience, which is not necessarily a natural quality in my young colleague over on the racing side; no shoes until this hoof has grown down healthy, and I think we'll apply a bit of my secret hoof oil. It can work miracles, but it's got to be applied every day.'

'I can see to that personally,' Abdul suggested.

'Great, I'll drop a pot of the stuff over this afternoon.' Andrew gave Alexander a hearty pat on the rump as the two men headed for the gate. 'What's his proposed schedule?'

'We'll need him racing again by September.'

Back in his office, Abdul went online in search of a supplement to assist with hoof growth. He knew exactly what he needed, remembering his first sight of the Persian Gulf as vividly as if it were yesterday. The sea was like a sapphire glistening beyond the haze of the desert. Abdul had closed his eyes and counted to twenty while his horse shifted its hoofs uncomfortably in the hot sand. When he opened them again the blazing blue sea was still there – it was no mirage. With a joy barely suppressed he looked to the horse master for permission.

'Go on, my boy. Get your feet wet.' The old man gestured towards the expanse with encouragement.

Abdul spurred on his tired mount and cantered over the last dunes to the beach, hanging on for dear life as the horse continued on into the water. Abdul slipped off his horse with a splash and dived into a wave, coming up laughing and spluttering from the unexpected taste of salt in his mouth. He was thirteen years old, and his parents had been dead for three years.

The old horse master sent him to collect seaweed, as much as he could find of the rich green kelp, hacking it off underwater with his father's knife. The seaweed was spread out on the sand overnight to dry, and in the morning they bundled it up and strapped it to Abdul's saddle. Long after the miraculous body of water had faded into the distance, Abdul kept craning around for one last look.

Returning to the present, Abdul shook his head lightly to clear the memories. He needed to find good-quality dried kelp, preferably whole so he could grind it into a powder. Added to apple cider vinegar and sprinkled over Alexander's feed, it should stimulate strong hoof growth.

Treating Alexander became a daily ritual. At 10.30 every morning Abdul would take Alexander's proffered hoof between his knees and pick the dirt out with his father's knife, which had not been out of hand's reach since Abdul was a boy. After checking Alexander's progress and his reaction to pressure, Abdul painted the strong-smelling oil onto the hoof, then gave the horse a scratch and spoke to him in Arabic of desert legends, fierce sandstorms and gentle winds.

7
Aboard the Sea Spirit, Nice, France

The French Riviera was the luxury playground to beat all playgrounds. The rich, the very rich and the wannabe rich all gathered here over summer, eyeing each other from the decks of their palatial boats and yachts. They rubbed shoulders in the casinos, trumped each other for coveted tables in chic restaurants and mingled occasionally with the ordinary folk who came to watch the spectacle.

Antonia shielded her eyes from the strong light reflecting off the water. She could just make out the ornate white facade and soft pink turrets of Nice's famed Hotel Negresco and the row of palm trees marking the Promenade des Anglais. Despite the warming sun she shivered slightly, wishing she were anywhere but here.

The swell hadn't been very noticeable on deck, but when she made her way carefully down the galley steps into a well-equipped kitchen, the distinct rise and fall of the boat became suddenly apparent. Two of the clients were talking in the galley and allowed her to squeeze past, the taller one groping her bottom for good measure.

'It all went smoothly; I have them both here for you. They're safe,' he said to the other man, who watched Antonia with interest.

'And our guests?'

'I think the entertainment will keep them happy for a while. One of them is already having a go.' The man indicated a cabin door.

'Good. I need them to sign off on the deal tonight. Give them anything they need, but don't let them know you've been playing delivery boy.'

Although the eighty-foot launch was impressive, it was dwarfed by the floating palaces moored in the nearby Monte Carlo marina. A few glasses of champagne contributed to Antonia's zigzag path down the corridor to the main stateroom. Without knocking she opened the door, and was confronted by a man's buttocks and the squeals of encouragement from the spread-eagled woman he was labouring into on the enormous bed.

Antonia gently closed the door, reluctant to get involved. Sent below deck on a mission she was eager to fulfil, there was the added benefit of being able to relieve herself in the process. She leaned against the glossy wooden panelling and thought for a moment. It was unlikely the package she was looking for would be in the stateroom at any rate, so it might be . . . She tapped lightly and opened the first door to her right.

The bed here was only queen-sized, but was seamlessly built into the room with intricate wooden detail. Boats always fascinated her – their watertight doors, the way everything was shut away or protected by brass railings should the weather get rough. Another wooden door led into an ensuite bathroom and she gratefully dropped her bikini bottoms and made it without accident onto the cool toilet seat. She gazed around the bathroom – again, everything was so carefully designed and executed with the utmost craftsmanship. As her eyes wandered, she caught sight of a man's leather toilet bag with the unmistakable Gucci insignia.

Antonia unzipped the bag and quickly rummaged through. At the bottom she found a parcel of silver foil, which opened to reveal two small vials of white powder. 'There you are,' she said in a broad American accent. 'Although there's not much of you . . . I might just take a little advance while I'm down here.' She flushed the toilet and stood carefully.

Making a fist, Antonia took a pinch of the powder onto her hand and lifted it to inhale. She suddenly stopped and looked suspiciously at the vial again. Antonia loved her champagne and coke, but unlike some of the other girls had no intention of trying anything harder. A sudden recollection of the client's instructions made her wonder if she'd found what she was looking for. What was it he'd said? 'You won't be able to miss it – it's as big as a bag of icing sugar.' She picked up one of the small vials again and examined it more closely.

Antonia dipped a finger into the powder and rubbed a little

on her gums. Immediately she spat it out, rinsed her mouth out and washed the traces of white from her hands. That wasn't cocaine. Examining her teeth in the mirror, she hunted around for some mouthwash. It was probably ice, she realised, and shuddered, remembering the effects on one of her once-beautiful friends, who had torn holes in her own skin trying to get rid of imaginary bugs.

Antonia carefully put everything back and closed the bathroom door. On one side of the bed she found some expensive Gucci luggage and unzipped one of the bags. 'Jesus!' she swore and pulled out a wad of cash, flicking through it with her thumb. The bag was stuffed with money, and she estimated there would be around one million euros – maybe more. She was about to help herself to a few notes as a tip, but her better judgement won out. People who carried around large sums of money were usually pretty ruthless about protecting it. No need to tempt fate. She carefully zipped up the bag and checked the second suitcase, which was full of clothes. A quick search resulted in a large bag of what looked much more like cocaine. 'Jackpot!' She bounded back up the stairs to the deck salon waving the bag and was greeted with cheers from the clients and other girls.

The party was now ready to start in earnest. One of the men pulled the bikini ties of a pretty French blonde called Mimi, exposing her impossibly large breasts. 'I think we just found our coffee table,' he quipped. Mimi stretched out on her back across the actual coffee table, wriggling herself into the most flattering position. 'I don't think you'll be needing those either,' he said, pointing to her tiny bikini bottoms. 'In fact, why aren't you all naked already?' he added, looking sternly around at the remaining three girls.

The men watched with obvious pleasure as the girls removed their bikinis and stood naked in the sunshine pouring through the windows. They all had magnificent bodies, with large pert breasts – some real, some clearly assisted – and were completely devoid of body hair. Mimi was the exception, her pubic hair manicured and dyed in a small pink love heart. She still lay across the coffee table, her tanned legs slightly parted. 'Don't move,' the first man commanded as he scooped cocaine onto her flat stomach. Expertly he used a black American Express credit card to create two straight lines of powder. 'Who's first?'

When no one moved, Antonia stepped up to the mark. She knelt down, bending from the hips to provide an excellent view for the clients behind her, picked up a neatly rolled hundred-euro bill and snorted two lines. A cheer went round and the next two lines were drawn on Mimi's thighs. This time one of the men snorted, blowing gently on the pink love heart as he finished, making the 'coffee table' squirm. Lines were drawn on her chest, too, and when they had all indulged, blue pills were handed out to the men. 'Ladies, we salute you,' said one as they all knocked back the Viagra like aspirin with swigs of champagne.

That was Antonia's cue to lead the way. She was paid huge sums of money for her expertise and it was time to go to work. 'Girls,' she instructed, 'I think Mimi needs a bit of attention.' Antonia switched her focus to the pink love heart with consummate acting skill, her own buttocks moving seductively in front of the men. The other girls enthusiastically joined in, marking the beginning of an afternoon dedicated to complete sexual indulgence.

In the early evening, the girls were given an hour back at the hotel to dress, and as they strode through the foyer in glamorous gowns, all heads turned. The men were already back on the boat, and as the girls stepped aboard in their evening regalia, the crew cast off and, once clear of the marina, put her into full throttle for the short cruise around to Monte Carlo.

As the group entered the casino, one of the clients took Mimi's arm and another motioned Antonia to his side as his escort. The house manager greeted them personally and led them through to a VIP table.

'Welcome, gentlemen, we're delighted you could join us this evening,' he said smoothly. 'It's always an honour to receive a visit from our foreign counterparts, and their guests.' The manager smiled at the girls, only too aware of their profession.

'We've come to steal all your secrets,' one of the men said, then laughed heartily. 'No, really, it's good to see a European operation.' He caught the unimpressed expression of the manager and stopped laughing.

'Congratulations on the Macau strip surpassing Las Vegas,' the manager said, smiling coldly before leaving them in the charge of an expert croupier.

Antonia's companion, an older Asian man, motioned for her to sit next to him, and traced his finger across the tattoo on her shoulderblade. 'Number eight is very lucky for the Chinese, so you will be lucky for me.' She didn't spoil the illusion by pointing out her tattoo was the symbol for infinity, which she'd had done straight after completing her accounting degree. Granted, it did look like the number eight on its side.

'Look,' he showed her his watch. 'It has a number with eights. Also very lucky. I wanted the number eight, or eighty-eight, but . . .' He shrugged. 'Someone beat me to them.'

All the girls looked at the watch, which had an unusual face. 'I've never seen one like that,' Mimi said. 'What is it?'

'A Frederique Constant Tourbillon. Very expensive. And tonight if I win a lot of money, I'll buy everyone a watch,' he joked, and turned his attention to the game of blackjack unfolding on the table.

Antonia was really annoyed when she came down with the flu the next morning. 'It's the airplanes and air conditioning in the hotel,' she explained to the pharmacist, who recommended vitamin C, paracetamol, cough medicine and bed rest, in a heavy French accent.

Fortunately, her room overlooking the beach had a small balcony and she was able to leave the door open for some fresh air. By the second day her body ached and she stayed in bed, half watching television, half sleeping, propped up on pillows, as lying down made her cough worse. By the third day she barely stopped coughing and the rattle in her lungs was pronounced.

'You sound awful!' Mimi exclaimed. 'I hope I don't catch whatever it is.'

The hotel concierge called a doctor that afternoon. Antonia was scared now. This wasn't like any flu she had ever experienced. Every part of her body ached, breathing had become torturous and when she blew her nose the discharge was frothy and yellow. She was too weak to answer the door when the doctor finally arrived and a bell boy had to be called to let him in.

After a quick inspection, the doctor dialled immediately for an ambulance. 'She's very ill and her lungs are full of fluid,' he explained to Mimi as the stretcher carrying a barely conscious Antonia was wheeled through the marble foyer.

The next morning she was dead.

8

Flemington Racecourse, Melbourne, Australia

There was a carnival atmosphere in the Chairman's Club at Flemington – an exclusive and expensive facility open to the privileged few. Contrary to appearances, the celebrations were less to do with the races on a wintery Wednesday and much more to do with spending the allocated food and beverage tab before the end of the racing season on the last day of July.

This had become something of an unofficial event on the racing calendar – Grange Hermitage Day. All those with exclusive membership had to use up what was left on their generous food and wine allowance.

Darcy had organised a table for four of his mates plus his trainer, Tom Carr, and a bottle of the great Penfolds Grange Hermitage, vintage 1996, was already breathing in the decanter. Darcy had a runner in the second race, and a win by his favourite filly would have topped off a great day, but it was not to be. Diplomatique had been pocketed in on the rails and with no chance of a clear run had ended in fifth position. But there was another reason Darcy had so fervently wished for the kudos of success. Sitting at a table across from him was a beautiful woman Darcy had never before seen at the track, and he had hoped to make a good impression.

Her tall, slender frame and flawless skin initially led Darcy to decide she must be a model. But her clothes were at odds with her appearance, being neither sexy nor quite fashionable. He was equally puzzled by the fact that she was sitting at the Racing Victoria table, deep in conversation with a bunch of administrators.

The Grange was poured, food served and Darcy's table selected a horse each for a first four flexibet for the next race. Tom played it safe and nominated the favourite, but Darcy included Carnivale, a long shot at twenty-five to one on a stable whisper, and backed it each way for good measure. Watching from the screen at their table, all six leapt to their feet when the field entered the home straight with Carnivale, the long shot, hooking out wide for a clear run.

'C'mon, Carnivale!' Darcy shouted.

'Don't lay in, you bastard,' Tom cursed as Carnivale reached the leader and moved too close, but the jockey straightened him without losing momentum and at the fifty-metre mark he sailed away and won by a length.

'You bloody ripper!' shouted Darcy and clapped Tom on the back.

The Racing Victoria contingent had turned around at the

sound of all the commotion and raised their glasses in congratulations. It was all the encouragement Darcy needed. He grabbed his glass and skipped over to their table.

'Gentlemen, good to see you enjoying yourselves instead of slaving away at your desks,' he said, shaking hands all round. As planned he was introduced to Dr Clea Reynolds, who stood and shook his hand firmly.

'Dr?' Darcy raised an eyebrow in surprise.

Clea Reynolds had seen that look a thousand times before. 'Yes, I'm a scientist with the Australian Animal Infectious Diseases Laboratory, specialising in zoonotic diseases,' she answered smoothly, watching Darcy squirm.

Clea had registered Darcy from the moment she sat down to lunch, thanks to a pretty blonde in a pale pink dress nearby. The blonde had been leaning over the table to display her ample bosom, and standing at any opportunity to show off long tanned legs in a desperate attempt to gain attention. Clea had turned to see who had commanded the girl's ardent interest and spied Darcy looking in her direction. He was very handsome, she had to admit. Now she knew his identity she stifled a laugh. It certainly explained the attention. 'I have, of course, already heard a lot about you,' she said, trying not to smile at his discomfort.

'All good, I hope?' Darcy said lamely.

'Varied reports, actually. Would you please excuse me for a moment?' Clea brushed past him and headed up the stairs.

'Allow me to assist you,' Darcy jumped in valiantly.

'To the ladies? I don't think I'll need much assistance, thank you.'

'Oh, I thought you were placing a bet.' Darcy was crestfallen at his own stupidity.

'I don't need help to place my bets,' Clea threw back over her shoulder as she walked away.

Chris Martin, the Chief Operating Officer of Racing Victoria, smirked. 'You're wasting your breath there, Darcy. She's a bit too serious for you.'

Clea sometimes enjoyed the disconcerting effect her appearance had on men, but often it was a professional hindrance. She wondered how much easier her life would have been if she'd been born a boy – certainly her two brothers were well established in their careers, while she'd just been overlooked for a promotion, even though she was an established international authority in her field. AAIDL had appointed a 51-year-old male scientist, whose expertise was in laboratory administration, to replace her former boss, Glen Collings. Clea could have done the job on her ear – hell, she *had* been doing it since Glen had recognised her ability. She couldn't help thinking how much easier it would be to have been born Darcy Ambrose-Taylor.

Clea's mobile phone rang and she paused to take the call, vaguely annoyed that on the one day she chose to get out of the lab and enjoy herself, the blasted thing wouldn't stop ringing. At the end of the call she dashed back to the table, pale and agitated but trying to compose herself.

'Gentlemen, I've had the most extraordinary phone call.

It seems we've just had a verified case of hendra virus,' she announced.

'Which state?' Chris asked anxiously.

'Well, that's the extraordinary thing. It was out of France – Nice, to be exact.' There was a shocked silence. 'Apparently the woman died almost a month ago of unknown causes and the coronial inquest has just concluded it was hendra.'

'But I thought hendra was only found in Australia – and only in New South Wales and Queensland?' Chris was dumbfounded.

'That's true; I'm amazed the French coroner was even able to recognise it.'

The news was distressing for them all. How could an Australian horse virus, transmitted by fruit bats, end up killing someone in France?

'Are there any horses involved?' asked Chris.

Clea shrugged. 'They don't know if the woman had any contact with horses, and I imagine if a horse had died of the disease locally it would almost certainly have been misdiagnosed. I'm guessing no vet in the south of France would be familiar with hendra.' It was still too early to call France so Clea would have to get onto the authorities later to clarify the situation.

Darcy suddenly appeared at her side again. 'I have a runner in the next race. Dr Reynolds, I was wondering if you'd like to come down to the mounting yard with me?' he asked hopefully.

Clea found herself torn between the opportunity and the intent, but the chance to get up close to the magnificent creatures outweighed her instincts. Clea loved horses. Downstairs, she leaned over the padded rails as the horses paced around the mounting yard, admiring their athleticism.

'Good afternoon, gentlemen.' Jockey Hayden Miller approached Darcy, Clea and Tom, who'd accompanied them. Hayden wore the Ambrose-Taylor colours of pale blue jockey silks with dark blue stars and a cap, and shook Darcy's hand while glancing admiringly at Clea. 'I hope you're having fun upstairs while I'm hard at work.'

'I told you to join us,' Darcy protested at the mock jibe.

'Can't, mate, I've got a runner in every race today and I'm out at Ballarat tomorrow. Another time, perhaps.' Hayden turned to Tom to discuss tactics. 'Now, boss, the speed will come from the top weight, and the number five, which is a front runner.'

'He's as green as grass, so expect a bit of star-gazing,' Tom warned. 'I'd keep him one out from the fence about midfield – I don't want him too far back or he might baulk at taking a run. They'll sprint away from him over this shorter distance, but we just want to see him coming home hard.'

'I'll hook him out in the straight and he can have a good gander at the grandstand and get it out of his system.' Hayden and Tom walked over to the parading horses. 'Don't bet the family farm!' Hayden called back to Darcy. Tom legged him up and he took up Spritzer's reins quickly as the horse became agitated and tossed his head around in protest.

'How's he going?' Darcy asked Tom, nodding towards Hayden.

'Yeah, he'll be fine – he's one of the best, and you simply

don't lose that skill easily.' They watched horse and jockey walk through the impressive wrought-iron gates, down the chute and onto the racetrack.

Hayden had been involved in a terrible race fall six months ago, when his mount broke its leg and crashed to the turf. While most of the field managed to avoid the catastrophe, one other horse came down as well, rolling straight over the prone jockey. With half a tonne of kicking horse on him, Hayden sustained serious internal injuries, concussion and minor breaks. He had returned to the racetrack only two weeks ago.

'He looks pretty strong,' Clea commented. It was bad publicity for the racing industry when one of its favourite stars had such a nasty fall and sat in rehab for so long. Everyone had seen the dreadful footage of the accident.

'The little buggers are so bloody brave. Can you think of any other job where you're constantly followed by two ambulances?' Darcy waved a greeting to another in-form jockey, who was riding the favourite. Clea was surprised to find Darcy so compassionate; for some reason she had assumed he'd be more self-interested. Darcy led Tom and Clea to the owners' viewing area and they sat down behind one of the leading trainers.

'I'm interested to hear your views on research and development funding for the racing industry,' Darcy said as Clea settled down next to him. 'I think we need to try again for a Cooperative Research Centre grant from the government – after all, most other agricultural industry groups have them. Cattle, sheep, pigs – why not horses?'

Darcy's conversation was not at all what Clea had expected. He had honed in on one of her pet subjects straight away, and slowly began to redeem himself from their initial conversation. She decided to tell him about the hendra case in France. 'That's an interesting question, particularly in light of a phone call I had a moment ago. If we had access to that level of funding we may be able to come up with some answers for hendra virus. There's been a case reported in France.'

'France? I didn't realise the virus was found overseas.'

'It's not.'

The lights flashed on the race barriers and their attention was drawn back to the race.

When the field jumped, Spritzer was away quickly. Hayden expertly manoeuvred him across the field from an outside barrier to take up a midfield position as the horses strung out. But Spritzer tossed his head in protest and over-raced with his mouth wide open when another runner came up on his outside. Darcy and Tom groaned. Hayden got the horse back under control and settled him between two horses until they turned for home. The back runners were making their move and in a moment poor Spritzer was in the thick of the field with nowhere to go.

'Come on, get him out of there!' Darcy exclaimed in frustration.

At the 200-metre mark, a break opened up in front, and Hayden urged the horse forward to take the run, but when another horse tried to go with him, Spritzer lost his momentum. The back runners swooped down to the finish line, leaving Spritzer flat-footed, finishing ninth out of a field of fourteen.

'Oh, well,' Darcy sighed. 'Out to the paddock for him.'

'Let's hope that toughens him up a bit. Do you want to wait and see Hayden?' Tom was heading back towards the mounting yard.

'No, I've got a glass of red wine calling me. I'll catch him on Saturday.'

Darcy led Clea back to the Chairman's Club and poured her a glass of wine from the decanter. They were soon deep in discussion about the impact the racetrack camber had on the structure of a horse's bones. One of Clea's close friends from her university days had become a research vet specialising in equine physiology, so she had some knowledge of it, and she was surprised to find Darcy had read a number of papers on the subject. Conversation flowed easily and Clea found herself trying to remember when she'd last enjoyed a discussion so much with someone outside her work.

At one stage Darcy leaned in close to draw a diagram in the back of her race book and Clea suddenly became aware of his physicality. She wondered for a fleeting moment what it would be like to be held in his arms – but no sooner had the thought crossed her mind than her defence mechanisms kicked in. Clea had spent her adult life avoiding romantic interludes guaranteed to end in pain, and she wasn't about to step beyond her emotional fortress today. Darcy's reputation as a womaniser was well known.

Clea finished her wine and noticed most of the Racing Victoria people had already left. 'You know, I really do have to get going. I want to contact France tonight and it'll take me well over an hour to get back to the lab in the traffic.' She stood and smoothed down her dress. 'It was nice meeting you, Darcy,' she said, shaking his hand. Then she picked up her bag and walked away.

Darcy was surprised; he thought they'd been getting on very well, and he had been hoping to find an excuse to organise another meeting. But just like that, she was gone.

Not to be deterred, he and the boys cracked open another bottle of wine. Darcy switched them from the Penfolds Grange to a Henschke Hill of Grace for a comparison and it held up well under the scrutiny. The winning owners from the last race had joined their trainer's table nearby to celebrate. The racing stable's marketing manager, Cathy, had been born into the industry and she knew everyone involved in racing both nationally and internationally. She greeted Darcy with a hug, but declined the offer of a drink.

'I can't,' she lamented. 'I have to look after my owners. But come and join us at the bar and I'll introduce you to my friend Amy.'

Amy was obviously out to turn heads in a short pale pink silk dress, which exposed her lovely tanned legs beautifully, with a sweetheart neckline that showed off her impressive cleavage. Darcy quickly discovered she was a budding young actress who had met Cathy during Italian classes.

The owners were a decent bunch of professional people who pooled their resources to breed and race their own horses from a band of six broodmares. Always mindful of selling stallion nominations, Darcy accepted their invitation to continue the celebrations at a popular bar and was delighted when Cathy and Amy agreed to come for one drink.

Amy was on to her second glass of wine when the conversation turned to Darcy's penthouse in a prestigious building. 'I bet the views are amazing . . . I'd love to see it,' she said seductively.

Amy was gorgeous and fun, and Darcy rationalised a little fling wouldn't hurt. He pulled her close and whispered, 'I could take you there now for a glass of champagne if you like, only I wouldn't want you to think I was trying to take advantage.'

'Maybe I wouldn't mind if you did.'

Darcy paid for the drinks, and offered Amy a lift home. Cathy was about to protest that her friend lived in the opposite direction when she picked up the sexual tension and sighed in exasperation. 'Look after her, Darcy,' she called out as they left the bar. Cathy didn't know who to blame – Amy for flirting so obviously with a catch like Darcy, or Darcy, who could be counted on not to miss an opportunity.

A couple of people stood on the pavement attempting to hail a cab, so Darcy crossed the road on the pretext of finding one going the opposite direction. But in a moment he drew Amy behind a tree and pinned her there with his body. 'Are you sure you want to come home with me? I can't promise I'll behave,' he breathed. Amy leaned forward and softly kissed his lips. They both knew what they wanted.

A short taxi-ride later, they arrived at Darcy's spectacular penthouse. 'Wow, look at the view!' Amy exclaimed.

'I think there'll be time to admire that later.' Darcy walked up behind Amy and kissed the nape of her neck confidently.

'But you promised me champagne!' Amy wriggled free, laughing.

'There'll be plenty of time for that later, too. Just think – you'll be able to admire the view, sip champagne, and as long as I can look at these,' he slipped his hand around and lightly ran a finger across her exposed cleavage, making her shiver, 'we'll both be happy.'

Amy turned around into his embrace and he kissed her deeply. She tasted of wine and faintly of garlic, but it was sexy. As their kiss became more passionate Darcy smoothly unzipped Amy's dress, pushed the straps off her shoulders and let the fabric fall to the ground around her stiletto shoes. He stepped back to admire her body. A pink lace push-up bra barely covered her nipples and the matching lace boy-leg briefs were completely see-through.

Darcy swept her up into his arms and she squealed in delight as he carried her to the bedroom and laid her on the Versace quilt of his king-sized bed. He slipped off her shoes and traced a path of kisses upwards from her ankle along her legs until he arrived at her panties. Amy groaned with pleasure.

He unclipped the clasp of her bra to free her beautiful full breasts and kissed down her flat, toned tummy until he found fabric. He rubbed her through the lace and said, 'I think it's time these came off, don't you?' Amy wriggled the panties over her curvy hips in a flash, and Darcy kissed the little rectangle of hair that had been left after a waxing. His hot tongue ventured further but only for a teasing moment. His fingers gently parted her thighs and began to stroke softly.

Amy was almost delirious with pleasure. Her hips moved involuntarily to aid Darcy's movement, signalling her arousal. He stopped and Amy took her cue, unbuttoning Darcy's shirt and running her hand over the bulge in his trousers. She looked at him with wide eyes. Her hand rubbed again and this time unbuckled his belt and delved into his boxer shorts. 'Wow, it's big,' she said so innocently that Darcy laughed.

'I have a feeling you're going to like it,' he murmured as she moved down the bed and took him in her mouth. Her technique wasn't brilliant, but it was hard not to enjoy the attention. After a moment he pulled her up the bed and whispered, 'I can't believe how much I want to be inside you.' Amy nestled on her back in anticipation.

'No, I want you on top, I want to watch your beautiful body.'

She knelt over the top of him now but seemed a bit unsure. He rubbed her softly again and her legs opened wider, allowing him to slip inside as she slid down with a gasp. Darcy pulled her forward, kissing and sucking her nipples until she lowered herself and began to move her hips rhythmically again. Amy's breasts bounced around as she increased her tempo, lost in the throes of pleasure, and when Darcy rubbed her swollen clitoris with his thumb she arched her back and moaned with the abandon of orgasm. Before the intensity subsided, Darcy manoeuvred so that he was above her, hooked her long legs over his shoulders for a few brief thrusts and found himself lost in immense pleasure.

After his heart rate calmed, Darcy climbed off the bed and disappeared into the kitchen. He returned momentarily with an elegant crystal glass. 'Your champagne, mademoiselle, as promised.' He bowed and handed her the glass.

9
Susanne Reynolds' Home, Glen Iris, Melbourne

Ernest bounded into his mother's kitchen carrying a laptop computer. 'Where do you want this, Mum?' he asked, while giving his sister a quick peck on the cheek. 'Hey, sis, you look glum. Why the long face?'

Clea ruffled her brother's hair and smiled. 'Just a few issues at work.'

'Just on the table's fine,' said Susanne Reynolds as she put a saucepan in the sink.

Clea watched as Ernest plugged the computer in and set it at the head of the table. 'What's that for?'

'You'll see.' Ernest turned the screen so it was facing the rest of the table, which had been set for Sunday lunch, a family tradition.

'Pour yourself a glass while I get this out of the oven,' Susanne suggested to her youngest son.

Ernest poured himself a large measure of pinot and clicked

his glass against Clea's. 'What are we having?'

'Lasagne. I even made the pasta myself.' Susanne lifted the heavy green enamel dish from the oven and a wonderful aroma filled the kitchen. 'Come on, you two, get yourselves to the table.'

Ernest fiddled with the computer for a moment and called up a number over Skype. Clea burst out laughing when she heard her other brother's voice answer and his face appeared on the screen. 'Surprise!' both boys called out in unison.

'Now I don't have to miss any family lunches. What are you guys having?' Robert asked enviously. 'The food up here is awful!' He was stationed in the mining area of the Pilbara in Western Australia.

Susanne served lunch and the family raised their glasses – Robert included, thousands of kilometres away.

'What's news? Did you get that promotion, sis?' Robert asked Clea.

'No, and I don't really want to talk about it.'

Ernest reached over and clasped his sister's hand. 'So that explains the glum look. I'm sorry, I didn't realise.'

'It's nothing,' Clea lied. 'But I do have something to report. There's been a case of hendra virus in France, of all places. A woman died. I'm investigating, but I honestly don't have any idea how she could have become infected.'

'Isn't hendra that bat disease?' Robert asked.

'Yeah, that's right. And that's not all – I met Darcy Ambrose-Taylor at the races.'

'*The* Darcy Ambrose-Taylor?' Susanne was impressed. 'What's he like? Handsome?'

'Well, yes, I suppose he is. He's not what I expected at all, actually. He was really interesting.'

'Are you blushing?' Ernest teased. 'You didn't fall for him, did you?'

Clea threw her napkin at him. 'Of course not. He might be interesting but he's still an arrogant playboy – not my cup of tea.'

'Is anyone your cup of tea?'

Clea retrieved her napkin and threw it at the computer screen.

'Okay, okay, I'm sorry,' Robert said, laughing.

10

Geelong Racecourse, Bellarine Peninsula, Victoria

Darcy smiled as he looked at the obligatory page-three photo in the newspaper of a racehorse in a party hat with a carrot birthday cake. It was excellent pre-spring publicity for the industry at a time when football dominated everything in Melbourne. August first was the official birthday of all Australian racehorses and Darcy was celebrating the occasion this year by watching one of his up-and-comers race at the Geelong racetrack.

Tom had suggested the provincial race for Dark Angel, a three-year-old gelding who needed to gain confidence on the track in a less pressured environment than his talent would suggest. The Geelong race meeting had been selected to give him an easy 'kill' in a lesser grade of horse. Dark Angel's sire, Hold That Tiger, had been crowned the Champion 2YO Colt of Europe for the 2002 racing season, and his grandsire was the extraordinary American stallion Storm Cat, whose service fee at stud reached such astronomical proportions that his owners had to hire a twenty-four-hour armed guard. Owing to Storm Cat's prowess as a sire of champions on both dirt and turf, Tom thought Dark Angel might relish Geelong's Thorough Track, an artificial surface composed of sand, wax and elastic fibre established for drought conditions.

From the 1300-metre start, it was a long back straight of 480 metres until the turn, which would give Dark Angel plenty of time to take up and hold a position. These were the days racehorse owners anticipated, the days when inside information gave a head start on the punt. Darcy planned to have a plunge on Dark Angel both on-course and with his corporate bookmaker.

His timing was cut a bit fine and the horses were already in the mounting yard when he found Tom and Hayden.

'So what are our chances?' Darcy said.

'I'd say they're still pretty good on exposed form,' Tom said. 'Are you having a bet?' Darcy nodded. 'Put a grand on for me, would you?'

While Hayden mounted up, Darcy wandered as nonchalantly as possible to the betting ring and placed bets on Dark Angel with a number of bookmakers, who immediately lowered the odds on his horse. He quickly pushed the speed-dial button on his phone for his corporate bookmaker and placed a larger bet. Tom was already in the stand when Darcy plonked himself down beside him.

'The favourite is that South Australian horse that won by three lengths the other day at Sale,' Tom said. 'My form man says it's good but the field was weak, it didn't beat much. We should have it all over him today.'

They trained their binoculars on the starting gates and watched as the horses jumped.

The horses went hell for leather down the back straight, which suited Dark Angel. Like his sire, he swept from the back of the field to claim victory over the favourite by a length. 'I think he's ready for town now,' Tom declared with a smirk.

The elation of winning a horserace anywhere, country or metropolitan, produced an addictive endorphin rush, and on this high, Darcy decided to call in on Clea Reynolds at AAIDL in East Geelong, only ten minutes from the track.

A centre for diagnosis and research, the laboratory also housed world-class biocontainment areas warranting high-security procedures. Darcy found himself at the security gate of the imposing grey structure explaining that, even though he didn't have an appointment, he was sure Dr Reynolds would see him.

'Who?' he distinctly heard down the phone when the guard contacted Clea's office, and although he now regretted his impulsive visit, he kept smiling confidently. The boomgate lifted and he drove through and parked. The security desk at the front of the building had already been appraised of his arrival, and after emptying all pockets Darcy walked through the metal detector, a visitor's badge pinned on his shirt, and waited.

Clea came out wearing a pair of old jeans under her white lab coat, but it looked as if she had just brushed her hair and applied lipstick. 'Darcy, what a surprise to see you here.' It was an understatement.

'I was in the neighbourhood and thought I'd drop in,' he said. Clea looked so skeptical he rushed on. 'No, really, I *was* in the area, at the racetrack – my horse just won the third.'

'Oh, I see. Well . . . congratulations,' Clea responded smoothly, but she was thoroughly thrown by his presence, and annoyed at herself for finding him so attractive. Men like Darcy were trouble. They were full of charm and promises, but wreaked havoc on the women who loved them. She couldn't help being flattered by the attention, but there was no way she'd let herself become involved with a man like Darcy.

'Perhaps we could talk somewhere?' he asked hopefully. 'If I'm not interrupting your work?'

'I can take a short break, I suppose.' Clea reluctantly led him down a few sterile corridors to her box-like office.

Darcy glanced around. There wasn't much here to give her away: a few stacks of neat papers, a large coffee mug and a framed photo of Clea with two young men and an older woman all bearing a striking family resemblance. In front of her computer screen was a report, and Darcy was able to see the telling word hendra. 'I read about the hendra outbreak in France you mentioned at the races. It was all over the newspapers,' he said.

'Well, it wasn't an outbreak, just one death, and no other reported cases. We still haven't been able to determine if there were any horses affected at this stage.'

'A mystery not even Dr Clea Reynolds can solve?' Darcy asked, smiling.

'I confess it has me completely stumped.' Clea fiddled with the papers on her desk. 'I've been able to verify it was the virus – but how it got there? I suspect we'll never know.'

'You'll have your work cut out for you if hendra can potentially pop up anywhere in the world,' Darcy said, picking up the family photo on her desk. 'So, you have two brothers?'

Clea removed the photo from his hands and put it back on her desk, but regretted her action when she saw the hurt look on Darcy's face.

'Surely you didn't come here to talk about my work, or my family?' Clea was still baffled by his unexpected visit.

Darcy explained that each year he organised a gala ball and auction with the proceeds donated to two causes: the jockey fund, which assisted the families of injured or deceased jockeys, and funding for equine research. He got her attention with the last point. 'I wanted to ask if you'd be my guest at the ball in two weeks' time?'

'It's certainly an excellent cause, but really . . .' She sighed and suddenly saw him again as the rich playboy. 'Darcy, you're very charming but I'm a pretty serious person, and I'm certainly not looking for a relationship – and even if I were, I'm not sure we have very much in common.'

Darcy stared at her for a moment, absorbing the rebuttal. 'There's no doubt you're a beautiful and interesting woman, but I think you've misconstrued my invitation,' he said quietly. 'As the host I take two tables each year and invite friends and industry people. The basis for my invitation was your work here at the laboratory. I apologise if it sounded like I was just asking to get you on a date. If that were the case, I'd have simply asked you to dinner.'

Clea's face flushed. She fervently wished she could take back what she'd said. Darcy stood and pulled a business card from his pocket. 'The invitation still stands, Clea. If you change your mind, let me know.' He put the card on her desk and walked out.

Clea rushed after him. 'It's a bit of a maze in here, I'll see you out.'

'Making sure I leave the premises?' She detected a note of humour in his voice, and felt a little better.

'Something like that.'

Darcy drove back to Melbourne berating himself for the way he'd handled the situation, but also annoyed with Clea. He'd barely met the woman and she was already presuming he was besotted with her. But Darcy had to admit there was a grain of truth in her presumption. Despite Amy's comely company, he hadn't been able to get Clea out of his head.

When he finally turned on his computer and checked emails that afternoon, he opened one from Clea with mixed feelings. It read: *Sorry for this afternoon, Darcy, you caught me by surprise. I feel very foolish. I'm writing to say I'd love to attend the ball as one of your many guests. Thank you. Clea.*

11
Jalal's Family Home, Dubai

Salah al Din bin Muntasir was a proud man. From humble beginnings in Saudi Arabia he had built his family's fortune on transportation and shipping, growing it from a few dubious trucks into a billion-dollar empire. He had moved his family to Dubai over thirty years ago, before the city began to blossom, and had worked hard to provide a good lifestyle for his only son. But now, when he should have been reaping the rewards of his success, he was struggling to hold everything he had created together.

Salah al Din was reclining on a sofa in one of the many rooms of his Dubai mansion when his beloved son Jalal entered the room and knelt anxiously by his side.

'Don't look so worried, it's just my blood pressure. Apparently I'm a little stressed.' He chuckled and patted his son's hand.

'You will be all right?'

'The doctors haven't written me off yet, although the women's fussing may well do the trick. But I have grave news on the business front. I'm struggling to get refinancing – the money simply isn't available.' He leaned back into the cushions.

'You'll just have to buy me some time,' Jalal pleaded. 'I know I can get the financing, I just have to finalise the deal first. I promise you, Father, I won't fail you.'

Salah al Din sighed. Everyone wanted time but it was becoming the scarcest commodity. The receivers were circling the Muntasir shipping company like wolves on the scent of a kill. They needed money fast as a stop-gap before Jalal's ambitious plan took place.

'How much equity in the company will you have to give away?' Salah al Din was reluctant to part with anything, but ever mindful that fate had taken away the luxury of choice.

'Whatever we lose in equity, we gain in a strategic alliance that could boost our profits by at least fifty per cent within five years.' Jalal knew his proposal was risky, but desperation had narrowed the alternatives.

'Tell me about Afifah,' his father asked. 'Have you spoken to Sheikh Faisal? Has he agreed to a wedding date?'

Jalal went quiet as his mother entered the room carrying a tray of nuts and herbal tea. He gave her arm a gentle squeeze and she smiled with delight. She was devoted to her only son. Jalal had entered the world at considerable emotional cost to his mother, but she would have had it no other way. The joy of holding him in her arms had outweighed all the grief. She touched Salah al Din's forehead and he took her hand in his own for a moment, before releasing it with a smile of great affection.

Jalal felt a cloud of worry descend as his thoughts returned to his father's question. He had been trying to resolve the serious issue of his wedding for months, but no amount of cajoling would convince the Sheikh to allow his daughter to marry before she finished her degree. Afifah had now made matters worse by deciding to pursue post-graduate studies. 'Once she is finished with her studies, she will become your wife, I promise you,' was the Sheikh's standard answer to Jalal.

'I have no answer for you, Father,' he said sadly. 'But I will do everything in my power to settle a date quickly.'

12

Kirtling Park Stud, Strathbogie Shire, Victoria

The winter weather had taken a turn for the worse, as if nature was intent on proving its force before the arrival of spring. Bitterly cold winds during the day and thick frosts at night battered the state, but the countryside was still crying out for drought-breaking rains, soaking and steady. The scant showers that had fallen were not enough to saturate the ground and swell the dams.

With the breeding season around the corner, Darcy was up at his stud working on stallion nominations. The pastures had a light topping of green from the last showers, but were still suffering. Darcy's property was on the river and he had irrigation rights, but he had always been taught it was best to keep horses on non-irrigated pastures. If the rains didn't come, though, he wouldn't have a choice.

His father had purchased the property twenty years ago and planted a beautiful garden around the graceful homestead, using natives and gum trees wherever possible. His foresight meant the garden was still thriving in the harsh conditions, and in the heat of summer provided cooling shade for the house.

Late in the afternoon Darcy heard a deep rumble. He leapt up from the piles of paperwork on his desk and bolted out the door. Ominous dark clouds broiled in the sky and scuttled quickly across the horizon, propelled by the force of a south-westerly wind. He rushed back inside and checked the weather bureau radar on the internet. There was rain coming.

He was standing outside the back door straining to see if rain was already falling a few kilometres away when he saw it – a great flashing sheet of lightning that lit up the sky. Darcy counted: one cat dog – two cat dog – three — and the thunder crashed. It was close.

When he reached the stables and located Paul, his stud manager, a flurry of activity was already underway. The storm, threatening and explosive, sent more streaks of light flashing across the sky. Staff secured a mob of two-year-olds who had been brought in for handling before going to the breaker. They were skittish with adrenalin and as charged as the air that swirled around them.

Paul tossed Darcy a couple of lead ropes and they dashed to the stallion yards just as the first drops of rain splattered onto the dusty ground. Darcy leapt into the yard of an older stallion and attached the lead rope to the nervous horse. At the gate he passed the rope to another staff member and the horse was led up to the stables.

Darcy had the second stallion under control and was relieved to see his stud manager passing the third stallion over. The rain started to come down in a slanted sheet, making vision difficult, but as he led the second stallion up towards the barn he could see most of his horses were safe. All of a sudden the hairs on the back of his neck stood up. There was still one horse out there.

A bolt of lightning came out of nowhere with a boom. Its jagged trajectory blinded Darcy for a moment and he stood frozen to the spot, his heart racing from the power of the electrical current that surged through the air. The horse he was leading reared and pawed the air then leapt forward, dragging Darcy with its sheer force. He tugged hard on the lead rope and brought the animal to a stop. A cry behind made him spin around and set the stallion off again. He shouted to one of the staff who was running down the hill, and together they brought the frightened horse under control. The stallion was led at a trot up the hill to the stables.

Darcy shielded his face against the stinging rain and headed towards the cry he had heard. Something was very wrong. His first-season sire Wigmore was down and his stud manager knelt on the wet ground over his thrashing body. The horse had taken fright when lightning struck his paddock gate and had tried to leap the fence. But he had slipped on the wet grass and caught his foreleg on the top rail, tumbling over and breaking it severely. He struggled in terrible pain on the ground, unable to stand.

Darcy ran back to the stables in the driving rain, unlocked a cupboard and took out a gun and bullets. He rushed back in a state of numbness and watched in silence as Paul loaded up and shot a single bullet into the horse's head. It was the kindest thing they could do.

Darcy stood beside his stud manager and stared at the majestic, still body of Wigmore while the storm continued unabated. Both hardened horse men wept tears of shock and sadness that mingled with the rain – so desperately needed but so cruelly given. Slowly they turned and walked away. There was nothing to say.

The freak accident shook Darcy to the core. Wigmore had been one of the stable stars. At two years old, he had won the Group Two Maribyrnong Stakes at Flemington, and at three, the Group One Caulfield Guineas. He had triumphed again in the Group One Chipping Norton Stakes at Randwick in Sydney. His stud career was assured by both his natural ability and strong breeding. Darcy had turned down a few offers for the stallion prospect, ranging from four million dollars early in his career up to fifteen million dollars after his second Group One win. In the end he struck a compromise deal with another Victorian breeder, who paid five million for one third of Wigmore.

Thoroughbreds had a frailty that belied their size and majesty. Almost everyone who bred them had been touched by tragedy, and, in a way, it made the triumphs on the racetrack more intense. It was a hard business. Darcy already had strong broodmare bookings for Wigmore, but now poor Paul would have to contact the mare owners and let them know the terrible news.

That night, while the storm rolled noisily around the sky and lit the windows, Darcy sat alone in front of the fire, nursing a glass of red wine. Here, surrounded by staff and horses, he could usually stave off the sense of isolation from his family far away in England. But this sudden melancholy was deeper than usual. It wasn't about being away from his family this time, it was about creating his own family – somewhere he belonged. He could pick up the phone and call a friend, but no one was there to share his bottle of wine and wipe away his tears.

Darcy couldn't put off the worst phone call any longer. He took a few steeling gulps from his glass and dialled his father.

The next morning Darcy was talking on the phone to Bahir. It was a comfort to speak to someone who knew how he felt about his horses. Bahir understood what he was going through. Paul appeared in the doorway and solemnly handed Darcy a sheet of paper, then turned quickly and walked away. Puzzled, Darcy watched as Paul crossed the lawn, still wet from rain, before unfolding the paper. It was a resignation letter. 'Bahir, can I call you back? Something's just come up.'

Darcy leapt into his boots by the back door and sprinted off after his stud manager. He gripped the man's shoulder and made him turn around. 'Please don't make me explain,' Paul implored, tears welling in his eyes. 'That was the hardest thing I've ever done – it's all in the letter.'

'I read the letter,' Darcy stated simply. He tore it up and threw the pieces into the cold wind.

'But it was my fault.' Paul was hurting deeply.

Darcy put his arm around the other man's shoulders. 'Paul, it was an accident, no one blames you – I don't blame you.'

'I shouldn't have had them in the yards, the forecast said there might be rain. He should have been safely inside, and now I've cost you millions of dollars . . .' Paul was beginning to ramble. He wiped a tear from his face with the back of a dirty hand.

'Now you're talking nonsense,' Darcy said kindly. 'He was insured for his full value, and I've already spoken to the insurance company. Look, Paul, you're my most valuable asset here. I don't know how I'd run this stud without you. But I can't insure you – I can only convince you to stay.'

Paul finally met Darcy's gaze, and took a deep breath to get hold of his emotions. 'Thank you, Darcy,' he said, and walked off.

Yvonne sat on a bench in the late summer sun, reading the newspaper. Heavy bumblebees droned around the nearby rubbish bin, and the scent of flowers wafted in the air. She shaded her eyes and looked up. Her son stood in his whites in the middle of the oval looking hot, but she knew he wouldn't be anywhere else – he loved cricket, like his father.

The other mothers had positioned themselves on another bench with their backs to Yvonne, as usual. She got the message loud and clear – she, a single mother, wasn't welcome amongst them. But she suffered the humiliation for her son's sake. He had so much fun playing, and the boys weren't to blame for the judgements and insecurities of their mothers. Tomorrow she'd be able to forget it all, too. She and her son would drive down to the family property for two blissful weeks of pure holiday, leaving London far behind.

She turned automatically to the sporting section and scanned the pages for racing news. A small headline caught her eye in the far corner: *Kirtling Park Stud Loses Stallion in Freak Accident*. It was Darcy's Wigmore. An overwhelming feeling of sadness welled inside her and she brushed an errant tear away from under her Dior sunglasses. Darcy must be upset – such a loss was devastating and she felt suddenly very close to him. Yvonne wished she could speak to him, but it wouldn't be right – not yet. Someday soon, though, she would have to talk to him. She shielded her eyes and stared out at her blonde-haired son on the pitch.

13

Royal Towers Complex, Melbourne, Australia

'Can I help you?'

Clea almost jumped out of her skin. She hadn't noticed the sales assistant standing on the other side of the rack.

'Do you have a special occasion?' the assistant persisted.

Clea confessed she was at a loss to know what to wear to a gala ball. Her own practical wardrobe didn't extend that far. The shop had come recommended as one of the best places for evening wear, and there were racks and racks of beautiful long dresses in every colour on display. Shopping was definitely not Clea's strong point, and if she could find a dress without having to traipse around for hours, she would be very relieved.

'You'd be a size ten, right?' The sales assistant was already pulling dresses off the rack. 'Do you have an idea of what you'd like?'

'Nothing too revealing.' Clea was holding up in amazement a canary-yellow dress with cut-outs down the side.

'This one would go beautifully with your eyes.' The assistant pulled out a pale blue empire-line dress with a rhinestone buckle under the bust. 'And this one doesn't look much on the hanger, but it's sensational on.' She held out a simple black dress with a sequined bodice, and then picked up a deep purple strapless dress with a ruffle down the high split, and a halter-neck satin dress in soft gold. Clea obediently followed the girl through to the change rooms.

The blue dress was tight across the bust, and while the colour was pretty, it lacked sophistication. The gold dress looked amazing, Clea had to admit, and flattered her tiny waist. She was admiring herself in the mirror when the assistant showed her another dress off the rack.

'Because you're so tall I think you can get away with this,' she said, holding up a red satin sheath dress cut on the bias, with a plunging cowl neckline.

'It's beautiful.' Clea reached out and touched the fabric. 'I'll have to try it.' She disappeared behind the curtain and re-emerged a moment later. 'Wow,' was all she could manage.

The sales assistant nodded in satisfaction. 'Yes, that's the one.'

Clea had decided to treat herself to a night in town for the occasion, and it made sense to stay at the hotel in the same complex as the venue. She checked into Royal Towers with her new purchase draped in a hanging bag, another shopping bag with a shoebox and an overnight bag in the grip of an over-eager bellboy.

Her room had an amazing view over the Yarra River. The huge

bathroom came complete with a television set over the bath for total indulgence. Clea flopped onto the bed and stretched out luxuriously. The room was a far cry from her functional apartment. With a sigh she climbed off the comfortable bed and hung up the dress. Fishing her new black strappy stilettos from the second bag, she wondered if she'd ever have cause to wear them again after tonight.

As with shopping, idleness wasn't a strong point, so Clea quickly changed into running gear, grabbed her iPod and pounded the busy footpath along the river in the direction of the Botanical Gardens. Running, either morning or night, was a ritual for Clea. The rhythmic fall of her feet inevitably restored her equilibrium. Once her mind had cleared after a couple of kilometres, she was free to focus on specific problems with a fresh clarity that often eluded her in the lab.

She had been puzzling over the strange occurrence of hendra virus in France for days, but she pushed the thoughts from her mind. Right now she needed to psyche herself up for the evening. It wasn't easy walking alone into a room of hundreds of people and Clea was beginning to regret her decision to buy the red dress; perhaps she would stand out too much. Darcy might think she was deliberately trying to attract attention to herself.

Clea picked up her pace to dispel this last thought. What Darcy thought was of no interest to her. She did find him attractive, yes, but really, it was just a passing physical reaction to a handsome man. Back at the hotel she slipped into her one-piece Speedo and did a few laps in the heated indoor pool.

The invitation said 6.30 for 7 p.m., so dressed and ready, Clea sat on her bed in her outfit, watching the news and waiting for the clock to tick over to 6.45. Her new shoes made her extremely tall and even more self-conscious, which wasn't helped when the lift door opened on a lower floor and a jockey and his wife entered, dressed in black tie. She followed them through to where a huge throng of people were enjoying pre-dinner drinks in the foyer of the function rooms at Royal Towers Casino. Clea checked her table number, grabbed a drink to calm her nerves and entered the fray.

A group of Racing Victoria executives waved her over and she joined them gratefully for a chat. A few moments later she spied a vet she knew well and squeezed through the crowd to chat to Zoe and her husband. By the time 7 p.m. came around she realised she knew quite a few people in the room and was feeling relaxed, or perhaps it was the sparkling wine going to her head.

Still chatting with Zoe, she walked into the function room, and gazed around in delight at the decorations. The tables were draped in silver organza over white tablecloths and set with magnificent twig and glass centrepieces.

Across the room Darcy was talking to a group of people and she headed in his direction, suddenly aware of admiring glances. Darcy stopped mid-sentence when he saw her and moved away from the group to greet her. 'I'm pleased you could make it.' He kissed her lightly on each cheek. 'And I know I have to take you seriously, but am I allowed to say you look stunning tonight?'

Clea was about to protest, but when Darcy held his fingers up to her lips in an intimate gesture, she simply said, 'Thank you.'

'I think we got off on the wrong foot – shall we call it a truce?' he asked affably. Before Clea could answer, a pretty young woman in a revealing black evening gown pushed between them and kissed Darcy soundly on the lips, before shooting Clea an obvious look of triumph. Clea was startled to realise it was the blonde from the Chairman's Club.

Clearly embarrassed by the display of affection, Darcy introduced the two women. Amy gave Clea a saccharin smile and shook her hand with little enthusiasm. 'Let me introduce you to a few others,' Darcy offered and led the two women to his table, where a group of guests were leaning on chairs and chatting.

When Darcy went to seat Clea next to his own place card, he realised it wasn't her seat – the place card was for the vivacious wife of a close friend. Puzzled, he checked the other cards and found Clea had been moved a few chairs away.

'Oh, I moved them so Suzie could sit closer to me,' Amy said cheerfully as she watched him. Darcy was caught. It would be rude now to switch the places back and Amy knew it. 'Besides, you said your friend from overseas might not make it and I didn't think you'd want an empty chair near you.'

'I said he might be running late,' Darcy said through slightly gritted teeth. 'I'm sorry, Clea, it seems there's been a mix-up,' he apologised.

As Clea moved to her place she couldn't help notice the smug look in Amy's eyes. So that was the type of woman Darcy dated, she thought – conniving, young and vacuous. It said a lot about the man. Halfway through entrée Clea was beginning to wish she hadn't come at all. The empty seat separated her from conversation down one end of the table, and Darcy's friend had his back half turned to her, talking to Amy. Clea picked at her duck salad feeling very awkward.

The MC, a retired champion football player with a love of horseracing, took centre stage to welcome the room, inviting Darcy to the podium to say a few words. Clea expected Darcy would be a confident speaker, and the way he bounded up to the stage seemed to confirm her assumption. However, when he began his voice was too quiet and he fiddled nervously with the microphone for a moment. He spoke hesitatingly at first, reading from a sheet of paper, but as he warmed up his enthusiasm for the subject began to shine through.

Darcy thanked everyone for attending and supporting a worthy industry cause. 'The loss of my stallion last week in such a freak accident brought home to me yet again how fragile these creatures truly are, but how robust an industry relies on them daily.'

Clea felt awful that she hadn't heard the news of Darcy's stallion, and her regret was made worse by the depth of emotion in his voice. He was obviously still distraught and she hadn't even realised.

Darcy's comments on funding for crucial research into equine diseases and physiology were concise and insightful. Clea looked around the room at the rapt audience, all of whom had a vested interest in the noble horse, and realised she was among like minds.

Darcy concluded by asking everyone to dig deep to assist the continued funding of equine research, before discussing industry assistance for injured jockeys and their families, a subject on which he was equally passionate.

As the applause died down and Darcy took his seat, the lights dimmed for a performance by a well-known singer, who appeared on stage in a white sequined dress. With her long hair flowing in soft waves, she looked like an angel and sang even more exquisitely. As Clea tried to catch Darcy's eye to offer her sympathy, she caught sight of a strikingly handsome man who moved swiftly through the room, clapped Darcy on the back and slid into the seat beside her.

'I see I timed my arrival to miss the speeches,' he said in charmingly accented English. 'Delighted to meet you – my name is Bahir. It seems I have the most fortunate seat at the table.'

Bahir was charming, and instantly made Clea feel at ease. As the main course of roast salmon was served, he explained he worked for a large Dubai racing stable and had been a close friend of Darcy's for many years. Bahir had dark features and healthy tanned skin, and was tall with an athletic build. His hazel eyes danced with laughter, and his vitality captivated Clea. She was almost disappointed when the head of the Rural Industries Research and Development Corporation leaned over and asked her about the mysterious case of hendra in France.

'Couldn't the woman just have come into contact with

someone who was already infected – an Australian?' Bahir asked naively.

'That's the mysterious part,' Clea explained. 'Hendra is a zoonotic disease with fruit bats as its host – and there's no vaccine or cure. The bats can infect horses and, in turn, a horse can infect a human. There's still a lot of research to be completed but we're almost certain hendra isn't transmitted from human to human. The woman must have come in contact with a horse, but I guess we'll never know.'

'Do bats migrate vast distances?' Bahir asked helpfully.

'Not these ones.'

Conversation was cut short by the dimming of lights. The MC took the stage once more and explained the main event for the evening – a karaoke fundraiser. Tables could bid for the right to hear key racing identities on stage singing, with the highest bidder choosing the song, although a professional singer would join the racing personality on stage for support. Clea looked around the room and noticed quite a few trainers looking distinctly uncomfortable; she cringed on their behalf and felt relieved that she would never in her life be in such a public position. She was perfectly capable of delivering scientific papers and lectures on her research, but the idea of making any other kind of public appearance sent her cold with fear.

The racing identities had agreed to participate weeks ago, so at least they knew what was coming. The MC drew the first name from a crystal bowl, and with a big grin, announced the name of one of Australia's prominent female trainers. The room erupted into applause and a spotlight followed the trainer up onto the stage. She looked amazing in a black satin evening dress and beamed confidently into the crowd. Bidding started at $1000 and quickly trebled in a frenzy of activity. The trainer encouraged further bids by announcing she would host a dinner for eight for the highest bidder.

The winning bid was $4500, and after some hurried consultation at the winning table, a voice called out the selected song – Aretha Franklin's anthem to female empowerment, 'Respect'.

When the applause finally died down after an enthusiastic rendition, the MC reached into the crystal bowl again and drew out a piece of paper. 'Well, this time it's our host! Darcy Ambrose-Taylor, would you please come up and do the honours?' For a fleeting moment, Clea glimpsed the look of horror that crossed Darcy's face before he plastered on a big smile.

'Come on, Darcy, you're a regular songbird,' Bahir quipped as his poor friend went up on stage like a lamb to the slaughter.

'Are you prepared to match the generosity of our previous participant?' the MC asked.

'Most certainly – I'll throw in dinner for ten.' A sudden flurry of activity between tables of women anxious to dine with such a desirable bachelor saw bidding rise quickly to $3500. But once the bidding died down and the winning table was announced, Darcy groaned. It wasn't a bevy of beauties; it was his own table full of mates. He knew they wouldn't let him off lightly.

Tom stood and declared in a loud voice, 'Lady in Red.' For a moment Darcy didn't catch the significance, but when he looked down at his table he suddenly paled. The bastards were ribbing him about Clea.

But he wasn't going to let it get to him. Darcy took a deep breath as the music started. He belted out the melody for all he was worth and, although slightly off-key, managed a reasonable attempt at the cheesy Chris de Burgh song, carefully avoiding eye contact with anyone at his own table.

Clea was mortified. Her beautiful red dress stood out like a beacon in a sea of black gowns. To her annoyance, when she could bear to watch Darcy's performance, he was smiling. He was enjoying her discomfort! Bahir gave her a quizzical glance and Amy looked daggers at her. It wasn't fair. Clea had accepted Darcy's invitation in good faith and now he was sending her up. But she had to handle the situation with dignity, much as she wished she could just get up and bolt from the room.

When Darcy rejoined the table he gave Amy a hearty kiss on her pouting mouth. But she refused to speak to him, and after a moment he stood up and moved towards Clea. 'Well done, Darcy,' she said and quickly excused herself from the table. Clea made sure she stopped to chat to Zoe on the way to the ladies so it didn't look like she was running away. The fundraising auction continued and there were only a few women checking their appearance in the mirrors. Clea angrily reapplied her new red lipstick, even more annoyed that it perfectly matched the dress. Most women would have been delighted at the attention, but it made Clea feel self-conscious, out of place and lonely.

She was sure the other women were staring at her and beat a hasty retreat back into the foyer, lingering for a while at the tables for the silent auction. But when she turned around, Amy had left the main room and was making a beeline for her.

'Wasn't that funny of Darcy's friends to choose a song about a dress I was wearing at a party the other night?' she said.

Clea suddenly realised how threatened Amy must be feeling to make such a ridiculous comment. 'It's Darcy's favourite colour, that's why I decided to wear red tonight,' Clea lied. As she walked off she was aware Amy was staring after her, concerned about how well she knew Darcy.

In the main room the band had struck up and couples were flocking to the dance floor. Bahir welcomed Clea back to the table with a warm smile.

'May I have the pleasure of this dance?' he asked. Clea joined him with relief and was soon laughing in his arms as they twirled around in an amateur jive. 'I thought you needed rescuing,' he confessed, speaking close to her ear above the music.

An unexpected shiver ran down Clea's spine. 'Thank you,' she mouthed back and laughed again as Bahir spun her around the dance floor.

The next song was more romantic and slow, and before Clea could escape, Bahir held her close. 'I didn't realise you and Darcy were such good friends.'

Clea laughed. 'We're not. We only met a few weeks ago.'

'But the song?'

'Yes, that was a bit embarrassing, but apparently it was in

honour of Amy.' Clea had no intention of spoiling this dance. Bahir held her with such confidence as they moved around the dance floor. She looked into his delicious hazel eyes and wondered if they would ever meet again after this night.

Clea was having fun, but a few songs later when the band took a break, she decided it was time to make a graceful exit. She thanked Bahir for being such lovely company and started to leave. Darcy, chatting to people at another table, saw her exit out of the corner of his eye. He dashed after her, not sure of what to say.

'Clea, I'm sorry if I embarrassed you, my friends —' he blurted out, but stopped short at her unimpressed expression. 'I hope you enjoyed the evening,' he finished lamely.

'Yes, thank you, Darcy, it was a very interesting night,' Clea replied coolly. 'I have an early start tomorrow, so enjoy the rest of your evening. Thanks again for the invitation.'

Back in her hotel room Clea angrily unzipped her red dress and let it drop to the floor in a crumpled heap. She felt so foolish and was annoyed with herself. Why on the earth had she allowed herself to be dragged into the games of a spoilt playboy?

Clea groaned and pushed the button that opened the curtains as she answered her mobile's insistent ring.

'Sorry, did I wake you?' said her brother cheerfully.

'What time is it?'

Ernest ignored the question. 'Looks like you were having fun last night – very glamorous. The social pages, no less.'

'What are you talking about?' Clea climbed out of bed and stepped over the red dress.

'He is rather good-looking, but you're the one who steals the show,' Ernest teased. 'It's page ninety-four of the paper.'

'Hang on, I'll see if they've delivered it.' Clea opened the door and found a copy of the weekend paper outside.

'Delivered it? I know you were at Royal Towers last night – but did you stay there too?' Ernest had a note of concern in his voice.

'Yes. By myself, thank you, stickybeak.' She closed the door, sat on the bed and flicked through the newspaper. 'Oh, no,' she groaned, staring at a photo of Darcy kissing her on the cheek. Clea hadn't even noticed the photographer, but they must've noticed her, because there she was – red dress and all.

'Anything you want to tell me?'

'No. Go away. I need coffee.'

'If you're in town today, want to catch up?' Ernest only hung up when his sister had agreed to have lunch.

14

Eclipse Stud, Hunter Valley, New South Wales

Ten days later, Darcy stepped out of the small plane onto the tarmac at Scone, New South Wales. Abdul was there to greet him and drive him the fifty kilometres to the farm. Despite the ongoing drought conditions over much of Australia, Darcy thought the pastures were surprisingly healthy, with a lot of nice green pick for the broodmares and early foals.

Australia was fortunately positioned with opposite seasons to most of the other major breeding centres in the world, which made it possible to breed to the best bloodlines in the world. The shuttle stallions ensured an internationally competitive racing and breeding industry.

Eclipse Stud shuttled their entire stallion roster. Seven stallions in all had flown south from the UK in preparation for the season – in two separate aircraft to satisfy the insurance company, who stood to lose a fortune from the dreaded possibility of a plane crash. Like a number of other major international thoroughbred horse studs, Sheikh Faisal had established a breeding stud up in the Hunter Valley, an area that had long been considered prime land for breeding and rearing racehorses. The stud's main purpose was to provide international bloodlines for his own large band of top-quality mares, and to build up a strong racing stable capable of dominating the Asia–Pacific racing region.

After a short but rough stint along a dirt road, which made Darcy reach out for the dashboard to steady himself, they arrived at their destination, heralded by uniform post-and-rail fencing sweeping into the distance on both sides of the road. Half a kilometre further the fence line was broken by a limestone wall angling into the main driveway. A large sign proclaimed 'ECLIPSE STUD'.

The stud was a thousand acres with the Hunter River running through much of the property. It had only been established two years before, and horses had been installed a year later, once the fencing and infrastructure were in place. It would take a while for the stud to establish its roots in the Australian landscape, but in the short-term the Sheikh was keen to breed a racing stable to compete in the prestigious Australian races. In particular, he had set his sights on the Weight for Age races such as the Moonee Valley Cox Plate and the BMW over 2400 metres at Rosehill, and the classics of the Derby and Oaks in both Sydney and Melbourne.

Abdul opened the imposing property gates electronically, barely slowing down as they zoomed along the vast driveway lined with young oak trees before pulling up at a substantial modern building shaped like a European-style stable complex. Through a large set of glass doors engraved with the Eclipse Stud logo, Darcy could see a great grassy quadrangle with a fountain in the centre.

Bahir stepped out into the sunshine from the office building and waited impatiently for Darcy to emerge. 'Leave your bags,' he suggested as Darcy pulled his computer and a dufflebag of clothes from the back seat. 'Someone else will deal with them. Come, I have a surprise for you.' Bahir ushered him around the corner of the building where two grooms were holding the reins of four saddled horses. 'I never understand why we drive around in cars when there is the pleasure of horseback.'

Darcy laughed and ruffled his friend's hair. 'You're always such a romantic, Bahir. Which one's mine?'

Bahir and Darcy mounted up and waited as Jalal appeared and he and Abdul leapt onto their horses. Bahir spun his horse around and cantered off down the roadway, as at home in the saddle as he was on two legs. Darcy spurred his horse to catch up and the two friends rode abreast down to the broodmare paddocks. Abdul and Jalal fell back at a distance to avoid choking on the cloud of dust kicked up from the dirt roadway.

Bahir slowed the group to a walk past his prized mares. 'Ah, my beauties, what bounty will you bear for me this year?' he crooned, admiring their pregnant forms.

The stallion section was immaculately manicured, with a large parade area of grass surrounded by a box hedge without a leaf out of place. Behind the lawn was an imposing stallion barn with large boxes for the stallions, all fully lined with wood panelling and rubber. At a slight distance from the barn was the serving shed, where the boys usually performed three times a day during the season if their libidos were up to it. Bahir and his company dismounted and proceeded on foot to the stallion paddocks. Eight half-acre squares were surrounded by high post-and-rail fencing and thick hedges of native trees and shrubs which acted as screens between paddocks to prevent antagonism among the territorial stallions.

'We'll parade them after lunch, but I wanted you to see them here first, free.' Bahir's affinity with his horses was very evident. The first paddock housed Napoleon, who had won both the Epsom Derby and the Arc de Triomphe. A deep bay horse, he picked casually at the grass before sauntering over for a pat. 'He still has a lot of letting down to go,' Bahir commented. 'I really think he'll suit the mares down here.'

Once at stud, a stallion developed into a much more powerful and heavier animal than his counterparts on the racetrack. Most noticeably, there was a dramatic thickening through the neck and shoulders. Napoleon had only served one season and still looked as if he'd stepped off a racetrack. Of course, in order to be fit enough to serve well over one hundred mares, the stallions had been in light training to tone up their muscles and ensure they would last the three and a half months before being sent home to the UK for a rest.

Despite Napoleon's placid appearance, all four men were experienced enough to know a stallion could display instinctively aggressive behaviour. Many an unsuspecting horse lover had had a hand crushed or finger badly bitten by a seemingly tame stallion.

In the next paddock, Bismarck gleamed like copper in the sunshine. At their approach he tossed his mane and reared, pawing the air, then galloped around the paddock before finally charging at them and stopping at the gate, half rearing again and arching his magnificent neck. Bahir smiled indulgently. Abdul called out to the feisty stallion in his native tongue and in an instant the horse walked calmly to the fence and greeted him with an affectionate headbutt.

'Abdul's the only one who can really handle him,' Bahir said.

Many years before in Dubai, the boy Abdul had been found in the Sheikh's stables after a huge sandstorm, curled up on the straw with a stallion as if they had known each other always. After much coaxing, the boy explained he had heard the horse in distress and soothed him with songs from the desert. Sheikh Faisal was intrigued. He sized up the boy and asked if he could ride. Before he could stop him, Abdul leapt onto the stallion's back, and without the assistance of a saddle or bridle rode the horse around the grounds as if it were an old hack. For his rare gift, Abdul became part of the Sheikh's household from that day. He was seventeen years old.

The seven-year-old son of Sheikh Faisal quickly became Abdul's shadow. Initially the young man tried to shake off his young devotee, preferring the company of horses, or solitude, but Bahir persisted, quietly following Abdul everywhere, careful not to get in his way. After a while Abdul began to relax in the little prince's company, answering his questions and teaching him about horses. Bahir became the little brother Abdul had left behind. But as Bahir grew older and more independent, he insisted his friend Jalal tag along. Under Abdul's patient tutelage both boys were superior horsemen by the age of twelve, when Bahir was sent away to a land far from home for his education.

As a special surprise for Bahir's first school holiday, and with the Sheikh's consent, Abdul organised for the two boys to compete in their first endurance ride, a gruelling race of eighty kilometres through the sand dunes.

Bahir was brave and resolute, even when a wind picked up and hurled sand in his face as he travelled between checkpoints, his valiant Arabian mount surefooted through the dunes. But Jalal struggled, and three times Bahir and Abdul doubled back to encourage him to complete the course. The two boys were the youngest riders in the race and arrived at the finishing line to great cheers from the spectators. Jalal lapped up the attention, but Abdul noticed that not once did he acknowledge the support of his friend.

Five of Darcy's broodmares had been allocated a visit to the first-season sire Bismarck and were already on the property waiting to foal down. Darcy had taken Abdul's advice and sent the four he'd suggested, but threw in a younger mare as well, as an experiment on type rather than pedigree.

The next paddock along from Bismarck held the English Ascot Gold Cup winner Mitterrand, another bay horse who stayed down the far end of the field and only acknowledged their presence with a few tosses of his head. The group inspected all seven of the stallions before mounting their hacks and cantering back to the office complex for a sumptuous buffet lunch in the boardroom.

After lunch, Darcy and Abdul stood under the shade of a gnarled peppercorn tree to watch the stallions parade. Two other broodmare owners and a bloodstock agent had joined them for lunch and had now staked out a position on the open lawn, each armed with a glossy stud brochure. Bahir was playing host, and Jalal talked to the agent, whom he knew well from international sales.

One by one the stallions were brought out and stood up in the correct pose, with all legs clear from the side view. Napoleon was in a particularly playful mood and fidgeted his legs back to square up every time his groom slackened the lead rope. Eventually the horse became tired with the game and struck out with his near fore.

'Just walk him,' Abdul called out. 'I don't think he's in the mood for posing today.'

'Is he sixteen hands?' Darcy asked as Napoleon was walked past.

Abdul remembered Darcy had a keen eye. 'Yes. I think he

may throw some refinement into your bigger-boned mares here in Australia.'

'Good, I have a mare I'd like to send. She's been a great producer, with six winners out of nine foals. I was going to send her to Wigmore,' Darcy said.

Abdul sympathised. It was terrible to have a stallion cut off in his prime. 'Let me know her details.'

Jalal and Bahir had moved off to the side and were admiring Bismarck as he made a grand entrance, rearing and tossing his head so his deep golden mane swished in the breeze. His groom Patrick was used to such behaviour, having travelled from the UK to stay with the horse, but struggled to get him under control. As Bismarck reared again Bahir made an almost imperceptible gesture with his hand, which Abdul picked up immediately and acted upon, firmly taking the lead rope from Patrick. Bismarck's front hoofs clattered to the ground and he gave Abdul such an enthusiastic nudge with his powerful head he almost knocked Abdul off his feet. He stood calmly when asked and mooched alongside Abdul as he walked circuits of the path.

'How many mares do you think we'll get for him in his first season?' Jalal asked hopefully.

'I checked the bookings today and he's already up to ninety, so I would assume around 120 outside mares plus thirty of our own.' Bahir turned to his friend. 'I keep forgetting this is the first stallion you've owned at stud,' he said, smiling. 'We're standing him at $35 000, but of course you won't see any returns until the foals are born under our usual contracts. We'll probably have to drop the service fee slightly for his second and third seasons, but I'm sure when his progeny step out on the racetrack and prove what they're worth we'll be able to increase it again.'

Abdul disappeared into the stable complex with a placid Bismarck, and Bahir joined Darcy under the tree as Mitterrand was led into the open. 'By the way, Afifah sends her love,' he said. Afifah was back at university, but had made her brother promise she could come with him to Australia on his next trip.

After a pause Bahir said casually, 'That Dr Reynolds who was at your table the other night, I'm guessing by the song you think she's a bit special?'

'That debacle! No, it was just Tom's idea of a joke. Not very funny, if you ask me. The last thing I need is a woman like Clea. Amy's my squeeze at the moment.' Darcy felt irritated just remembering that night. At least the make-up sex with Amy had been worth it.

'The little blonde thing?' Bahir asked with a level of surprise, and it was only then Darcy realised where the previous question had been leading. Bahir was interested in Clea. Well, so be it. Let him see how far he could get with that cold fish.

'Amy's a sweet girl, and she's certainly more than a little blonde thing,' he said defensively. But the truth was Darcy had been annoyed by Amy's behaviour at the ball and he was relieved to be going overseas soon.

Jalal joined them in the shade and for once Darcy was pleased, since the conversation about women ceased abruptly, as if Bahir didn't want anyone to know his thoughts. Darcy shifted the subject back to the safe topic of horses.

'Jalal, you must be so pleased with Bismarck. Not only did you get the glory on the racetrack, but it looks like he'll fire up the serving barn as well,' he said amiably.

'I have had a lot of success on the racetrack, thank you, Darcy,' Jalal shot back. 'I may not be like you, managing all your father's stallions, but I'm not a complete novice.'

Darcy was at a loss to understand how his friendly comment had been so misconstrued. 'I'm sorry, I was only complimenting you on such an impressive animal,' he said, an edge in his voice.

'Let's take our other visitors to meet some of the new foals,' Bahir suggested, diffusing the building tension. The rivalry between his two closest friends saddened him greatly. Jalal's jealousy was the root cause, but Darcy could also say and do stupid things that inflamed the situation.

Abdul led the party on foot across to the nursery stables, from where the high-pitched whinnying of foals and the guttural reassurances of their dams rang out.

'This little fellow is in with a hernia.' Abdul allowed them to stop and admire a perky little steel-grey colt, who stood bravely next to his mother instead of hiding behind her bulk. 'The dam has already produced two Group winners, so this colt has a reputation to live up to.'

In the next box the foal was laid out cold on the fresh sawdust, his mother watching over him carefully. He had a bandage on his fetlock where he had knocked himself while trying to stand on his wobbly stick-like legs.

The filly in the third box had just had a periosteal strip performed on her leg to correct her conformation. The dam put her head over the stable door at their approach. Bahir stopped and spoke to her gently. She lifted her nose and he blew softly into her nostrils, which widened to take in his scent. Abdul had taught him to 'breathe' with a horse when he had been a young boy. Given far away from any classroom, that lesson taught him the spiritual connection with a horse that made your soul soar with freedom. Bahir had been in awe of Abdul then, and in many ways he still looked on him with a sense of wonder.

15

Stallion Barn, Eclipse Stud, Hunter Valley

A half moon threw soft light on the path, intermittently disappearing behind scurrying clouds, and a strong cool wind from the south whistled past Jalal's ears. He stopped and listened, turning his head to catch the sound of soft music. Lights blazed fifty metres away in the staff living quarters. Reassured, he continued on his path to the stallion barn.

Jalal made this nocturnal pilgrimage every night in Australia. He found sleep an elusive mistress in this faraway country. Closer to the barn, the smell of horses was both familiar and comforting; he could hear their hoofs fidgeting on the sawdust with dull thuds. He paused to let his eyes adjust to the interior darkness, then moved purposefully to the far stable. Bismarck turned to greet his customary visitor and listened intently while Jalal spoke softly in Arabic to reassure him. Abdul might manage the stallion with ease in the sunlight, but in the dark Bismarck belonged to Jalal.

Salah al Din had little to do with horses, and frowned upon the indulgence of horseracing. But Jalal had learned to love horses under the masterful tutorship of Abdul, and he aspired to breed champions in the way his father aspired to succeed in business.

Bismarck moved closer, his velvety muzzle inquisitively inhaling his night-time visitor's familiar scent. Sadness welled up deep within Jalal's chest. Entrenched within his soul was an ocean of respect for the horse. If only these visits could go on forever. But Jalal would soon have to go back to Dubai and desperately try to salvage something out of the wreck of his family's fortune.

He made his way gingerly to the feed room, hands outstretched in the dark. The barn cat Tatiana had already skewered three mice with her razor-sharp claws, and she sat quietly with saucer-like eyes, bloody bodies at her feet, smugly aware of her invisibility. Jalal fumbled around for a moment then found a bale of lucerne hay. He pulled out an armful and headed back to the stable, inadvertently kicking over a feed bucket on his way. Tatiana leapt onto the feed bins and knocked off a metal scoop. Up in the rafters there was a loud squeak and the flapping of wings, before all settled back into silence. Jalal, heart pounding, was now aware of the nocturnal creatures on watch.

The moon reappeared and a soft light filtered into the airy barn as Jalal held out his offering to Bismarck, smiling as the horse crunched the sweet hay.

*

At the noise in the barn, Abdul tensed. He was doing a routine check of the mares ready to foal down, ensuring their foaling alarms were all activated in order to alert staff when they lay down to give birth. The noise could have been anything and there was no sound of distress from the stallions. But he felt something imperceptible, a presence out of place, and decided to investigate.

Tatiana wrapped herself around his leg affectionately as he reached the side door. He bent to scratch behind her ear, feeling the vibration of her purr through her soft fur. She was worth her weight in gold, this little feline, the best mouser he had ever found. Her ever-important task was to prevent the horse feed from becoming contaminated by mice. From inside the barn, Abdul heard a voice, soft and secretive, and he moved stealthily towards the sound, concealing his presence in the gloomy shadows. The voice was coming from Bismarck's stable. A man was leaning on the stable door, and when he spoke again Abdul recognised Jalal's voice. Abdul knew Jalal often came down to see Bismarck at night, and he was about to tiptoe out and leave the man in peace with his horse when he caught some of the one-sided conversation.

'My family started from nothing and built an empire,' Jalal told Bismarck. 'Throughout my life I've had almost everything I could wish for, but if I lose it all tomorrow, my most important possession has been you.' Abdul could see Jalal stroking Bismarck's mighty head. 'To think a boy from Khadelem could conquer the world's great racetracks with such a champion,' Jalal breathed in amazement.

Abdul staggered back, then ran as quietly as he could from the barn and sank to the ground in the deep shadows against its exterior. Jalal spun around at the scuffling sound but was reassured by the silence that fell. Just a mouse or cat, he thought. He gave Bismarck one last pat and quietly left the stables, pausing for a moment as the moon reappeared, and heading for the path to the stud residence.

Abdul watched from the shadows, his breathing shallow. *Khadelem.* It was a shock to hear the name of that poor little village, so very far away. He put his hands over his eyes in an effort to block out the memories, but was overpowered by the horror. The blood, the screams, the lifeless eyes of his mother, which haunted his dreams.

16

Prince Of Wales Hospital, Sydney

Three days after Darcy's visit, Prince Bahir fell gravely ill. He was running an extreme fever, had difficulty breathing and had a hacking cough that brought up alarming traces of blood. The local doctor checked his patient briefly before ignoring Bahir's weak protests and ordering an ambulance to take the prince to Sydney immediately. Jalal intervened, insisting an air ambulance would be faster, and within the hour Bahir was in a helicopter racing towards the city.

Bahir was barely conscious but maintained his grasp on Jalal's arm. With such shallow breaths his lips were turning blue, a startling contrast against his tanned skin. Jalal clung on to his friend as if his own strength could pull Bahir from the brink of death. On arrival at the hospital Bahir was hooked up to a ventilator in the intensive care unit while tests were run to determine the nature of the illness. An infectious-diseases specialist was already on standby, as the severity of the condition in someone so fit and healthy suggested a rare and deadly infection. Dr Jonathan Craic examined the patient then questioned the doctor and Abdul briefly.

'Has anyone else fallen sick around him?' Both men shook their heads.

'When did the symptoms first appear?'

'Two days ago – only two days and look at him!' Abdul was distraught.

The specialist moved back to Bahir's bedside and gently opened his mouth. There were traces of foam around his lips and a few flecks coming from his nostrils. Dr Craic turned quickly back to the men. 'Tell me, are any of your horses sick?'

'One of the stallions is ill, but they've just come out of a long period of quarantine.' Abdul was almost defensive, as though he thought he could be at fault in some way.

Dr Craic sprang into action. 'I need to test for hendra virus immediately,' he barked at the presiding doctor. 'Hendra can cause severe respiratory failure, including haemorrhaging and oedema of the lungs, or it can lead to meningitis. You'll need to X-ray his chest immediately and run a CT.'

Bahir was moaning in pain. Jalal held his hand, unsure of whether he was still conscious, but a faint squeeze told him Bahir was still with them.

'I will attend him with you,' he insisted when the orderlies put up the sides of the bed and wheeled it from the room. He walked quickly alongside, a hand reassuringly on the sick man's shoulder. 'I am here, Bahir, I will always be here with you. I will not leave your side,' he whispered, thinking back to so many years ago, when they had watched their blood mingling with the desert sand. Blood brothers would never be parted.

Abdul paced the floor of the waiting room outside the intensive care unit like a caged tiger, until he could take it no longer. He faced Mecca, fell to his knees and began to pray.

Patrick the stud groom sat in the straw of the veterinary box weeping, with Bismarck's powerful head in his lap. Only two days ago the stallion had started to show alarming symptoms of ataxia, a dysfunction of muscle coordination, and this morning the vet had drained twenty litres of fluid off the horse's lungs. By the afternoon Bismarck was no better and had sunk moaning to his knees, before toppling over in the straw. His huge body laboured under every breath, his soft nostrils flaring to suck in as much oxygen as possible. He seemed comforted by the groom's soothing words, recognising a friend.

There seemed no hope now. The vet was trying everything he could, and frantically consulting vets at the Hunter Valley Veterinary Hospital over the phone. Bismarck made a soft noise and tried to lift his head. Patrick supported his weight and encouraged the horse to try to stand. 'Come on, boy, you can do it, get up, Bismarck!' But the stallion lay back down, panting for air.

His great lungs heaved anther moment, and then suddenly all was still. Bahir and Abdul's favourite stallion lay dead, his glassy eyes staring into oblivion. Patrick hunched over his body sobbing.

Dr Craic burst through the doors of the intensive care unit. 'I have positive confirmation of hendra virus,' he called out to the attending staff. 'Instigate maximum infectious protocols immediately.' Fortunately the attending doctors and nurses had all donned protective masks, gloves and gowns when Dr Craic first mentioned the virus. 'Do you know where the other man is? Your friend?' Dr Craic asked Jalal urgently, who pointed numbly to the waiting area, incapable of speech.

Dr Craic found Abdul on the floor praying. 'Prince Bahir has hendra virus,' the doctor said. 'We can treat his symptoms, but not the virus. It will have to run its course, I'm afraid. We'll do the absolute best we can here. Meanwhile, I need you to contact the horse stud urgently. The sick horse will be contagious to anyone attending it. Do you understand? You must warn everyone to stay away from the horse and you must alert the authorities straightaway. Anyone who has had contact with the horse must come to hospital immediately, even if they're not showing any signs of illness – and I'm afraid any horses that have had immediate contact will need to be destroyed.' Dr Craic spun around and went back to his patient.

Abdul stared after him in bewilderment and disbelief. He vaguely recalled reading about the virus, but couldn't believe it could strike down a healthy young man like Bahir. Abdul pulled himself together. Bahir was in good hands, now he had to act quickly to save the horses.

The racing industry heard of Bahir's illness and Bismarck's death through an alert from the Australian Government's Department of Primary Industries. Not long after Bahir, Patrick had been rushed to hospital critically ill with meningitis and the stud vet had shown mild flu-like symptoms and was under observation. Mitterrand, the stallion in the box next to Bismarck's, had also shown signs of congestion in his lungs and with great reluctance had been euthanised.

Sheikh Faisal had flown to Australia immediately and was now a permanent fixture by his son's bedside. The Sheikh and Jalal made sure Bahir was never alone, their dedication touching the hearts of the hospital staff. The Sheikh had learned, like so many others before him, that while money and power assured many things, the truly important things in life could never be bought. Health and happiness were priceless. Now he was praying for his son's life.

As Bahir began to recover slowly, Jalal allowed himself to grieve over the loss of the mighty Bismarck. He would probably never again own a horse of that calibre; never again see his own glory reflected in the eyes of a horse.

Ten days later Patrick was lying in hospital with a heavily bandaged head. Emergency surgery had removed the fluids accumulating between his brain and the surrounding membranes – a procedure that amounted to having holes drilled in his skull. Thankfully, Patrick was well drugged up and had been mostly sleeping for the past week.

He woke to a light pressure on his arm, as a nurse in protective clothing gently woke him and explained that someone had come to see him. She stepped back and Patrick saw Prince Bahir in a wheelchair, an intravenous drip by his side and a mask and gown protecting him. He looked pale and drawn and as he spoke he lost breath quickly and had to pause.

'They tell me you are strong and will pull through this well, Patrick,' he said as he moved a little closer to the bed. 'I'm so very sorry this has happened. Rest assured that all your medical expenses will be looked after, and as soon as the doctors think you are well enough to travel we will send you back to your family for a few months break, with full pay.'

'Thank you, Prince,' Patrick answered slowly. Even in his groggy state he was relieved at the news. A stud groom didn't command a huge salary and he would have struggled through this time without his employer's generosity and care. 'The horses?'

'All the other stallions have tested negative. It was just our beautiful Bismarck and Mitterrand who suffered.' Bahir's eyes filled with tears.

'I stroked his head to the end,' said Patrick. 'He didn't die alone . . . That horse meant everything to me.'

'I know. No one could have cared for him better. Rest now,

I will come and visit again soon.' The nurse, who had stood quietly by during their exchange, wheeled Bahir out of the room. Patrick lay for a while with tears rolling down his face.

Abdul was cleared of the virus, and once he knew Bahir was out of danger, he reluctantly agreed to return to the stud to help manage the crisis. The Sheikh and his family were all Abdul had in this world, the only people he could truly trust. The thought of losing Bahir was unbearable, after having lost so many close to him. Unable to sleep, the old urge crept up on Abdul again and he finally gave in, unrolling his swag in the stables at night, the comfort of the horses' presence lulling him finally to sleep. But even there he wasn't completely safe, as horrific images flashed before his wearied eyes. Long-ago scenes he had blocked out seemed to haunt him, awake and asleep.

Agents from the Department of Agriculture, Fisheries and Forestry settled in at Eclipse Stud for a lengthy investigation, sharing their findings with the Department of Primary Industries. Forensic experts hoped to determine the exact cause of the contamination, and a microbiology expert had been called in from the Australian Animal Infectious Diseases Laboratory. The whole stud was put under strict quarantine until further notice.

Darcy was horrified when he heard of the drama unfolding in the Hunter Valley and contacted Abdul immediately to offer his assistance. He was already booked on a flight to Sydney to visit Bahir in hospital and confirm with his own eyes that his friend was going to pull through. Darcy suggested he could drive up to the stud and help Abdul manage the crisis, but Abdul wouldn't hear of it.

'Stay away, Darcy,' he warned. 'Until I can be sure no one else will get sick, I'm certainly not allowing you up here. The Sheikh and your father would never forgive me.' He was right – there really wasn't anything useful Darcy could do, except provide some comfort to Bahir at his bedside.

17
Eclipse Stud, Hunter Valley

On her way through Sydney en route to Eclipse Stud in the Hunter Valley, Clea made a visit to the hospital to see Bahir. It was only when she heard of the virus outbreak that she'd realised he was not just a handsome friend of Darcy's, but Prince Bahir, son of Sheikh Faisal. She told herself she was visiting in the name of science, but deep down, she knew it was more than that.

She knocked tentatively on the hospital room door and entered to find Bahir looking frail, propped up on pillows with his drip arm resting on a cushion. He smiled weakly when he saw her.

'I'm sorry to disturb you, Bahir, but I'm going up to your stud this afternoon and wanted to say how very sorry I am.'

'Please, come in.'

Clea hadn't realised there was anyone else in the room, but when she stepped forward she saw a man sitting in an armchair. The family resemblance was clear.

Sheikh Faisal introduced himself and shook her hand. 'I might leave you two alone for a moment.'

Clea was surprised that a man as powerful as the Sheikh looked like just another anxious father in this hospital setting. She had imagined someone more aloof.

As Sheikh Faisal left the room he touched Clea lightly on the shoulder and whispered, 'Please, not too long, he's still very weak.'

Out in the corridor the Sheikh leaned against the wall for a moment. He was exhausted from worry and lack of sleep. He headed for the cafe to get some food and coffee, and to call Yvonne. He needed someone to talk to – she wasn't a parent, but he knew she would understand.

Inside the room, Clea turned to Bahir. 'How are you feeling?'

Bahir gestured for her to sit in the chair by the bed. 'I confess I've been better.'

'You look —'

'Awful, I know.' He smiled again and Clea saw the charming man she'd first met. 'Please tell me you can stop this spreading. We've already lost two stallions and it's just been devastating.'

'I'll do my best, Bahir,' Clea reassured him.

As Clea left the hospital room, she almost bumped into a man who resembled Bahir in height and appearance, though his face held none of Bahir's charm. 'Who are you?' he demanded.

Clea explained her presence in the hospital, and Jalal introduced himself as Bahir's closest friend and advisor. 'It would be best if you tell me about anything you find.' He handed her a business card. 'Anything at all – I may be able to help.'

Clea stood for a moment in the wintery Hunter Valley sunshine, feeling warmth soaking through her protective biosecurity suit before entering the stables. It took her eyes a moment to adjust to the change in light. Each stable had an elaborate engraved brass plate on the door and she walked past each one, tracing the names with her finger until she found Bismarck's. There was a terrible poignancy about this empty stall. Clea ran her heavily gloved hand lightly over the horse's name and the Arabic phrase inscribed underneath, and closed her eyes as if to conjure up his image.

'It means, "God took a handful of southerly wind, blew his breath over it and created the horse". It's a Bedouin legend.' Abdul, watching Clea from the shadows, stepped forward.

'It's beautiful,' Clea breathed. 'But you shouldn't be in here without proper protection, it's still not safe.' Abdul had caught her by surprise.

'I didn't mean to startle you,' he apologised. 'My name is Abdul Aniza, I'm the managing director here at Eclipse. Perhaps you could brief me on your initial findings later this afternoon?'

She nodded, struck immediately by his intensity, and watched as Abdul walked from the stables. Clea guessed he was in his forties, although his face was weather-beaten – a man of the land.

Clea checked her oxygen supply; she would take no risks in the contaminated area. She stepped inside Bismarck's stable and walked carefully around the deep impression of the dying horse indented in the straw. Squatting down, she rummaged around with large tweezers, finding a few likely pieces of straw. It had, of course, already been tested in the autopsy, but another sample wouldn't hurt. She removed a sterile container from her kit and dropped the samples inside.

Next she carefully examined the walls, looking for some evidence of how the virus had infected Bismarck. Bats were unlikely to roost in the barn, as all the daytime activity would keep them away. Perhaps a stray bat had winged its way in and somehow left droppings or urine in this stable? Clea looked around for a clue. If a bat had got in here it would have passed through either the internal or external iron bars of Bismarck's stable.

Clea stepped outside the stable again and looked carefully at the small ledge outside the bars. She took a hand-held UV light from her equipment bag and flicked the switch. It wasn't the greatest forensic technology, but it did show up traces of bodily fluids and other substances hard to detect with the naked eye. The light shone over the ledge and bars, showing all variety of marks and splodges. But one smudged area stood out – a few flecks of brilliant white, clear as day under the light. Clea carefully scraped the area with a swab and deposited her findings in a small sterile container.

A mobile laboratory with all the necessary equipment had arrived from the National Centre for Biosecurity, which was attached to the Australian National University. Any samples discovered on site could be safely identified and stored in the mobile unit using the correct biocontainment protocols.

Clea extracted the sterile containers from her equipment bag and switched on the electron microscope. It came complete with an isolation box, which she opened and carefully placed the specimens inside. The case sealed tight and was airlocked by a pressure container, but two holes sealed off with thick rubber gloves on either side of the rectangular box allowed Clea to insert her hands and work with the materials. Within a few minutes, she had expertly prepared a slide of the suspect white substance to view under the microscope. This was placed into another smaller container inside the isolation box that would become a vacuum, allowing optimal viewing conditions.

Clea stared at the microscope screen. There was always a story to be told from the structure of a virus. Hendra virus was one of the two viruses that made up the genus of henipavirus, in the family paramyxoviridae – the other being the nipah virus. Both viruses occured naturally in fruit bat populations, but the bats themselves had a natural immunity, acting only as hosts – though capable of infecting a number of animal species.

As a scientist, Clea had to admire the simplicity of the virus's structure. Embedded within the membrane were attachment spikes of protein, which secured the virus to the surface of the host cell, and fusion spikes, which allowed it to release its deadly contents directly into the cell.

Perhaps that was what she loved most about the microbiological world in which she was immersed. No emotions, no mistakes, just genius nature at its simplest and most effective. In comparison to this world of order, humans were flawed, not just because they could be invaded by an invisible army of viruses, but truly, intrinsically flawed.

Clea's head jerked up from the screen. She checked the slide carefully then examined its contents again. The white substance she had collected had nothing to do with bats, but contained a protein and salt in a powdered form. Amazingly, traces of the hendra virus appeared to be fused with the substance. Clea's gut instinct told her something was very wrong.

Showered and back in civilian clothes, Clea made her way to the stud office complex. She wanted to talk to Abdul again in more depth, and after a few minutes wait, he appeared and led her to his office. He sat quietly watching as she explained her role in the investigation, making her uncomfortable with his silence.

Abdul was still grieving for Bismarck, his hopes and dreams for the horse in tatters. Such a cruel death. And now they had sent him some pretty young woman to work out how the tragedy had occurred.

'Is there some solution you would typically give to the horses that combines proteins with salts?' Clea asked, following up her startling discovery.

Abdul thought for a moment. There were so many feeds, solutions, veterinary procedures and inoculations he didn't know where to start. There was no easy answer. 'I'll have to look into it,' he answered gruffly.

Clea glanced at the clock behind Abdul's desk and realised it was already 6.30 p.m. She was tired and hungry and couldn't really achieve much more for the evening. It would be better to wait for Abdul's answer. 'Thank you. I look forward to hearing what you find out tomorrow,' she said. 'I'll leave you in peace for the rest of the evening, but could you point me in the right direction for my room tonight?'

Abdul was embarrassed that he had not extended the correct hospitality. He left her in the charge of the receptionist; she would manage it far better than he could.

Clea was staying in the guesthouse, a single-storey modern building set on a slight hill with soaring glass windows looking over the stud. There were two separate apartments here, both private, and Clea knew some of her colleagues from the government team were housed in the apartment on the other side of the building. Her bag had already been placed on the king-size bed and she grabbed a warmer jumper from its depths as the night air cooled.

Over a simple dinner of roast chicken with chat potatoes back in the office complex, Clea and the government boys compared notes. Hendra outbreaks had only ever occurred in Queensland and northern New South Wales, east of the Great Dividing Range that swept down the eastern coast of Australia. If disease-carrying bats had migrated into the horse-rich valleys of the Hunter the situation could be critical.

Back in the guesthouse, Clea realised how much she was enjoying working out in the field. Being here somehow vindicated all the hours of work she'd done in the sterile environment of AAIDL. Here she was surrounded by magnificent horses free to roam in their paddocks, as opposed to the poor laboratory animals whose miserable lives were shortened for the advancement of other species and ultimately humans. Tomorrow morning she would get up early and go for a run around the property to make the most of the beautiful surroundings. But for the moment something was troubling her and she couldn't quite put her finger on it.

More than a year had passed since she had last examined the hendra virus kept in biosecurity at AAIDL, but she was very familiar with its appearance. That was it! Clea's curiosity got the better of her and she threw her coat and shoes on to go back to the mobile laboratory.

The guesthouse was silent and most of the lights were out as she quietly closed the door. Once away from the glow of the windows she waited for a moment as her eyes adjusted to the dark – the moon was casting a faint glow, certainly enough for her to find her way to the mobile lab. She stumbled along the path, a cool wind blowing the smell of pastures her way. Her feet crunched along the gravel surrounding the stallion barn, but she stopped suddenly, hearing something close by. Clea held her breath and waited. There it was again, the sound of singing in a foreign language, which made it seem even more mysterious on this dark night.

Clea crept silently towards the stallion paddocks, towards the music. Drawing closer, she saw Abdul leaning against a paddock gate. He was stroking Napoleon's head and the stallion seemed entranced by the lullaby.

Clea decided not to spoil this private moment. She turned to creep back towards the path just as Napoleon nickered a greeting to the intruder. 'It is a song of my ancestors,' Abdul said. 'It seems everyone wishes to visit my horses under the cloak of darkness,' he added under his breath.

'I'm sorry, Abdul, I didn't mean to disturb you. I was just getting my computer.' Clea felt embarrassed, as it seemed clear both man and horse had sensed her presence some time before.

'My people were nomadic tribesmen,' Abdul continued, ignoring her apology. 'We would sing this song to the horses at night to calm them. Do you understand the bond between my people and Allah's great gift, the horse, Dr Reynolds?'

'No, I don't suppose I truly do.' Clea moved closer and cautiously patted the stallion's strong head.

'These creatures are blessed; they are as wild and free as the desert itself. They have carried us to safety across the sands for centuries; they are our friends. To an Arab, the horse is the spirit of all that is wise and good. We must stop this virus, Dr Reynolds. You have to help me.'

'I'll do everything I can, I promise.' Clea finally broke the spell and walked quietly away. Silence fell across the paddocks again. But as she climbed the steps to unlock the door of the mobile lab she could hear Abdul singing softly again, and envied him the passion he felt in his heart for the mighty horse.

Abdul watched her slender form disappear into the dark.

What could she ever understand of his life, his Bedouin background, the loss of his parents? She had been raised in the West with a luxurious life mapped out before her. Abdul had lost everything. Even the memory of his parents had faded over time, their laughter and love overshadowed by the ghastly vision of their deaths.

They were Bedouins, steeped in the traditions of their ancestors, eking out a subsistence living on the fringes of the vast desert. Seven families made up a group that was part of a larger tribe, or Qabila, and Uncle Ghalib was their appointed leader. In tribal society everyone had their place, but once his parents were dead Abdul felt like an outsider floundering in the sand, struggling to come to terms with his loss and profound sense of alienation. He found solace with the horses.

These wonderful, free-spirited creatures recognised the grief of the boy and offered him gentle affection. The old tribesman who had tended them for forty years recognised a kindred spirit in Abdul – a boy with the soul of a horse. Abdul had found a place in the harsh desert world, and for the first time his uncle seemed pleased.

Abdul became a fearless horseman. He slept with his equine family under the blazing sky and the old man taught him songs from times past, songs to settle his charges as the desert wind blew cold and battered their small fire. Abdul tended the horses, learning to groom, feed, handle their tack and equipment, and manage their feet and health.

Before Abdul's parents died, his uncle had become sick with

an illness that robbed him daily of his physical force. The tribe settled on the outskirts of Khadelem village so that Ghalib could see out his life in comfort and care. But the disease was in no hurry, and by the time the tribeswomen took up the grieving wail, the tribe had all but assimilated into village life.

The new leader had less power, as modern conveniences had broken down centuries of tradition in a matter of years. But he had enough power left to make the one decision that would affect Abdul's entire future – he sold the horses to buy a beaten-up wreck of a truck. Abdul left the tribe forever that night.

18

Breeding Season Opening. Eclipse Stud

Up early the next morning, despite having stared at the computer screen for hours the night before, Clea helped herself to the breakfast provisions in the apartment's kitchenette and brewed a plunger of coffee. She ate her cereal and toast gazing out over the property and then treated herself to a morning jog.

The grounds were immaculately kept: all the fencing perfect, the roadways neat. A few early foals, looking awkward on their impossibly long legs, peeked out from underneath their mother's tails at the strange new world of blue skies and green pastures. They were adorably cute but, despite Clea's encouragement, they were too young to venture far from the safety of their relaxed mothers. A brand-new foal was stretched out in the morning sun fast asleep, its stumpy tail and near foreleg twitching occasionally in dreamland.

The female occupants of other paddocks waddled over for some attention, their pendulous bellies swaying as they ambled in the sunshine. The system of paddocks allowed the mares to be moved closer and closer to the foaling-down paddocks, which were floodlit and monitored at night, as they approached term. The mare in the paddock closest to the broodmare stable complex was leaning slightly on the gate and Clea was amazed to see a tabby cat curled up on the warmth of her broad back and basking in the early-morning sunshine. She reached over and patted the contented creature, who stretched in appreciation, her claws carefully sheathed.

For a moment she wondered if Darcy's stud was this idyllic, but pushed the thought from her mind. She needed to solve a problem.

Clea jogged along the roadway between paddocks, focusing on her breathing. The rhythm would clear her mind. After half an hour she was struck by a thought and sprinted back to the guesthouse to change as quickly as possible. The sample she had taken from the stable yesterday should make sense of the issue.

Inside the mobile unit, she prepared the straw she had collected from Bismarck's stable for examination. The virus illuminated the electron microscope's screen. She hastily switched the unit's computer back on and inserted a USB device that contained the pictures of the virus collected from the stallion's autopsy. Unsurprisingly, the virus in both images was the same strain, with an identical shape: a lateral eclipse with a bulbous end.

The hendra virus was pleomorphic, meaning it could take on a variety of shapes. Cells from the same strain of virus, however, maintained the same shape. The hairs on Clea's arms prickled with recognition as she realised where she had seen that exact shape before.

The investigators from the Department of Agriculture, Fisheries and Forestry looked at her in surprise. 'Surely it's just a coincidence that the shape is the same as your lab sample,' one of them ventured. 'Besides, we found bats last night. We had to travel a distance up the river, but there was a big roost of them, so I think we can safely say we've found our culprits.' An expert bat handler had been called in to assist in trapping and testing these local bats for the hendra virus.

'Think about it, Dr Reynolds. How could the virus have even escaped from your laboratory, let alone wound up here? It's simply not plausible – not with the level of biosecurity you have at your facility. Surely the strain of virus you have at AAIDL could also occur in hosts in the wild?'

Clea had to agree. It was a bizarre coincidence, but the local bats seemed to be carrying the same strain that AAIDL had locked away in their Geelong lab. Abdul had already confirmed the stallions had all been recently subjected to booster inoculations, and a syringe squirted before injection could account for the traces of viral transport medium. Bahir had simply come in close contact with Bismarck once he was infected. Case closed. She toyed with the idea of phoning Darcy for his opinion, but decided to ignore her gut instinct in favour of the empirical evidence.

Clea dialled her mother instead. She had rushed up to the Hunter Valley without letting Susanne know about the trip. Sure enough, her absence had already been noted.

'I called you twice last night at home, and this morning too. You could have let me know, darling, I've been worried.'

'Sorry, Mum. The mobile reception's really bad up here, I'm standing on the highest hill to call you now.'

'You be careful. I don't like the sound of that hendra virus one bit.'

Clea had had this conversation many times before. 'You know I'm always careful. The funny thing is, Mum, I'm really worried about the *source* of this outbreak. It doesn't quite make sense — Mum?' The signal had dropped out.

Clea stayed on for an extra day to conclude the investigation, and discovered the following day, September first, was the opening of the breeding season. Although the stud was still under quarantine, there were enough broodmares already on the property ready for service. When the alarm went off at 5 a.m., Clea jumped out of bed, showered and dressed, tying her long hair back in a sleek ponytail. Noises could be heard coming from the serving barn, which had been cleared and fully sterilised in preparation for the first day of the stud season. Grabbing a cup of coffee, Clea strolled in the pre-dawn darkness to the stables.

The barn lights revealed numerous stud workers already in attendance. Inside the barn was a large sawdusted area with a vet crush to manage the horses and a padded enclosure with a gate for access. At the back of the barn was an area partitioned off for safety. Abdul waved her over as she neared.

'You must stay close to me,' he warned. 'The stallions can be boisterous on the first day.'

In the grey light of first dawn Clea heard the sound of hoofs on the path as the first broodmare was brought up to the serving barn. High on his toes and looking around in bewilderment was a young foal, sticking close to his mother and dodging any handlers. The mare was fully in season and agitated by the attentions of the teaser pony in preparation for her encounter with the stallion. As the mare came closer the piercing squeals of the excited stallions in one of the adjoining barns were almost deafening. One of the stallions lashed out in his box, his hoofs hitting the walls heavily. 'Get down!' a groom yelled as the stallion reared up and struck at the bars.

Abdul led Clea into the serving barn to the partitioned area at the back. The mare and foal were brought in after them and the foal secured gently in the padded area by a well-cushioned gate. He called out to his mother, who whinnied in fear and excitement. The mare stood with her back to the door while lead shoes were fixed to her back hoofs to prevent her kicking the stallion as he approached. The handler grabbed a twitch and attached it to the soft part of her muzzle, twisting until it was tight and making the mare grimace and freeze. Another handler pulled her partially shaved tail out of the way.

Screams and snorts preceded the entrance of Napoleon, who was prancing on his toes, his neck curved over. As he entered the barn he reared and lashed out. His penis was fully extended, bouncing comically underneath him as he was led closer to the mare. He sniffed at her and raised his head in the air, baring his teeth in appreciation. With a handler on either side he leapt awkwardly onto her back and found his own way in. It was all over in a few seconds, and as he dropped back to the ground placidly one of the handlers announced, 'Five pulses . . . not bad.' Napoleon was led back to his stable and the mare, released and reunited with her foal, was led away.

'Is Attila in next?' Abdul asked one of the grooms, who nodded. 'He's a first-season sire,' he turned and explained to Clea. 'They need to be taught the procedure and he'll probably be quite nervous, so you'll need to move back and remain very quiet.'

The second mare and foal were led into the barn to a chorus of excitement from the stallions. Once the mare was secured, a lovely young stallion entered excitedly. He was almost black, with a striking white blaze down his nose and two white socks on his forelegs. He was led up to the mare and allowed to have a long sniff and mooch around. Twice he half bounced up but hesitated, unsure of himself. In the wild, young colts learnt by observation, but there was no such luxury afforded to young thoroughbreds.

After a while two handlers assisted him on one of the half-hearted bounces and he found himself on top of the mare. His foot-long penis seemed to have a life of its own as it banged around at the mare's hindquarters, completely missing the mark until a gloved hand acted as a guide. Once inside he threw back his head and almost fell off. Attila thrust once, twice, then promptly fell asleep and began to slide from the mare's back.

Clea couldn't believe her eyes. He hadn't even finished the

job! Before the horse could topple heavily to the floor and injure himself the grooms applied their shoulders to keep him upright and woke him up. He jumped down and began to give it a second shot.

'It will be very good if he can figure it out this time, but we won't pressure him, he has to learn and gain confidence,' Abdul whispered. 'A young horse can often suffer a narcoleptic incident like that – some quirk of nature.'

Attila's second attempt failed, and he lost interest and was taken back to his stable. 'We'll try him again this afternoon, if he's ready,' Abdul explained as he led Clea out of the barn in the lull between stallions.

Clea found it a fascinating insight into this strange man's world. 'How many mares do they serve in a day?' she asked.

'We aim for three services a day,' Abdul said. The actual number of mares per day was dependent on the cycling of his book of mares, and a busy stallion who could maintain his virility and interest often served four per day. Top commercial stallions served anywhere between one hundred to 200 mares per season. 'Bismarck was already booked to serve 120 mares for his first season.' Abdul sighed. 'I will miss him, he was a great character.'

'Very valuable, too, I imagine?'

'Well, yes, but it is hard to value the experience of owning such a champion in dollars and cents. There is great passion in horseracing and breeding – when money is not an imperative, the passion overrides everything else,' Abdul explained.

Before she could stop, Clea found herself asking the question that had been tormenting her since the previous night. 'Could there be a reason why anyone would have wanted Bismarck dead?'

Abdul gave her a strange look. 'Why would you ask a question like that? He was a horse, not a politician or gangster.' They had walked out of earshot of the other staff.

'I know the official ruling will be contamination in some form from the fruit bats in the area,' Clea said slowly. She wanted to tell him about her own suspicions, but his gruff manner was off-putting. Then she remembered the man in the moonlight, singing to the animals he loved. 'Abdul, I want you to keep a sharp lookout around here. I may be jumping at shadows, but I *know* that strain of virus – it's the same one I've seen in my laboratory. It's either a remarkable coincidence, or —' She broke off. 'I probably shouldn't even have mentioned it.' She turned to leave.

Abdul gently held her arm. 'Thank you, Dr Reynolds. Thank you for caring.'

19
Sheikh Faisal's Residence, Mayfair

Yvonne had already slipped out of bed, brushed her hair and put on some light make-up when the Sheikh stirred and yawned. She sat on the bed, aware her silk robe had opened enough to expose a breast. 'Good morning.' She gently touched his arm. He had flown back from Bahir's bedside in Australia to London the day before. 'Did you sleep well?'

Sheikh Faisal stretched and smiled – she was a beautiful sight to wake up to. He lifted the bed covers and she climbed in, snuggling into his embrace. The Sheikh had been impressed with Yvonne since their first encounter. She was classy and smart, an excellent lover, and best of all, she loved horseracing as much as he did. He slid his hand into her robe and cupped her full breast, stroking the nipple until she sighed with pleasure.

'I've been thinking. We're a good match, you and I,' he said.

Yvonne laughed and ruffled the hairs on his chest. 'You only say that because I love horses.'

The Sheikh smiled. He enjoyed her playful nature. 'Maybe it's time to sort out an arrangement that would suit us both?'

Yvonne held her breath. The Sheikh had already been very generous; if he would just provide her with a level of financial security, she would be so relieved.

'I'd like to take an apartment for you, closer to here. Somewhere appropriate. And of course, I will give you an allowance, something befitting the status of my mistress.'

Yvonne was delighted. This was moving faster than she had hoped. 'So that's what I am, your mistress? I think I like that.' She rolled over on top of him and kissed his lips. 'But how often will I see you?'

'You can travel with me anywhere but the Middle East. We'll go to all the major race meetings together, and the horse sales.' He sounded so excited. 'And when we're not together and you're in London, my car will be at your disposal.'

Yvonne smiled, imagining the looks on the faces of the other mothers at school when they saw her pull up in a chauffeured Bentley. She couldn't wait to tell her son. Perhaps the other kids would stop picking on him and treat him as an equal.

'I'm so happy,' she said softly, gazing at her lover. 'Where will we go first?'

'Have you ever been to Australia for the Spring Racing Carnival?'

'No, but I've always wanted to go!' Yvonne sat up in excitement and her robe slipped off her shoulders. She smiled as the Sheikh admired her body.

He pulled the robe off completely and rolled on top of her. Yvonne folded her legs around his torso, feeling his erection as she guided him inside. He entered her slowly, sliding in a fraction at a time, until she thrust her hips up to take all of him.

Yvonne's world was secure again, and the sense of empowerment was dizzying.

20

Sheikh Faisal's Palace, Dubai, United Arab Emirates

Early in the dry desert morning Darcy climbed into the back seat of a chauffeur-driven black Maybach 62 and cruised through the quiet streets of Dubai to the palace of Sheikh Faisal.

Darcy had broken his journey to London on the Sheikh's bidding. Hearing of the tragic loss of Wigmore, the Sheikh was offering a five-year-old beautifully bred stallion as a replacement. Casanova had performed well at Group One level, but the Eclipse stallion roster was already overloaded with his bloodline, so the Sheikh was offering him as a shared arrangement to stand at Kirtling Park Stud in both Northern and Southern hemisphere seasons. It was a very generous offer.

A year had passed since Darcy's last visit to the shining jewel of the United Arab Emirates, and she was still resplendent, despite the effects of the economic downturn. As he drove from the airport it was difficult to determine if the empty building sites were gearing up for the day or had been abandoned – investors were apparently walking away from their off-the-plan deposits in droves as global property prices tumbled.

Startling reports had filtered home from this playground of the rich, as high-flying ex-pats lost their jobs and abandoned their expensive cars at the airport with the keys left in the ignition and letters of apology in the glovebox.

But the Downtown Burj Dubai area showed every sign of life. The 160-storey building that would claim the title of world's tallest tower was close to completion. More cranes clustered around the Dubai marina in the distance. Darcy gazed in amazement at the flurry of construction taking place in the city. The economic meltdown had finally hit Dubai, but much of the building continued, as if all the cranes that had fallen silent in the rest of the world had been sent to this city of ceaseless self-invention.

The financial downturn seemed far away as the Maybach turned into the Sheikh's palace, a property of such extraordinary splendour and opulence it took Darcy's breath away each time he visited. The driveway to the magnificent wide marble entrance staircase was lined with fountains tiled in lapis blue and gold mosaics and the enormous entrance hall of elegant marble had a high domed ceiling. Here Darcy was greeted by the Sheikh's personal assistant, Hassan.

'Welcome back to Sheikh Faisal's home,' Hassan said, shaking Darcy's hand warmly. 'Come, I'm sure you are tired from your journey and would like to rest.' Hassan led Darcy down the main hall to the next reception area, where a sweeping marble staircase dominated the room. 'The Sheikh apologises deeply for not being here to greet you personally. He returns from London this afternoon and asks you to dine with him.'

Hassan led Darcy into a lift to one side of the staircase and pushed level two. Turning right when the doors opened, they continued down a thickly carpeted corridor until they reached a door labelled Chantilly, after the famous French racecourse, and entered an extensive guest suite. 'I believe you've stayed in this room before?' Darcy nodded. 'You are most welcome to use the main pool if you would like to relax.'

'Actually, I might do just that . . . A bit of sunshine and a swim will do me good.'

A young man dressed in a pale blue cotton tunic and pants appeared at the door carrying Darcy's luggage. Hassan introduced Sariyah, Darcy's valet for his stay. 'Sariyah will help you with anything you need. Now I'm afraid I must get back to my duties, if you will excuse me?' Darcy thanked Hassan as he walked out the door and closed it lightly behind him.

'Can I get you any refreshments, Mr Ambrose-Taylor?' Sariyah enquired in perfect English as he placed Darcy's luggage on the floor.

'I think I'll take coffee by the pool.'

'Your robe is in the bathroom,' Sariyah offered, and busied himself pouring a glass of iced water from a pitcher on the desk. Darcy went into the bedroom and changed into his board shorts, then threw on the Versace towelling robe and slippers provided. He gathered together his sunglasses, cap and a book, before Sariyah led the way out of the palace and down a garden path.

The pool was as spectacular as the palace's interior. Designed like a palm tree to replicate Dubai's astonishing man-made islands, the 'trunk' was twenty-five metres long and perfect for a morning swim. 'Branches' sweeping out from one end connected to the main pool with small bridges. Real palm trees dotted around the lawn provided shade, and there were three Bedouin-style tents set up as cabanas for protection from the desert sun. The pool was tiled in the same lapis lazuli and gold mosaics as the front entrance fountains, making it look particularly inviting.

It felt strange for Darcy to be here without Bahir. They had swum in this pool together so many times, but it would be a while before Bahir would be capable of such physical exertion.

Darcy swam for half a kilometre to relieve the stiffness of travel, and when he got out, Sariyah returned with a silver tray of coffee, a bowl of neatly sliced exotic fruit and a small basket of fresh pastries. Surrounded by such lavishness, Darcy found himself wondering what Clea would make of it all. He suspected even she would be seduced by the beauty and luxury of the palace.

He shook the thought from his head, annoyed yet again by how Clea seemed to infiltrate his mind. He couldn't understand it, especially since Amy had been so . . . accommodating.

But his fling with Amy was never going to last. It had ticked along for several weeks and Darcy had grown quite fond of her, but it was time to move on – this trip had offered an opportune excuse for a gentle break-up.

'Do I have to get up?' Amy had pouted beautifully on the morning of his departure, tangled naked in his sheets.

'I thought you had to be at the studio by 9 a.m.?' Darcy asked, buttoning his shirt.

'I know, I'm late.' Amy sat up. 'It's just that I'm going to miss you so much while you're away.'

'You don't really want to be with an old codger like me. We've discussed this, sweetheart.' He drew her into his arms. 'Anyway, you'll forget me as soon as you walk out that door. Now, are you going to get up and have a shower or do I have to carry you in there?' He scooped her out of the bed as she giggled in protest, carried her to the ensuite bathroom and deposited her in the shower recess. 'Be careful or I'll turn on the cold water too,' he said, laughing.

Over time, this scene had become all too familiar to Darcy. He always stated his intentions clearly up front, and reiterated them regularly, but when it came to the crunch, girls always had other expectations. Especially of his wallet. Amy was fun and he enjoyed her company, but she had never been a serious prospect. He wondered if he would ever meet a woman who was.

By mid-morning the Dubai sun was searingly hot and the humidity so high it was too muggy even to sit in the shade of the palm trees. Darcy went to his suite, showered, changed and had Sariyah organise a car.

Darcy directed the driver to drop him off at the gold souk in Old Deira, the perfect place to find a present for his stepmother's upcoming birthday. The souk was a huge covered market where accented Westerners in shorts and T-shirts rubbed shoulders with Arabs in traditional dress. The women's burkhas covered them from head to toe, and hid expensive designer clothes and glittering jewellery. Much of the jewellery on offer was twenty-four-carat gold in local designs – the kind of jewellery that jangled hidden under the long sleeves of the modest Muslim women. But it was also possible to find more classic pieces that would suit Darcy's stepmother's taste.

Darcy searched around for a while, soaking up the ambience – people haggling over prices, languages clashing, and the aroma of thick, barely drinkable coffee filling the air. Finally he found a pair of gold earrings he was sure Julia would love, with teardrop sapphires in green, blue, pink and yellow dangling from fine gold chains. Darcy enjoyed haggling, so he sipped a gooey coffee and bartered away until a deal was struck at less than half the original price – a sign of the economic times.

Feeling pleased with himself, Darcy had lunch in one of the many restaurants inside a large shopping mall, thankfully air-conditioned, and on a full stomach browsed through some of his favourite labels: Gucci, Hugo Boss, Dolce & Gabbana and Paul Smith – all on sale. It was late afternoon by the time he arrived back at the palace.

Darcy declined Sariyah's suggestion of a coffee, still buzzing from the muddy Arabic brew, but gratefully accepted a beer and settled back to relax before dinner. Although Dubai was part of a Muslim country, alcohol was discreetly served to Westerners and widely available in restaurants, hotels and nightclubs.

He was surprised by a knock at the door, but delighted to find it was Bahir's younger brother Khalid. The two men greeted each other warmly.

'I just had to come and say a quick hello,' Khalid said as he accepted a glass of Coke from Sariyah and sat down. 'I'm sorry I wasn't here to greet you this morning, but I had to go to Qatar early. It's a wonder I didn't bump into you at the airport.'

'Are you joining us for dinner tonight?' Darcy asked hopefully.

'Of course. I'm looking forward to it. Tell me, have you seen mu brother? We're all so worried about him. I was going to fly over to be with him, but . . . well, someone had to look after things back here while Father was gone.'

Darcy smiled. Bahir and Khalid had a rather quarrelsome relationship, unique to siblings, but Darcy knew Khalid adored and admired his older brother.

At the appointed hour, dressed and refreshed, Darcy was led down to an elegant room where Sheikh Faisal was relaxing on a sofa. Darcy greeted his host formally and with deep respect.

'Sheikh Faisal, I am overjoyed to return to your country, but sorrowful that I have arrived before your son Bahir was well enough to travel back to his family.'

Sheikh Faisal rose from his chair and clasped Darcy to his chest. 'You are welcome, Darcy, always. Bahir is recovering well and will return to us shortly.' The Sheikh had only returned from Australia once the doctors assured him Bahir was well into recovery.

'A terrible misfortune, Sheikh Faisal. I am ashamed such a thing happened in my country.'

The Sheikh looked searchingly into his eyes for a few seconds, making Darcy wonder at the pause. 'I lost my prized stallion, but thankfully not my son. Let Allah be praised for his mercifulness.' Khalid entered the room and after Sheikh Faisal had settled back into the sofa, the two younger men took a seat opposite.

'Have you heard any more from Bahir?' Darcy asked.

'He's as well as can be expected. He is a healthy young man, and they looked after him with great care in Sydney, as you know. Jalal has stayed by his side and updates me twice a day, as Bahir always tells me he is fine.' The Sheikh sighed. 'Jalal will tell me the truth – he is like family.'

'I spoke to Bahir just before I left and he seemed very frustrated with hospital life.' Darcy smiled. The last thing his friend was able to cope with was being cooped up inside under the instruction of doctors and nurses. At Oxford, even when it snowed, Bahir took long walks to enjoy the fresh air, and could often be found sitting on a bench somewhere rugged up with a book.

Sheikh Faisal understood exactly what Darcy was alluding to. 'That is good, it means he is well,' he said laughing. 'And I doubt they will be able to keep him in much longer.'

'What about the stud?' Khalid asked. He was not as passionate about racing as Bahir and had been too busy with the family's other businesses to catch up on the news.

'It's still under quarantine but the disease has passed. We were able to start stud season two days ago with the mares already on the property.'

The conversation moved to horseracing and the Global Sprint Challenge. With his sprinter, Spartan, the Sheikh had already won two legs of the series: the Golden Jubilee at Royal Ascot and the July Cup at Newmarket. The Japan leg, the Sprinters Stakes at Nakayama, loomed large on the calendar, but Japan had reported cases of equine influenza and the Sheikh was still reluctant to risk one of his best horses.

'Spartan's win at the Golden Jubilee was so impressive, I'm sure he can take out the series, but if he gets stuck there . . .' he mused.

Before dinner, Sheikh Faisal insisted on taking Darcy to see the stallion Casanova in the stables. He was a magnificent animal, bred from a mare who had already produced two successful stallions. Darcy had difficulty hiding his pleasure.

'He'll make an excellent addition to the Kirtling Park stallion roster. I can't tell you how much my father and I appreciate this gesture. But are you sure it still works for you, now you've lost Bismarck and Mitterrand? We'd understand, of course, if you've changed your mind.'

'No, their deaths only make us more top-heavy with Casanova's sire line. We're looking at a few American options to add to our roster. There's a first-season sire who's performed particularly well that we have our eye on. He stands at a small farm in Kentucky.' The Sheikh hoped a generous offer would convince the owners to part with him.

When Khalid wandered off to look at the horses on the other side of the barn, the Sheikh had an opportunity to ask Darcy something that had been puzzling him.

'Darcy, you must have made quite an impression on our mutual acquaintance Yvonne Green. She mentions you regularly and asked me to pass on her regards.' The Sheikh scrutinised Darcy's face for a reaction, but saw nothing except genuine surprise.

'I've only spoke to her briefly at the races, but that's kind of her to think of me. Please pass on my respects,' Darcy said tactfully, wondering what he had done to warrant Yvonne's attention. The last thing he needed was for the Sheikh to think he was interested in his new mistress. But the Sheikh seemed satisfied with his response and the subject was dropped.

21

Alchemy Nightclub, Dubai

The Hummer pulled into the driveway of a major hotel and Darcy stepped out onto the red carpet. Khalid had convinced him to come out for a drink at one of Dubai's most famous nightclubs. 'Just one,' Khalid said. 'I won't keep you out too late.'

The pair now sauntered through the lobby to an exclusive nightclub, where Khalid gained access in front of a queue comprising curious tourists and beautiful women. As they passed into the glowing depths of the club, Khalid pointed to a stunning girl with long straight blonde hair, a strapless Dolce & Gabbana dress and the latest Gucci handbag. 'She comes with me,' he instructed the bouncers, and the girl was let through the queue and fell in obediently behind them.

Zayd Farouk was watching from across the lobby, envious that the two men had been given instant access. More than anything, he wanted to command such respect wherever he went, and if his plan paid off he would certainly rise higher than he could have hoped. Not that he wanted to waste his time chatting up pretty girls in nightclubs. That wasn't his scene – too much trouble for not enough reward. The junior concierge approached and handed Zayd an envelope, smiling as he received a large tip for his trouble. Zayd walked to the elevators and tore open the envelope. There was a security key inside and a slip of paper with the number 2132.

He let himself into the room quietly and was delighted to see a busty blonde sitting on the side of the bed, naked except for a sheer black baby-doll negligee and a black leather collar. This was more like it. He threw a wad of money on the floor and commanded her to pick it up.

Music pumped out from the dance floor, which was crowded with gorgeous girls showing off their talents. The young and beautiful from around the world had flocked to Dubai for the high wages and glamorous lifestyle, and those remaining were clinging on to that ideal with gritted teeth. Dubai especially attracted the party girls, who loved the generosity of the myriad multi-millionaires who frequented the nightclubs. If you examined the scene closely, Darcy thought, it was only a step or two removed from prostitution. Girls came to wriggle around on the dance floor and attract the attention of the rich men; the men showered them with gifts, bedded them and, if they were lucky, kept them as mistresses for a while. None of these girls had any hope of a marriage proposal from their suitors, no matter how enamoured they were. But if everyone knew the rules, did it really matter?

Khalid was led to a roped-off area with a circular red leather booth, and Bollinger champagne and diet Coke appeared at the table. 'What's your name again, beautiful lady?' he asked the blonde girl, who had positioned herself next to him on the sofa.

'Candy,' she replied, with a Canadian accent.

'Oh, that's right – you're as sweet as sugar. Are those your friends?' He pointed to the three girls waving to Candy from the dance floor. 'Why don't you go and join them for a while and let us appreciate you, then you can bring them over for a glass of champagne.' He patted her firm bottom as she left the table. 'I think she's free at the moment, but the redhead is taken. Pity, she's rather striking, don't you think?'

Darcy glanced over at the girls, who were all dancing as seductively as possible to get their attention. The tallest girl had long, dark red hair and a stunning figure, which she was showing to great effect in cropped tight pants and a skimpy silver top. Darcy watched for a while as the girl made eye contact with him and moved her body rhythmically for him to appreciate.

Khalid noticed his gaze and warned, 'He's very possessive. That's him over there.' A handsome, bearded man of around forty sat with a younger man and three girls at another roped-off booth.

'He seems rather preoccupied,' Darcy commented hopefully,

as the man whispered into the ear of the pretty blonde beside him and stroked her shoulder.

'That's his prerogative, although I think she's taken a bit of a liking to you, too.'

The redhead hadn't taken her eyes off Darcy. Khalid signalled with a champagne glass and Candy and the other girls made their way over to the table.

The redhead introduced herself as Portia, in a delightful English accent. Her skin was as luminescent as moonlight and her generous lips were enticing.

'I haven't seen you here before,' she said to Darcy, almost pushing one of the other girls out of the way as she sat down. 'Are you a friend of the Sheikh's?'

'I suppose you could say I'm a friend of the family. You obviously come here often?'

'It's one of the best spots, and besides, Mukhtar likes to come here and show off.' She looked over at the other table in time to see Mukhtar kissing the blonde on the lips. Portia frowned and sipped her champagne.

Khalid was already deep in a flirtatious conversation with a brunette on one side and Candy on the other.

Portia turned back to Darcy and smiled. 'So, what line of business are you in?'

Darcy decided to play with her for a while. 'Oh, I'm an accountant.'

'Don't believe a word of what he says.' Khalid cut in, overhearing. 'He's Darcy Ambrose-Taylor.'

Portia looked impressed. 'From *the* Ambrose-Taylor family?'

'Well, now my cover's been blown, yes. Only son, actually, at your service.'

Portia quizzed him on the length of his trip, where he lived, and where he was staying. 'My place,' Khalid interjected again, with an uncanny ability to flirt with two girls and simultaneously eavesdrop on another conversation.

'Come on, all this champagne makes me want to dance.' Portia giggled and dragged Darcy reluctantly to his feet, leading him into the crowded centre of the dance floor.

The music pulsated like a physical force as they danced dangerously close. Darcy was usually a little self-conscious on the dance floor, but not here – Portia had caught him in a seductive web. Her blatant interest in his position and wealth made him feel strangely free and very powerful – a potent aphrodisiac for any man's ego. Dubai was the ultimate rich boys' fantasy.

After two songs with Portia's lithe body rubbing against his, Darcy retired to the discretion of the table, guiding the redhead in front of him for cover. She seemed very pleased when they sat back down, fully aware of the effect she had on men. Khalid was surrounded by four girls now, with his arms around the closest two. 'Did it get a bit too hot on the dance floor for you, my friend?' he teased.

'This is a very hot country,' Darcy said, grinning.

'But all is not perfect in paradise, is it, Portia?' Khalid intoned. 'Now who would like more champagne?' He quickly changed the subject before Portia could respond.

'What did he mean by that?' Darcy asked quietly over the squeals of the girls.

'Shall we go outside for a while?' Portia led the way while Darcy followed with their drinks. The balcony overlooked Dubai Creek and a slight breeze moved the fabric draped from above, which provided softly curtained areas around deep sofas. Moroccan-style candles were dotted around the low coffee tables, creating an intimate atmosphere of golden lighting. Finding a quiet corner, Portia slipped off her Chanel shoes and curled up on a sofa.

'So, what's going on?' Darcy asked.

Portia felt that she could trust Darcy, and was desperate to share her grief with someone sympathetic. 'Did you hear about the girl who died of a rare virus in France? It was in all the papers.'

Darcy was surprised. 'Do you mean the girl who had hendra virus?'

'Yes, that's right,' Portia said, gazing sadly down at her glass. 'She was my friend. At least, we were really close . . .' The sentence slipped away. She looked around the lounge area to ensure they couldn't be overheard. 'When I first arrived, I was an accountant working in investment banking.'

'Now that you mention it, you do look a little bookish,' Darcy teased, and gently swept a strand of hair from her cheek.

Portia began to tell Darcy her story. She had come to Dubai looking for a new adventure after a relationship disaster in London. She worked hard for the first year, but then she met Antonia, who was also an accountant at the bank, and was introduced to the other side of Dubai. Portia was an instant hit in the nightclub scene, with her exotic red hair.

Antonia had explained to Portia how it worked for beautiful Western women – you flirt, leave them wanting more and get showered with expensive gifts. The key was to play hard to get. The men were competing with each other to show off their wealth and score the hottest girl, and the girls were in competition for the most expensive presents. But despite their appetite for foreign women, none of these wealthy locals would offer a permanent relationship. There was no security, but everything to gain.

Portia was soon swept up in this glamorous world, but Antonia was already in too deep. 'It's all about the sex – you have to hold off and make them want you. When you concede, the game is pretty much over,' she'd said. But Antonia didn't play by the rules. She became too readily available. Once she crossed over, it was too late – she couldn't come back. She stopped kidding herself about what she was really doing and made a profession of it instead.

Portia explained that Antonia had a number of major clients who would fly her around the world for their entertainment, including that fateful trip to the French Riviera. 'I think she may have become expendable.' Portia stared intently into Darcy's eyes.

'Do you think her death was deliberate?' Darcy was incredulous.

'She sent me a text.' Portia pulled her Prada mobile phone out of her bag and showed him the message: *hi p, in french riviera. don't like it – something's going on – back soon. a.* 'A few days later she was dead.'

Tears welled in Portia's eyes, spilling down her cheeks, and Darcy felt an overwhelming desire to kiss them away. The damsel-in-distress act, whether real or not, was certainly working. Portia looked so frail, curled up like a schoolgirl on the sofa, with the candles casting a glow over her pale skin. But he could see genuine fear in her catlike green eyes.

He tried to reassure her. 'Do you know if she came into contact with any horses? She could've just been in the wrong place at the wrong time.'

'No, it's impossible. Antonia was allergic to horsehair. She had to take antihistamines just to go to the racetrack.' Another tear trickled down Portia's cheek.

Darcy was intrigued. From his knowledge of hendra, a person had to come in very close contact with a horse. Bahir had obviously contracted it by 'breathing' with Bismarck, as he liked to do. At such close quarters the poor stallion had infected his owner. But if this girl were allergic, then none of it made any sense. Thinking of Clea and her investigation, he asked Portia to give him a call if she had any more information, and gave her his phone number. It was a perfect excuse for continued contact with Clea – and Portia.

'Well, that's a turnaround. I haven't had to call a guy since I've been here!' Portia entered his number into her phone.

'If it makes you feel better, I was going to ask you for your number, anyway.'

'So you could ask me out on a date?' Portia asked flirtatiously.

'Something like that.' Portia was exotic and exciting. Darcy knew he wanted to see her again.

Khalid suddenly appeared. 'There you are, Darcy, I've been looking everywhere. Come on, it's time to leave these lovelies. I've got an early meeting and I'd better not yawn my way through it.'

'Are you taking the girls back with you?' Darcy asked hopefully.

'Are you kidding? Do you think my father would approve?' Khalid laughed heartily.

Darcy turned to Portia to say goodbye, but she just blew him a kiss and walked off.

He lay between the cool sheets of his bed later that night, thinking. Could someone have used hendra virus to kill Antonia? And why? He had a disturbing feeling that the death of Bismarck may somehow be connected, but dismissed it as a conspiracy theory. Who would want to kill a stallion? He finally fell into a deep sleep and awoke the next morning to the smell of brewed coffee, feeling refreshed.

22

La Grenouille Restaurant, Dubai

Darcy was waiting in the bar of the elegant French restaurant when Portia appeared laden with designer-store shopping bags. They had agreed by text to meet for lunch, as Portia had some new information about Antonia's death. Darcy jumped up and gave her a kiss on the cheek. 'Had a little shopping spree did we?' He laughed at the myriad labels being wrestled into the cloakroom – Gucci, Fendi, Chanel, Prada, Versace and Hermès.

'It had to be done,' Portia explained earnestly. 'Once Mukhtar moves onto another girl he asks for your Amex back. I just thought I'd better get in before he did. He doesn't care – it's all a game to him.' She sat down in the chair offered by the waiter.

'You look lovely today, even lovelier than last night.' Darcy meant every word. Portia was dressed in an elegant black pencil skirt with a beautiful soft green silk blouse, high court shoes and a necklace of large Tahitian pearls. Her eye-catching hair was tied back and draped over one shoulder.

She scanned the menu and suggested they start with some caviar and oysters. Darcy added two glasses of Bollinger champagne to the order.

'I managed to get on to Mimi, one of the girls who used to work with Antonia. She's not the brightest and I thought she might speak to me,' Portia said. 'Can you believe Mimi actually thought Antonia had died from a cold? She must have been living under a rock! Anyway, I said I had been contacted by the police and they had agreed to leave Mimi out of the investigation if she told me everything.'

'And she believed that?' Darcy asked incredulously.

Portia laughed. 'Mimi's clients don't pay for her intelligence and conversation.'

Mimi's information was sketchy. She was flown to Nice to entertain a group of men for a few days, but couldn't recall many details that would help. The girls charged astronomical fees for a trip like that, and rarely asked questions. One night after a visit to the casino, two Asian men in the party signed a bundle of documents, and they all shook hands. Mimi thought it looked like a business deal.

But there was some hope of getting more information. One of the men had been a regular client of Antonia's and had now switched his attentions to Mimi. 'But you don't want the gory details.' Portia looked at Darcy's hopeful face. 'Trust me, you really don't want the details.'

Mimi was only told his first name was Zayd, and Antonia was no longer alive to shed any light on his background. But Mimi promised to tell Portia if she found out anything else.

Darcy spooned sour cream on a blini, added some caviar, finely chopped egg and spring onion, and placed it in his mouth, appreciating the wonderful mix of flavours. Then he raised his champagne glass. 'To my intrepid investigator, Portia.'

Portia raised her glass sadly. 'To Antonia, may she rest in peace.'

During the rest of their meal Darcy questioned Portia about her life. She was raised in Chelsea in a quiet, respectable family, and her dream was quite suburban – to work for a number of years, get married and have a child or two.

'Is that still your dream?' Darcy asked.

'Yes, I think so. A lot of my friends back home have kids now. I'm sure I'd want children with the right man. What about you?' she tossed back at him.

Darcy was thrown. 'I haven't really found the woman I want to settle down with. I suppose when she walks into my life, I'll know. As for children? They come with the territory, don't they? The thought of nappies and nannies is pretty daunting, but with the right person it must be wonderful, or else people wouldn't do it.'

'Are you a bit of a romantic?'

'I'm definitely a romantic, no doubt about it.' He reached over and kissed her hand, making her laugh and blush at the same time.

Portia's apartment was in a salubrious neighbourhood not far from the palace, so she accepted Darcy's offer of a lift gratefully. Darcy assisted her out of the car, leaving the driver to manage her shopping. 'I think I'll have to help you upstairs with those,' he suggested.

'Okay, but just to the door,' Portia cautioned and strode into the foyer, leaving Darcy to carry all the bags.

'You must have a nice view,' he commented when she pushed the lift button for the fifteenth floor.

Portia unlocked her front door and opened it wide for Darcy to drop the bags in the hall. His duty discharged, Darcy took her hands, and when she didn't protest, wrapped them around his waist so their bodies were pressed together. He gently held her head in his hands and kissed her. He looked deep into her eyes and kissed her again, this time with more passion, until finally he broke away. 'Are you going to be at the racetrack on Thursday night?'

'Yes, I'm a guest of Prince Khalid.'

'Well, I'll see you there. Call me if Mimi remembers anything else between now and then.'

In the mirrored walls of the lift Darcy carefully wiped off Portia's red lipstick, and was composed by the time he climbed back into the car for the five-minute ride to the palace. Feeling confident he would be visiting the apartment again, Darcy was careful to take note of the route home.

Clea picked up her mobile and checked the caller ID. It was a number she didn't recognise.

'Hello, Clea Reynolds speaking,' she said guardedly.

'Clea, hello. It's Bahir.'

Clea was momentarily rendered speechless, and in her silence Bahir forged on.

'I wanted to thank you for all your help up at the stud,' he said, sounding stronger and more like the man she had first met at the gala ball.

'Are you out of hospital?' she asked hopefully, finally finding her voice.

'They discharge me tomorrow and I'm going straight home to Dubai. I can't wait to get out of this place.' Bahir looked around his hospital room at all the flowers sent by well-wishers. He had asked the nurses to take most of them to cheer up other patients, since his own room had begun to resemble a florist, but had kept flowers from the Australian Prime Minister and from his close friends.

Darcy had sent him a Japanese-style arrangement, complete with a miniture zen garden of sand. The card read: *The sand will remind you of home.* Bahir reflected that a life-threatening illness made you realise what was truly important in life, and the people you cared about the most.

'I still plan to come back to Australia later in the year for the Spring Racing Carnival, so perhaps we can catch up then?' Bahir asked Clea.

'I'd like that very much. Give me a call when you're back in town.' For a moment Clea wondered if she should tell Bahir what she had discovered in the Hunter Valley, but decided against it. The hendra virus outbreak had been solved to the satisfaction of everyone else – a terrible coincidence and nothing more.

When Bahir hung up, Clea sat staring at her computer screen. She had wanted to be a scientist ever since she lost her father – to study the deadly viruses that robbed people of their loved ones. Her father had died from viral pneumonia when she was only thirteen. Strangely, Clea had never wanted to be a doctor – her drive had always been to find out the cause of a virus and stop it dead in its tracks, so no one would have to go through the agony her poor mother had suffered. Of course, it had been difficult for Clea and her brothers, but Susanne had lost the man she loved more than life itself; for the sake of her children she had struggled on. Even as a young girl, Clea realised her mother had changed forever, as though half of her were missing.

In her heart, Clea feared that intensity of love, feared the thought of ever loving someone so much you could never be the same again without them.

23

Sheikh Faisal's Stables, Dubai

Sand was the enemy in Dubai. It invaded the golf greens, sat like a dirty brown smudge in the glistening swimming pools and created a tiresome task for many poor labourers – sweeping. The winds blowing from the west lifted a veil of sand to hang suspended in the air, permeating clothes, hair and eyes with grit.

Sand was the reason there were so few horses bred in Dubai, despite the healthy racing industry, and racehorses were kept in air-conditioned stables. Sand colic was often a fatal condition, especially in foals.

The humidity struck Darcy as soon as he left the palace and crossed the vast expanses of lawns and ornamental gardens to visit the stables. July and August were the worst months, but the moisture still hung heavy in the air in September, and his clothes were soon drenched in sweat.

Bahir would arrive any minute now with his nurses, Jalal and Abdul, who had fussed over him on the long flight home, and

Darcy knew the Sheikh would want to see his son immediately. Darcy would head back to the palace once Bahir had settled into his room. He was hoping to see his friend in good spirits for the opening of the racing season, and he knew that no matter what the doctors instructed, Bahir would insist on attending.

The Sheikh's stables were always a wonderful distraction, and Darcy was keen to visit Casanova again. The horse would serve his first season at Kirtling Park Stud in Newmarket, as he was too late for the Southern Hemisphere breeding season.

Darcy walked the length of the exercise pool, designed so horses could easily walk down a ramp, swim thirty metres, then walk out the other side. It was excellent for both fitness and cooling off. The stable complex consisted of four large blocks, each fully enclosed and air-conditioned to keep out the heat and humidity. Each stable was roomy, as its occupant rarely spent time in a paddock.

Darcy entered the first barn, nodded to the workers, and strolled along admiring the breeding listed on each stable door. These horses were the cream of the crop. Bought at yearling auctions around the world for huge sums of money, or bred by the Sheikh's own superior broodmare band, they were the envy of horse devotees all over the world.

Darcy stopped by Casanova and patted his grey head, but suddenly became aware that all the stud workers were quietly putting down their equipment and disappearing.

'Darcy!' Afifah called, appearing in the stable entrance. 'What a surprise!' She was wearing a modest long-sleeved tunic of pale pink with magnificent silver embroidery, white slim-fitting trousers, and a pink and silver chiffon scarf over her hair. 'How many days have you been here without seeing me?' She rushed to his side and gave him a quick kiss on the cheek before her chaperone, Basmah, came panting in behind her. The chaperone didn't seem surprised to see Darcy. She smiled and moved politely to the other side of the stables where she could keep an eye on her excitable charge but allow the pair to talk in peace.

'Well, little princess, I didn't realise you were here. I thought you'd still be locked up at gloomy university, studying until you need glasses.'

'Don't tease, you know I'll never need glasses,' Afifah said coquettishly. 'I'm so pleased to see you. Does this mean you're staying for the opening of the racing season?'

'If you're going to look as beautiful as always I wouldn't miss it for the world,' he replied, indulging her vanity.

Afifah beamed, then a scowl crossed her pretty face. 'That woman of my father's talks about you too much for my liking.'

'Yvonne? So I've heard, although I can't for the life of me think why.'

'So you're not interested in her, then?' Afifah asked casually.

'Me? What? I've barely met the woman, for heaven's sakes. I do sometimes wonder what goes on in that pretty head of yours.'

Afifah patted the grey horse for a while as silence momentarily fell. 'Do you ever wonder anything else about me?' she suddenly asked shyly.

Darcy was taken by surprise. He wasn't too sure where this conversation was going. 'Well, I wonder how your studies are going, I wonder if you're behaving yourself, I wonder if you'll ever remember my birthday and send me a card . . .'

'But do you ever think of me?' Afifah insisted, then looked embarrassed and crossed to a stable opposite to pat a bay horse, keeping her back to him. 'I think of you,' she shot back over her shoulder. 'Not just as my brother's friend – I think of you as a man.'

While Darcy was still trying to think of a subtle way to answer such a direct question, Jalal stepped out from one of the side doorways with a face like thunder.

'Afifah!' he called.

She spun around, anger in her eyes. 'What are you doing here, Jalal?' she demanded.

'I saw you coming over this way . . .'

'You were spying on me again, weren't you? You're always spying on me!'

'Be quiet!' Jalal roared, his face red with fury. He paced menacingly towards Darcy, who stood his ground. 'Afifah belongs to me. She's mine, do you hear? You are not to so much as look at her again without my permission.' Jalal grabbed a shovel used for mucking out the stables and advanced on Darcy.

'Don't be ridiculous, Jalal, I've known Afifah since she was a little girl. She's like a sister to me!' Darcy looked around quickly to see if there was anything he could protect himself with in reach.

'Leave him alone!' Afifah screamed and fled the barn with her chaperone in tow.

Jalal lost his aggressive stance, threw the shovel at Darcy and ran out of the stables after Afifah. He caught up with her by one of the many fountains scattered through the grounds, grabbing her wrist and spinning her around.

'Let go of me,' she hissed.

'I heard you.' Jalal was spitting with rage. 'I heard you in there, talking to him like some cheap whore.' He grabbed her shoulders and shook her until her teeth rattled. 'If you want to be treated like a whore then that will be *my* prerogative when you are my wife.'

'You're hurting me,' Afifah sobbed. 'Let me go. I'll *never* love you.'

'You will learn to love me,' Jalal whispered back menacingly.

'Let her go,' Darcy commanded, striding up behind them.

'You stay out of this,' Jalal said, without taking his eyes off Afifah. Darcy stood firm next to two stud grooms who'd accompanied him and the weeping chaperone.

'I said, let her go, Jalal.'

Jalal stepped back and Afifah flung herself into her chaperone's arms. Darcy stood glaring at Jalal, the grooms fidgeting nervously behind him. Jalal glared back, then turned on his heel and stormed off. Darcy turned to Afifah.

'Are you all right, princess?'

'You can't tell Father,' Afifah wailed, afraid Darcy would get the blame. 'No one can tell him. It's all my fault!' And she ran off in the opposite direction, with Basmah trying valiantly to keep up.

Darcy gazed after Afifah's running form and wondered if this was actually all *his* fault. Had he misled Afifah into believing his affection for her was romantic instead of brotherly? Darcy knew he would need to tread very carefully or he could risk losing Bahir and his whole family.

He walked back to the palace, hoping Bahir had arrived, and luckily he had just been settled in his bedroom. When Darcy walked in, Bahir's face lit up, and he held out his arms to hug his friend.

'I don't need you all hovering around me,' Bahir said patiently to his mother and the servants who were still hovering. 'Father has said the doctor will be here any moment, and I have everything I need.'

Bahir's mother retreated quietly to the far side of the room and sat down after shooing out the other women. She was not going to leave her son's side.

'How are you feeling?' Darcy asked, noticing how tired his friend appeared.

'The flight took it out of me, I'm afraid. I still feel pretty weak, but so much better.' Bahir looked around the room. 'It's so nice to be home at last.'

Darcy couldn't bring himself to tell Bahir of the altercation with Jalal just yet. Bahir needed rest, and the story could wait until they were able to speak in private. The door opened and Sheikh Faisal walked in with the doctor in tow. Darcy excused himself and promised to visit in the afternoon after Bahir had had a chance to rest.

24

Jalal's Family Home, Dubai

Salah al Din was sitting at his desk when Jalal entered the room. 'Son, I heard that you had an argument with Afifah at the palace. Please put an old man out of his misery and tell me it is not true.'

Jalal gazed out the window angrily. News travelled fast, and bad news travelled at the speed of light. 'It wasn't my fault. Darcy was trying to seduce her and I had to protect her honour,' he lied.

'Have you spoken to her since?'

'No, but she'll get over it. It's best she knows how much I care for her and that I will always protect and defend her.'

'This marriage is so important to our family.' Salah al Din stood up and gripped his son's shoulder. 'Particularly now. When you are married, all will be well. You will have such influence and power that I have no doubt we can pull ourselves out of this nightmare.' He looked down at the paper before him, and Jalal suddenly realised it was a notice of demand from the bank requiring the company to provide other financial collateral security, or they would put the company into receivership.

Jalal looked at his father in dismay. 'I thought we had more time.'

'Not enough, it seems.' Salah al Din handed him the papers. 'Son, you must go and apologise to her. Buy her something pretty, you know how much women love gifts. And speak to Bahir, he may have influence over his father in this matter.'

Salah al Din gazed at his son for a while. Jalal had such a quick temper, which was also his father's greatest shortcoming. It didn't pay for Afifah to see that side of him now. There was no doubt Jalal loved her deeply, but he would have to mind his attitude until they were safely married.

'I'll do my best, Father.' Jalal's mind was a whirl. Where would they find more money? The deal he was working on was taking time as the new investors conducted their due diligence. His man was due back any day now to report on progress, and he had already indicated the news was positive. But he couldn't speed up the process.

'You have to do better than that, son. The Sheikh already loves you, it's true, but it's imperative that you become an official family member. Then he will do everything to protect your honour and position.'

A son could not ask for more devoted parents than Jalal's, and the one thing he could give them in return was fast slipping out of his grasp. Jalal's marriage into the Sheikh's family had always been his father's dream. If the mainstay of their transport empire went into receivership, Jalal knew there would be no hope of Sheikh Faisal allowing the marriage to proceed.

He went to his rooms to change into something appropriate for the race meeting that night, but found himself staring at the walls. His head was reeling, with secrets and lies. He knew he needed more money to keep the company afloat, and he knew where to get it, but at what cost?

Jalal walked into his wardrobe and selected a suit and tie, but stopped as he rummaged through a drawer for cufflinks, his hand hovering over a sandalwood box concealed at the back. After a moment's hesitation, he opened the lid and pulled out some old papers. They were records showing that he, his parents and grandparents had been born in Khadelem, a small village in Saudi Arabia, not in Riyadh as they claimed. It was his family's secret.

Salah al Din had paled when Jalal, at sixteen years old, mentioned his discovery. He searched his son's face to see if he had uncovered the awful truth, but could see only the curiosity of a teenager.

'We do not speak of the place,' he warned Jalal. 'My business would suffer if this truth were known.'

'But what is the truth?' Jalal had insisted.

Salah al Din hesitated. 'I am ashamed of our background, which was far humbler than I have led people to believe. If our true background was known, our success in business would be compromised severely.' He put a hand on the boy's shoulders.

'You must destroy those papers, Jalal. Do you promise?' The boy nodded his head.

But now, as an adult, Jalal couldn't help wondering if there was more to this family secret.

25

Nad Al Sheba Racecourse, Dubai

Nad Al Sheba Racecourse was announced from a distance by a halo of light reaching out into the night sky. An oasis of lush green turf and grounds, it formed a modern retreat from the dust and construction sites of Dubai for locals and expats alike. Built by the ruling family of Dubai, whose passion for horseracing was internationally renowned, Nad Al Sheba hosted the richest race in the world, the Dubai World Cup, with a purse of six million US dollars to the winner.

From the back seat of a car in the Sheikh's convoy, Darcy took in the stadium and the building excitement. He was reminded again how much he loved the spectacle of thoroughbred night racing. Countries like Dubai, Hong Kong and Singapore raced in the cool of the evening out of necessity, but night racing was also a successful event in Australia, where the Moonee Valley Racecourse operated both during the day and under lights.

The Sheikh's party moved slowly through the Millenium

grandstand. Jalal supported Bahir, who had insisted on attending the track despite his fragile health. The view over the brightly lit racetrack was magnificent from their second-floor box, which was already filling with guests. Bahir settled into a chair overlooking the track, assuring Darcy he would only remain for the first few races, then make a quiet exit back to bed.

'Keep an eye on Abdul for me, would you, Darcy?' Bahir murmured quietly as Darcy went to find him a glass of mineral water. 'I'm worried about him. I fear the death of the stallions has hurt him more than we know.'

Darcy returned to Bahir with a drink, only to find Jalal had already provided one. Jalal leapt to his feet as if to defend Bahir from Darcy's presence. The look in his eye was far from welcoming.

Darcy had promised Afifah not to say anything of the confrontation in the stables, although he was sure her father would blame Jalal and not his own daughter. But these were family politics, and he thought it best to just keep an eye on the situation from a discreet distance.

Abdul was standing to the side of the box and Darcy was only too happy to join him to find out which of the stable horses would run well that night. Abdul answered, but his heart wasn't in it, and he kept staring in Bahir's direction. After a while Darcy left him to his own thoughts, deciding he would pick a quieter time to talk about Bismarck.

Refreshments and canapés were served as the horses entered the barriers for the first race. No gambling of any kind was allowed in Dubai on religious grounds, and Darcy always felt a little lost without the ability to place a bet, as if the intrigue of the race were somehow diminished. In Dubai he would often find a kindred spirit and place side wagers of cash or bottles of expensive Bordeaux wines. But he would never do so in Sheikh Faisal's presence – and besides, one glance at the guests in the box told him they were unlikely to come to the party. He sighed and put down his empty beer glass. He found his thoughts inevitably drifting towards Clea, and had to remind himself that Portia was on the course tonight.

After his host had left to visit his horses in the mounting yard, Darcy slipped away. The lift doors opened on the fourth level of the grandstand, where Khalid was hosting a number of senior executives and other guests in the Gulfstream suite. The box was directly in front of the lifts and Portia must have been watching for Darcy, because she stuck her head out of the suite and waved.

'There you are, Darcy.' Khalid clapped Darcy on the arm as he entered. 'Couldn't stay away, hey?' he added, winking and indicating Portia, who was fetching the new arrival a drink. 'I hear Bahir has risen from his sickbed. I'm surprised Father allowed it – Bahir's the golden boy of our family, you know.' Khalid gazed around the room as Portia passed Darcy a beer. 'Okay, I'll leave you two in peace, I know when I'm not wanted.' He made his excuses quickly, having spied a pretty blonde girl who looked a little lost.

As soon as they were alone, Portia told Darcy that Mimi had remembered another detail. 'I'm not sure it's of any use, but one of the Asian men had an expensive watch. Mimi said it had a special lucky number.'

'I have no idea what that means, but thank you for passing it on,' Darcy said thoughtfully, taking a sip of beer.

They watched the next race in the Gulfstream suite before Darcy took Portia's hand and led her to the lifts. He had a plan to ensure the Sheikh had no anxiety where his new mistress was concerned, and Portia's slinky white dress should leave him in no doubt. They stepped out on the second level and were about to walk into Sheikh Faisal's box when she pulled back.

'I can't go in there,' she mumbled.

'Why ever not?'

'Because I wouldn't be welcome,' she protested, but Darcy took a firm grip on her hand.

Afifah was standing with her father in the middle of the room, and when she saw Darcy approaching, holding hands with Portia, a look of pain crossed her face and she fled to the bathroom, followed by one of her friends.

'Ah, who do we have here?' Sheikh Faisal appraised the striking woman in Darcy's grasp and raised his eyebrows admiringly at Darcy.

'Sheikh Faisal bin Hashim bin Asad al Azim, may I introduce Portia Blackton. She works in finance,' Darcy added.

'I'm charmed.' Sheikh Faisal shook Portia's hand. 'Please, enjoy my hospitality – and tell me, who you think is going to win the next race?'

Portia looked nervously down at her form guide and suggested the favourite.

'Excellent! You have picked one of my horses, so I hope you're right.' The Sheikh moved over to the window as the horses loaded into the barriers.

'There, that wasn't so bad, was it?' Darcy teased Portia as a waiter handed them both a glass of champagne. Bahir had already slipped away from the racetrack and Jalal appeared to have escorted him home.

After the last race, Darcy and Portia followed the Sheikh and his entourage back to the waiting line of cars. 'Take a car for yourself, Darcy,' Sheikh Faisal called out as he climbed into the back of the first car.

'Shall I take you home?' Darcy asked Portia, and offered his arm to lead her to the tail end of the convoy.

When the car pulled into Portia's driveway, she turned to Darcy. 'Would you like to come up for a nightcap?' she offered casually.

'Most certainly.' Darcy was out of the car in a flash, beating the chauffeur to Portia's door. He escorted her into the building, pulling her close in the lift. Once in the apartment, he kissed her face gently. 'I wanted you from the moment I saw you,' he whispered in her ear.

'And what makes you so sure you can have me?' she responded, arching towards him.

'This.' Darcy's lips met hers and they kissed for a long time, letting the intensity build. Finally they parted and Darcy gazed into her green eyes. 'So, is that an invitation to stay?'

Portia pressed her body against his and wrapped her arms around his neck. 'Yes,' she whispered and sought out his lips again. Still locked in an embrace, she manoeuvered both of them over to a chaise and climbed on top of him, kicking off her shoes. 'The question is, are you game enough to stay?'

'Oh, I think I can handle the situation,' Darcy said confidently, but when he went to wrap his arms around her body, she gently drew them behind the chaise instead. Suddenly he felt cold metal on his wrists and before he could protest, Portia had handcuffed his hands to the chaise. For a moment he was startled, and wondered if he was in any danger. But a moment later, smiling and straddling him, Portia unzipped her dress and pulled it over her head to reveal a taut, athletic body in a sexy pink and white push-up bra and matching G-string. As Darcy appreciated her toned curves, Portia undid the pins in her French roll and shook her glorious hair down around her shoulders.

There was no emotion in this sexual game, just pure lust. All Darcy could focus on was Portia's amazing body so close to his own.

'Now I can do whatever I want with you,' she said, smiling wickedly and kissing him again. Slowly she unbuttoned his shirt and kissed his chest. Darcy was very obviously turned on, and she lightly stroked his crotch before unbuckling his belt and removing his trousers. 'I'm going to enjoy this,' she said appreciatively.

Portia straddled his groin again. He wanted to touch her but the handcuffs prevented it. Portia reached behind her back and unhooked her bra strap, before leaning forwards over Darcy. Her breasts were nicely curved and full and she gasped as his tongue encircled her nipple.

Darcy figured if she could play rough, then he could too. He bit her nipple, taking her to the border between pleasure and pain. Portia moaned in response. She was on fire – he could smell her excitement – but she was in charge, and he could only succumb to her desires.

She kissed him deeply again before running her tongue down his chest and stopping at his shorts. Sliding off to kneel beside him on the floor, she pulled these off now and his erection sprang out of its bondage. With a sigh of satisfaction she slowly took him deeper and deeper into her mouth until he could have sworn he was all the way down her throat. It was Darcy's turn to moan now as she sucked him expertly, bringing him to the brink of climax. Just before the point of no return, she stopped.

'That was amazing,' he managed to say. 'But don't stop!'

'Oh, I haven't finished with you yet.' She smiled. 'I just thought I'd give you a little break to collect yourself . . . for this.' Portia stood up and wriggled her panties down her hips. Her body was smooth and beautiful.

She stepped over the chaise with a leg on either side, giving him a wonderful view as she lowered herself down until he was positioned against her. Darcy watched in fascination as she slid his cock in until he was deep inside. 'I can feel you all the way up here,' she pointed to the soft feminine curve of her belly. She leaned over, teasing him without moving her hips. Darcy desperately wanted her to move – he wanted to feel the friction and couldn't bear the tension much longer. Eventually she began to gyrate her hips slowly, and after a little of this tantalising movement, she leant back, pushing down hard, and began to ride him in earnest.

Portia was magnificent – so sexually self-assured, so seductive, and Darcy was in seventh heaven as he lay cuffed to the chaise. He watched, fascinated, as her desire reached a peak. Still moving, Portia began to moan, and threw her head back with a cry as she came. Darcy was desperate to reach his own peak but she wouldn't let him.

'Oh, no you don't, not yet,' she laughed, still panting from her exertions. 'I plan to enjoy you for a lot longer yet. That was just round one.' She slipped off him and patted his aching cock. 'You're going to have to wait your turn.'

26

The Library, Sheikh Faisal's Palace

The library had always been a refuge for Bahir. He could lose himself for hours in the pages of pedigree books, searching for significant ancestors and crosses in all the champion racehorses of the world. His health was improving and he felt stronger each day, but the virus had been more debilitating than he was willing to admit.

He had pulled up the website for AAIDL and was reading Clea's biography, feeling very impressed, when he heard the doorhandle turn, and quickly closed the page.

It was Afifah who carefully opened the library door, concerned he might be napping, and she smiled radiantly upon seeing her favourite brother awake. She had brought him a glass of sweet peppermint tea and gently rested the back of her hand against his forehead to check his temperature. Bahir had always adored his beautiful, headstrong sister, and she returned his love as she had done from when she was a little toddler, reaching up her chubby arms to be lifted into his protective embrace.

'You're looking a bit better this morning,' she noted. 'The colour's coming back to your cheeks.'

'It will take more than some errant bat disease to knock me over. I'm made of tougher stuff than that.' Bahir watched as she sat in the leather armchair opposite his sofa. There was something troubling her – he had detected it the moment she walked in the door.

'I'm planning to continue with my studies, isn't that exciting? My lecturers are very keen for me to do a Master's degree.' She was avoiding his gaze.

'I'm proud of you. You must be doing very well.' Afifah had everything going for her – position, intelligence and beauty, but Bahir knew too well that none of that necessarily made one happy. He took a few sips of tea. 'And what about your marriage? Does this mean you will postpone it further?' he asked casually.

'Father says I can finish my studies before I marry,' she replied defensively. 'Who knows? If I do well I might even complete a PhD and become *Dr* Afifah Azim.'

'Don't you mean Dr Afifah *Muntasir*?' Bahir queried gently, suspecting he had struck at the root of her trouble. Afifah went silent and stared for a long time out the window. 'So perhaps this degree is a means of stalling the inevitable?'

Tears sprang to Afifah's eyes. 'I don't want to marry Jalal,' she admitted softly, still unable to look at Bahir.

'Afifah, my dear sister, everyone gets cold feet about marriage.

Jalal loves you very dearly. He will be a good husband and you will always be close so I can make sure you're happy.'

'But I don't love him,' she said.

Bahir creaked out of the sofa and knelt before his sister, wiping her tears away. The door opened suddenly and Hassan peered in, apologising when he realised he was disturbing them.

'Come.' Bahir offered Afifah his hand. 'We must be careful with such a delicate conversation. Walk with me and we'll talk. You can trust me, Afifah. I will always look after you.'

They walked slowly out to the palace grounds, where they were sure not to be overheard. Bahir steered his sister down a shaded arbour path alongside the lapis-blue fountains. 'Tell me, what's changed your mind? You were so excited about the betrothal when it was announced.'

'I was much younger then and I didn't know anything about life. Jalal was like a brother to you and I had always looked up to him, so it seemed right.' She tossed a leaf from the green vines into the fountain and watched for a moment as it spun into the whirlpool of a spout. 'But I'm older now. I've lived away from home and I have friends all over the world. I know now Jalal and I will never be compatible.'

Bahir thought for a moment. 'Marriage in our world isn't about the perfect vision of love you see in the Hollywood movies,' he cautioned. 'It's about respect and a mutual path through life. But with that can grow love – a very satisfactory love – and there will always be the bond of children.'

'It's all right for you men – you marry, and as soon as you get bored you go and find a mistress. We can't do that, we're stuck with our husband for the rest of our life!'

Afifah's words rang true, and Bahir didn't insult her by denying it. He had the freedom to pursue someone like Clea, married or not, but Afifah's romantic life would be determined by their father.

A bougainvillea scattered its luminous purple flowers into the blue water, where they bobbed on the ripples. Afifah sat lightly on the edge of the fountain, sighing deeply as she fought back tears.

'I think perhaps there's something you're not telling me, Afifah?' Bahir clasped her hand.

She turned to look Bahir full in the face, her expression grave. 'Yes. I am afraid of him,' she whispered.

Bahir was stunned. He and Jalal had played together, prayed together, studied together, raced and ridden and travelled together. Jalal certainly had a volatile temper, which had got them both into all sorts of trouble when they were younger. But never in Bahir's wildest dreams could he imagine his friend hurting Afifah. He gazed into the distance and remembered his second endurance race as if it were yesterday. After the success of their first attempt, the two boys had been allowed to compete without the watchful eye of Abdul.

Riding together, they slid exhausted from their mounts to struggle up a steep dune as the sun rose high in the sky. At the top they looked out over kilometre after kilometre of undulating dunes, other riders mere pinpricks in the distance. Before they remounted, Jalal grabbed a sharp knife from his saddle and slashed it across his finger, crying out at the unexpected pain. He handed the knife to Bahir, who did the same, and their blood pooled into the sand – blood brothers until death.

Bahir drew Afifah onto her feet and they continued to amble down the shady path, arms linked. If his instincts were correct, there was still something she was concealing from him. 'Is there someone else?' he asked as carefully as he could.

Afifah spun around to hotly deny his accusation, but she could not. 'If I tell you anything, you have to promise on our mother's life to take it as a secret to the grave,' she said intently.

Bahir looked solemn. 'I promise.'

'I am in love,' she confessed, with a mixture of shame and bravado.

'Is this boy of our faith?' Bahir asked and Afifah shook her head sadly. 'Please tell me nothing has happened to disgrace you?' he went on urgently, turning her to face him so he could look into her eyes.

'Nothing has happened – nothing at all. We haven't even spoken of it. I would never do something to bring disgrace on my family!' she added vehemently.

Bahir breathed easy again. There was no damage done, just the fancy of a young girl.

'You know Father will never allow you to be together. It's not possible, Afifah. For your sake, and his, you have to give this nonsense up now. Trust me, it will only lead to pain.'

He could feel her body slumping against his in resignation. 'I know,' she admitted sadly. Reaching the end of the arbour walk, they crossed the driveway near the gates and walked back up the other side, Afifah silent in misery and Bahir wondering when his little sister had become a woman.

'You must help me, Bahir. If you love me you'll help,' she finally pleaded.

'What can I do?' he asked helplessly.

'Make Father release me from my betrothal to Jalal.'

'If it's what you truly wish, I will speak to him when the time is right, somewhere away from everything surrounding us here,' Bahir promised. But in his heart he hoped Afifah and Jalal would reconcile. He would give them some time before speaking to his father.

27
Edge of the Desert, Dubai

Jalal leaned back against the cushion of brilliant green leaves, hidden from sight behind the arbour. He had left his father discussing business with the Sheikh to come and seek out Afifah – and apologise. He hadn't intended to eavesdrop, but she had looked so distraught that he just had to know what she was telling Bahir.

Jalal's heart was beating so fast he could hardly breathe. He had loved and coveted and waited for Afifah for years, and now she was casting him aside. Darcy had destroyed any hope he had had for happiness and Jalal would ensure he paid the price. But Bahir's betrayal stung much deeper. How could he stand there, calmly, and agree to Afifah's demands without a word of support for his friend? He should have been angry, should have stopped Afifah before she had uttered those terrible words. Jalal felt abandoned by the family he had come to love as much as his own.

He slipped quietly across the gardens towards the palace. What if Bahir convinced the Sheikh to annul the betrothal? All Jalal's ambitions of power, prestige and position would be thwarted. He *needed* this marriage. As the Sheikh's son-in-law he would finally be Bahir's equal in status, and would guarantee the survival of his family business. His sons would be the grandsons of a Sheikh.

He had to talk to Bahir, to reason with him. This marriage couldn't fall through – Jalal simply wouldn't allow it. Rescuing his family business became even more critical – with no financial prospects, there would be good grounds for the marriage plans to be dropped. He couldn't allow any reason to be found to release Afifah from her promise.

Jalal was more resolved than ever on his course of action to salvage the Muntasir shipping company. The new partners would bring with them access to new ports, and the company would prosper. There would be a wedding. And with that wedding would come more shipping contracts, promised to Jalal by the Sheikh. Newly determined, he entered the palace to find his father and the Sheikh enjoying coffee in one of the many sitting rooms.

Abdul was returning from the stables when he saw Jalal creeping around the side of the palace. He had been watching him for days now, although he was not even sure why. Somehow Jalal was connected to that small village so many heartbeats away. Somehow he had awakened memories that the boy Abdul had buried deep in his subconscious, where they couldn't be reached, where they couldn't paralyse him with fear.

Jalal entered a side door, keeping a close watch on the palace but not looking behind him. Abdul entered a moment later from the same door, but found only staff in the majestic marble corridor. Voices led him along to the second door on the right, which stood open as a maid served a fresh pot of coffee, the delicious smell lingering in the air. A voice he recognised well was discussing the hendra outbreak in the Hunter Valley.

'So do they know much about this strange disease?' Salah al Din asked.

'I believe there is still much to learn. They're not even sure which animals can be infected. There is a scientist studying the case, so perhaps some more light will be shed on the virus soon.' The Sheikh was able to be philosophical now his beloved son was out of danger.

Abdul peered in and saw the Sheikh and Jalal, sitting with a man he had seen many times before, but something about this man's profile froze Abdul in his tracks. For the first time Abdul recognised Salah al Din for who he had been.

The blood rushed to Abdul's head, adrenaline coursing through him. He stood in the open doorway clenching his fists, trying to prevent the child within him from running, from fleeing his memories. Sheikh Faisal looked up and saw his trusted manager.

'Abdul, is there something you wish to discuss?' he asked, assuming there was an issue in the stables.

Abdul stared wildly for a moment, his mouth open but no words coming out. He shook his head and forced himself to retreat as slowly as he could as the Sheikh gazed after him with a puzzled expression.

There was only one place Abdul could think of to escape. He sprinted across the gardens to the riding stable and yelled at a groom to bring him a horse float immediately. A beautiful white Arabian horse named Qamar, after the moon, nickered a greeting. Picking up Abdul's tension, the horse stamped his feet and tossed his head. Bahir's horse called out now, as the excitement and fear Abdul had brought in with him permeated the stables. A bay gelding reared and lashed out at the stable door, the chorus of whinnying growing to a crescendo and bringing groomsmen running to check the commotion.

Abdul entered the stable and Qamar dropped his head low to paw at the straw. Abdul quickly slipped on a bridle and led the horse out to the float, sending the groomsman back to collect the rest of Abdul's gear.

Driving out the palace gates, Abdul's head was whirling. He couldn't think straight, but pointed the car towards the desert and found himself amidst the dunes half an hour later. He expertly tacked up Qamar, then leapt into the saddle. The Arabian horse danced around near the car for a moment, his magnificent neck arched, then horse and rider whirled to face the freedom of the open desert and took off in a gallop. Abdul leaned close to the neck of his horse and shouted encouragement, speeding up their flight. Excitement flowed through man and beast alike, Qamar's powerful muscles rippling as he sped through the sands with his silver tail and mane streaming in the wind.

As one with the magnificent creature, Abdul no longer had to think, and the sense of overwhelming foreboding began to fall away from him as it had done so often before on horseback.

28

Ambrose-Taylor Residence, Knightsbridge, London

Darcy was awoken by the unmistakable sound of a sports car careening around the corner of the elegant residential street below his bedroom window. A shrill toot of the horn heralded the arrival of his father and stepmother, and probably awoke the entire neighbourhood. Darcy sat up and looked at the time. It was 7 a.m. and he had been soundly asleep for nine hours. Car doors thudded, followed by the front door, and finally there was a pounding of feet as his father took the stairs two at a time and burst into the bedroom.

'Sleepyhead!' he exclaimed. 'How are you? Train for Doncaster leaves at 10.35 but I'm sending Roger on ahead with the luggage, so get your gear together pronto. Your stepmother's organising breakfast for us all, so shake a leg and I'll see you downstairs in a jiff.' He finally drew breath and allowed Darcy to speak.

'Hi, Dad, how are you?'

'Same old, same old. Now jump out of there, let's get some

tea into you . . . or do you prefer coffee? I can't remember, but never mind, we've got both, of course – you can take your pick.'

He bounded out of the room and ran lightly down the stairs again, leaving Darcy shaking his head. His father really was incorrigible. It was always the same when Darcy came to stay with his parents: his father talked at a million miles an hour and his stepmother fed him as if he hadn't eaten in months. He'd flown back from Dubai three days earlier for the St Leger Stakes at Doncaster, but Henry and Julia had been staying with friends in the country.

Darcy threw on a silk dressing gown and went downstairs to the kitchen. There he greeted his stepmother warmly with a big hug and kiss, and she fussed around making tea *and* coffee, just in case, as well as crumpets. His father fired questions at him about the horses and his travels, and barely waited for him to answer before he shot the next one out. And so it went for a hectic half and hour until Henry suddenly looked at his watch, announced he had a coffee appointment, and barrelled out the door. He would meet Darcy at King's Cross Station at 10.30. A moment later they heard his Jaguar XKR roar into life and zip off down the road.

Darcy looked at Julia and laughed. 'I see nothing's changed! How on earth do you put up with it?'

Julia smiled indulgently. 'I've got used to it, and besides, he's always like this when you first come home. He misses you terribly.'

'Well, finally, can I ask how you are? You're looking very well.' Regardless of the hour Julia always managed to look elegant.

Darcy adored his stepmother and felt very fortunate to have her. His parents had separated just after the family moved to

England when Darcy was sixteen. It had been a difficult time; Darcy remembered feeling isolated and alone in a new country and new school while his parents fought. Over the years, his mother had mellowed and given up the pills and alcohol that had destroyed her marriage. She had been living in Milan for the last six years. Maybe he would surprise her with a visit – and this time perhaps they would find some common bond.

Henry had met Julia at the races, after dallying with a string of lovers designed to ease a broken heart. He had sworn to never marry again, but found himself proposing a year and a half later. Darcy clicked with Julia from the moment they met, which had made Henry very happy – not to mention Darcy, too.

Henry and Julia were two equals who complemented, loved and respected each other, and in Darcy's eyes, their marriage was as perfect as he imagined a marriage could be.

'I'm terrific, never been better. Your father's had a few niggling problems but nothing to worry about. If anything, I think he enjoys his life more as he gets older,' Julia mused. 'Now, would you like another cup of tea, or should I leave you alone to get organised?'

'I certainly don't need any more tea or I'll be waterlogged,' Darcy said, grinning. 'But I could definitely do with a shower.'

'Just tell me one thing first, because I'm dying to know . . . Is there anyone special at the moment?'

Darcy rolled his eyes at his stepmother. 'You are so predictable,' he teased. 'But no, I'm afraid I haven't found you a daughter-in-law yet.'

Not long after, toting a small leather satchel carrying his form guide, newspapers and other necessities, Darcy jumped on the Underground and made his way to King's Cross station to meet his father. As usual, he had cut it a bit fine, and while striding towards the platform for Doncaster he glanced at his watch, a Frederique Constant Tourbillon that had been a special gift from his father for Darcy's thirtieth birthday. It was a beauty, the perfect present from a man who viewed punctuality as a high virtue – a watch whose precision was considered one of the best in the world. Each Frederique Constant Tourbillon was individually numbered, with only 188 in existence, to match the number of components in each watch. Darcy had no idea how Henry had got it, but his watch was number eight. Needless to say, Darcy wore his Tourbillon with great pride.

Henry was waiting impatiently by the first-class carriage and waved Darcy onboard with a scowl. The train jolted and moved off as they took their seats, but there was thankfully no further comment from Henry on punctuality. Father and son were both stylishly dressed in well-cut suits and chic ties, and each sported a trench coat over his arm, just in case.

The train ride to Doncaster was always relaxing for both father and son. Although they'd discussed the hendra outbreak at breakfast, Henry was keen to know more and was very concerned for the horses at their Victorian stud.

'As far as I know there has never been a case any further south than the Hunter Valley,' Darcy explained.

'But the girl in France?' Henry queried.

Darcy had wanted to keep his suspicions to himself until they could be further substantiated, but he found himself blurting out the story to his startled father.

'Why would anyone want to kill a stallion, for heaven's sake?' Henry responded. 'I think you've let your imagination run a bit wild, son. Tell me, is this girl in Dubai pretty?' Darcy resented the patronising tone and changed the subject.

Roger was waiting with the Bentley as they left the station, and he drove them to the Doncaster Racecourse. Here Henry and Darcy met up with a group of friends who had gathered at this September meeting for over twenty years. The people of Doncaster turned out in force for the annual Ladbrokes St Leger Festival, and down by the racetrack a cheerful atmosphere presided. Henry and Darcy settled quickly into the time-honoured rhythm of betting and drinking between races.

At the end of what proved to be a very successful day of punting, Darcy and his father freshened up after the track and met again in the local pub, where a crowd had gathered. Darcy was feeling the effects of too much excellent French wine, so he switched to a pint of beer to last the distance. This night in the pub was something of a racing ritual amongst Henry's friends, and the evening often spilled over into the morning. It paid to pace yourself. Darcy had first been invited to join his father at the Doncaster carnival when he reached the legal drinking age, and the trip had been treated as a rite of passage into manhood and serious racing. He wouldn't miss it for the world, and with their runner tomorrow likely to win the big race, not even the Southern Hemisphere breeding season could keep him away.

An Irish bloodstock agent broke into song across the bar, and everyone joined in the chorus to the end. Just getting started, the Irishman struck up another tune, his voice strident with alcohol. Darcy took the opportunity to go to bed – he and his father had taken rooms upstairs as they always did. His head was already hurting from the fine wine and he staggered up the rickety stairs and down the narrow corridor with hands out to prevent himself careening into the wall.

Safely in the small, stuffy room, he splashed cold water on his face, and drank a few glasses of water. He then slipped into bed and switched off the lamp, gripping the sheets as the room did a slow revolution. Thoughts of Clea slipped easily into his mind. Portia had distracted him for a few days, and he had to admit it had been a hot few days, but his mind had stubbornly returned to Clea. He shook his head to dislodge the vision of her in the red dress, and immediately regretted the gesture as the room lurched unsteadily on its circular course once again. Clea had made it clear she wasn't interested. She was a lost cause, Darcy told himself sternly, as his eyes drooped shut.

It was the fourth and final day of the Ladbrokes St Leger Festival, and the day of the world's oldest classic race, the St Leger Stakes. The Ambrose-Taylor Stable had Christopher Robin, the favourite for the 3000-metre race for three-year-old colts. The St Leger had once held more prestige as a race to make a stallion's name, but in recent times, as speed was increasingly valued over stamina, it had lost some of that gloss.

Henry had been hoping to avoid a clash between Christopher Robin and Genghis, a powerful colt from the Eclipse Stable. Genghis was earmarked to compete in the staying races of Europe, but at the last minute he had been entered into the St Leger field. Henry suspected the change of heart was based more on the long-standing friendly rivalry between the two stables than programming for the horse, and the Sheikh's beaming face confirmed the suspicion.

'Today we find out who has the best three-year-old stayer,' he said, greeting Henry and Darcy. 'Your horse may be the favourite, but Genghis is race-fit and the distance should suit him perfectly.'

'We'll see, my friend, we'll see,' Henry responded to the challenge.

Watching the racing and festivities from a corporate marquee, Darcy had managed to avoid any conversation with Yvonne, but as his father and the Sheikh wandered off to speak to another acquaintance she materialised next to him in a magenta dress.

'At last I get a chance to talk with you,' she said familiarly, and linked her arm in his to draw him out onto the lawn. Darcy glanced back over his shoulder towards the Sheikh and his father. Yvonne followed his look and smiled. 'You know, I've known your father for a very long time,' she said and waved as Henry caught sight of them.

'I didn't realise,' Darcy answered uncomfortably. It was only a matter of minutes before the Sheikh spied their tete-a-tete, and he fervently hoped it wouldn't be misconstrued.

'Yes, we go back a long way – lots of history.' She seemed to be warming to her topic.

'Your family raced a lot of horses, didn't they?' Darcy was keeping a close eye on her champagne glass. It would be an excellent excuse to move away with some politesse.

'Yes, that's how I met your father. We were introduced by a trainer. We had a very good colt at the time, Inimitable, and your father was keen to purchase him as a stallion prospect.'

Darcy clearly remembered the occasion. It had been around the time of his parent's divorce, two years after they'd separated, and Henry had been forced to let the deal fall through while he sorted out his personal life. As it turned out the horse hadn't performed too well at stud, although his daughters were producing good progeny. Darcy watched as Yvonne finished the last sip of her champagne and quickly insisted on bringing her another. As he walked back into the marquee the Sheikh brushed past him and rejoined Yvonne. Relieved, Darcy sent a waiter out with a fresh glass and found his father by the food, where a chef was preparing Peking duck.

'I didn't realise you'd known Yvonne for so long,' Darcy said offhandedly and was surprised when Henry looked at him sharply.

'Why, what did she tell you?'

'Nothing. To be honest I was trying to get away. The last thing I need is for the Sheikh to think I'm trying to steal his woman.' Darcy rolled his eyes for effect.

Henry relaxed, and handed Darcy two Peking duck pancakes on a small plate. 'Try these, they're very good.'

Later in the day at the horse stalls, Sheikh Faisal and Henry compared their two runners for the big race. Darcy was surprised to find Abdul there too, as he hadn't seen him all day. As the horses proceeded to the mounting yard, saddled up and ready to race, Darcy went on ahead with Abdul.

'I haven't had much of a chance to see how you're going after the hendra deaths,' he began tentatively.

Abdul looked surprised. 'I've been preoccupied with other things lately,' he said. 'I must admit it's taken my mind off the tragedy.' Abdul walked in silence for a while, thinking. He desperately needed to reach out to someone with his fears, someone he could trust. He couldn't broach the subject with Bahir or the Sheikh — they considered Jalal family. He knew Darcy was no friend of Jalal's; he had watched the friction from the sidelines for years. Perhaps Darcy could help him. But he simply didn't know where to start.

'Abdul, it seems like something's troubling you. Is there anything I can do to help?' Darcy asked.

It was the opening Abdul needed. 'It's Jalal and his father,' he began slowly. But how could he explain? What if he was wrong and Salah al Din had nothing to do with the death of his parents?

'What about them?' Darcy said encouragingly as Abdul fell silent again.

'I don't think he's who he says he is,' Abdul stuttered out, thinking of Salah al Din. The Sheikh and Henry were catching up to them and Abdul looked around in a panic.

Darcy was intrigued but realised he wouldn't get any more out of Abdul for the moment. There would be time later. The mounting yard was crowded with hopeful owners, trainers and jockeys, and Henry and the Sheikh split up to discuss tactics.

The race unfolded to suit Christopher Robin, who had taken a trail behind Genghis one out and three back. The pace was slow for the first mile, but at the 1400-metre mark the back markers started to make their move. Christopher Robin and Genghis hooked out into the clear and had caught the leaders by the 100-metre mark. From there, the two superior colts pulled away and battled it out to the line. The Ambrose-Taylor jockey threw everything at it as they approached the winning post, flattening out on Christopher Robin's neck so the horse could stretch right out in a tight finish. The judge called for a photo finish and everyone waited anxiously for the result to be posted. Darcy was sure the bob of the head favoured Christopher Robin on the outside, and in a moment his hopes were confirmed.

The celebrations went on long and hard into the night, and Darcy and Henry climbed aboard the train the next morning for the short trip back to London feeling rather fragile.

Abdul had returned to the Newmarket stud straight after the race, angry at himself for trying to involve anyone else in his business, especially Darcy. As night fell he left the warmth of the house and paced the farm in the dark, inhaling the musty autumn air. The vixen barked to her cubs a little way off as Abdul walked down the laneways, checking each horse in the paddocks on either side. He began to relax as the animals moved to the gates to greet him. This was his family. He had left everything else behind in a windswept desert, in another country and another time.

29
Mimi's Waterfront Apartment, Dubai

Mimi rushed back to her apartment from lunch. She had a client at 4 p.m., one of the many who enjoyed the discretion of her home. She quickly put down her shopping bags and went to 'the office', as she called the bedroom she used for entertaining – as opposed to her real bedroom on the other side of the apartment. Mimi unwrapped a small red and white striped parcel and held up a deep red balconette bra and beautiful matching French knickers.

She peeled off her casual dress and flat heels and removed her underwear. She was about to put on the expensive new set when she remembered her impending visitor had enjoyed playing rough at their first encounter. Sighing, she carefully laid the red lingerie in a drawer full of lacy pieces and pulled out an older black set. Her clients paid a fortune for the privilege of using her body, and her underwear paid the price.

Decked out in a black bra, French knickers, garter and

stockings, she selected a red silk robe from the wardrobe and some high stiletto heels. In the bathroom she tousled her hair sexily in front of the mirror and applied red lipstick. Her final touch was to add a squeeze of lubricant, to give her client the impression of excitement.

Although Mimi didn't mind the rough stuff – it paid incredibly well – this particular client did frighten her a little. She had first encountered Zayd during the trip in the Riviera and it had taken weeks before the bruises disappeared. This was his first visit to her home and she hoped his previous enthusiasm had been due to the sea air.

There was a rap at the door and with one last check in the mirror, Mimi opened it. Zayd walked into the room and made sure the door was closed before pulling out a wad of cash and throwing it disdainfully on the dining table. 'You look like such a whore,' he said gruffly to Mimi. 'Let me see you properly.' He yanked the cord of her robe and pushed the red silk off her shoulders so it pooled on the floor at her feet.

'I'm going to make you earn every cent of that money.' He pushed her head towards the cash, making her stagger across the room and almost topple over on her heels. Then he grabbed her arm, dragged her into the bedroom and shoved her onto the bed. Mimi rolled expertly to avoid putting lipstick all over the clean sheets.

Zayd unbuckled his belt and let his trousers fall to the floor, then instructed her to remove his shoes. As Mimi moved to the edge of the bed she could see he was already turned on. 'Look at you,' she taunted. 'You can't wait to get a piece of me, can you?'

She reached back to unclasp her bra, but Zayd stopped her, grinning. He pulled a sharp knife from his jacket and flicked it open. Mimi looked suitably afraid, even though she'd had a feeling this was coming – it had been the same the first time. He reached over to cut the bra right between her breasts, and with one slice her bra fell to the floor. Zayd closed the knife and began squeezing her breasts together, pinching her nipples so sharply that she cried out. Finally he sat on the bed in front of her, flicking open the knife again to run it softly up and down her inner thighs, forcing her to open her legs.

In a flash he cut her knickers off, leaving just her garter belt and stockings. He touched her pink love heart almost tenderly for a moment, then sliced through the four garters holding up her stockings. Dropping the knife on the bed, he grabbed the top of her stockings and yanked until they ripped down her legs.

'You were made to please a man, and this is how you should always be – naked and ready,' Zayd said. He pulled off his own underwear and pressed her down until she knelt on the floor, grabbing her hair and forcing her face into his groin.

Mimi knew she was very good at giving head, and she could feel his excitement grow as she sucked him off, stopping occasionally to circle the head of his cock with her tongue. Her jaw was aching before he finally instructed her to get onto her hands and knees on the bed. She did so as demurely as possible, her legs together and no arch in her back. Predictably, Zayd grabbed her thighs and pulled them apart.

'I want to see what I've paid for, whore,' he said, his excitement making his voice hoarse.

Mimi curved her spine to show her body at its best angle. Grabbing her hips he pushed into her frantically, at first unable to control himself, but eventually slowing to a more manageable tempo.

Taking a handful of her hair he jerked her head back and demanded, 'Tell me how much you want it, bitch. Tell me how much pleasure you get out of being fucked.'

'Oh God, I've been wanting it all day, Zayd.' Mimi told him what he wanted to hear.

He slapped his body into hers violently for a few strokes but was too turned on to keep up the pace. 'Tell me what you fantasise about.'

'Your big cock inside me and all over me. I want you to fill me up with your come. I want you to rub it all over my breasts.'

He was beginning to lose it now, so Mimi faked an almighty orgasm to please him.

After a few more thrusts he flipped her over onto her back and knelt over her chest. Pushing her large breasts together he slid his cock into her cleavage and spurted his pleasure onto her face. Then, with a moan of contentment, he rolled off and lay back on the bed.

A few minutes later Zayd was in the shower. After wiping the mess off herself, Mimi tiptoed towards his trousers and grabbed his wallet. With heart pounding, she searched through until she found a credit card. His full name was Zayd Farouk, and she had promised to tell Portia as soon as she found out. She replaced the wallet carefully, but his watch fell out of the pocket as she did so. She stared at it for a moment, recognising the brand. On the back was an inscription: *To Lady Luck!* Mimi quickly checked the water was still running in the bathroom, then picked up the phone and dialled Portia's number.

Zayd appeared in the bedroom doorway, dripping wet and unnoticed. He wanted Mimi in the shower with him, but now, bizarrely, she was on the phone. Something was going on, and he quietly ducked beside the bed to eavesdrop. He heard it all.

30
Eclipse Stud, Newmarket, England

The stud was down a narrow, undulating road with ancient stone walls on either side, making it virtually impossible for two cars to pass. The day's intermittent showers were punctuated by bursts of sunshine, and it was in a pool of golden light that Darcy pulled up his dirty Range Rover outside the main house, where Bahir was waiting.

Bahir came bursting out of the door and greeted Darcy warmly with a clap on the back and a bear hug, looking much more his usual vigorous self.

Darcy gave him a mock punch in the arm for his efforts. 'Hey, you're looking pretty good for someone who was on death's door a moment ago – are they feeding you molasses or something?'

'Come on, I've organised lunch. I can bore you with my health while we eat.'

The decor inside the eighteenth-century manor house was predictably horsy. Winning photos adorned the walls, interspersed with a few paintings – also of horses – and *every* available surface, be it sideboard, mantel or occasional table, was crammed with trophies.

'Here we are.' Bahir threw open the door to a room flooded with light from the glass bifold doors that led to a patio. The sunlight streamed in and reflected off the crystal glasses on the table in dazzling prisms of light. A sideboard groaned under the weight of a smorgasbord of dishes: wood-smoked Scottish salmon, foie gras, quail stuffed with prunes and pine nuts, lamb cutlets with a herbed crust, a selection of crisp salads and a pungent cheese platter.

'You really *are* feeling better.' Darcy looked on in amazement as Bahir passed him a plate and piled his own high with food.

'Hospital food has given me a great appetite for anything that doesn't arrive on a plastic tray. And besides, I have to build my strength back up.' He laughed and motioned for Darcy to sit.

'So where's the entourage? I don't think I've ever seen you here alone before,' Darcy commented.

'You're right, I've just sent them all off to lunch in Newmarket at the Rutland Arms. That reminds me, I am an awful host . . . Would you like a glass of wine?' Darcy shook his head politely. 'You don't need to refuse on my account,' Bahir said, laughing. 'Lord knows you didn't at Oxford.'

Bahir didn't mention he had sent all the others away to avoid Jalal, who was applying pressure to set a wedding date. He had not discussed with Jalal the conversation he'd had with Afifah, but repeated his father's wish for Afifah to marry after she finished studying. He couldn't deny he felt disloyal to Jalal, but blood ties would always be stronger for him than those of friendship.

After lunch Bahir suggested going to the stables for a tour. On the way across the large expanse of lawn between the manor and the stables, Darcy's mobile phone rang.

'Darcy? Is that you? It's Portia.' Her voice was distressed.

'Portia? Are you okay?' Darcy said, startled to hear from her.

'Darcy, I think Mimi is dead,' she said hysterically. 'I heard her and now I can't get her on the phone.' She burst into tears and it was a moment before she could speak again.

'Tell me what happened,' Darcy encouraged.

'She rang to tell me the client Zayd from the boat had turned up again, and this time she'd found out his full name, only he must've still been there because she screamed, and then all I could hear was her gasping for breath. He picked up the phone, and I could hear him listening, so I hung up. Darcy, I don't know what to do, I'm really scared.' Portia's voice was shaking with fear.

'You need to get to the police now,' Darcy instructed, and briefly filled Bahir in while Portia waited on the line.

Bahir pulled out his mobile and dialled a number, speaking urgently in Arabic, then he took the phone from Darcy. 'Portia, you must speak only to Lieutenant Kassab when you go to the central police station. I have informed him you are on your way. He is well known to our family and can be trusted. Now, go.' He handed the phone back to Darcy.

'Don't worry, Portia, you'll be safe once you get to the police.

Jump in a taxi right now and don't stop anywhere,' Darcy warned. 'What did you say the man's name was again? The one with Mimi?'

'Zayd Farouk. I should have known it was dangerous,' Portia moaned. 'I should never have got her involved.'

'You weren't to know,' he reassured her, but quietly wondered if their prying had sent the girl to her death, or if she had already been a marked woman. 'Mimi lived on the edge – she knew the risks.'

Portia stifled a sob and hung up. Darcy hoped she would be all right.

Bahir was sitting silently, gazing into a roaring fire in one of the drawing rooms, when a car crunched to a halt on the gravel driveway. Abdul and Jalal came quickly through the door.

'What's this I hear?' Jalal demanded. 'You are somehow involved in the disappearance of a prostitute? Do they know who's responsible?'

'Yes, they have his name. Darcy's friend Portia is sure she heard the girl being killed. It's all so awful.' Bahir looked tired.

'Be careful, Bahir,' Jalal cautioned. 'You can't afford to get your name mixed up in some sordid lover's fight.'

Jalal went to the study to make a few phone calls, so Bahir suggested to Darcy that they try to make that tour of the stables they had planned.

The chill of an autumn afternoon permeated Darcy's thin jumper as they walked across the damp lawn. The horses were being led back from the paddocks into their stables and were nickering for feed. They were creatures of habit, and most content when following a set routine. The groomsmen were throwing on night-time rugs to keep out the cold and buckling the straps around their restless charges, who stamped their feet, impatient for the meal run to begin.

Bahir led Darcy down the row of horses, pointing out favourites until they stopped at the last box, where the stud vet was examining a striking dark brown horse with a wide white blaze down his face.

'Is there something wrong, Jeremy?' Bahir asked.

'Peter noticed an unusual discharge,' Jeremy answered, indicating the groom holding the horse. 'I'm sure it's nothing serious, but Sampson was off his feed this morning so I'm not leaving anything to chance.'

'This is Sampson, the Arc de Triomphe winner,' Bahir told Darcy. 'He's the best Weight for Age Classic horse in the world right now by Timeform ratings.'

'That's odd.' Jeremy was listening to the horse's breathing through a stethoscope. 'His breathing is pretty laboured; he must have a chest infection. I'll run some bloods immediately but in the meantime, as a precaution I'll put him straight on antibiotics. Peter, I'm sorry, but no sleep for you tonight – I need you to be on two-hourly checks through the night and to let me know if his condition worsens even marginally. I'm sure it's just an infection of some sort, Prince. It can't be travel sickness as he's been here for a good three weeks now.'

'Keep me informed?'

As they watched, foam began forming in the horse's nostrils until he snorted it all over the groom.

'I don't like the look of that,' Jeremy said. 'Let's isolate him just in case. Take him down to the vet stables, Peter, I'll take blood down there.' Jeremy stepped aside as Peter led the horse out of the main stables, hoofs clopping on the path outside.

'I think you should take a few more precautions, particularly with the groom,' Bahir warned. 'That foamy substance . . . it looked just like what happened with Bismarck. But there's no way it could be hendra, could it?'

'No, there's never been a case of it in a horse outside Australia,' Jeremy said confidently.

'I couldn't have . . .'

'From my understanding of the virus, Prince, horses can pass it to humans but not the other way around. There's no way you could have —' Jeremy paused mid-sentence. The thought that Bahir might somehow still be carrying the hendra virus was frightening indeed.

'Can we test?'

'I'm not even sure of the testing procedure but I'll make some phone calls immediately and find out. Excuse me, Prince.' Jeremy rushed off after Sampson, leaving Bahir frowning and staring at an empty stable.

Remembering what had happened at the Hunter Valley, Bahir checked the adjacent stable and discovered, to his dismay, that

Drake, the stable's best sprinter, was housed there. If it *was* hendra then Drake had been directly in its deadly path.

'Maybe this is my fault,' he said eventually, looking distraught.

'Don't jump to any conclusions yet,' Darcy cautioned. 'As long as you protect your staff and get to the bottom of it right away, that's all you can do for the moment.'

'I think we should go back to the house and shower and change right now, just in case. Believe me, you don't want to go around catching this thing.' Bahir started back across the lawn for the house and Darcy followed in silence.

They quickly showered and put all their clothing in plastic bags and sealed them as a precaution. One of the staff took away their shoes and disinfected them.

'Some visit this has turned into! I'm so sorry, Darcy.' Bahir was morose.

'This couldn't be the same,' Jalal comforted Bahir, once he'd heard the news. 'How could the virus be all the way over here? It will just be a cold and tomorrow everything will be all right.' Jalal looked carefully at his friend. Bahir seemed tired and upset, but there were no signs of illness.

Bahir finally dragged his eyes from the dancing fire in the sitting room. 'I'm so sorry for you too, Jalal. Drake means a lot to us both.'

'Don't worry about me.'

A meal of roasted meats and vegetables was prepared, but no one had much appetite. Eventually Bahir was summoned to the phone to speak to Jeremy, who had quarantined himself in the veterinary quarters with the horse.

'The news isn't good, I'm afraid. I've spoken to our vet in Australia and the symptoms are very similar to hendra. I also sent the grooms to check the temperatures and breathing of the other horses in the stable and Drake is the only one showing symptoms. I've shifted him down here now too.'

Bahir was understandably worried about his staff. 'Are you all taking enough precautions?'

'Yes, although I'll keep a very close eye on Peter – he's the one at most risk. With your permission, I'd like to fly the scientist who attended the stud in Australia out here as soon as possible.'

'Of course.' Despite the circumstances, Bahir felt an unexpected sense of happiness at the thought of seeing Clea again. She had left a lasting impression on him.

31

Terminal Three, Heathrow Airport, London

Thirty hours later, Clea stepped out of customs at Heathrow. She felt a knot of anticipation in her stomach, and told herself it was a reaction to the prospect of an international hendra outbreak. But deep down she knew it was about Prince Bahir. His charm and sexy eyes the night of the gala ball had enchanted her. The thrill of his arms holding her firmly on the dance floor had lingered long after the music had faded.

Abdul and another man were waiting for her at the gate and hurried her along a corridor.

'I wasn't expecting to see you again so soon,' Clea said to Abdul as they paced along a travelator.

'We are very grateful you have come so quickly. Bahir is worried sick.'

'He's not ill himself this time, is he?' Clea asked anxiously.

'No, but this horse is very important to us all. It couldn't be the virus again, could it?' Abdul looked like he hadn't slept for weeks.

'I can't really say until I've had a chance to examine the situation carefully,' Clea answered cautiously. 'Where are we going?' They seemed to be getting further and further away from the main section of the airport. She had assumed a car would be waiting for them somewhere.

'To the helipad. The prince wants you there as fast as possible, and the roads in the UK . . .' He left the sentence unfinished.

Arriving at the helipad, they were ushered into a golf buggy that sped across the tarmac to a large twin-engine helicopter poised for take-off. As soon as they climbed on board and buckled in, the helicopter lifted upwards and set off towards the north-east of England.

Abdul seemed caught up in his own thoughts, and the noise of the helicopter prevented easy conversation anyway, so Clea gazed out the window, feasting her eyes on the lush landscape – it had been a long time since she had seen anything like that depth of green.

By lunchtime they landed on an expanse of lawn at the horse stud and Bahir rushed out of the manor to greet her.

'Thank you so much for coming,' he shouted over the noise of the helicopter rotors. 'We're all so worried, as you can imagine. I'll get someone to put your bags in your room, but if you wouldn't mind going straight to the stables?' Bahir's anxiety was evident.

'Of course, there's no time to waste.' Clea retrieved her briefcase and laptop bag from the pilot. Bahir tried to follow her towards the stables, but Abdul stopped him firmly.

'I'll let you know as soon as I find anything,' Clea promised.

'Come up to the house when you can, I'll be waiting.' Bahir watched as Clea left.

Despite the sense of urgency, Clea allowed herself a moment of delight at seeing Bahir again as she put on full protection gear. She entered the small set of stables that made up the vet's quarters, set up with a couple of stalls, two vet crushes, an office and a small lab. Jeremy rushed out to greeted her wearing a face mask and protective clothing, much to Clea's relief.

'Dr Reynolds, thank you for coming so quickly. I'm out of my depth with this one.' Clea shook his hand. 'Here are our two patients, and this is Peter, who has been with Sampson the whole time.'

Clea cried out involuntarily when she saw Sampson. He was staggering to stay upright and his breathing was dreadfully laboured. Flecks of foam kept appearing on his soft muzzle. His eyes rolled back in pain as he tried to draw in enough oxygen to fuel his impressive frame. Clea checked him over quickly.

'I'm afraid all clinical signs point to hendra, as you said over the phone, but I'm still at a loss as to how he could have been infected. Do you have the bloods? I'm going to need an electron microscope to have a look.'

'We took the precaution of alerting the authorities and they've sent in a MBU, luckily.' Jeremy led her to a side door. The mobile biosecurity unit, a large truck, was parked alongside the vet area, and the lab driver, hidden behind his protective gear, appeared as they approached. 'You know, it's ironic, the Sheikh kicked in three million pounds to sponsor the biosecurity initiative when it was struggling to get funding. Now we're actually using it. I just hope to God we're wrong about the virus.'

Clea placed a reassuring hand on his arm. 'I'll do everything I can.'

She was relieved to see the state-of-the-art equipment neatly installed in the truck. It was far superior to the Australian mobile lab she had used in the Hunter Valley. She would have every chance to get this issue under control and hopefully save as many horses' lives as possible. For a moment she gazed sadly at the four vials of blood, two horse and two human, which were already awaiting testing. But after a moment she got a grip on herself and, taking the first vial, went to work quickly, only pausing after an hour to request a thermos of strong coffee to keep the jetlag at bay.

The whole stud was in suspense. The main gates were shut and anyone trying to enter or leave the property was prevented by order of Defra, the Department of Environment, Food and Rural Affairs, who had stopped just short of imposing an official quarantine restriction while awaiting notification from Clea.

Sheikh Faisal was in London, and furious. 'I want you out of there immediately,' he insisted to his son over the phone. 'I don't want you anywhere near that disease again.'

'Father, I'm not a child,' Bahir said gently. 'We're taking all precautions, and I must stay here until we work out what this is. Besides, Defra won't allow anyone to leave the property.'

'I still don't like it one bit. I'm sending in a doctor just to be on the safe side.' Sheikh Faisal was adamant.

By 3.45 p.m. Clea had determined without a shadow of a doubt that she was dealing with the hendra virus. But not only was it hendra – it was exactly the same strain as in the Hunter Valley. 'Jeremy, it's hendra,' she told him as she stepped out of the MBU. 'You're now officially in quarantine. Both Sampson and Drake have tested positive. I've already notified the authorities.'

Jeremy was shocked. 'What do we do with the horses? How do we treat them?'

Clea turned away for a moment, her eyes filling with tears. There were no miracles. When she turned back, Jeremy saw the sadness in her eyes and slumped into a chair, defeated.

'Jeremy, I'm so sorry. There's nothing we can do. You'll have to put down both horses as swiftly as possible to prevent any further spread.' Clea pulled up a chair next to the devastated vet. 'You did everything you could,' she reassured him. 'Because of your quick actions the rest of the horses will probably be all right. You should be proud of yourself, if that's any consolation.' Clea knew it wasn't – these horses were prized athletes and beautiful animals, and their untimely deaths were a tragedy.

'What should I do with the other horses?'

'Start taking bloods. As Sampson was in the end stall, it's unlikely he spread the virus far. Was he in contact with any other horses besides Drake in the twenty-four hours before you noticed his condition?'

'No, he and Drake have adjacent paddocks,' Jeremy answered,

desperately hopeful Clea was right and the tragedy could be contained to two horses.

She rested her hand against his forehead and was relieved to find his temperature normal. 'Well, in the meantime, we should be worrying about you, too. You've tested clear but this virus is unpredictable. And where's Peter?'

Jeremy suddenly realised he hadn't seen the groom for a while, and called out frantically. After a moment Peter's head popped out from a hay storage area and he came towards them rubbing his eyes. Jeremy rushed over to support him. 'My God, Peter, are you all right?'

'I'm fine, I was just taking a nap,' Peter said shyly. 'I figured you didn't need me for a moment.'

Clea immediately checked his forehead for a temperature. 'No shortness of breath or headaches or feeling unwell in any way?'

Peter shook his head. 'I'm fine, honestly. I was just so tired after staying up most of the night.'

'We were only exposed to the horse for a very brief time before taking precautions.' Jeremy still looked concerned.

'Okay, well, you two may be very lucky. But even though you're clear I want you both to go to hospital this afternoon. This virus is deadly and I'm not taking any chances with either of you.'

In fresh protective clothing Clea strode over to the main stable, armed with her trusty equipment bag, and went straight to the bars of Sampson's stall. Using her UV light Clea checked the bars for any traces of the mysterious powder she had found before, and caught her breath. It was clearly visible. She bagged a sample, then checked Drake's stall, which seemed clear. Clea was beginning to believe her initial instincts were right – there was some other force at play, and these outbreaks had to be deliberate. In Australia she'd been able to quell her concerns as there was enough empirical evidence to suggest natural causes, but here in the UK an outbreak of hendra had to be treated with the utmost suspicion.

Heading back to the MBU again, she tested the powder and came up with traces of protein and saline with the virus attached. It was the same strain she had found in the Hunter Valley – and the same strain that was stored for research purposes in the AAIDL facility. She needed to speak to Bahir immediately.

Clea emerged from the MBU and began to head back to the house. Halfway across the lawn, Jalal was waiting for her. 'Dr Reynolds, we met in Sydney. Jalal bin Muntasir. If there is any way Bahir is in danger I need to get him away from here now,' he said vehemently. 'His father would never forgive me – and I could never forgive myself – if he fell ill again.'

'There's nothing I can prove without further testing,' Clea said cautiously. 'But I have found evidence to suggest how the virus was transported to the UK.'

'Have you mentioned this to anyone?' Jalal demanded.

'No. I still need to complete my testing. At this stage it's just a hunch,' she admitted. 'If I have solid proof this time, they'll have to take it seriously.'

Jalal stopped in his tracks. 'Are you telling me there were suspicions about the source of the outbreak in the Hunter Valley?'

Clea hesitated, and answered cautiously, 'I'm not prepared to jump to any conclusions until I've studied all the evidence.'

The guard at the doorway to the manor barely looked at Clea as they passed from darkness into a pool of light in the hallway. Jalal ushered her into a warm sitting room with a fire crackling cheerfully in the hearth, and the occupants all stood as she entered.

'Dr Reynolds, we are so pleased you could come so quickly, we're really at a loss here,' Bahir said, as he smiled deeply into her eyes.

Clea was suddenly very conscious that she had jumped off a long-haul flight and gone straight into a laboratory, and had not thought about how she might look.

'Please, sit,' Bahir said, gesturing for her to join him on a deep leather sofa. 'Abdul, could you please organise Dr Reynolds a drink?' Bahir looked at her questioningly.

'A glass of water would be lovely,' she responded, noting a glass already on the coffee table. 'Please, call me Clea, Dr Reynolds sounds so . . .' Clea trailed off, unable to find the words, and met Bahir's gaze. He was really very handsome.

At that moment Darcy walked into the room smiling and greeted her with a quick kiss on the cheek. Clea's surprise showed on her face. 'Bet you weren't expecting me,' he said cheerfully. 'I'm ubiquitous, you know.'

'I thought of calling you from the Hunter Valley – I knew you'd be interested in my discoveries,' she confessed. 'But —'

'But the whole red dress incident got in the way.' Darcy finished her sentence smoothly. 'Bloody horse trainers have a warped sense of humour sometimes – getting up at three o'clock every morning makes them a bit soft in the head. I think we can put it to rest now, can't we?' He smiled gently. 'Please?'

Clea couldn't help but smile back. 'It's in the past. But now we have to look at the present and it's very serious, I'm afraid.'

'What can you tell us, Clea? We are all in shock,' Bahir said.

'Well, I can definitely tell you it's hendra virus, although how it got here is beyond me.'

Jalal jumped to his feet. 'That's impossible!' he challenged.

Clea ignored his outburst. 'Two horses are infected, but as Jeremy acted so swiftly I think the risk of it spreading is minimal. I've already notified Defra so you're now in full quarantine.'

Jalal was pacing the room. 'It must have been brought over by —' he stopped and stared at Bahir, a look of dismay on his face.

Bahir caught his eye for a moment, but remained calm. He turned back to Clea. 'And my staff?'

'At this stage there are no clinical signs of illness, but I'm sending them to hospital to be on the safe side. Bahir, I will find out how this happened,' Clea promised.

'I certainly don't want anyone else going through what I went through,' Bahir said, grimacing. 'Is there any news of Sampson and Drake yet?'

Clea hesitated. 'I'm afraid both horses must be put down immediately to stop the spread of the virus.' She saw the look of distress and profound sorrow on his face. 'I'm so very sorry for your loss.'

Darcy thought immediately of Abdul having to deal with the death of two more magnificent horses, both with stellar racing and stud careers ahead of them. Abdul's mysterious confession at Doncaster had been part of the reason for his visit to the stud, but so far he hadn't had a chance to speak to him alone.

'I need to take some blood from all of you,' Clea continued as calmly as she could. 'I've brought my kit here, if you'll permit me?' It was ghastly to think Bahir could be infected again.

But he was one step ahead. While Clea had been in the stables, the helicopter had collected an infectious-diseases specialist from London who had drawn blood from each of them for Clea to test. Given the infectious nature of hendra, it was imperative for Clea to test the blood immediately and she prepared to leave again.

'Let me walk you over,' Bahir offered. 'I promise I'll only go to the stable door,' he added, as everyone began to protest.

'I'll come too,' Darcy said. 'I can't bear just sitting around not knowing.'

'I'm sure Dr Reynolds only needs one escort,' Bahir said firmly before Darcy could stand.

Bahir and Clea carried the blood samples across the darkened lawn towards the flaring lights of the stables. 'Does Darcy often come to stay with you?' Clea asked to fill in a silence that had suddenly become awkward.

'His stud isn't very far from here so we see each other a fair bit in England. Dubai, too, when he's not busy mooning over some pretty girl he's picked up in a nightclub.' Bahir shot Clea a look but couldn't read her reaction in the dark.

After a moment he changed his tone. 'I need you to be very honest with me, Clea.' Bahir was walking close enough for her to feel the warmth radiating from his body. 'Could I have somehow brought the virus with me?' He stopped and turned to face her, his eyes full of anguish.

'No! You mustn't blame yourself. There is no evidence to suggest a person can pass on the hendra virus in any form,' Clea answered emphatically. They walked on quietly for a few paces. 'But I must tell you when I was at the Australian stud, I found something that could indicate the infection was deliberate,' she said frankly.

'The infection of the horses or me?' Bahir asked sharply.

'The horses.'

'And this time?'

'I need to check your blood sample quickly. Do you feel all right?'

'Perfectly healthy.'

They parted twenty metres from the vet's quarters and for a moment Clea watched as Bahir walked briskly back towards the house. She wondered how it must feel to have cause to fear for your life.

In face mask and suit, Peter was standing protectively with Sampson, almost as if he could stave off the inevitable by preventing anyone from getting near. Jeremy had already prepared the lethal injection and was approaching Sampson's stall. Clea could hear the rotors of the helicopter starting up outside, like the drone of a giant insect, ready to take the two men to a hospital in London once they had completed their sorrowful task.

'You can't kill him,' Peter protested with tears in his eyes. He patted Sampson, but the horse didn't respond – his eyes were rolling around and his head was low. 'You mean everything to me, don't you, boy?' Peter sobbed, stroking the horse's forelock.

'We have no choice,' Jeremy told him. 'If there were any other way . . . I promise he'll be at peace in a moment. The disease will kill him anyway, and he'll suffer even more before it does. You don't want that, do you, Peter?'

Peter wrapped his arms around Sampson's neck and choked back sobs. 'We're doing this for you, my boy,' he whispered. He pulled himself together and held Sampson's head while Jeremy carefully pushed the needle into the vein on the horse's neck and released its deadly dose into Sampson's bloodstream.

Clea braced herself as Sampson dropped to his knees unconscious and then toppled over into the hay. Both vet and groom stared for a long moment at the lifeless form at their feet, before moving reluctantly to Drake's stall to repeat the procedure.

Clea entered the MBU brushing away her own tears, but she didn't have time for sentiment. Into the night Clea worked through the samples, one by one, to confirm that Bahir, his staff and guests were clear of the deadly disease. Later that evening she staggered up to the manor and collapsed exhausted into one of the guest rooms that had been made up for her arrival.

32

The Manor, Eclipse Stud, Newmarket

The mood at Eclipse was sombre. The loss of two stallions was a major blow both emotionally and financially. The bodies had been destroyed, but at Abdul's request, their ashes were returned to Bahir in wooden boxes. When the time was right they would bury these great athletes on the stud by way of remembrance.

Abdul was in shock and kept to himself, but Bahir tried to maintain a brave face and ensure everything was being done to find the cause of the virus.

Two days after Clea's arrival tempers were fraying behind the scenes. One of the maids had left work the day before complaining of a migraine and fever, and Amanda the housekeeper was covering Sharee's work as well as her own. She was furious.

There was so much to do with the prince, his guests, the Australian scientist who had just arrived, and of course with all the extra disinfecting required to ensure the deadly disease didn't spread amongst them all. The younger staff members were threatening to walk out, afraid they would get sick, and it was left to Amanda to keep them all on the job. With Sharee lazing away at home, Amanda delegated extra work to the remaining staff members, who were already run off their feet. And of course the service had to be seamless, with everything perfect for Bahir.

By lunchtime Amanda was at her wits' end. Horrified at the incompetence demonstrated by a girl unused to serving food, she realised there was nothing for it but to roll up her sleeves and do the job herself. The guests were seated when she appeared from the kitchen carrying a silver salad bowl in one hand and a dish of steaming baby potatoes in the other, placing them carefully on the table.

As she left to bring in more dishes, Bahir touched her arm lightly. 'Amanda, you shouldn't be doing this,' he said quietly. 'Are we understaffed?'

'We have one girl off sick. Don't worry, Prince Bahir, at least this way I know it will run smoothly.'

Clea overheard the conversation. 'This girl who's sick, do you know what the problem might be?' she asked with a sense of foreboding.

'She says it's flu, but I suspect it has more to do with a big night on the town,' Amanda answered crisply.

Clea's face had turned pale. 'Where is she now?'

'Is something the matter?' Amanda asked, seeing Bahir and Clea stare at each other with unconcealed dismay.

Bahir and Clea excused themselves from the table and came

with Amanda out to the kitchen. 'The girl, where does she live?' Bahir demanded.

'In the village. I have her details here somewhere.'

'Call her immediately, please.' Bahir waited fidgeting as Amanda found her address book and dialled the number.

'There's no answer,' she said eventually. 'I'm sorry, sir, but you know how irresponsible the young can be . . .' Amanda suddenly put the phone down and stared at them wide-eyed. 'Oh, no. The virus?' she whispered.

'Call an ambulance,' Bahir instructed.

Meanwhile, Bahir and Clea readied themselves to leave. Amanda scribbled Sharee's address down on a piece of paper. The driver was roused from the garage and Clea collected protective gear from her kit bag. She and Bahir gave directions to the driver and a pair of security guards drove ahead in a separate vehicle.

The door of the little whitewashed cottage was bolted from the inside, and there was no response to their urgent knocking. One of the guards wrapped a jacket around his arm and with a single expert blow, broke the glass on a window then unlatched it. Clea made him wear a mask and gloves before he climbed inside to open the door. The cottage was tiny and it didn't take long to find Sharee lying on the kitchen floor. Her eyes stared ahead unseeing. Life had drained out of her, leaving only the material shell. They all stared in dismay as the wail of an ambulance drew near.

Clea cleared the scene and prevented any further contact with the body until the police had arrived and been briefed. She carefully took a swab from the body and drove with Bahir back to the MBU at the stud for analysis. It took less than half an hour to confirm it was unmistakably hendra.

The police had by then arrived at the manor and were questioning staff and guests, but no one could recall seeing the girl visiting the horses.

Peter was still at the hospital under observation, but was able to answer their questions by phone. After much coaxing he confessed Sharee and he had a thing going. Further coaxing determined that she would sneak down to the stables to be with him on her breaks.

After a tense buffet dinner Clea excused herself and headed off to bed. She was deeply disturbed by the girl's death. She had studied viruses for years to try and prevent this kind of tragedy, and she blamed herself.

On the second floor she searched briefly for a light switch, but gave up and paced along the corridor to her room in the dark. Footsteps followed behind and for a moment she hoped it was the prince, but when she turned she found Darcy.

'I just wanted to make sure you got to bed safely,' he mumbled.

'Thanks, Darcy, I'll see you in the morning.' She firmly closed her bedroom door. Bahir's dig about girls in nightclubs had reminded Clea of the truth about Darcy. He didn't seem capable of lasting long without a pretty girl on his arm and in his bed. She wasn't about to get in line.

Darcy stood staring at the door for a moment. Clea seemed

as determined as ever to shut him out. He sighed and retired to his own room.

Zayd was exhausted. He had been on the run since that dreadful moment in the whore's apartment when he realised his identity had been compromised. He had disposed of her body at the bottom of a building site, covering it with sand and gravel. The concrete was due to be poured that week and he fervently hoped no one would dig her up before then. Killing her had been a bad blunder – he probably could have bought her silence, but rage had stopped him from thinking straight. It was a pity – she had been a good fuck.

On the instructions of his employer, Zayd had made his way to London by plane and train in order to cover his tracks. Tonight he was holed up in a hotel room in Waterloo awaiting orders, but he hoped the phone wouldn't ring. He needed a decent night's sleep in order to keep his wits about him.

A few hours later Clea awoke with a start as the door to her bedroom closed gently and a floorboard groaned in the corridor. Heart pounding, she reached out and switched on her bedside lamp but the room was empty. Suddenly anxious, she checked under the bed, in the cupboards and in the bathroom, but there was no sign of anyone. She was about to climb back into bed, telling herself it had been a dream, when something caught her eye. Her briefcase was open and had been moved, and papers were sticking out as if someone had rummaged through them. Clea distinctly recalled closing it properly before she went to bed. Someone *had* been in her room.

The corridor was empty but there was light coming up the staircase. Throwing on the warm cashmere guest robe, Clea crept softly down the stairs to the sitting room where the glow of a lamp shone out of the half-closed door. Bahir jumped as the door opened and Clea realised he was as on edge as she was.

'You couldn't sleep either?' he asked, putting down a leather-bound book.

'Bahir, I think someone has been in my room,' she said quietly, trying to keep the fear from her voice. 'My briefcase had been searched while I was asleep.'

Bahir motioned her over onto the sofa. 'We'll call security immediately.'

'I'm not sure what good that will do, but I feel unsafe upstairs now,' Clea said nervously.

Bahir picked up his mobile phone and dialled a number. A moment later there was a tap on the door and one of the security guards appeared and positioned himself outside to keep watch.

'I've asked him to stay outside your door when you go back upstairs,' said Bahir reassuringly. 'Now that you feel safer, can I get you a cup of tea? I was just about to get one for myself.'

'Do you have peppermint?'

Bahir went to the kitchen and reappeared carrying a silver tray with a silver tea set and fine bone-china cups. Clea flicked through the leather-bound book he'd been reading. It was about the art of falconry.

'Falconry is my other passion,' Bahir said simply.

'I've never seen it practised,' Clea admitted.

'Then you have missed out on a magnificent sport. The peregrine falcon can swoop on prey at over 300 kilometres per hour. It's an astonishing sight. When I was a child my father used to take me to the fringe of the desert on horseback to hunt. They were our best times together. When I was sent here to school it was always one of the first things we did when I went back home in the holidays.'

'There must have been a huge contrast between boarding school and home,' Clea mused.

Bahir laughed. 'Yes, all this greenery hurts my eyes after a while and I long for the shifting sands and the shimmering light of the desert.'

'What was Dubai like back then?'

'It was much less sophisticated.' Bahir gazed into the fire that still smouldered in the hearth. 'A simple city perched on the land where the desert meets the sea. Now it's all different – it's a magnificent city, one of the greatest in the world.'

'I'd love to go there one day. The closest I've ever been is in transit on my way here.' Clea sighed. She longed to explore some of the more exotic corners of the world.

'Then you shall come, and I will be your guide.' Bahir said, flashing his enchanting smile.

They sipped tea in a comfortable silence.

'How about you, Clea? Did you grow up in Australia?'

'Mmm, I've pretty much lived in Melbourne all my life – not quite as cosmopolitan as Dubai, but it's a good city. I'd love to live overseas at some stage. Australia is just so far from everywhere else.'

Bahir hesitated. 'And . . . is there a man in your life? A woman as beautiful as you should be protected by a good man.'

'Not barefoot and pregnant too, I hope?' Clea laughed.

'No, I'm not such a traditionalist.' He stood up and pushed back a burning log that was threatening to tumble out of the hearth. When he sat down, he was closer than before. 'I find you a very intriguing woman.' Bahir reached out and touched the back of his hand to Clea's cheek.

The warmth of his hand sent a shiver of sensation through Clea's body and she found herself gazing into his eyes, unable to look away. Finally Bahir broke the moment and looked down.

'I will leave you now,' he said, with a hint of sadness.

Clea did not want to go back to her room, and Bahir assured her the guard would stay on duty wherever she was. The sitting room seemed suddenly empty when Bahir softly closed the door. Clea curled up on the sofa, reluctant to move and break the spell he had cast on her. She had spent most of her life pushing away anyone who came too close. But Bahir's world was so fascinating, so exotic, he had sidestepped her careful barriers and captivated her. Despite her misgivings, it felt so natural. She stared into the fire until sleep overtook her once more.

Clea awoke with a start early the next morning, completely

disorientated. The fire had long ago burned itself out. She stretched her stiff neck and sat up. The voices that had woken her were coming from outside the window, and she carefully pulled the heavy velvet curtain to one side and peered out into the grey light of dawn. Darcy and Abdul were talking near the window, both rugged up in warm coats and scarves. Clea ducked behind the curtain; she had no wish to speak to Darcy this morning.

'I've been worried about you ever since we spoke at Doncaster,' Darcy was saying. 'And now, all of this . . . How are you, Abdul?'

'I'm fine, thank you,' Abdul answered gruffly. 'Now, are you coming with me to look at these horses or not?' He stomped off across the damp lawn towards the paddocks with Darcy in tow.

Clea dropped the curtain and went to the door. The guard was sitting across the hall and smiled as she motioned to him that she was going back up to her room.

'You said something about Jalal and his father the other day,' Darcy persisted, his hands thrust deep in his pockets.

'It was really of no concern,' Abdul replied. He had decided to keep his own counsel. This was private, and Darcy couldn't help.

'I feel so sorry for Jalal losing Bismarck. Bad enough to lose any stallion, but when it's your first . . .' Darcy continued, trying to engage Abdul on the subject.

'And now Drake,' Abdul added, deep in thought.

'Drake? I didn't realise Jalal had any ownership in Drake. He certainly has had a lot of luck on the racetrack.' But Abdul would not be drawn any further and for the rest of their brisk morning walk, their conversation was taken up with a discussion about the upcoming carnivals.

Clea opened her bedroom door carefully, as if something might fly out in her face. The room was empty, and the only evidence of her night-time intruder remained the open briefcase. She wondered what they were looking for. A chill went through her body and she ran a hot shower to warm up. As the soothing water cascaded through her long hair, Clea decided that today she would speak to the police – it was worth making her concerns known.

With her hair wrapped up in a towel, Clea stepped from the bathroom and stared around the room. The threat to human lives from hendra was very real, but what if it was also deliberate? What if the person who searched her room last night was in possession of the virus? What if they had come back while she was downstairs? Not wishing to touch anything, she threw on her robe and a pair of shoes, pulled off the towel and shook out her hair. In a moment she was dashing out of the house across the wet lawn.

As she rounded the corner of the MBU, Abdul and Darcy were walking back from the opposite direction.

'Clea! Are you mad? You'll freeze out here.' Darcy rushed towards her and draped his coat over her shoulders. 'What on earth are you doing?'

Clea's teeth were chattering from cold and she gratefully accepted the gloves Abdul passed over. 'Maybe I am mad, but I need my equipment quickly.' She was fiddling with the key to open the MBU.

'Couldn't you at least have put something warm on first?' Darcy asked incredulously.

Clea turned to face him. 'Darcy, I think someone may be using the hendra virus to target people, and I think I might be one of the intended victims. I have to get my equipment and check my room.' She left Darcy and Abdul standing, open-mouthed, as she threw a few items into a kit bag and grabbed protective clothing.

'I'm coming with you,' Darcy insisted, following her back up to the house at a trot.

When they reached her room, Clea held up her hand to stop him. 'You can't come in, it's too dangerous. Go and wake up Bahir, quickly, and tell him not to touch anything. I'll have to check your room as well.' She pulled on the protective gloves and mask and fished the UV light from her bag, closing the door behind her. Her heart was racing and she paused by the door for a moment to calm herself. She had to think scientifically, and push aside the feelings of fear and disgust that were rising inside. This was like any other case, she told herself. Stay detached.

Her curtains were still closed, making the UV light more effective. Clea began by casting it over her briefcase and papers, but nothing showed up. Next, she tried her suitcase, carefully peeling back layers of clothes, but apart from discovering she had accidently added a tissue to a load of washing, her suitcase seemed clear. She crossed to the bed and shone the light across the covers, drawing a blank there too. She looked around the room for other likely places and swung the light across a glass and water jug next to the bed. With a sharp intake of breath, Clea saw that they were lightly dusted in white powder, invisible to the naked eye. She picked up the glass carefully and held it closer to the UV light. The brilliant white flecks of powder stood out, speckled on the glass. She took a sample, sealed it up, and left the room.

Bahir and Darcy were waiting for her in the corridor. 'It's not looking good. Call the police immediately, I'm going to check your rooms.' Clea followed Bahir to his bedroom and went in by herself. She swept the room carefully, but thankfully found nothing. Darcy's bedroom was also clear. But while she found no obvious signs of powder, there was no guarantee it wasn't there.

She went back to Bahir and Darcy, who were waiting in the corridor. 'No one is to enter these rooms. In fact, you'd better get everyone together now and they can wait for the police in the sitting room. Tell people to come out of their rooms just as they are and that they're not to touch anything,' she instructed. 'I'll be down at the MBU testing.'

When Clea returned with a positive match to hendra from the glass in her room, just as she feared, she found the police had assembled everyone outside the building and had called for a team of forensic experts. She drew Bahir and the senior officer to one side and quietly explained her findings. 'I'm sure I didn't touch the water, but there were fingerprints in the powder on the jug handle. Can you think of anyone else who might have touched it?' she asked as calmly as possible.

Bahir thought hard for a moment, realising the importance of the question. He looked around for Amanda and motioned for her to join them. 'Amanda, I need you to think carefully. Which of your staff had access to the guest room Clea is occupying?'

The housekeeper's face went ashen. 'Oh, no.' She put her head in her hands. 'I sent Sharee up there before she left for the evening to check the room. She called in sick the next day.'

Bahir looked shaken. 'She must have . . .' He couldn't finish the sentence.

Clea instinctively put her arm around him as if to protect him from her next words. 'I'm afraid this is a case of murder.'

33

Eclipse Stud, Newmarket

Hordes of media were clamouring outside the gates of the stud, inflamed by reports of the death of a woman and two top racehorses struck down by an exotic disease carried by bats and only found in Australia. The tabloid editors already had their headlines: *Vampire Virus Slays Champions* and *Deadly Bats in the Belfry*.

Photographers were climbing the perimeter walls with telephoto lenses as police questioned guests again and cordoned off the scene. The security guards tried their best, but now the news was public, their valiant efforts were in vain. Every news program was already running footage of the two horses winning major races, and a photograph of Sharee taken during her school days was being shown everywhere.

Bahir decided someone needed to make a statement to the press, and he asked Clea, given that she was the best qualified to speak from a scientific point of view. Stepping outside the gates was daunting for Clea, as cameras and microphones were shoved in her face. It took a moment to quell the mob so she could answer the questions being fired at her in concert.

'I am Dr Clea Reynolds from the Australian Animal Infectious Diseases Laboratory,' she began bravely, as soon as she could be heard. 'I've been brought in to verify the virus that has killed two horses and one person —'

'How quickly does the disease spread? Will the whole of Newmarket be put under quarantine?' a journalist broke in.

'Hendra is only passed through close contact. It's not an airborne virus, so there is no immediate cause for alarm. The virus has been contained on this stud,' she said with great authority, but privately questioned the truth of her statement. If someone was deliberately spreading the virus there was no telling where it might spring up.

'So the virus was passed to the horses by Sheikh Faisal's son, who came into contact with it in Australia?' another journalist speculated.

'No, we don't think so. There's no evidence to suggest that hendra can pass from humans to horses – or to any other animal for that matter,' Clea answered clearly.

'But a stud representative has already confirmed the disease was brought from Australia by Prince Bahir,' the journalist responded aggressively.

Clea flailed for a moment, wondering who would have briefed the media before her. 'I am unaware of anyone else on the stud with scientific knowledge of this virus, and reiterate that humans cannot pass the virus to horses,' she repeated firmly.

'Are you denying the virus only occurs in Australia?'

'No, I'm not —'

'Then how did it get here and kill two horses and some poor maid if it wasn't brought over by Prince Bahir, who we know suffered for many weeks in a Sydney hospital with hendra?'

Thankfully, Sergeant Will Robinson, the investigating officer, stepped in at that moment and restated Clea's position. With the assistance of a security guard Clea retraced her steps to the gate and was swamped again by cameras.

'Do you have any further comment, Dr Reynolds?' The most persistent journalist thrust his microphone at Clea.

'Who was the stud representative who spoke to you earlier?' she asked.

The journalist referred to his notebook. 'Jalal bin Muntasir, representing Eclipse Stud.'

The gates closed, and Sergeant Robinson and Clea rejoined the staff and guests on the lawn. Clea found Bahir and drew him aside.

'Did you give Jalal permission to talk to the media?' she asked.

'No – is that what he did?' Bahir looked around and saw Jalal talking to the police. 'I'm afraid he does like to take the limelight a bit, but there's no reason why he can't speak on behalf of my family or the stud.'

Clea was about to explain otherwise, but bit her tongue. Jalal was, after all, Bahir's close friend.

She kept an eye on Jalal until he had finished with the police and then approached him quietly.

'Can I ask why you informed the media Bahir was to blame for the virus, Jalal?' she challenged him out of earshot of the others. 'I thought you were his friend.'

Jalal looked surprised. 'I'm not sure what you're talking about.'

'You spoke to the media!'

'Well, someone had to, it was a circus out there. Does Bahir have a problem with that?' he asked a little smugly.

'No, but I do,' Clea retorted. 'You know nothing of this virus and yet you've led the media to believe Bahir has spread it here in England.'

'No, they can't be saying that.' Jalal seemed genuinely surprised and Clea began to regret her tone. 'I never said such a thing.'

'Well, the media seem to have got the wrong story somehow. Let's hope I have set the record straight. Before you speak to anyone else it might be best to clarify any scientific questions you have with me,' Clea suggested more kindly.

The police had dusted her room for fingerprints but suspected those found were mainly her own, and the forensics team had not found any more evidence of the virus in the house, although their investigation continued. When Sergeant Robinson was free Clea asked if she could have a private word, and they moved into the library, since the house was now cleared, and sat down to talk. Clea filled him in on her suspicions as quickly as possible.

The sergeant clarified a few points regarding timing before

he asked the obvious question: why would someone be trying to kill Clea? And what might they have been searching for in her room?

'Perhaps they were looking for the information I'm about to give you,' she said, and handed him a few sheets of paper. He flicked through them and looked to Clea for an explanation.

'The first page shows three photos of the hendra virus taken from a microscope. The first is from the recent outbreak in the Hunter Valley, Australia; the second is from the horses here and the third is a picture of the virus stored at AAIDL,' she told him.

The sergeant looked baffled. 'They all look the same to me,' he said.

'That's the point! They're the exact same strain of the virus, with exactly the same shape!'

'Meaning?' He still wasn't following her.

Clea took a deep breath and started slowly. 'The hendra virus is pleomorphic, so each strain of the virus has a slightly different shape. Given the identical nature of the strains found in the Hunter Valley and here, I believe both outbreaks originate directly from the virus held at AAIDL. Look at the second sheet of paper. It shows traces of protein and salt solutions that were found in both stables where the initial infection occurred. It can't just be a coincidence.'

Sergeant Robinson stared intently at Clea as she continued. 'A viral transport medium often contains protein to stabilise the virus, and an antimicrobial agent in a buffered salt solution. The only difference here is that the medium is in powdered form, not a solution.'

The sergeant finally realised the enormity of her explanation. 'Why didn't you report this in the Hunter Valley?' he asked incredulously.

'I did, but the line of least resistance won out. There were bats nearby and bats equal hendra – case closed,' she said sadly.

The sergeant stood up and walked to the window. 'Do you imagine the virus escaped accidentally from your laboratory?' he asked.

'I would say that's virtually impossible.'

Sergeant Robinson turned back to her. 'Would you mind staying in here a moment? I want to send in the head of my forensics team so you can explain this information again.' He waved the sheets of paper and walked out.

Clea's mind was preoccupied with the overwhelming question of whether the virus had been stolen from AAIDL. Slowly it dawned on her that she would be a prime suspect – who else had access? For a split-second she glanced out the window for an escape route, then shook her head at her own stupidity. She had nothing to hide.

Clea was deep in thought when Sergeant Robinson returned with a forensic scientist who had already examined Clea's data. 'You look worried, Dr Reynolds,' he commented.

'Yes.' Clea paused, momentarily unsure. 'I realise I have another piece of information that might be of use.' She paced the room, aware the sergeant was watching her closely. 'My colleague – my boss, actually – took up a position in the UK rather suddenly a few months back. It was unexpected and happened very quickly.'

Sergeant Robinson nodded slowly but didn't take his eyes off her face. 'And did this colleague have access to the hendra virus?'

'Yes.'

34

Sage Cottage, Kent County

Kent was called the garden of England for good reason. Its green rolling countryside, orchards and market gardens were a beautiful contrast to the grime of London. Dr Glen Collings' cottage was down a quiet country lane near a magnificent estate that had once belonged to a relative of Jane Austen, where it was believed she penned one of her famed novels. The police had already visited Dr Collings' workplace, a laboratory situated in a brand-new industrial park, and had discovered he hadn't turned up to work that morning. A check of Dr Collings' bank accounts hadn't revealed any unusual spending, his only extravagance being a lease on a Mercedes. Now, armed with a search warrant, they hoped to find the doctor at home.

Past the imposing white mansion, the police followed the lane off to the left, over a quaint stream with a stone bridge, to a picture-book cottage nestled beneath an ancient oak tree. There was no response to the jangle of the bell by the door and the police fanned out, not sure what to expect. The back door was unlocked, and two officers entered, guns drawn in caution.

The ceilings were low and a steep staircase led up to the first floor. The stairs creaked with age as one of the officers headed up and investigated the bedroom carefully. There was no need for such caution, though – Glen Collings was not going anywhere. Hanging from a beam in the roof, he'd been dead for hours.

Bahir and his guests were officially cleared of hendra, following Clea's tests, and were allowed to head back to London, which was a great relief for all. Bahir was beginning to feel like a target on his own stud, especially since he'd been filled in on the investigation instigated by Clea. He insisted Clea stay with him at the family's Mayfair mansion, and Darcy and Jalal joined them in the helicopter, leaving the others to navigate the crowded motorways.

The sprawl of London was breathtaking from their bird's-eye vantage point as they travelled south. Their flight path took them over the towering modern buildings of the City, and along the sparkling Thames, which they followed down to Battersea on the south bank past the Tower of London and London Bridge. Darcy and Bahir pointed out landmarks to Clea, who gazed in awe at the metropolis.

Two impressive cars were waiting as the helicopter landed at the Battersea Heliport, a beautiful sleek midnight-blue Bentley, complete with a liveried chauffeur, and the Ambrose-Taylor

Bentley with Roger behind the wheel. Darcy said his goodbyes and drove off towards Knightsbridge. Bahir turned to Clea.

'I can't express to you how appalled I am that someone would try to kill you – let alone in my home. This whole business is so upsetting. I keep thinking about that poor girl Sharee and how she didn't deserve to get caught up in my mess. She was so young.' Bahir's eyes were glistening with tears. 'I've spoken to her family, but there's nothing I can do to bring her back.'

Clea put her hand on his arm. 'It wasn't your fault.' It was the only comfort she could offer. 'We'll find out who did this.'

'I don't want to face my father yet,' Bahir said. 'He's so worried about me and I don't have any answers. Would you mind if we do something to take our minds off this tragedy?'

'Like what?'

Bahir thought for a moment. 'How about I take you shopping?'

'But what for?' Clea protested. 'I have everything I need.'

The smile returned to Bahir's handsome face. 'You really are an unusual woman, Clea. Shopping is always a good distraction, and it will make me feel better. Let me make up this awful situation to you. Because of me, you almost got killed.'

Clea glanced down defensively at her plain tailored pants and shirt. 'I suppose my wardrobe might seem a little boring to you, but I'm quite capable of buying my own clothes, you know.'

Bahir's only answer was a smile, and within twenty minutes they were in New Bond Street. Holding Clea's hand tightly in case she tried to escape, Bahir gazed up and down the street.

'Hmm, let's see. Versace isn't quite your scene – too out there. You'd look wonderful in Dolce & Gabbana, very sexy. Let's not forget a Gucci bag, and perhaps a bit of Burberry – you can't argue with a trench coat, it's very practical!'

He led her into the Dolce & Gabbana store and proceeded to select clothes from the rack for her. An eager sales assistant came over and began helping, pulling out coats and dresses, pants and shirts, and before she could protest, Clea was in the changing room trying on piece after piece of exquisite clothing and parading in front of the mirrors. Together they selected a slinky black dress, a chic trouser suit, two blouses and a light coat that Bahir declared was perfect for the races.

All of this was organised as Clea changed back into her own clothes, and the purchases were packed in suit carriers to be collected by their driver.

Her face was flushed with a mixture of excitement and embarrassment. 'No one's ever bought clothes for me . . . It doesn't seem right. When am I going to wear such glamorous things, anyway?'

'Tonight for starters. I think the dress will be perfect. Now, let's see – Gucci is next.' Bahir was not going to be discouraged from his mission.

Despite the horror of the last few days, Clea found herself relaxing as she walked alongside this remarkable man. So this is what it feels like to be rich, she thought. The Gucci store was amazing, and she felt overwhelmed until finally, on Bahir's prompting, she selected a black leather handbag, matching wallet and a pair of killer black heels. The next stop on their whirlwind shopping tour was Burberry, and she had to admit, the trench coats were fabulous.

'Enough!' Clea said laughing as they hit the pavement again. 'I don't think I've ever bought so many clothes in my life!'

Bahir twirled her around on the footpath. 'But there are so many more shops!'

'No, I can't take any more, honestly. You'll just have to accept I'm not a very good shopper.'

'And this coming from a woman who looks like she belongs on a catwalk! All right, I'll compromise, just one more shop.' Bahir looked up and down the street. 'More shoes?' he mused. 'Or another handbag or . . . Chanel!' And before Clea knew it he had led her into the Chanel store.

While Bahir talked to the sales assistant, Clea glanced at a few price tags and almost fell over. 'Can we go?' she whispered. But the sales assistant had already been worded up and was showing her a range of accessories impossible to refuse. Clea's final and reluctant selection was a new-season evening handbag, some sensational tortoiseshell sunglasses, a pair of beautiful cream and black shoes and a matching belt complete with a signature enamel camellia.

'*Now* can we stop shopping?' Clea said, glowing with pleasure as they left the shop. 'You promised!'

Bahir looked at his watch and rang for the driver.

'Where are we going now?'

'Harvey Nichols of course, for lunch. And if you happen to see anything while you're there . . .'

But they had only just been seated when Clea's mobile rang. She was completely unprepared for the news she received and paled visibly as she listened intently. Glen Collings was dead, in what looked like a suicide, and the police needed to speak to her immediately. Instead of Harvey Nichols, Bahir had his driver take them straight to New Scotland Yard, in nearby Westminster. The case was now being conducted out of the Specialist Crime Directorate Homicide Command, and a murder investigation team had been assigned.

Glen's cottage in Kent was still being investigated, but so far there was no evidence of the hendra virus, only a suicide note discovered on his computer. Clea was handed a printout of the note at the station soon after she was seated in a small room. She steeled her emotions, but for a moment couldn't bear to read the words before her.

I can't live with myself any more, knowing what I have done. I didn't realize anyone would get hurt. Death is my only option now.

Clea stared at the paper for a long moment. That was it? A man she knew so well had died and that was all he left behind to account for his actions? She studied the words again. 'He didn't write this,' she declared.

Senior officer Inspector Angus Sutherland, who had been standing in the room, sat down opposite as she pushed the paper across the desk towards him. 'How can you be so sure?'

'Glen was a total perfectionist in everything he did. It just doesn't make sense that the last thing he wrote would be incorrect.'

Inspector Sutherland was intrigued and scanned the paper again. 'What's incorrect here?'

'It's the spelling. Glen only ever used English spelling – he was really pedantic about it. But if you see that word,' she pointed to the word *realize*, 'it's spelt the American way. He would never have done that. Glen always used to say there was only one correct spelling – the English way. You can ask anyone who worked with him.'

'We're already treating his death as suspicious,' Inspector Sutherland said. 'The autopsy might shed some light, of course.'

'How . . . how did he die?' Clea asked hesitantly.

'He hanged himself in his bedroom.'

Clea flinched at the shocking image of a man she had worked with for five years – the man who had recognised and nurtured her talent. The light-hearted happiness she'd shared with Bahir during their shopping expedition dissipated into the grey London sky.

35
Sheikh Faisal's Residence, Mayfair

Clea broke into tears as she told her mother the dreadful news the next morning. Susanne was shocked and very concerned. Someone had tried to kill her daughter. She had also been particularly fond of Glen and, Clea suspected, had always hoped something would spark between the two of them. Clea had just managed to compose herself when her mobile rang.

'You were right, Dr Reynolds.' Inspector Sutherland spoke briskly. 'The autopsy has shown strong sedatives in Dr Collings' bloodstream, which could still be consistent with suicide. But there were also traces of skin under his fingernails, which indicate a struggle, and a small contusion to the left side of his skull, which could have been from falling over, or from his body being dropped. We think it is likely Dr Collings was already unconscious before he asphyxiated.'

'You mean someone . . .' Clea found she couldn't finish the sentence. To be sitting in one of the luxurious light-filled rooms of Bahir's Mayfair mansion, listening to this news, seemed so unreal. Glen had been murdered. 'Why would someone murder him?' she asked finally.

'At this stage we believe it's closely linked to the hendra virus outbreaks both here and at Eclipse Stud in Australia.'

Bahir walked into the room as Clea hung up. 'What's wrong?' he asked as soon as he saw her pale face.

'Glen was murdered.' Clea fought back her tears and for a long moment allowed herself to be comforted by Bahir's embrace, tears of grief and shock wetting her cheeks. Slowly, she pulled herself together.

Bahir picked up a pile of mail, forwarded to London from the stud, and began sorting the letters. 'Seems everyone except me has been receiving letters.' He sniffed a pink envelope, scowling. 'This one's for Darcy, and if I'm not mistaken that's my sister's handwriting.'

Clea caught a waft of heady perfume as Bahir placed the letter on the sideboard. Clea suddenly felt irritated. It seemed obvious that Darcy had some sort of thing going with Bahir's sister. How could he behave like that, when he was a trusted family friend?

Bahir handed Clea a next-day-delivery envelope and she looked up at him in surprise. 'I told you everyone except me received mail.'

Clea recognised Glen's handwriting instantly, dropping the letter onto the coffee table as if it were scalding hot.

'What is it?' Bahir asked.

'It's from Glen.'

'Don't open it, I'll call the police.'

As Bahir dialled the number, Clea heard a car pull up outside. It was Darcy, and Clea had never wanted to see him less. By the time the police arrived, he'd been filled in. They all watched the package being carefully opened. It contained a letter and a USB device.

Clea,

I'm sending this to you for safety. I'm afraid it doesn't show me in a very good light. I've done something so terrible, something that goes against everything we stand for, and I can hardly bear to think of the censure in your eyes. I was weak, but have already paid the price in guilt a thousand times over. It was my fault that innocent girl and those horses died. When I saw you on television I realised that my star scientist was the one trying to determine how the hendra virus reached the UK. Well, I've saved you the trouble – all the information you need is here. I'm sending it to you for safekeeping, but if, as I suspect, my time is limited, you will need to act quickly. My contact was Zayd Farouk.

I sold myself for thirty pieces of silver and now I realise I will pay dearly for them.

Forgive me.

Glen

While Bahir went off to grab his laptop Darcy noticed Afifah's letter on the sideboard and picked it up in surprise. He sniffed it as if it would bite, then swiftly pocketed it, glancing around the room. His eyes met Clea's steely gaze and his face turned red. What did she know? He had assumed Afifah's crush would pass. But after the incident in the stables, he realised the matter needed to be handled very carefully.

The room fell silent as Bahir inserted the USB into his computer. It proved to contain digital recordings from conversations held on Skype between a man identified as Zayd and Dr Glen Collings. The police and Bahir, Clea and Darcy all crowded around the computer to listen. The first recording was muffled, as if both men were wary of speaking over the connection.

Glen: I don't really wish to discuss . . .
Zayd: The offer is now one million euros.
Glen: (pause) One million?
Zayd: And relocation.
Glen: The relocation we discussed? I would be in charge of the laboratory?
Zayd: Yes, it's all arranged.
Glen: I'll have to think.
Zayd: No. I need your decision now.
Glen: (pause) Tell me again what you require?
Zayd: A sample of both the hendra virus and the EI virus from your lab. How much EI would we need to infect a population of 1400 horses quickly?

Glen: Very little. It's a virulent virus that's airborne and lives on hard surfaces. The virus will do the spreading for you.

Zayd: Okay. Do we have a deal?

Glen: (long pause) Yes, we have a deal.

The recording ended and Bahir quickly clicked on the second one, without waiting for anyone to ask.

Glen: I'm all set, have you organised the money?

Zayd: Yes, it's ready. It will be waiting for you in London. My people will be in contact exactly one week after you arrive.

Glen: How do I know you'll give me the money?

Zayd: You'll just have to trust me.

Glen: (long pause) So, 4 p.m., Bangkok airport. How will I know it's you?

Zayd: Don't worry, I'll make contact.

The recording ended as Clea sat in shocked silence. It was Glen's voice, but she simply couldn't believe he would sell out for money. It didn't make sense.

'How close were you to Dr Collings?' Inspector Sutherland asked gently.

'He was my boss for five years and also a friend,' she answered automatically.

'Do you have any idea why he would have done this?'

Clea looked up, shaking her head in bewilderment. 'He was dedicated to his work and led quite an austere lifestyle. I didn't think money was important to him at all. But he must've needed it for something – otherwise he wouldn't have taken such a risk.' Tears sprang to her eyes and she quickly looked away. Bahir took her hand and held it, the warmth of his skin comforting against her own.

'And I don't understand the connection between hendra and EI – equine influenza,' Clea continued tearily. 'Hendra can kill, but EI is just a flu-like virus that passes through the horse population much the same as our own flu. Older or weaker horses may die from complications, and the very young can be affected, but it's usually all gone in a few months.'

'Could you play the first recording again?' Darcy asked, and they all sat in silence listening to the two voices plotting. 'I think I know what they're referring to,' he announced excitedly once the recording finished. 'There's really only one static horse population of around 1400 horses – it's such a specific number, it immediately got me thinking.' He had their undivided attention. 'The Hong Kong Jockey Club. Think about it: the horses are all stabled in close proximity to each other, and the virus would spread like wildfire.'

'But what would it achieve?' Bahir asked.

'I don't know. I haven't figured out that part yet,' Darcy confessed. 'It would certainly shut down racing there for a while, but I don't see how any of this is connected.'

'We should get onto Hong Kong immediately, just in case,' Bahir said. 'Could they vaccinate their horses against EI quickly?' he asked Clea.

'I'd be suprised if the population wasn't already vaccinated, particularly after the Japan outbreak and then the one in Australia,' she said slowly, trying to piece together the information in her head. 'Unless —' She stopped mid-sentence. 'I need to contact AAIDL immediately and find out if we can determine exactly which vial of the virus is missing. I'm sure Glen would have covered his tracks well, but it's worth a try.'

As with the human flu, equine influenza had different strains, and the correct vaccine needed to be administered in order to prevent an outbreak. Viruses were kept under the tightest security controls at AAIDL and Clea had no idea how Glen could have removed the two in question without detection. It might prove impossible to distinguish which serotype was missing, but logic told her it would probably be from the Newmarket outbreak in 2003. Most horses were vaccinated against the more recent strains, but would be unlikely to have immunity to the Newmarket strain. Providing the correct vaccine to Hong Kong was imperative. She suggested to Inspector Sutherland that they make immediate enquiries about vaccine stockpiles.

'Are you absolutely sure it's Hong Kong? I mean, surely there are 1400 horses in plenty of other places?' the inspector asked Darcy.

Darcy explained the Hong Kong Jockey Club system, which was restricted by space availability to around thirty trainers who could have a maximum of sixty horses in their stable. The right to race a horse in Hong Kong was determined by a ballot system amongst the 20 000 members of the HKJC, and the horse population was kept consistently at around 1400.

While Clea and Inspector Sutherland called AAIDL to warn them of the theft, Bahir joined Darcy by the window. 'I assume that letter was from my sister? I recognised the handwriting,' he said softly, so they couldn't be overheard.

'Yes, I'm afraid so.'

Bahir looked him in the eyes. 'Does she often write to you?'

'No, Bahir, I can explain. It's all rather embarrassing, actually . . .'

Now I understand, Bahir thought. But his voice hardened as he said, 'Darcy, if you've laid so much as a hand on Afifah —'

'It's not what you think, Bahir,' Darcy protested. 'You know I've always thought of her as a little sister, but she seems to have developed a crush —' His explanation was cut short when the inspector hung up the phone and turned to face the two men as if they were conspiring behind his back.

After Darcy left the mansion that afternoon, he mulled over the EI conundrum in his mind. The billon-dollar juggernaut of Hong Kong racing would be halted in its tracks by an outbreak of EI – but who stood to gain from such a disruption? There were certainly easier ways to nobble an individual horse, or even a stable.

The connection between the deadly hendra outbreaks and a plot to spread EI had Darcy completely mystified. He turned over all the information he had in his mind, but got nowhere. The police had so far drawn blanks with the name Zayd Farouk, although they had his voice on a recording. He was the main suspect for Glen's murder, and was also being searched for by the Dubai police in relation to Mimi's disappearance. But so far, there was no sign of him. It was frustrating. The only link Darcy could come up with was the Asian man on board the boat Mimi had mentioned, the man with the numbered watch. If only they could work out his identity, it might lead to something.

Once home Darcy sat for a moment in the study, contemplating just how to break the awful news of the possible plot to the CEO of the Hong Kong Jockey Club. He glanced down at his watch. It would be 10.30 p.m. in Hong Kong. With great reluctance, he scrolled through his contact list and was about to dial James Gregory, when he dropped his mobile phone and took his watch off.

Why hadn't he thought of it before? He was blind to what was on his own wrist. He too had a numbered watch – was it possible that the Asian man had worn the same series? He dialled Portia's number quickly. She was in a bar having a drink before dinner and couldn't hear him until she moved away from the crowd outside onto the footpath.

'Portia, it's really important. Did Mimi ever tell you the brand of the watch the guy on the boat was wearing?'

It took Portia a moment to catch on to the urgency in Darcy's voice, and she paused before she answered. 'Yes, and I'll never forget it. It was the last thing she ever said to me before —' Portia broke off for a moment before she could continue. 'It was a Frederique Constant Tourbillon.'

36
Yvonne's Apartment, St James, London

Sheikh Faisal gazed out the car window as his driver navigated the quiet streets of St James. He was tired of endlessly discussing resource prices in these tough economic times and needed a distraction. Yvonne was perfect. She knew how a mistress should behave.

Tonight he would visit her new apartment. The one-year lease was paid in advance and after that he would see. So far, she had played her cards right. The Sheikh stepped from the car and his driver handed over a large box tied with a bow, a smaller present resting on top. The Sheikh enjoyed making his women smile with unexpected gifts. It was part of the privilege of wealth.

Yvonne answered the door in a slinky black cocktail dress and the diamond necklace that had been his birthday present to her. Her hair was flowing loose and her dark red stilettos clicked across the intricate parquetry floor as she led him inside. The decorator had furnished the apartment in an elegant mix of old and new, with a few quirky artefacts for good measure. All the candles in the main room were lit and their soft light was reflected in a large, ornate mirror positioned above the fireplace.

A gasp of delight escaped Yvonne's lips when she opened the large box and discovered a three-quarter-length white mink coat of exquisite quality. Holding the soft fur to her cheek, she practically purred with pleasure. The second smaller box contained a beautiful lace lingerie set, and with a sexy smile Yvonne excused herself, taking her gifts into the bedroom.

The Sheikh was admiring a pair of shell fossils set between candles on a side table when the phone rang, but it was clear Yvonne had no intentions of picking up this evening. The answering machine clicked on in the next room and a boy's voice called out clearly. The Sheikh could hear easily.

'Mum? Mum, pick up if you're there, it's really important.' There was a pause as the boy presumably waited for the phone to be picked up, then, 'I need to talk about my pocket money, Mum. It's not fair all my friends have so much more, I feel like such a loser. Mum, you *have* to call me back as soon as possible, all right?'

The Sheikh's expression was thunderous when Yvonne reappeared wearing the mink coat, and she immediately dropped her smile.

'I didn't know you had a child,' he said coldly.

'You didn't ask,' Yvonne answered lightly. When the Sheikh continued glaring at her without comment, she added, 'He's thirteen years old and away at boarding school. He'll never be in your way, darling.'

'Whose child is he?' the Sheikh demanded.

'Oh, that's ancient history,' Yvonne soothed. 'His father pays for his education, so there's no financial issue. I'm much more interested in discussing us.' She moved closer to the sofa with a touch of hesitation.

'I must warn you that if you fall pregnant to me, it won't work. I will take the child and you will be left with nothing. Is that clear?' His harsh tone stung her like a swarm of wasps, and a mixture of anger and sadness welled up in Yvonne's chest, but she knew her role and could act it to perfection.

'Of course, darling, but you know I would never do that to you. My son was an accident and I was young and foolish.' She smiled. 'Now, let's move on to more interesting topics shall we?' Yvonne unbuttoned the mink and shrugged it off her bare shoulders, exposing a gorgeous black lace corset complete with suspender belt, French knickers and stockings, all trimmed with pink bows. 'Thank you for all my presents . . . do you like them?' she asked huskily as he admired her body.

'My mistress deserves nothing but the best,' he said possessively and Yvonne relaxed a little, knowing how much he desired her. He stood closer and slipped the mink completely off her so it fell to the floor, running his finger along the curve of her cleavage. 'Now turn around and let me see you properly.'

Yvonne turned slowly. After he had admired her firm, tanned curves he embraced her from behind, one hand on her breast and the other hand delving into her lacy knickers. 'I like what you've done with the apartment.' He kissed her lightly freckled shoulder.

Yvonne laughed and pressed back into his groin, feeling his rising desire. 'Such a beautiful coat deserves a gift in return, don't you think?' she asked and turned to face him. Slowly she knelt in front of him, unbuckled his belt and licked her lips.

37
Raymond's Restaurant, Chelsea, London

Late in the afternoon, Jalal sat in a cafe in Mayfair waiting for Bahir. He had been anxious to speak to him again about Afifah, but the events of the last few days had overtaken them all. It was better here, on neutral territory, and away from the Sheikh, who Jalal fervently hoped still had no idea of his daughter's heart.

Jalal sipped his coffee, nervous despite having requested the meeting. Bahir soon arrived and Jalal spoke hesitantly as he clutched his cup. 'I felt I needed to explain about the argument Afifah and I had not long ago. I know you would have been told of it, Bahir.'

Bahir nodded, but said nothing. He had been going over and over the idea of Darcy and Afifah, but hadn't yet been able to work out if it was all one-sided or if Darcy returned her affections. Marriage would be out of the question – or would it, if Afifah were free to follow her heart? The matter needed to be handled with great delicacy.

'It was foolish, really. I saw her with Darcy and became jealous.' Jalal tried to read Bahir's expression, but he was giving nothing away. 'You know how much I love her. How much I've always loved her. You can't blame me for feeling a bit possessive – after all, she is going to be my wife.'

Bahir leaned forward and spoke quietly so they couldn't be overheard. 'Jalal, I still don't know what went on between you and Afifah, but I'm not sure that one argument is the problem. You know I love you dearly, and have always wanted us to be brothers, but Afifah . . . Afifah is so special to me. I couldn't bear to see her unhappy.'

'Has she told you I make her unhappy?' Jalal knew the answer.

'You have to understand, Jalal, she's been educated over here – she wants love, not just a good marriage. And I can't say I blame her. If there's any chance she can find love, I have to try to help her.'

Jalal was stunned. Bahir was choosing Darcy over his oldest friend. Jalal had never imagined it would come to this, but maybe they hadn't been as close recently as in the past. Perhaps Bahir and his family had always thought he wasn't good enough to marry into royalty. He was so angry for a moment he couldn't find any words.

'I'm sorry, Jalal,' Bahir said quietly.

'Please don't speak to the Sheikh about this,' Jalal begged, calming his fury. 'I need this marriage, Bahir, I need it more than you can imagine. Promise me you'll give me some time to change Afifah's mind.'

'I'll do my best, but I can't promise.'

Even this request, Bahir could not grant him. Jalal's feelings of rage and powerlessness surged. 'You'll regret this, Bahir,' he warned, his eyes flashing with hatred. 'Our friendship will be destroyed forever.'

Bahir was taken back by the venom in Jalal's voice, and suddenly wanted to get away from his friend. 'I hope not. I hope one day you will see why I must act for Afifah. I'll give you a few weeks, but I doubt you'll change her mind.' Bahir stood up, paid for the coffee and left, while Jalal remained staring out the window.

At least he had a few weeks. Bahir must not speak to the Sheikh or all would be lost.

Clea was being swept off her feet and she knew it. This wasn't her world, but it was a wonderful world of invisible servants, sumptuous houses and chauffeur-driven cars.

It felt like a dream, but Clea refused to believe in dreams. For now, the police had requested she remain in England, but she knew it would soon be over and she would have to return to Australia and resume her everyday existence. Tucked in the back seat of Bahir's Bentley, surrounded by the smell of new leather, it was easy to forget. Clea gave herself permission to go with the flow.

She turned heads in her new designer clothing as she entered a Michelin-starred London restaurant, and for the first time under such scrutiny felt confident instead of self-conscious. Bahir ordered a glass of vintage champagne and a soda with a twist of lime for the two of them.

'I'm so relieved we're alone tonight,' he said, leaning back and gazing at her over the table. 'I want us to enjoy this evening and not focus on what has been happening. All these ghastly deaths make me realise how important it is to enjoy every minute of life. Although, to tell you the truth, I'm not quite sure of myself with you.'

'Well, don't look to me for help,' she smiled. 'I've got absolutely no idea what I'm doing here.' Clea was grateful she would not have to talk about Glen this evening. Thoughts of him would just bring on a fresh set of tears.

Bahir gave a shout of laughter and leaned forward again to take her hands. 'You're not particularly good at the romantic part, are you? It's always straight to the point. Are all scientists like that?'

Clea was laughing now too. 'You're right, I'm great with a virus, but when it comes to men . . .' She shrugged.

'Well, I just love being with you, so how about you leave the romancing to me?' Bahir chuckled, and smoothly changed the subject. 'Clea is an unusual name – where did it come from?'

Clea explained her mother's love of books, and that although Susanne had never travelled, books were her window to the world. Clea had been a central character from a series of four books set in Egypt, each written about the same events but from a different character's perspective.

'Egypt, I like that. Has your mother travelled yet?' Bahir asked.

'No, I still haven't convinced her – I think she might be a bit afraid, actually. I'd love to send her to Paris or Rome . . .' Clea smiled. 'You must find this so strange. You've had everything you wanted your whole life, but as a child I had nothing. I've worked hard my whole adult life to help put my younger brothers through school and university.'

Bahir looked puzzled. 'What about your father? What did he do?'

Clea's expression changed and Bahir instinctively reached out to hold her hand. 'My father died when I was thirteen years old. You know, it's sad, my youngest brother hardly remembers him.'

'I'm so sorry. That must have been very hard for you and your family.'

'My brothers are very successful now,' Clea said brightly, moving away from the painful subject. 'Robert —'

'After?'

'Robert Louis Stevenson, of course. Robert's an engineer in the mining industry and, as you can imagine, very well paid. And Ernest —'

'Hemingway?'

'Spot on. Ernest is in IT and doing very well also.' Clea's eyes shone with pride.

'Back to the romance,' Bahir said seriously. 'Have I told you I get lost in your eyes?'

Clea almost choked on her champagne. 'Do you find lines like that actually work?' she asked, laughing. 'Do women fall over themselves to jump into bed with you?'

Bahir started to laugh too. 'No, to be honest they usually jump into bed for my title and wealth. That's why I find you so fascinating. You have your own life, worlds away from mine, and you don't seem to care about my status or my money. There are not many people who would have handled themselves as well as you have over the past few days. You have a real strength about you, Clea.'

Clea looked embarrassed by his very genuine compliment. 'Do women really throw themselves at you?' she asked, a little intimidated by the thought. Bahir nodded sheepishly. 'No bloody wonder, when you go around taking them on shopping sprees! That's a dream for most girls.'

'But not for you?'

'No, please don't get me wrong. I love my beautiful new clothes,' Clea said quickly. 'But my real motivation in life is to find vaccines that will save agricultural industries a lot of heartache.'

'You want to see your name up in scientific lights?' Bahir smiled.

'Something like that. Anyway, in my line of work the white lab coat is *so* this season that I don't really need a fashionable wardrobe,' she said flippantly.

Over entrée the conversation inevitably turned to horses. Bahir explained his father was one of the first in his immediate family to become involved in horseracing. The culture of racing was already strong throughout the Middle East with Arabian horses, endurance races and camel racing, but once the ruling United Arab Emirates families became heavily involved in horseracing, they built beautiful racetracks and stables that were the equal of anything in the world. Sheikh Faisal had moved from Qatar to Dubai to follow his own passion for racing and established the stud farm in Newmarket to stock his racing stable. Bahir had been at home on a racetrack by the time he could speak.

'Tell me about Abdul,' Clea asked. 'He intrigues me – he has an amazing connection with the horses.'

'We joke that he is a horse and takes his real form at night, galloping in the moonlight. When I was about ten I actually believed he could, and would watch from my window night after night, hoping to see him change form. One time I saw as clear as day a white horse galloping from the stable complex across the gardens, but I've never found out if it was real or the fancy of a child. Abdul knows the language of the horse.'

'Like a horse whisperer?'

'No. Abdul knows and speaks wild horse. He knows why they shy when we see nothing, he knows what it is to gallop with the wind in his mane, he can see the world through the eyes of a horse. He started as a teenage boy in our stables when he appeared out of the desert one day with no past. We're all still in awe of him.'

'When I first suspected there was a deliberate element to the hendra virus outbreak in Australia, I wondered about Abdul,' Clea confessed. 'But seeing him with horses made it impossible to imagine he could ever deliberately inflict harm upon the creatures he so loves.'

'Abdul? Never!' Bahir stated vehemently. 'And he loves my family even more than he loves horses.'

Bahir ordered another glass of champagne for her. Clea would have preferred a glass of wine, but she was in his world now, and in Bahir's world women drank champagne. It was a delicious vintage drop with a fine bead that tickled her tongue. 'Anyone would think you're trying to get me drunk,' she said flirtatiously, looking over the rim of her glass.

'I'm hoping my own powers of seduction are more potent than alcohol,' he replied, looking at her longingly.

Clea gazed back, wondering what it would be like to be kissed by him. Their dinner continued until they were one of only two couples left in the restaurant, both reluctant to break the mood of the evening.

Clea's mobile rang in the car on the way home and a quick check confirmed it was her mother. Not wishing to have such a romantic evening disturbed, she dropped the phone back into her new Chanel handbag without answering.

Bahir opened the car door in front of the Mayfair mansion and held out his hand to assist Clea from the seat. His touch was thrilling and neither of them released the contact as they walked into the house. Bahir led her up the marble staircase to her room and slipped them both quickly inside, closing the door quietly. Clea turned around, unsure of herself, and found Bahir tantalisingly close.

'I wanted to say goodnight before I went to my room.' His voice was husky and his body pushed against hers as he walked her slowly backwards, as if they were dancing, until her legs hit the bed.

'What kind of a goodnight are you giving me?' she asked brazenly. Bahir brushed an errant strand of hair from her face and slowly drew her lips to his in the softest, most sensual kiss Clea had ever experienced. Finally he broke away, but desire overcame him so fiercely that he kissed her again, his tongue seeking hers, and breathlessly she responded. There was an urgency to their passion, as though recent events had shaken them both more than they cared to admit.

Bahir kissed Clea's neck and she arched towards his hot lips, feeling every touch with heightened awareness. He lifted her off the ground and Clea wrapped her legs around his waist, responding to a crushing kiss that seemed to stop all time and thought. Clea had never felt so exposed, succumbing to the powerful passion of this man, and the sensation was exciting. She felt feminine and alive as his hard body pushed against their combined layers of clothing.

Still locked in an embrace, Bahir unzipped her dress and placed her on the bed. He pulled the dress off and gazed at her bare, beautiful breasts before shedding his clothes and tumbling onto the bed – the contact of skin on skin making them both burn harder with desire. Bahir teased Clea's hard nipples with his tongue until she moaned softly, wanting more.

His hot kisses trailed down her slim stomach and he slipped a hand inside the flimsy material of her panties, quickly finding the moist evidence of her arousal. Bahir lifted Clea's hips off the bed and slowly slipped off her knickers, caressing her gently until she could take it no longer. She had to be possessed by Bahir.

'God, Clea, I want you so much,' Bahir whispered in her ear, making her body shiver as his cock pushed against her thighs.

She parted her legs and lifted herself so he could slide inside in one powerful stroke that took her breath away. Bahir held her gaze as he thrust inside again and again, their two bodies moving in rhythm. Clea felt as if he could read her every thought – as if he could see right through her. As Bahir's tempo increased Clea met each thrust as vigorously as he exacted them, wanting to be taken by this man, utterly filled with this man who thrilled her so intensely.

Clea wrapped her legs more tightly around Bahir's body, wanting to pull him deeper inside, needing to feel completely satiated as she reached a euphoric crescendo. She was finally overwhelmed by a wave of pleasure that shook her body so powerfully she thought it would never end. Bahir's eyes never left her own as he reached his own climax.

38

Khadelem, Saudi Arabia

The shimmering road seemed endless as Abdul bumped along in the hire car on the uneven surface. He had been driving for hours and his eyes were aching from fatigue. He slowed the car as a camel and her calf cantered along the side of the road before veering back into the desert, the dust raised by their great hoofs hanging suspended in the still air. The car's air conditioning was in mortal combat with the sun beating down outside, and the heat further exacerbated Abdul's weariness.

He wondered what he expected to find. Why had the past dragged him back, when he had sworn many years ago never to return?

The town of Khadelem spread out before Abdul in a valley surrounded by rocky hills. He stopped the car and stared in disbelief. The once dusty village of ramshackle dwellings that had sprung from the desert as haphazardly as weeds had grown into a town. Sealed roads were graced with street lights. Traffic flowed in and out of the town and buildings of four stories and higher cast welcome shade into narrow streets and winding alleyways.

Abdul struggled to get his bearings as he drove slowly through the town, craning his neck in amazement at the urban sprawl. He left his car by the side of a main road and continued on foot, sure his instincts would return, but nothing seemed familiar in this place. Suddenly he rounded a corner and found a well sitting in the middle of a square, with a random collection of children, dogs and old men sharing the shade of a nearby tree. He knew this tree, his initials were carved deep into the wood like a brand. Abdul turned and shaded his eyes against the sinking afternoon sun. He set off down an alleyway on the other side of the square, recognising a building here and there, until he halted abruptly by a six-foot stone wall that shielded a house from the prying eyes of passersby.

He ran his hand lightly over the warm stone as if it could transport him back. The iron gate was steadfastly locked with a rusted padlock, so Abdul examined the wall again. His adult feet no longer fitted into the cracks he had used to scale the wall as a child, but the advantage of height meant he could get a grip with his hands on the top and scramble up. The house behind the wall was derelict: the heavy wooden door sagged open on its hinges, and the garden kept lush and green had shrivelled to dust a long time ago. The window was broken – had he done it? He couldn't recall. There was a blur in his memory as if a kind hand had smudged across it to grant him some peace.

Abdul lowered himself into the abandoned garden and stood silently, clenching and unclenching his sweating fists. Fear rose in him and made his legs tremble and he stood stock still, waiting. A wind picked up through the streets behind, blowing an empty soft-drink can along the alleyway, but the noise was drowned out by the pounding of his own heart reverberating in his ears. Suddenly the broken window swung out at him in the wind and Abdul recoiled as if it were a cobra within striking range.

He stepped through the door, ducking under a collapsed beam, and walked into the front room. A broken chair lay on its side in a pile of sand in the corner, and everything else had been stolen or burned long ago. Abdul closed his eyes and pictured the room as it had once been, draped in carpets with large cushions on the floor around small brass tables. He had entered only once as a child, but had watched from the wall outside until every inch of the room was etched into his memory. He turned around and pushed aside a hanging piece of plaster. The safe was where he remembered. It had been hidden by a picture once, and he vividly recalled watching as it had been opened with a long iron key and a wad of money extracted. Blood money.

Abdul kicked around the floor, looking for evidence of the struggle, but the desert had cleansed the house for good. He carefully climbed up the decrepit stairs to the floor above, and located a small prison-like room with a narrow, high window. From outside below he had wished his mother goodnight every evening after dinner, accompanied by his father. He looked out the window and imagined what it must have been like for her, separated from her family for those long, lonely months. Then he saw a marking in the shadow behind the door and pulled the door ajar. Scratched into the surface was a pattern of marks, and he quickly realised they represented each tortuous day that had passed. There were so many. He reached out, but couldn't bring himself to touch them.

Suddenly his head started spinning with memories. He had to get out, had to escape this place that haunted his subconscious. He ran down the stairs as if the devil were at his heels, one foot crashing through the rotting wood and gashing his ankle, which bled as he staggered through the streets trying to get back to the car. He didn't make it. His legs buckled underneath him by the well in the square and he dry-retched over and over, dimly aware of people gathering around him, but only seeing his mother's eyes until he passed out.

When Abdul came to he found himself in the sparse interior of a modest house, propped in the corner on cushions. Dazed and confused, he stared at the curious faces of young children watching him intently. An older man entered and shooed the young ones outside. An elderly woman approached and offered Abdul a foul-smelling potion to drink. He pulled a face, but she gestured for him to try it and he found it wasn't as bad as the smell suggested. The warm liquid soothed his stomach immediately, and his temples stopped throbbing so he could think again.

'How did I get here?' he asked in Arabic.

'You were in the square and they called for us,' the man answered slowly.

'Are you a doctor?'

'No.' The man held out Abdul's driver's license, which had

been removed from his wallet, and pointed to his name. 'You are one of us,' he said simply, and Abdul realised with a sense of amazement that these people were from his tribe.

The old man Jassim explained he was Abdul's uncle on his mother's side, and that much of their tribe had remained settled into village life in Khadelem. 'The desert is an unforgiving mistress,' he said, his kindly smile showing half his teeth missing. 'You are a ghost to us, Abdul. You were lost in the desert, and we thought you were dead. But here you are.' He clasped Abdul's hands and grinned again.

'I had to come back,' Abdul said softly.

'Yes. You were already a ghost before you left. Now to be a whole man, you must face this place again. Do you remember?' Jassim asked.

'Only parts of it – the visions come to me when I sleep. The horses . . .' He looked away.

'The horses protect you. They always have. But now you must face your own tragedy so that you can trust people too.'

Abdul nodded. Somehow he knew he had to confront his past here, where it all happened. Jassim began the story and Abdul listened, desperate to piece together the puzzle of his childhood.

The tribe had moved to the outskirts of the village when their leader Uncle Ghalib fell ill. The women loved the convenience of the well and congregated around it daily to gossip in the shade of the tree. The village people were wary of the outsiders, these nomads from the desert who dressed differently and kept to themselves, and as time went on tensions arose, sparking heated debate amongst the village elders.

Ghalib lingered on, pale and thin but still leading his people from a tent outside the crumbling village walls. The village doctor visited daily at first, but after he diagnosed a wasting disease, his visits became less frequent. Ghalib needed medicine from one of the larger cities, but it would cost money.

Abdul's mother Hasna was considered beautiful by the Bedouin, with her curvaceous figure and light eyes, and she attracted the attention of the villagers as she walked to the well from the campsite with a baby on one hip and a water bucket on the other. Abdul's little brother was only fourteen months old at the time, while his sister was six and Abdul was nine. One day Hasna was approached by a village woman and invited to escape the cruel sun in the cool depths of her home. Hasna hesitated, but decided if she could befriend this woman it might help dissipate the mounting tension between the nomads and villagers.

The house was behind a thick wall that protected it from the desert winds and Hasna was delighted by the garden of trees and fragrant plants. She sat on plush carpets gazing out into this private oasis, her baby son asleep in her lap, and talked to this kind woman Najwa, who brought her peppermint tea and dates.

On her third visit to the house, Hasna heard how her friend was unable to bear a child and how she and her husband were broken-hearted by this cruel twist of fate. Najwa's husband said he loved her too much to take another wife, but this was Najwa's greatest fear, for if another wife bore him a child she would surely be supplanted in his affection forever. The only solution she could imagine was to convince her husband to pay an able-bodied woman to secretly bear them a child whom they could pass off as their own – a woman who had already had the proof of a son.

Hasna was thoughtful on her trip back to the campsite and stopped by the main tent to check on Ghalib, who was resting during the heat of the day. 'How is he?' she enquired of the chief wife.

'Not good,' the wife responded, drawing Hasna away so they wouldn't disturb Ghalib's sleep. 'The pain is getting worse and nothing I give him seems to help. Without money there is no hope of medicine, but even if we sell everything we own there will not be money enough.'

Hasna busied herself making tea for the exhausted chief wife. As they quietly sipped the hot liquid she repeated the strange conversation she had had with Najwa. A gleam of hope crossed the chief wife's face.

'How much money were they offering?' she demanded.

'I didn't ask, but she said it would be a lot,' Hasna answered, surprised.

The chief wife sat deep in thought for a while, then turned to Hasna with a sweet smile. 'You are young, healthy, strong and you have borne two sons,' she said.

Hasna was horrified at the implication. 'No woman takes on the burden of childbirth lightly,' she finally answered. 'I have a family and a husband to care for, I cannot do this.'

But the news of Najwa's offer spread through the campsite

like pestilence and by the time Abdul's father Rashad sat down for his evening meal with Hasna, a group of men had gathered. Still clutching his tin plate, he was dragged away from the camp fire for a conference. Bewildered at the turn of events, Hasna herded the children into the family's tent and kept them around her while she waited for Rashad to return. But it was not a man who entered the tent some while later.

'It has been decided,' the chief wife said quietly, and she ushered Hasna into Ghalib's tent, where a crowd of men sat around their frail leader.

Hasna knew her fate before another word was spoken; Rashad couldn't look her in the eye and his face was red from crying. A man on either side had a hand on his shoulders, as if to restrain him from running out of the tent and taking his wife with him.

'Hasna, my child.' Uncle Ghalib spoke with more strength in his voice than his appearance would suggest. 'You must tell us where this woman and her husband live. We will speak to them and see what price they are offering for this small service.' As if bearing and giving birth to a child was easy, like fetching water from a well.

Hasna slowly and defiantly shook her head.

'Would you deny me the medicine I need to live?' Ghalib asked her harshly. In that instant she could see pain and suffering burning like hot coals through his eyes.

Hasna fell to her knees and begged her husband to put a stop to this madness. She wept and implored the stone-faced wall of men to protect her from such degradation and dishonour.

But her tears were in vain. By the next day a bargain had been struck, an upfront payment that bought the required medicine, and Hasna was dragged to the pleasant home in the middle of the night, her mouth gagged against her screams. Ascertaining paternity was imperative, so for the first month she was locked up in the small room and left untouched, to ensure her husband's baby wasn't already growing in her womb.

Najwa wanted to keep her company during the long days and nights of dust storms that heralded the beginning of summer, but Hasna refused to speak to her and eventually her visits tapered off. At first, Najwa's husband would fling open the door irregularly and inspect Hasna like a chattel, demanding to know her private woman's business, but his visits increased as he became fascinated by her beauty, and she suffered the humiliation of him touching her body. On one of these occasions he carelessly left the door open, and Hasna saw Najwa watching from the shadows with a look of spite on her face as her husband stroked the soft skin on Hasna's arms.

Her only saving moments were when Rashad and her children appeared each night at the wall outside and spoke softly to her in the moonlight. 'I will love you no matter what happens,' Rashad repeated over and over again, as if he had to convince himself. 'We will be together again.'

When her monthly cycle came, it was impossible to hide it and with a look of triumph Najwa announced to her husband that Hasna was ready for impregnation. He had been waiting so long for this prize that he immediately agreed to his wife's conditions.

Until Hasna fell pregnant he could have her as often as he liked, but to ensure there was no intimacy in the act, Najwa insisted he took Hasna from behind only, and she was to remain clothed.

The pent-up frustration of a month showed on Salah al Din's face when he entered the room on that first night of many, and Hasna cowered in the corner, afraid and shamed. She tried to duck past him, but he closed the door and she distinctly heard the lock slipping into place from the outside. She tried to beat Salah back but he grabbed her slender wrists and pushed her over the rail of the bed, pulling up her clothing and exposing her at last to his sight.

'You people live like animals out in the desert, so I'll take you like an animal,' he growled, his voice full of lust and contempt. In a moment he was inside her and Hasna cried out in pain, tears burning down her cheeks as he brutally took his pleasure and left her crumpled on the bed like a rag doll, motionless with shock.

The next night she was ready for him, brandishing a wooden slat she had torn from her bed. She swung at him but he caught the splintered wood and laughed at the attempt. 'Fighting spirit, I like that – a good trait for my son.'

Night after night Salah al Din abused Hasna upstairs while his wife sat calmly waiting below, and during the heat of the day he would often appear once again, revelling in his virility. Hasna prayed for a pregnancy so the humiliation would stop.

Six weeks of torment had passed with no sign of Hasna's cycle. To her immense relief, she was pregnant, and the visits ceased as abruptly as they had begun. Hasna was allowed to move around the house now that paternity was assured. It felt good to stretch her legs again, even if it was only to sweep the floors and thrash the sand out of the carpets.

Najwa had begun to stuff her clothing with rags when she left the house so it appeared she was with child, and no one was allowed to visit. The village would assume the baby was Najwa's when he arrived. The only people who would know the truth would be the Bedouin, but once their leader was healed, they would surely move on.

As her belly grew Hasna was treated more kindly by Najwa. She was fed well and didn't have to work too hard. One special day she was even allowed visitors, and she clung to her husband and children as if they were lifelines.

The baby inside her was strong. Hasna allowed Najwa to rest her head on her rounded belly and croon soft words to the child inside, feeling with delight when he kicked out or rolled over. Hasna willed away the months until she was full term, and finally delivered a healthy baby boy in the cold hours before a weak winter dawn.

The next night Rashad came to visit, but Hasna's happiness at seeing him soon turned to horror when she realised he was demanding more money from the Muntasir family. 'You have forever disgraced my family – we have to leave this place and start a new life,' he implored. 'You must help us with more money, you owe us that much.'

Najwa put a defensive arm around Hasna and the nursing baby and stared at Rashad coldly, while Salah looked impassive.

'We had a deal and it won't be changed now,' Salah said calmly. 'You should have thought of the consequences and negotiated at the beginning – now it is too late. The child is ours and you will not get any more money.'

At these words, Rashad became enraged. He went to grab Hasna's arm but Najwa stood firmly in the way. Hasna struggled to her feet but was pushed back into her chair. Abdul watched hidden from the shadows of the wall outside as Salah al Din struggled with his father, and just as Salah was about to be overpowered he grabbed an iron pot holder from the hearth and smashed it into Rashad's head. Abdul's father toppled in slow motion, his eyes rolled slowly upwards and a cascade of blood flooded down his face.

Hasna screamed hysterically, reaching out for her husband, but Najwa held her back. Abdul was frozen in horror and couldn't call out, even when he saw Salah grab his mother's arms and shake her violently to stop the screaming. Hasna was on the floor now, and Salah al Din grabbed a cushion and held it tightly over her face. Hasna struggled and thrashed about for a long time, but eventually went limp. Salah cautiously moved the cushion and felt her pulse. Hasna's sightless eyes stared out the window.

Najwa reached for the crying baby and picked up the child. 'Now no one can ever claim you, my son,' she whispered, wrapping him tightly in a shawl.

'We must leave now,' Salah al Din instructed as he moved shakily towards the safe, opening it to remove wads of cash. 'Take only what you need.'

In a moment they had left the room, gathering anything valuable and clothes by the armful. Abdul threw a rock at the window and it shattered, but his parents were still lifeless on the floor. In terror and rage, he tumbled off the wall and ran like the furies were on his heels to raise help. But when the tribesmen arrived in force not long after, the roar of an old truck leaving on the unsealed road out of the village gave evidence of the Muntasir's murderous flight. Abdul was carried back to camp and never spoke of his parents again.

His sister and little brother were taken in by other families, but Abdul struggled to become close to anyone again. He abandoned everyone when he fled into the desert.

Abdul stared at Jassim for what seemed like eternity. Finally, after so many years of buried pain, the pent-up tears of grief flowed freely down his cheeks.

'The death of your parents has never been avenged. We couldn't go after them – we only had horses,' Jassim concluded. He sat quietly and comforted Abdul into the night.

39
Kensington High Street, London

Darcy wandered into an expensive jeweller in Kensington, hoping to find what he was looking for. After a few moments, a well-dressed man behind the counter asked if he could be of assistance.

'You don't seem to stock any Frederique Constant Tourbillon watches,' Darcy said.

'We're restocking at the moment, I'm sorry. If you don't mind me saying so, the one on your wrist is a beauty,' the shop assistant said admiringly. 'May I take a look?'

Darcy handed him the watch and the assistant checked the number stamped on the dial. 'Number eight. Very special. If you ever tire of it, I could certainly find a buyer.'

'Actually, I'm trying to find the number eighty-eight or 188 Tourbillon. I want to buy one of them as a special gift for my father – he's very superstitious,' Darcy lied. 'Is there any way I could find out who might own those numbers?'

The assistant wasn't sure, but excused himself and came back with the store owner. The owner sized Darcy up quickly and could smell a big commission coming his way. 'It won't be easy to find those numbers,' he warned. 'But I have some sources in Switzerland. I could try and see what I come up with. You'd have to pay a high price for either of them, but definitely more for the last Tourbillon in the series.'

Darcy opened his wallet and took out a business card, which he passed to the man. 'Money is no object.'

Clea wasn't sure what to think when she discovered Darcy would be her travelling companion on the long flight home. She was still shell-shocked by the deaths of Glen and Sharee, reeling from her tryst with Bahir, and exhausted from lack of sleep. The attempt on her life made Clea wake during the night in a cold sweat, and even Bahir's warm embrace couldn't put her fears to rest.

'I'll apologise now for any snoring,' Darcy tried to joke as they checked in at the first-class Qantas counter, but neither of them were in the mood for frivolity. He was pleased to have Clea's company on the flight. So much had happened, and it was comforting to be with someone who understood.

Clea and Bahir had said goodbye back in Mayfair, to avoid the predictable parting scene at the airport. He had promised to join her in Melbourne in three weeks' time for the Spring Racing Carnival. Clea missed him deeply already.

'Come on, let's see if some shopping can cheer us up,' Darcy suggested as they received their boarding passes, leading her towards a large duty-free area reeking of the clash of a thousand perfumes.

Clea followed, still too weighed down by the gravity of recent events to argue, even though shopping was the last thing on her mind. She felt overwhelmed by the bustle of the duty-free shoppers, the strong lights and the myriad of superfluous products on offer. All she could think of was that neither Sharee nor Glen would have need of any of this again. She gave up her browsing and found Darcy wandering aimlessly in the aftershave section. 'Any suggestions?' he asked half-heartedly.

Clea had always loved the Chanel perfumes and selected the Egoiste Platinum, which Darcy bought, before they headed to the first-class lounge to relax before their flight.

Seated next to each other at the back of the first-class cabin, they settled in for the long haul to Singapore. Lunch was served after take-off and they relaxed into a conversation about the thoroughbred industry as they sipped on excellent Australian wines, a Cullen semillon sauvignon blanc from Margaret River and an aged Katnook Prodigy shiraz from the Coonawarra. It was obvious they were both avoiding the bigger issues.

'Do you go to the races often?' Darcy asked, trying to turn the conversation to more personal matters.

'I don't really get much chance,' Clea confessed. 'But I love horses. My father always used to say he would buy me a horse. I don't know where he thought we'd keep it.'

Darcy was intrigued. 'So you didn't get a horse?'

'No. My father died.' Clea stared down at her glass.

'What happened?'

Clea didn't know whether it was the wine or the cocooned confessional ambience of altitude, but she felt strangely comfortable with Darcy. She told him of her father's early death.

Darcy put a hand over hers in sympathy. 'I can't imagine how awful it would be to lose a parent like that.'

Clea found Darcy's hand reassuring. 'It's my mother you should feel sorry for. She never got over it. I can't ever imagine loving someone so much. But you're so lucky with your family; Life has been easy for you.'

Darcy stared off into space for a moment. 'You know, I learned a long time ago that everyone has a cross to bear, and it's always relative to their own life.'

Clea looked at him curiously. 'What's yours?'

'My mother. After she had me she tried desperately to fall pregnant again but couldn't. Dad took her to every clinic and specialist around the world but nothing worked. She became very depressed, which led to prescription drugs by the handful – and alcohol. To this day I still can't fathom addiction. My father adored her, but in the end he couldn't be with her. She became someone else, someone we couldn't recognise.'

Darcy looked so sad Clea had to resist the urge to fling her arms around him and comfort him. It was true – you never knew what burdens people carried, even when their life seemed perfect.

'What happened to her?' Clea asked.

'She lives comfortably in Europe now, and has been on the

wagon for a number of years. I think it all improved when she stopped feeling sorry for herself and started to think about others. I've lost count of how many orphanages and schools she's helped set up in poverty-stricken countries. Now she has hundreds of children and I guess she's happy.'

'Are you close?'

'We have a good relationship now, but for a long time it was really strained. I think she resented Dad for finding another woman to love, and felt betrayed by my friendship with Julia, my step-mother. Perhaps I could have handled it differently, but I was only a teenager.' Darcy looked up and gazed intently into Clea's eyes until she had to lower her own. 'I know it was the hardest thing for my father to walk away. But then he found such happiness with Julia. I really hope that one day I can find a relationship half as good as theirs.'

Clea grimaced. 'So you're telling me you're a true romantic at heart, despite the playboy exterior?'

'Something like that.'

Darcy was a little stung by her sarcasm, but was more concerned with his growing feelings towards her. He knew he was falling for Clea, and had been since the moment they met. It wasn't fair. Bahir was his best friend and Darcy could never act against his interests. But Bahir couldn't give this beautiful woman the life she deserved. Despite himself, Darcy reached out and gently stroked Clea's cheek. She looked at him with such confusion that he immediately regretted the intimate gesture. What a fool he was to have lost this beautiful woman forever.

40

Ascot Festival, Ascot Racecourse, England

Alexander the Great leaned his muscular frame against Abdul for a scratch and was rewarded with a vigorous rub on his favourite spot on the neck. The prolonged spell in the paddock had done him good; his coat was dappled with health and glossy before his winter coat would begin to show through. He was excited to be back at Ascot and stamped impatiently, nickering to his stablemate in the next stall.

Abdul placed a hand on Alexander's knee and the horse obediently lifted the foot for inspection. The stud farrier, Andrew McPhee, wouldn't have missed this day for anything; he watched as Abdul removed his old carved knife from his pocket and scraped away a compression of straw and sawdust to examine the troublesome hoof. Abdul tapped around the T-bar shoe with the knife handle and looked up at Andrew with a grin. 'You've worked wonders, Andrew! It's strong and healthy.'

'We've worked wonders,' Andrew corrected him. 'I've no doubt your old recipes helped him as much from the inside as I did the outside. I don't think that shoe will be left on the turf today.'

Dropping the hoof Abdul scratched the horse's neck again, and Alexander rested his heavy head on Abdul's shoulder with a sigh of gratitude. Today Alexander would compete against some of the best milers in Europe in the Group One Queen Elizabeth II Stakes at the Ascot Festival. Abdul wasn't expecting Alexander to win, but hoped he would be running on well and could show them he was ready to enter quarantine with the rest of the Sheikh's horses travelling to Melbourne for the Spring Racing Carnival.

Alexander was saddled up for the race with a strapper leading him out of the stall when Abdul saw the Sheikh and Bahir crossing the gardens towards the horse stalls. His heart beat faster when he saw that Jalal and his father were strolling beside them. He panicked for a moment and grabbed Alexander's lead rope from the strapper.

'Best if I take him out today,' he grunted at the startled man and led the horse away as fast as he could.

'Is that Abdul leading the horse?' Bahir asked in surprise as he changed course for the parade ring. 'Is there something wrong?' he called out to the farrier.

'No, the horse is in tip-top shape,' Andrew called back as they left him standing by the stalls.

Once the jockey was safely mounted and the trainer had given final instructions, Abdul handed the lead rope back to the bemused strapper and took a place in the grandstand away from the owners' viewing area. From his vantage point Abdul trained his binoculars on Jalal and his father, feeling a cold shiver when their faces appeared so large and close in his lenses.

He studied Jalal's face carefully, as if there might be some mark or sign of his violent arrival into the world, but found only a face that bore a striking resemblance to Salah al Din. No matter – they couldn't outrun him this time. For all their giant transport industry, there wasn't a single clapped-out truck that could speed them away from the truth now.

Abdul was jolted back to the present when the gates opened, launching the horses and their riders onto the turf with a compelling force. He switched his binoculars back to the track and watched with satisfaction as Alexander took a position midfield and seemed to be travelling effortlessly. With such a crack field of milers, the runs came thick and fast and Alexander went with them, looming on the outside, his neck stretched long as he powered to the finish line to take third place: an excellent return to form and a reward for all their efforts to get him there today. He would travel by float from the track directly to quarantine, and in a fortnight's time would make the long flight out to Australia.

41

Spring Racing Carnival, Melbourne

The Australian Rules football season was finally over, and Melburnians put away their knitted scarves and football guernseys to focus on the glamour of the racetrack. The mounting excitement made Clea feel even more lonely and foolish as she waited for Bahir to arrive. He could have any woman he wanted – why would he choose her?

She decided not to share her romance with her family, but they knew something had changed.

'Were you perhaps a little closer to Glen than you've admitted?' her mother asked over coffee one day.

'No, Mum, he was my boss, nothing more.' Susanne had been staying with Clea more regularly since the tragic deaths in England. It was a relief for Clea to have company. She felt so alone and so far from Bahir, but when the flowers started arriving she sent her mother back home.

Her family wasn't deterred by her denials. 'Mum says

something's going on. Care to explain?' Robert asked one evening as Clea was putting yet another bunch of flowers in water with the phone jammed between her neck and shoulder.

'I'm just a bit down, that's all,' she said. 'I just wish there was something I could have done for Glen before things got as desperate as they did.'

'You can't beat yourself up about something you didn't know about.'

'But that's the problem, Rob. I *did* work out where the virus had come from, I just didn't act on it.' Clea had gone over her notes again and again. But nothing was going to bring Glen back.

'Sis, we're all worried about you. What if someone still wants you dead?'

'Don't, Robert!' Clea knew there was an edge of fear in her voice.

'Okay, you know I'm always here if you need to talk to me,' Robert offered. 'Lord knows I could do with some decent conversation in this place. Just call whenever you need to.'

Finally, by mid-October, everything was coming together. Bahir was arriving that morning for an extended stay over the Spring Racing Carnival. Clea would move into his hotel with him and commute to the AAIDL facility as required, but a lot of her work was now up in Melbourne. The lab had been able to determine that Glen had stolen a vial of the Newmarket strain of EI and they were now busy vaccinating the horses in training with the correct vaccine. In order to prevent speculation and panic leading up to the Spring Racing Carnival, the vaccination program was conducted as secretly as possible under the guise of a precautionary booster.

Clea had a daunting feeling that she'd been caught in a whirlwind of fantasy. It had all happened so quickly, and she was worried that Bahir would quickly tire of her. The persistent knot in her stomach tightened as the day wore on, before she could get away and meet Bahir at the hotel.

He had already called earlier, on landing. 'I can't wait to see you. Promise me you'll stay at Royal Towers with me? Or you can have your own suite if you'd prefer?' he'd added, ever the gentleman.

So it was all settled, but still Clea couldn't shake her nerves. She raced home from work early that afternoon, changed into a few different outfits before deciding on the Dolce & Gabbana trouser suit Bahir had bought her in London, threw toiletries and clothes into a bag and emerged from her apartment building to find a seven-series BMW and driver waiting patiently. An hour and a half later she walked into the plush foyer of Royal Towers and approached the front desk.

'Oh yes, Dr Reynolds, Prince Bahir is expecting you. I'll escort you to the Platinum Club.' The elegantly groomed young concierge led her to the lifts and keyed her up to the fortieth floor.

The young man led Clea through a luxurious black marble reception area, nodding to his colleagues sitting at mahogany desks on either side, to a large lounge with tables and comfortable sofas. Soaring ceilings supported cascading chandeliers and the view through the two-storey-high windows was breathtaking.

Bahir had positioned himself so he could watch the entrance and stood up immediately, his face beaming. He moved across the room as if pulled by the force of gravity and despite an audience of guests and staff, lifted Clea off her feet and twirled her around in excitement. 'I've missed you so much,' he said in a low voice, and planted a lingering kiss on her lips.

Clea suddenly noticed Abdul and two other men sitting nearby, and broke away from the prince's embrace. 'I'm sorry, have I disturbed you?' she asked anxiously.

Bahir laughed and led her by the hand over to the group. 'I know you and Abdul are old acquaintances. May I introduce you to my trainer, John Gallows, and the jockey who will ride for us through the carnival, Derek Robinson – this is my Dr Reynolds.' He gave her waist a squeeze as she reached out and shook hands with the two men.

Derek was slight in stature but his handshake was positively brutal. The strength of his grip reminded Clea how immensely powerful a jockey needed to be to manage the explosive force of a thoroughbred weighing in at half a tonne.

'Shall we have a drink with the boys before I show you upstairs?' Bahir asked, and Clea nodded politely, even though she longed to be alone with him.

A glass of Moët was produced along with another round of drinks for the men, who were discussing the potential field for the Cox Plate. The favourite was a New Zealand Weight for Age performer who had successfully raided the race the previous year. On the next line of betting were a mare from Queensland and a four-year-old horse who was unbeatable in the rich autumn races in Sydney.

Abdul wasn't fazed. 'Remember, this is a race for champions, so it will be hard to beat Alexander if his foot holds out.'

'How are your horses going?' Clea asked.

'They've done well despite their travels. Only Sun Tzu has lost a bit of condition. He dropped twenty kilos on the flight to Melbourne. But I reckon we'll show you Aussies what a few serious horses can do,' John said, chuckling.

'Don't get all superior on us.' Derek was defensive. 'You know our horses are as good as yours in the UK.'

'Sprinters, I'll grant you, but we're experts in the staying races. Our two horses in the Melbourne Cup have already won over greater distances than the two miles. But half the local field will be trying it for the first time.' John could be right, although Derek wasn't going to concede the point.

'If I get the urge to come out and watch track work tomorrow morning, I'll let you know,' said Bahir, standing up to signal his departure. 'But I'm sure this jetlag is going to hit me hard. We'll leave you to it, gentlemen.' He led Clea through the Platinum Club and to their room.

The Sandown quarantine facility allowed the imported horses a chance to continue their training while under strict quarantine rules, ensuring they didn't lose too much condition after their travels. The daily schedule for the Eclipse Stable team was a holiday compared to the usual early mornings. The luxury of a 7 a.m. start was only possible because they were not in competition with other horses for the track. Apart from the Eclipse team of five horses, there were only six other horses stabled at Sandown. Every morning a crowd of journalists arrived at the track, keen to take photographs and find out snippets of information about the international interlopers.

Now the quarantine period was over, the five Eclipse horses were stabled at one of the major racing stables at Flemington Racecourse, and track work began considerably earlier. The lights in the stables were all switched on by the time the Eclipse team arrived in the pre-dawn, the horses neighing or pawing the ground as the army of strappers scurried around, preparing them according to a tight schedule. At least Abdul and his crew had only five horses to consider, but each one needed to be groomed, geared up, and stretched before they ventured out of their large sawdust stalls onto the rubber-rock surface that cushioned their footfalls.

The Eclipse Stable horses were all competing in the distance races, but Alexander the Great was their best shot, a champion classic distance horse who had been surpassed only by his dead stablemate, Sampson. Alexander had been brought out to Australia specifically to challenge the Tatts Cox Plate, the best Weight for Age race in the Southern Hemisphere. His stablemate, Nelson, would be outclassed in such a strong Cox Plate, and would probably race in the Group One Emirates Stakes on the final day of the Flemington carnival. Caesar Borgia was aimed squarely at the Caulfield Cup. He had a turn of foot that could see him outsprint many a staying horse over the 2400 metres, but that was his limit. The final two horses, Sun Tzu and Marengo, were outright stayers preparing to run the 3200 metres of the Melbourne Cup. Their lead-up race would be the Caulfield Cup, where Abdul expected them to run home strongly at the finish. It was an impressive stable this year, and anticipation built as the carnival loomed closer.

Clea was astonished by the luxury of the villa secreted away at the top of the hotel tower. Never in her wildest dreams had she imagined people actually lived like this. She'd only got as far as the huge living room before Bahir pulled her into his arms. Clea felt her body melting into his and became lost in a dizzying kiss, full of the longing of separation.

Clothes were shed as if of their own accord until the two lovers sank gratefully into the sofa, their naked bodies connecting and moving in a primal rhythm – the tempo adjusting naturally to pace the satisfaction. Being with Bahir felt so natural and real.

When the overwhelming wave of passion had subsided, Bahir gallantly retrieved two thick white Versace towelling robes from the bathroom and watched in amusement as Clea wandered around the rooms like a kid in a candy shop, clad only in her robe. 'Do you always stay in suites like these?' she finally asked.

'Yes, but I've never really thought about it. I suppose I just take this for granted,' he answered with genuine surprise.

'Maybe you should try out a standard room so you can

appreciate this more.' Clea laughed and sat down behind the antique desk in the study. When she stood her mood had changed. 'I really don't belong here, Bahir. I've worked so hard to get where I am – this is . . . it's a world beyond my comprehension.'

'Well, my darling Clea, speaking of your world, I've taken the liberty of booking a suite for your mother for a night – I know it's not exactly the travel she's craved, but it's a small start.'

Clea looked at Bahir in amazement. It was such a thoughtful gesture, it took her completely by surprise. And it was his way of bringing their worlds just that little bit closer. Then reality kicked in. 'You can't meet my mother!'

'Why ever not?'

'I told you, she's not at all what you're used to. And besides, she'd faint if I asked her, or even told her about you.'

'So I'm a secret?' Bahir teased. 'Don't you think your mother would like to meet the man you're in love with?' Clea rolled her eyes and piffed a cushion at him. 'I'm serious! I want you to ask her to dinner tomorrow night – and the hotel room will just go to waste if she doesn't use it because I'm not cancelling it.'

'Okay, okay, but don't say I didn't warn you.' They walked back to the living room and Clea snuggled up next to him on the sofa, incredulous that Bahir had mentioned love. Could this be real? The scientist took over from the romantic and assessed the evidence. The fact that he wanted to meet her mother suggested serious intentions. And downstairs he had introduced her as *my* Dr Reynolds. Perhaps, for all their differences, it really could be love? Clea pushed the thought from her mind, and reminded herself that something that seemed too good to be true usually was.

Dinner was brought up to Bahir's villa from the kitchens of one of the hotel's restaurants. They were served large New Zealand oysters steamed with chilli and lemongrass, lobster san choy bau, and barramundi in a light soy and ginger sauce. It was a wonderful evening, but when Bahir yawned for the umpteenth time, overcome by jetlag, Clea announced it was time he went to bed.

Clea didn't fall asleep right away, but lay awake for a couple of hours, feeling the warmth of Bahir's body against hers. She wondered what she had done to deserve this magical romance.

42

Caulfield Cup, Melbourne Racing Club

On the morning of the Caulfield Cup, Clea put on a beautiful lavender and black silk dress and a black hat of feather quills and straw. At the last minute she realised her sensible black work bag simply wouldn't cut it and raced down to one of the hotel's boutiques, where the sales assistant helped her choose a patent leather clutch. She clipped back along the marble floor of the hotel lobby in her Gucci heels just as Bahir and Abdul emerged from the lifts.

Clea fell in alongside Bahir and smiled as he entwined his little finger with hers. Caulfield racetrack was a twenty-five-minute drive from the hotel, although they were held up in the racing traffic, which gave Clea a chance to appreciate the signage displaying the names of past Caulfield Cup winners that heralded their approach along the main road. There was total gridlock but the driver managed to navigate into a gateway in front of the main administration buildings where Bahir had arranged access, and they were greeted as they got out of the car by the club chairman.

As they were led up to the private boxes Clea looked around at the scores of young girls dressed to impress and balanced precariously on sky-high heels, making them appear as long-legged as the fillies in the mounting yard. Despite a distinctly chilly spring wind, they displayed plenty of fake-tanned flesh, a smorgasbord for the roving eyes of all the sharply dressed boys, who wore bravado in their smiles. The day was as much a celebration of beauty and the glorious promise of youth as of the race itself, Clea reflected. No wonder the carnival attracted such huge crowds.

A group of politicians and businessmen, keen to make contacts in the Middle East, were already in Bahir's private box, along with Darcy and several racing luminaries.

'Hello, my friends, long time no see,' Darcy joked and clasped Bahir on the shoulder. He gazed admiringly at Clea before giving her a kiss that lingered for an extra second on her cheek, and then he turned to shake Abdul's hand warmly. 'Now I know you don't bet, but what's my chance of getting some guidance from you today?'

'I'd be delighted to help – as long as you don't hold it against me if I'm wrong.' Abdul was in a good humour, believing their horse to be a good thing for the main race.

'I never win at the races. Perhaps you'll bring me luck, Abdul,' Clea teased as a flash of pride crossed Abdul's usually stern face.

Abdul proved to be as precise as one of Bahir's hunting falcons, selecting winners with uncanny accuracy. Darcy and Clea reaped the benefits, but when they complimented Abdul on his skill, he dismissed it modestly as luck. In fact, Abdul had spent all his spare time that week analysing distances, track success, times, trials, trainers and jockeys. Based on his research, he was confident the Eclipse runner, Caesar Borgia, would run well in the Cup today.

From the glassed-in seating area in the front of the box Clea had a great view of the immense crowd. Fashionably dressed racegoers teemed around the mounting yard in front of the grandstand, studying the form and craning to see the horses as they paced around the yard. The lawn areas were packed with picnic revellers and every available box in the grandstand was full.

Later in the afternoon, the chairman escorted Bahir's group down through the crowded members' bar and out into the mounting yard, where Caesar Borgia was being led around by a strong strapper. John Gallows found Bahir amongst the throng of excited owners and trainers and explained the race tactics while the group watched the stable star moving placidly around the ring. Sun Tzu and Marengo came down the walkway from the stalls alert to the noisy crowd, but they were seasoned performers and remained relaxed, joining the circle of horses moving to their correct saddlecloth position so that all the horses paced around in order.

The jockeys appeared in their bright silks, and huddles were formed before the call of 'Mount up, riders,' sent them sauntering over to their horses to be legged up into the saddle.

Caesar Borgia was getting frisky, tossing his head around, and seemed eager to stretch his legs on the turf. The strapper unclipped his lead and let Derek steer out onto the racetrack, leading the field with the number one saddlecloth.

The mounting yard thinned out as owners and trainers moved to the designated seating behind glass in the grandstand to watch the race. Bahir and Clea were escorted to a private committee viewing area; the rest of the group found a seat with the other hopeful owners.

Caesar Borgia jumped well from barrier three at the start of the race and quickly slotted into fourth place one out from the rail and one back from the two leading horses. Derek's instructions were to stay away from the rails, where he might be deliberately jammed, or have difficulty getting a clear run when the field sprinted to the line.

The horse was travelling beautifully, relaxed and under no pressure – even when a few of the back markers moved up to his outside as they hit the turn into the straight. For a moment he was bottlenecked, but a path cleared in front at the 200-metre mark and as the leaders began to tire, Derek clicked him up and sprinted past, breaking away from the field by two lengths to the roar of the crowd. Derek had a quick look over his shoulder at the 100-metre mark and could see no obvious rivals, but just at that moment the favourite, Diamond Cutter, burst through the field and came bearing down on him in a few strides. Caesar Borgia caught sight of his rival before Derek reacted and accelerated, the two horses running neck and neck to the finishing post, but Diamond Cutter reached it first by a short half head in a nail-biting finish.

Bahir joined his racing team, clapped John on the back and kissed Clea in exuberance. 'Well done!' he exclaimed. 'We came very close, but second place in a Group One is worth celebrating.'

The placegetters came back into the mounting yard once the excitement had subsided a little and took up their respective positions. The steward's grey horse led the winner a way up the straight, to the applause of the crowd, then into the mounting yard to a barrage of media. Bahir led Clea over to the winning owners where they shook hands and congratulated the delighted group, before joining the Eclipse team next to Caesar Borgia.

Darcy was talking to his horse trainer, Tom, on the viewing steps nearby but watching Clea with Bahir over Tom's shoulder. He felt an intense knot of jealousy twist inside him. Tom looked behind him to see what had attracted Darcy's attention just in time to see a laughing Clea pat Caesar Borgia's neck. When he turned back to Darcy the suffering and confusion in Darcy's eyes was so intense Tom quickly looked away again, knowing he had stumbled on a moment of deep emotion.

Tom rested a hand on Darcy's arm. 'He's your best friend,' he said simply.

'I know,' Darcy answered with deep resignation.

*

That evening, Susanne applied her make-up in the opulent bathroom of her Royal Towers suite. She couldn't help feeling disappointed that Clea had kept her romance with Prince Bahir a secret from her family, even though it was out in the open now. She hoped Clea knew what she was doing.

Susanne sighed as she stared in the mirror, one hand resting on a gleaming strand of pearls around her neck. Her struggle to raise three children on her own, sometimes barely able to put food on their plates, was etched in her face. In her youth she had been considered a great beauty, and traces of that beauty still remained. Her skin was translucent, her cheekbones high and her eyes clear and bright blue. She had always joked with her children that the crows' feet around her eyes were from laughing too much, but in reality it was the opposite.

She wondered how she would have managed without Clea's help. Wise beyond her years, Susanne's young daughter had provided the emotional support Susanne had desperately needed after her husband died. Clea had taken charge of her younger brothers, and by the time Susanne shook off her mantle of grief, the household was running smoothly again – although there was an emptiness that never truly went away.

Her children were her life and, in a way, the hardship of their upbringing kept them all close and in harmony, like a concerto where the beauty of the music was in the sum of the parts.

When Clea knocked at the door to take her mother downstairs she was thrilled to find her elegantly dressed in a simple black dress with heels, upswept hair and soft make-up. 'Mum, you look fabulous,' she said, and hugged her tight.

They had dinner in the upstairs private room of a renowned French bistro in the complex. Conversation flowed, Bahir's natural charm quickly putting Susanne at ease. At the end of the night Clea walked her mother back to her suite and sat for a moment with her.

'Darling, he's wonderful – truly wonderful and very much in love with you, I think. How do you feel about him?' Susanne asked cautiously.

'I'm sorry, Mum. I should have told you when I got back from England.' Clea gave her mother a hug. 'I really think this is serious,' she said nervously. 'I've never felt like this about a man – and I think he feels the same way about me.'

'Oh, darling, I'm so happy for you.' Susanne tried to hide her reservations as Clea hugged her goodnight and went back to her villa. Susanne sighed. She could see so many barriers – religion, distance, culture – but her daughter had looked radiant.

The next morning, Clea knocked on her mother's door, expecting her to be ready for breakfast. Bahir was planning to join them if he could, but was checking final arrangements for his family's arrival. When the door opened, Susanne was still in her bathrobe, looking dishevelled.

Clea was shocked by the look of anguish on her face. 'Mum, what is it?'

'You don't know, do you?' Susanne sat down on the bed and took Clea's hand. 'I know it's not our business, but Ernest rang me first thing this morning.'

'Is he okay?' Clea was seriously alarmed. Her mother was usually so composed.

'He did a full internet search on Prince Bahir,' she said softly. 'I'm sorry, darling. I didn't ask him to, I promise, but he was worried about you.'

Frustration flashed across Clea's brow. Her family could be such meddlers sometimes. Why couldn't she run her own life? 'Mum, I appreciate your concern, but I Googled him myself when I got back,' Clea reassured her mother. 'The only information I found was about horseracing.' But she was troubled when tears sprang to Susanne's eyes. Her mother seemed to be struggling to speak, before she finally turned to Clea and looked her straight in the eye.

'Bahir is married, Clea.'

Bahir wasn't in the villa when Clea rushed in to grab her belongings. She couldn't bear to spend another minute in the hotel, and scribbled a short note for Bahir, her hands shaking, leaving it on the desk. Susanne met her in the lobby downstairs and they drove in silence to the family home.

43
The Platinum Club, Royal Towers

Later that morning, Sheikh Faisal, Yvonne and an entourage of security guards, a private secretary, a chef and a personal valet arrived in Melbourne, followed a few hours later by Prince Khalid, Afifah and her chaperone Basmah; family policy dictated that they never all travelled on the same flight.

Bahir greeted his family in the Platinum Club reception, embracing his father, clapping his brother hard on his back and spinning his sister around. Afifah was elegantly dressed in Western clothing. 'They've let the songbird out of her cage.' He kissed her on both cheeks. 'You look radiant – obviously long-haul flights suit you well, sister.'

'Actually, Bahir darling, I'm so tired. I want to go to my room immediately and take a nap.' She pouted prettily then smiled when one of the Platinum Club managers took his cue and ushered them all towards the elevators.

Once the guests had been shown to their respective villas,

Bahir chose to stay behind with his sister for a while, sitting on the bed while she chatted happily about the trip and her plans.

Finally Bahir interrupted her. 'Afifah, I have someone special I would like you to meet in Melbourne.'

Afifah looked searchingly at her brother. 'Bahir! Not you too! It's bad enough I have to travel with father's puffed-up little mistress, who thinks she's *so* superior. You know I love Jameela – you'll break her heart if she finds out. Don't expect me to be your mistress' new best friend, because I'm not interested.'

'You really are such an innocent, aren't you?' Bahir marvelled.

'No, I'm not!' Afifah answered indignantly. 'I was educated in London like you. I'm not innocent – and I'm not naive. I'm just loyal to my friends. One day this might be my husband talking to his younger sister about his new mistress, and how would you feel then?'

Bahir ignored the comment. 'Clea will be joining us at the races and other functions, so promise me you'll at least be nice?'

Afifah sat down on the bed beside him. 'So it's that public already? I've assumed you've had other women before, but you've always been so discreet. I expect it of Khalid – he's always hanging out at nightclubs with the Euro trash – but you, Bahir?'

'I'm afraid I'm falling in love,' Bahir answered quietly.

'Are you, brother? Are you really? I can forgive you if it really is love – although I daresay that will make it much harder for Jameela when she finds out . . . Don't worry, I won't ever tell her,' she added hastily. 'What did you say her name was?'

'Clea. Dr Clea Reynolds.'

'Okay, when I meet this Clea woman I promise to be very sweet and not at all judgemental.'

'Thank you, darling, I knew I could count on you.' Bahir stood to leave. 'I'll leave you in peace for some beauty sleep. Would you like to have lunch later?'

'I'd love to but — Could it just be the two of us? Khalid is giving me a hard time as usual, and Father is so busy at the moment I know we'd rush in, gobble up our meal and have to leave.'

'I'll see what I can do.'

Bahir went and knocked at his father's villa and found him talking heatedly on the phone as Hassan fussed around, setting up a laptop and organising diaries and paperwork. Bahir sat patiently until his father was free.

'You look well, son, I think this country agrees with you — or is it the women?' Sheikh Faisal teased and was rewarded with one of Bahir's charming smiles. But he was soon distracted by urgent business matters from Qatar, so Bahir wandered out and visited his brother in the next-door villa.

'You're doing the rounds like you own the place,' Khalid said tersely. 'Isn't it typical that you've come to Australia a number of times and I've been stuck in Dubai working myself into the ground.'

Khalid's jealousy of his older brother was a barrier that stood between them. Bahir resisted the urge to ask how Khalid managed to work so hard and yet spend most evenings in the nightclubs, parading around with the latest hot girls. There would be bastard Khalids sprouting up all over the place soon.

'Perhaps you'd like to come out tonight?' Bahir asked.

'I'll see. Someone has to work around here.'

Bahir sighed and got up to leave.

'That was a quick visit, brother, am I boring you?' Khalid said antagonistically.

'Sorry, Khalid, I have a few things to do myself. I'll see you later.'

He assumed Clea had already left to go to the racing stables. She was personally handling the EI vaccinations, and the work was non-stop in order to give each horse both their initial shot and a booster a few weeks later. He decided to go to the hotel gym for a workout. He glanced into the office but emails and phone calls could wait.

Feeling refreshed after an hour at the gym, Bahir knocked on the door of his sister's villa a while later. The sound of high heels on marble preceded the door being thrown open. Afifah gave her brother an affectionate kiss on each cheek.

'You did it? It's just the two of us?' Bahir nodded. 'I'm so happy! I feel like I haven't spent any time alone with you for ages.'

Bahir admired his sister in the lift. Her long, dark hair hung down her back, straight and sleek and glossy. She was wearing a pair of tight designer jeans, black lizard-skin peep-toes, a pale blue satin shirt, and a black Dolce & Gabbana bomber jacket. An elegant diamond necklace sat high around her throat and a Louis Vuitton charm bracelet rattled engagingly on her wrist, matching the LV bag slung casually over her shoulder. She was a beautiful, well-dressed woman, and Bahir glowed with pride as they left the hotel to meet the waiting car.

At Zest, an impressive seafood fusion restaurant perched above Melbourne's Federation Square, Afifah was the object of many a glance, but no one stared for too long once they caught Bahir's protective glare and noticed a burly bodyguard positioned at the bar.

Bahir smiled indulgently as his sister primped at the table, loving the attention. 'I've missed you,' he announced suddenly and reached out for her hand.

Afifah paused until the waiter had taken orders for lemon squash and handed out menus before she quietly removed her hand from her brother's. 'Now, are you going to tell me what's going on?' she asked.

Bahir blanched at the direct question. 'What do you mean? There's nothing happening of any interest to you besides lunch, the races and a nice visit to Australia.'

'Bahir, don't be so condescending. You know I'm not stupid – at least that's what my lecturers at Oxford tell me and I choose to believe them.'

'Darling, of course you're not stupid. You know how proud I am of you. I just don't know what you're talking about,' he lied.

'You're not very good at this.' Afifah smiled. 'Something's going on, Bahir, and I want to know what it is. We've lost four of our best horses over the last few months to hendra, you contracted the virus yourself when you were over here, and some scientist turned up dead in England, not to mention the maid . . . Do I need to go on?'

Bahir sat back in his chair and contemplated his sister for a while. The waiter erroneously believed it was his cue to take their orders and the interruption gave Bahir a moment to think. Once they were alone again he answered carefully, 'To be perfectly honest, I'm at my wit's end with all of this. It's just so awful. Four people have already died —'

'Four? I thought it was only two – our maid, and the scientist who stole the virus in the first place.'

Bahir explained what he knew of the deaths of Antonia and Mimi to his sister, reasoning she would find out about them sooner or later. 'The police are still investigating the links but they think this man Zayd Farouk is just a henchman. He managed to escape from Dubai after the second girl's suspected murder and the police in the UK believe he was most likely Dr Collings' killer. But the only proof they have at the moment is his voice on the recordings and Dr Collings' letter. So, I'm afraid, we're no closer to working out who is behind it all, and why. But, my darling little detective sister, let's not spoil a good lunch with such a sad conversation.' Bahir felt frustrated and frightened that the killer was still on the loose, but he didn't want to scare Afifah.

Realising she wasn't going to get any more information from her brother, Afifah changed the subject. 'So what's on the agenda tonight?'

Relieved the conversation had changed tack, Bahir imparted the dinner plans, followed by drinks with Darcy in the city.

'It will be lovely to see Darcy again,' Afifah breathed.

Bahir leant across the table and grasped his sister's hands. If there was a chance to deter her from this course of action, he had to take it. 'You must stop this Darcy nonsense, Afifah. It will never amount to anything, you know that. At this stage I don't think Father knows, so there's no harm done.'

'Bahir! I'm not interested in Darcy!' Afifah protested, blushing despite herself. 'I just like him, that's all – he *is* one of your closest friends. Don't you want me to like him?'

'Yes, but as a sister and nothing more,' he cautioned her.

'Have you spoken to Father yet about my marriage?' she asked quietly, eyes downcast.

'No, I'm waiting for the right opportunity. But poor Jalal came to me and explained what happened between you. He's quite desperately in love with you, you know.' Bahir looked hopefully for some change of heart but his sister's eyes clouded over.

'He's in love with the idea of me,' she spat out. 'And perhaps even more in love with the connection to this family. Bahir, you promised. I *can't* marry him.'

Clea had berated herself all day for being such a fool. She was learning the hard way that rich men led very different lives. Bahir was busy with his family today, so her absence probably wouldn't even be noticed until later. And even then, she had no idea what she should say to him.

Susanne was fussing around as if she were a sick child, and eventually Clea announced she was going to the stables to distract herself. By early afternoon she could no longer avoid the issue, no matter how engrossing her work. Anger and sadness flared up alternately, but eventually anger won out and she picked up the phone to dial the person she was most furious with.

'Why the hell didn't you tell me he was married?' she demanded when Darcy answered the phone. 'You just let me make a fool of myself – some friend you turned out to be!'

'Clea, I'm so sorry.' Darcy really didn't know what to say. 'It wasn't my place —'

'Darcy, he's *married*.' She spoke the word as if it were one of her viruses.

'You have to understand, it's different for Bahir,' Darcy said, trying to explain what he had long understood. 'He comes from a very different culture, and marriage to a good Muslim girl was always going to be part of the deal. That doesn't mean he cares for you any less.' Darcy fervently wished he could speak his mind, but his loyalty to Bahir prevented the words from forming in his mouth.

'I'm such a fool,' Clea said, her voice beginning to crack, and she abruptly hung up.

Darcy tried calling her back but she wouldn't pick up. He left a message and then left her alone.

Clea knew she was being irrational. She had written a note telling Bahir not to bother getting in contact, but the only thing she wanted was to hear his voice. Late in the afternoon, when she still hadn't heard from him, Clea was beginning to wonder if he cared about her at all. She left the stables and drove back to her mother's house – she couldn't bear to be alone right now. When she opened the door she was suprised and relieved to find

Bahir sitting in the lounge room with her mother, who quietly got up and left so they could talk in private.

Bahir hesitated. His instincts told him to take Clea in his arms and kiss away the pain visible in her eyes, but he restrained himself. Bahir pulled Clea's letter from his pocket and placed it on the coffee table.

'Clea, I can explain, although I'll understand if you never want to speak to me again.'

'Why didn't you tell me?' she demanded.

'Because I foolishly assumed you already knew,' he answered lamely. In his world, infidelity was a way of life and the lure of money ensured there were always women prepared to play the game. 'You're very different to other women I've known, Clea.' He moved around the table and took her hand.

'Bahir, you are a married man, and I'm not that — I'm not that sort of a woman.'

'My wife was fourteen when we were betrothed, and I was twenty. It is the way of my culture – it is the way of my family. Ours is not a love match, it's a traditional marriage between two people who will hopefully grow to love and respect each other. Unfortunately, I've spent most of my life in the West, growing up with your customs and expectations. I want to fall in love . . . and I want to fall in love with you.' Bahir wore his heart on his sleeve.

Clea looked him in the eye. 'But you're *married*,' she enunciated clearly, as if he had a hearing problem.

Bahir smiled sadly. 'Most of the time my wife and I don't even live in the same house. I hope she will give me sons, as it is my father's wish, and I have affection for her, but we don't share our lives.' Bahir tentatively encircled Clea in his arms. 'You see an obstacle, and I only see you.' He was relieved to feel her body relax slightly against his. 'We can work this out if you'll just give me a chance, I promise.' He kissed her lips softly over and over until she responded.

It went against everything Clea believed in, but it was hard to ignore the sincerity in Bahir's voice. He had opened her eyes to a sophisticated world of wealth and power and perhaps, just perhaps, there really was a place for her in that world. Bahir and Clea left together after saying goodbye to Susanne, but Clea avoided looking at her mother's face, fearing her disappointment.

Clea had just enough time to change before joining Bahir in the Platinum Club where Sheikh Faisal, his family and the racing team had already assembled. Clea felt very self-conscious in light of what she now knew and avoided Bahir's extended hand, but was reminded of the different values of his world by the presence of Yvonne, who greeted her warmly like a co-conspirator.

'Father, you remember Clea?' Bahir asked.

'Of course, who could forget your beautiful face!' Sheikh Faisal exclaimed and stood up to clasp Clea's outstretched hand. 'And your intelligence,' he added suavely.

Khalid stayed seated but greeted Clea with such obvious

admiration that Bahir was immediately irked. Afifah stood and smiled warmly at Clea.

'It's lovely to meet you. Bahir has told me everything about you – all good, I promise.'

Just then Darcy came in and momentarily hesitated on seeing Clea. He greeted everyone cheerily but gave Clea a raised eyebrow that sent the colour rising to her face. Afifah watched the two of them with narrowed eyes. She was relieved that Jalal had been detained on business in Dubai and wasn't due to arrive until Friday.

The Platinum Club concierge escorted them down to a private dining room in one of Melbourne's better-known restaurants. Afifah managed to snag a seat next to Darcy at the table and seemed oblivious to the discomfort on his face. Clea was seated between Darcy and Bahir – not the combination she'd hoped for. Luckily Darcy was too engaged talking to Afifah to bother her.

After the meal the group split up. Sheikh Faisal and Yvonne went back to the Platinum Club for some time alone, the racing contingent headed to a favourite bar of the racing industry, although they couldn't convince Abdul to join them, and Bahir, Darcy, Clea, Afifah and Khalid wandered off to a cocktail bar in one of Melbourne's famous city laneways. There was no need for Basmah, Afifah's chaperone, when Afifah was with her brothers.

'Okay, little princess, what can we get for you?' Darcy asked Afifah indulgently, then regretted using his pet name for her when Bahir scowled from his deep leather armchair.

'I'd love something creamy and yummy – but of course with

no alcohol,' Afifah said, before turning to Clea. 'So, I want to know all about you! My brother is clearly head over heels about you, so you must be very special.'

'Oh, I don't know about that,' Clea said, embarrassed.

'She *is* very special,' Bahir said. 'You have to help me convince her to move to London. Geelong is too far away.'

'Australia is too far away!' Afifah quipped.

'No criticism from you, thanks, princess – you've just landed here and you've already got an opinion. Don't forget I live in Melbourne for most of the year,' Darcy said.

'Well, if you've chosen to live here it must be okay,' Afifah corrected herself with a hint of sarcasm. 'Perhaps I should come and live here too?'

'Why the hell would you want to live here?' Khalid said before Darcy could respond.

'Because, dear brother, they serve such wonderful cocktails!'

'You might think being flippant is endearing, but it's not – it just makes you look stupid,' Khalid said spitefully. 'In fact, you shouldn't even be here tonight. I wonder what Jalal would think about his future wife hanging out in a bar like a street walker.'

'Don't speak to her like that,' Bahir warned his brother.

'You should know, Khalid, since you spend so much time in bars,' Afifah taunted back.

'Okay, that's enough! We're supposed to be having fun!' Darcy interrupted before the conversation could get worse. 'Tell me, Khalid, what do you think of Alexander the Great's chances on Saturday?'

'I wouldn't know. Father and Bahir are the horse specialists. Ask them,' he answered sulkily.

Afifah poked out her tongue. 'You're such a party pooper.'

Khalid stood up. 'Actually, if you'll all excuse me, I have some business to attend to.'

'Oh, for heaven's sake, sit down and stop acting like a child,' Bahir said, but Khalid turned on his heel and marched out the door.

Bahir went to follow him but Afifah grabbed his arm. 'Let him go, he's such a spoilsport. We'll have more fun with just the four of us.'

'I don't doubt that, I'm just worried about what he might say to Father. I don't want to cause you any trouble, little one.'

'It'll be fine. As long as I'm with you and in full view of the BG.' She indicated the bodyguard watching from the bar.

'You know, I don't understand why you two are so mean to Khalid. You're lucky to have a brother, even if he can be a pain in the arse,' Darcy said unexpectedly, but before anyone could comment he stood up. 'Come on, let's change the atmosphere – who wants to go to a new place that's just opened? It's a bit rowdier but good fun.' Darcy downed the rest of his martini and fixed the bill while the others polished off their drinks.

The hour was well past midnight when Clea and Bahir found themselves standing awkwardly back in the entrance hall of the villa. Clea was unsure of herself, but Bahir tenderly took her face in his hands and kissed her lips. He led her to the bedroom, her hand firmly in his grasp as if she'd slip away like a sylph.

But Clea's desire overwhelmed reason and she willingly stepped into his embrace for a long passionate kiss, feeling his hard body pressed against hers. Bahir cupped the outline of her breasts through her dress and she gasped at the sheer thrill of the sensation. She slowly unzipped her dress and let it fall to the ground, while Bahir slipped her bra strap off her shoulder and lightly kissed the curve of flesh above the lace of her lilac bra. Sensing no resistance, he reached around and undid the clasp, peeling back the lacy fabric as if he were unveiling an exquisite gift. Clea wanted to feel his lips against her skin more than anything, but a voice inside her head was telling her to stop, and before she knew it she had articulated it out loud. 'Please stop,' she whispered again.

Bahir sighed and kissed her again. 'I understand,' he whispered back. 'Take your time, Clea. I'm sorry about today.'

Bahir was such a wonderful man, but now it felt like there was something missing. Clea didn't want to be the other woman, no matter how different the culture. And she still felt ill at ease in this world of wealth and privilege. Her eyes were being opened to a world where rich men behaved as if the common rules didn't apply. Darcy seemed to change women on a whim and Bahir sought love outside his marriage as if that were perfectly normal.

Bahir slipped quickly into a deep sleep, but Clea's mind was a whirl of thoughts and emotions. She didn't sleep for a long time.

44

Gymnasium, Royal Towers, Melbourne

Clea punished herself early the next morning on the running machine, turning up the speed and the gradient each time she thought of Bahir until she was sprinting fast uphill. She wasn't some naive twenty-year-old, but a grown woman. For as long as human civilisation had existed, there had been such things as arranged marriages and infidelity. In Bahir's culture a wealthy man often had more than one wife, Clea reminded herself, but that thought did little to make her feel better.

As long as Bahir remained distant from his wife, both emotionally and physically, perhaps she could handle the situation. Ultimately it was her business and hers alone, and no amount of stares from Darcy or disapproving looks from her mother could sway her if she chose to stay with Bahir. She simply couldn't walk away now. Too much of her heart had been invested.

The debate was still raging in her head when, hot and sweaty, she returned to the change rooms for a quick steam and shower before breakfast. The steam room was already activated and Clea was a little annoyed that someone else was in there, but stripped off and wrapped a towel around her body. She was winding her hair up into a knot when the door opened and a lithe, tanned figure emerged, reaching for a towel. When the person turned around Clea realised with dismay that it was Afifah.

'Oh, hello!' she said, squeezing moisture from her long, wet hair. 'I thought I'd be the only one up at this hour – jetlag, you know. I don't know how you Australians travel all the time if you know you're going to be so messed up when you get there.'

'You get used to it, I suppose,' Clea said with a weak smile.

Afifah hung her towel outside a shower cubicle and turned on the cold water. Clea hung her own towel outside the steam room and stepped inside. She stretched out on the top bench, enjoying the sensation of being enveloped in a foggy swirl of heat.

The door opened and Afifah stepped back inside. 'I hope you don't mind – I always have three steams and three cold showers, it makes my skin feel so good.' She settled in the opposite corner, the thick steam providing a cover for their naked bodies.

The women were silent for a few minutes as the steam billowed out into the room again, increasing the temperature.

'Please forgive me for saying this, but I'm curious about why you're with my brother,' Afifah began before realising the question didn't sound right. 'I mean, I understand why you're attracted to each other. It's just that you're not like the other women.'

Clea knew immediately that Afifah was talking about the Yvonnes of the world. 'No, I'm not,' she said, deciding honesty was the best policy. 'I've only just found out Bahir is married, and now I don't know what to do. I've never been in this situation before,' she added awkwardly.

Afifah was silent for a while. 'It's so different for you Western women – you can marry purely for love. We must marry the man who is selected for us and hope that love will grow. But even if I had your freedom I wouldn't want to take another woman's husband.'

'I hadn't thought of it that way,' Clea said, although she had been thinking of nothing else.

'Perhaps you should,' Afifah said gently. 'Please don't get me wrong, Clea. I think we could be friends, and of course I see the way Bahir looks at you. But his wife Jameela is a beautiful young woman who loves my brother dearly. She knows and accepts that he will never be faithful to her and that most of the women are just passing attractions, like Yvonne is for Father – but you're different. You would break her heart.'

'I don't know what to say.' Clea was sitting up now, trickles of sweat rolling down her body, her mind a mass of confusion. Suddenly Bahir's wife had a name, and it made her even more real.

'Then don't say anything,' Afifah said. 'Just think of me. I can never be with the man I love and will have to marry someone I'm afraid of, if my brother can't stop the marriage. Even then, the new man my father chooses may not be someone I will love or desire. But I will do my best, and pray every day that he doesn't meet a woman like you and give up on me.'

Afifah stood up and opened the door. In a moment she was gone, leaving Clea staring after her through the curling steam.

Bahir found his father in the villa after breakfast working through a list of emails with Hassan.

'What is it, son?' Sheikh Faisal enquired as Bahir hesitated in the doorway.

'May I have a word with you?'

'Of course, always.' The Sheikh looked at his eldest son.

'I'm sorry, Hassan, but it's a private matter.' Bahir watched as Hassan beat a swift retreat out of the room.

'Hassan already knows most of my business,' the Sheikh commented dryly.

'Of course, Father, but this concerns Afifah.' Bahir sat down in the chair opposite his father. 'And it's about Jalal.'

'Somehow I get the feeling you're not about to tell me he'll make a fine son-in-law,' Sheikh Faisal surmised. 'What's troubling you?'

Without giving away too much of his sister's confidence, Bahir calmly explained their conversation by the fountains over a month ago in Dubai, and his promise to bring the issue to the Sheikh's attention. 'I can't bear to see her unhappy, she's such a beautiful beam of sunshine. Surely there's something you can do?'

Sheikh Faisal stroked his beard for a moment. 'And this incident at the stables can be corroborated by others?'

'I've already questioned the chaperone and it seems Afifah's story is true.' Bahir deliberately left out Darcy's part in the episode. He didn't want Darcy entangled in family affairs.

The Sheikh stood and paced the room. 'On the one hand, I consider Jalal to be like my own son,' he said, thinking aloud. 'But on the other, I could never allow my beloved Afifah to make a bad marriage. Have you spoken of this to anyone?' he asked Bahir sharply.

'Of course not, Father,' said Bahir, offended, and the Sheikh softened his voice.

'Thank you for coming to me, son. Rest assured that I will do what's best for my family.'

45

Training Stables, Cranbourne, Victoria

The task of vaccinating all horses in the main training centres of Victoria was a large one, and Clea was behind schedule. She got up early and despite Bahir's encouragement to come back to bed, left the hotel before 7 a.m. for the one-hour drive to the Cranbourne training track. Zoe greeted her at the first stables, and the two women vaccinated all the equine occupants, entering the details manually in a spreadsheet as they went. A Racing Victoria representative had accompanied them to handle the inevitable questions. They were trying to keep the process under wraps, but it was proving difficult.

Clea could hear the trainer getting more and more exasperated with the answers he was receiving. 'But if there isn't any threat, why are you vaccinating all the horses?' he asked for the third time.

The Racing Victoria representative kept his cool. 'Just think of it as an insurance policy for the Spring Racing Carnival.'

It wasn't the best of explanations, but it would have to do.

Zoe was one of the few vets who'd been fully briefed, and she looked at Clea and grimaced. 'I doubt we'll get many horses done in Mornington by the time we've finished up here. Looks like we'll be down there tomorrow. You weren't doing anything, were you?'

Clea laughed. For once in her life, her work wasn't taking top priority. She had every intention of getting back to the hotel by early evening. Her brother Robert was in town on one of his visits home from Western Australia, and she had agreed to meet him for a drink.

Later in the day, Clea quickly tidied herself up in the hotel room and dashed downstairs to the bar. Robert was sitting on a stool with his back to her, drinking a dirty martini. She snuck up behind him and put her hands over his eyes.

'Aren't we a bit too old to play that game?' Robert gave his sister a hug. 'You look good,' he said appreciatively.

'And you look suntanned. I hope you're using sunscreen out there.'

'You sound like Mum.' Robert ordered two more martinis. 'Now, tell me what's happening in your life.'

Clea looked down at her nails and realised they were still dirty from handling horses all day. 'Did Mum put you up to this?'

Robert put an arm around his sister. 'That's a bit unfair. We're all worried about you, sis. You haven't spoken to any of us since —' He broke off, not wanting to upset her.

'Go on, say it. Since we found out Bahir's married. Anyway,

we all thought it was too good to be true.' There was an edge of bitterness in her voice.

'What are you going to do?' Robert asked gently.

'I don't know.' Clea took a long sip of her drink. 'I honestly don't know how I got myself into this mess. The problem is . . .' She paused, looking into her brother's eyes. 'I think I'm in love with him.'

'Is it him or the whole prince thing?'

Clea looked away again. 'You know me better than that, Robert.'

'Sis, we're all here for you, whatever your decision.' Robert put his glass down. 'Can I meet him?'

'No. At least, not yet.' Clea wondered if her family would ever understand if she chose to remain with Bahir.

46

Darcy's Penthouse, Melbourne

The next evening the Sheikh and his two sons left the hotel to attend a dinner organised by industry heads in a private room at Melbourne's finest Chinese restaurant.

Clea was pleased to be left alone with her own thoughts. It had been a long day at the Mornington stables, and she took a relaxing bath and ordered up room service. When her mobile rang she looked at the screen suspiciously; she was still avoiding her mother's numerous calls. But it was Darcy.

'I knew Bahir was out tonight so I thought I'd ring and see how you are,' he said.

'I'm fine, why shouldn't I be?' Clea answered defensively.

'I don't suppose you want to have dinner somewhere casual tonight? It would give us a chance to talk.'

'I'm not sure that we have a lot to talk about, Darcy,' Clea responded, but then regretted her tone. None of this situation was Darcy's fault. 'And besides, I've treated myself to a bath and room service is on the way,' she added more kindly.

Darcy tried to push the image of Clea's naked skin glowing from a bath out of his mind. 'Are you going to the cocktail party tomorrow night?' he asked.

'I believe so. I'll see you there. Good night, Darcy.'

Darcy checked out his refrigerator and found the usual bachelor selection of beer, cheese and dips. He sighed and picked up the phone to order some takeaway from a Thai restaurant around the corner. But before he'd even dialled, the buzzer on his doorbell rang sharply.

To Darcy's immense surprise, it was Yvonne. On seeing her face on the security monitor, Darcy toyed momentarily with the idea of pretending he was out, which was one of the perks of living in a high-rise building, but curiosity got the better of him and he pushed the button to let her in downstairs.

'This is an unexpected pleasure,' he announced as he opened the door a minute later. 'Come in, I was just pouring myself a drink.'

'I'm sorry to burst in on you like this, Darcy, but I needed to see you alone,' Yvonne said as she followed Darcy to the kitchen. 'There's something I have to tell you.'

Darcy was wary but intrigued, and motioned for Yvonne to sit on the deep leather sofa facing the view. He brought over two glasses of white wine, a crisp New Zealand sauvignon blanc, handed one to Yvonne and propped himself in a vintage Eames chair nearby. 'Well, I'm a good listener,' he encouraged.

Yvonne sipped her drink and stared into its contents for a long while. 'There's no easy way of saying this, so I'll just come straight to the point; please forgive my bluntness. Many years ago I had an affair with your father.'

'Okay,' Darcy said slowly. 'I know my father had lovers after he split with my mother. I didn't know you were one of them.'

Yvonne wouldn't make eye contact. 'Actually it was a little later than that.'

It suddenly dawned on Darcy what she was implying. 'You mean you two had an affair after he was married to Julia?' he asked incredulously.

'Well, it was just before the wedding. I was young and full of myself. I really believed it meant something and that he wouldn't go through with the marriage.'

'All right, this is getting weird.' Darcy felt the blood rushing to his head and stood up to gaze out the window at the city lights. 'So you had an affair before they got married. Really, Yvonne, I'm not sure why you're telling me this now. Why dredge up the past?'

'In your father's defence, I think he had cold feet about getting married again, and I guess you could call what we had more of a fling than an affair, although I took it seriously. Darcy, I'm not proud of what I'm telling you. It certainly wasn't one of my finest moments, but you need to know because there were consequences, and your father has no intention of ever telling you.'

'What *consequences* could possibly interest me now?' Darcy asked, trying to remain calm.

Yvonne looked him in the eye and said quietly, 'You have a brother.'

The simple phrase was like a physical blow, and Darcy gasped as though winded. He opened his mouth to speak but no words came forth.

'I'm sorry, Darcy. I didn't want to upset you, but I thought you had a right to know. I just couldn't keep the secret any longer – not now that I've met you.' Yvonne stood and placed her glass on the coffee table. 'I'm sure you'll need time to think this through by yourself. I'll leave you in peace.'

Yvonne was halfway out the door before Darcy found his voice. 'How old is he?'

'He's thirteen. His name is Philip.' And she closed the door behind her.

Darcy wanted to call out after her but was unsure of what he would say. The doorbell buzzer roused him from his state of incredulity. So much for a quiet night in. To his amazement he saw Afifah on the security monitor and, without thinking, buzzed her up. It wasn't until she appeared at his door that he realised something was wrong. 'Where's your chaperone?'

'I gave her the slip, but I'm wondering now why I bothered.' Afifah stormed inside and spun around to confront him. 'How *could* you, Darcy?'

This was turning into quite an evening. Darcy took a long sip of his wine before responding. 'You know you are never allowed to be alone in the presence of a man who is not a relative – even me. You must leave right now, for both our sakes. And how could I *what*?'

'What has she got that I haven't?' Afifah's green eyes darkened.

'Ah, you saw Yvonne.'

'Yes, and now she's going to tell Father that I've come here and everything will be ruined!' Afifah burst into tears and Darcy took her in his arms without thinking.

'I'll speak to her, you silly girl, but I doubt she'll be telling anyone about her visit. Please don't go around jumping to conclusions. Yvonne came to discuss a private matter, which is none of your concern, and a million miles from what you're implying.' He brushed a tear from her hot cheek.

'So . . . you're not together?'

'Not now, and not ever – she's definitely not my type.' He laughed at Afifah's wide-eyed stare. 'What's this all about, little princess?' he asked her gently, tilting her chin to look searchingly into her eyes.

'Darcy, I can't marry Jalal because I'm in love with you,' she exclaimed and burst into a fresh flood of tears.

Darcy wrapped his arm around her shoulders and led her to the sofa. He had known this would come to a head sooner or later, and he needed to act with great diplomacy. 'My dear princess, I'm not worthy of your love.'

'Don't you love me?' She looked so endearing with her tear-stained eyes and flushed face.

'You know I do, but not in the way you want. I will always be here for you and I'd give my life for you, but you and I can never be together. You know that.' He brushed the hair from her eyes.

'I can't marry Jalal,' she said with a quivering bottom lip.

'Have you spoken to your father or Bahir?' Darcy agreed with her wholeheartedly. This beautiful star should never be dimmed by such a man. Afifah nodded. 'Then if you like I'll speak to them also, on your behalf.'

Afifah looked sadly down at her hands and gave a little shiver. 'Then you can't ever love me?' she asked quietly.

'Not the way you deserve.' Darcy hugged her again and felt another shiver run through her body. 'Here, I'll get you something warmer to put on.' He stood up and went to the bedroom to get a jacket, but when he returned Afifah was gone.

Later that night Darcy tossed and turned in bed, unable to sleep. *He had a brother*. The news was shocking, but he really didn't know which part caused him the most anguish – that for all these years his brother had existed without him knowing, or that his father had kept it a secret. If Darcy acknowledged this half-sibling then Julia would discover the truth, and such a truth could well destroy their happy marriage. But if he didn't, then this little brother – Philip – would travel through life as Darcy had, alone. More than anything he wished he had someone to confide in, someone to help him through this emotional labyrinth, someone who would understand. But there was no one.

47
Government House, Melbourne

A cocktail reception in honour of the Sheikh's visit had been organised by the racing industry at Government House, set in the middle of Melbourne's glorious gardens. A collection of racing identities, politicians and businessmen were already crowding the elegant rooms when Sheikh Faisal and his party arrived.

The Governor and his wife greeted them at the impressive entrance, and the party proceeded down a line of people, shaking hands in order of official importance. By the end of the line Afifah and Clea turned to each other, trying to stifle the laughter welling up inside. The two princes and Darcy, more used to such receptions, handled the situation with great diplomacy, speaking to each person individually and warmly greeting members of the racing industry who were well known to them.

Yvonne was the last in the party and didn't appear very happy, despite the pendulous rubies large as pigeon eggs hanging from her ears. Clea made a point of approaching Yvonne as soon as the formal introductions were over, but the Sheikh's mistress was not in a mood for friendly conversation. The Sheikh was chatting amiably with some important businessmen and looked like he couldn't care less where Yvonne was.

'Take a good look,' Yvonne warned Clea, a note of bitterness in her voice. 'This is what it will be like for you, too. Bahir is wonderful and charming but don't kid yourself – you're expendable, and he will never marry you.' She drained her glass and looked around for another. 'But listen to me, I shouldn't be complaining. At least I get to travel with my man, which is more than I can say for his wife.'

'I really don't think it's quite the same for me,' Clea protested.

'Oh, really? You think you're so different? The best you can be is his mistress, and I'm here to tell you that it can be a thankless and lonely task.' The Sheikh was moving on to another group and Yvonne hurried to join him.

Clea watched her for a moment and sighed. Suddenly Bahir was beside her. 'Come here, my beautiful Dr Reynolds. I want to introduce you to some of my Australian racing friends.' He led her by the hand over to a group of people chatting with Darcy, some of whom she had already met.

'Block your ears, Bahir,' Darcy warned. 'The boys and I are having a little wager, perhaps at your expense. They say Alexander won't be fit enough for the race tomorrow and will finish out of the placings against the local horses. I beg to differ – they haven't seen what this horse is capable of.' He turned to the men. 'I'll see your fifty and raise it to a hundred-dollar stake. Who's on?'

'Not me,' said the Moonee Valley chairman. 'I'd never bet against a horse with such a tremendous Timeform rating!'

'But we don't know if he can handle your track,' the Victoria Racing Club chairman said. 'So I think you can count me in.'

Further wagering was interrupted by the Governor, who stepped onto the podium to welcome his guests. Darcy moved off to the side to collect another drink and when he turned around he saw Yvonne standing nearby. His mind was racing with questions and he wanted to know everything and nothing. He moved alongside her and was rewarded with a surprised smile.

'I have something for you,' she whispered as the Governor spoke about the Spring Racing Carnival and its importance to the city of Melbourne. Yvonne unclasped her Judith Leiber panther-shaped crystal clutch and pulled out an envelope. She quickly slipped it into Darcy's suit pocket and moved away towards the Sheikh, who was scanning the room for his mistress.

Darcy meandered casually through the crowd and slipped out a side door onto the terrace. He peered into the ballroom, a magnificent and ornate room that had accidentally been designed a foot larger than any room in Buckingham Palace, which had been a source of great pride in the new colony. He passed along a covered verandah where a few smokers greeted him hopefully. Their numbers were dwindling and extra comrades prepared to stand in the cold to get a nicotine hit were more than welcome. Darcy politely declined and moved away from their haloes of grey fog, walking across a lawn to lean against a low wall at the end of the terrace, gazing out across the darkened spring garden to the city skyline beyond.

Light spilled around him from a wrought-iron lamp, allowing him to make out the features of the young boy in the photograph he had pulled out of the envelope. Darcy stared long and hard. There was no doubting the family resemblance. All of a sudden he felt terribly alone. His world was in turmoil and the only person he wanted to confide in had chosen to be with his best friend.

'You too?' The woman in his thoughts suddenly emerged by his side.

Darcy jumped at her unexpected arrival. 'I'm out of sorts tonight,' he confessed, his heart pounding in her presence. He gazed at her beautiful face in the soft light, and admitted to himself for the first time that he was in love. 'What's your excuse?'

'Yvonne,' Clea said simply, knowing Darcy would understand. Watching a mistress in action had terrified her. Yvonne had been like a mirror held up to her face and the reflection wasn't particularly flattering.

'You know I love Bahir, but you deserve so much more than a life of playing second fiddle to an unloved wife,' Darcy said quietly.

'I'm not sure you're the best person to be giving advice about love,' Clea said indignantly. 'You seem to change women like you change your socks.'

'Only because I haven't found the right one,' Darcy answered. 'Clea, whether you believe it or not, I care about you and I don't want to see you get hurt. This relationship with Bahir isn't you.'

'Why is everyone so quick to judge me?' Clea responded angrily.

Darcy turned back to the city lights, feeling more confused than he had ever been before. 'I'm sorry, I have no right to lecture you,' he said softly. 'I just wish . . .' There was so much he wanted to say, but loyalty to his friend held his tongue. After a moment Clea walked back across the lawn and into the building.

When Darcy finally returned to the function he found Clea firmly by Bahir's side, but noticed she was drinking champagne like it was going out of fashion. He sought out Abdul's company, not wishing to disturb her further. At least he could be assured of a sensible conversation with Abdul; right now, all the women around him were bewildering.

The photo felt like it was burning a hole in his pocket, a caustic hole of betrayal, secrets and lies. Henry and Julia's marriage, which Darcy had held up as an ideal, was changed forever by Darcy's knowledge of Philip's existence. Henry had diminished in Darcy's eyes. After all these years, he still didn't have the courage to deal with his illegitimate son. Darcy wondered if his mother's breakdown had anything to do with the way his father had handled the situation.

Yvonne had been a young woman when she bore Henry a son in secret, and what a mess it had made of her life; she was surrounded by all the trappings of wealth, but had no real love. And Philip didn't have a father.

Darcy found Abdul quietly sipping juice in a corner and

breathed a sigh of relief. 'Tell me something about horses, Abdul, I'm sick of people.'

'They have very good memories,' Abdul answered thoughtfully, his mind far away.

Darcy glanced at him sharply, realising Abdul was also caught up in his own world.

'Do you know when Jalal is due to arrive?' Abdul asked.

'He arrives tonight, but the flight from Hong Kong gets in late, otherwise I'm sure he'd be here.' The thought of Jalal sticking to Bahir's side like glue suddenly irritated Darcy. 'He wouldn't miss an opportunity to be part of the Sheikh's entourage if he could help it.'

Abdul snorted in agreement, then after a moment asked, 'Is the princess all right? I hate to see her so sad.'

Darcy could see, even from a distance, that Afifah wasn't her usual bubbly self. It was as if the lightness of youth had taken flight and left her anchored to the ground. Nonetheless, she was radianat in a Chloé white crystal-embroidered shift dress that glittered in the chandelier light.

'I followed her the other night,' Abdul said simply, and put a hand on Darcy's arm. 'I trust you, Darcy, but others might not, and she would be the one to suffer.'

'Thank you, Abdul. Believe me when I say I only have her best interests at heart . . . She's the sister I never had,' he answered honestly. But this wasn't a conversation Darcy wanted to have now. His emotions were bubbling away just under the surface, and he was fuelling them with wine as the drinks waiter did another sweep of the room. Darcy knew it was time to leave. He said a few goodbyes as he finished off his glass, carefully avoiding Bahir and Clea.

The cool night air was a welcome relief and Darcy went home the way he had come, on foot, across the damp lawns of Kings Domain gardens. The homeward journey was like his life; there were plenty of well-lit, easy paths, but Darcy always seemed to choose the darker, more difficult way home.

Staring out restlessly across the city from his penthouse, he decided to go back to Royal Towers, although he wasn't sure why. He was unsettled in his apartment and walked to the hotel, hoping to bump into Clea. Instead, it was Bahir he met in the hotel foyer, chatting with other members of the entourage who had also left the party.

'Darcy! We lost you,' Bahir exclaimed. 'Are you coming to join us for a coffee? Clea's already gone to bed, I'm afraid, but Jalal has arrived; I'm going straight up to meet him.'

Darcy saw his chance. 'No, I'm just catching up with someone at the bar,' he lied. 'I'll see you all tomorrow.' He watched as they entered the lift up to the Platinum Club. As soon as the door closed, he picked up the house phone and dialled Bahir's villa.

'Could I come up for a moment, please?' he said when Clea answered. 'I need to talk to you.'

In a moment the lift doors opened to reveal Clea, still in her evening dress. She swiped the security key to reach the villa, pressed the lift button and turned to look at him. It was obvious she'd had a few too many drinks, but her voice was clear.

'I don't even know why I agreed to let you up. Surely it could wait until tomorrow?' The lift arrived and she unlocked the door to the villa, turning on a few lights.

'I'm sorry. But I didn't know who else to turn to,' Darcy said. He reached into his pocket and pulled out the photograph, handing it to Clea.

'Who is this?'

'My brother.'

'I didn't know you had a brother,' she said, sitting on the sofa.

'That's the point. Neither did I, until last night when Yvonne told me. Clea, I don't know what to think – I'm so angry with my father. I just can't believe he'd keep such a secret for all these years and deceive everyone – me, Julia and this boy Philip.'

'This is Yvonne's child?' Clea asked in surprise. 'What are you going to do?'

'I don't know. If I acknowledge my own brother now, Julia will know the truth and it would break her heart. For all these years, I thought their relationship was amazing, but it's all been a lie – a terrible lie.' Darcy sat next to her, his shoulders slumped.

'You have to speak to your father.' It was the only advice Clea could give. She suddenly realised how lucky she had been to grow up with her brothers. It would have been so lonely without them.

Darcy took the photo from her hand. 'When I look at him I see myself, and I know I can't just turn my back. He's my brother, my flesh and blood.'

'Then I think you know what you have to do.' Clea looked towards the door and Darcy caught the gesture.

'I should leave. It's just that . . .' He stopped at the door and gazed into her eyes. A moment of electricity passed between them and he knew that if he kissed her, she wouldn't resist. 'Clea . . .' Their lips met softly, and when Darcy felt her body relax momentarily in his arms, he was completely overwhelmed with the intensity of his feelings and crushed her body against the wall with his muscular frame.

His masculine scent was powerful and Clea's temples were throbbing so she couldn't think straight. 'Darcy!' She pushed him away.

'I'm sorry,' he mumbled, and opened the door. 'You're probably not going to like this, Clea, but I'm falling in love with you.'

Clea pushed the door gently closed behind him and leaned against the wall, shaking her head in disbelief.

Abdul couldn't rest knowing Jalal was somewhere in the hotel. He resigned himself to another sleepless night and paced his room, flicking irritably at the television channels. Finally he settled down at his laptop and logged in to deal with emails from all over the world.

Apart from the daily stud reports, an email had arrived from Weatherbys Insurance, one of the largest brokers in equine bloodstock. It detailed the insurance payout for the two horses struck down in the UK: Sampson, owned one hundred per cent by

Eclipse Stud, had been insured for twelve million pounds, and Drake, owned fifty-fifty with Jalal, had been insured for ten million. Abdul stood up and did another circuit of the room, feeling stifled in this box in the sky. Was it just a coincidence that two horses part-owned by Jalal – Bismarck and now Drake – had been killed by the deliberately administered hendra? He dismissed the speculation. Dr Reynolds had discovered the powder containing the virus in Sampson's stable and no traces of it in Drake's. It was unthinkable that a man so close to Abdul's adopted family could consider slaughtering his own champion horses. But there was one key connection that was troubling him – if he could only find the answer. He settled back at the computer. Abdul had to think clearly and remain focused on the critical issue for him, which had nothing to do with hendra or EI. It was personal. Jalal would pay for the crimes of his father, but if Abdul happened to find evidence that his hand had struck down the stallions, Jalal would pay even more dearly.

48

Cox Plate Day, Moonee Valley Racing Club, Melbourne

Prince Bahir couldn't get back to sleep. He had awoken at 4.30 a.m. from a nightmare and it took a while to shake off its lingering, clinging fear. A deep sense of foreboding settled over him like a miasma. Fear made him restless and he eventually climbed out of bed, careful not to wake Clea, made himself a plunger coffee and switched the television to CNN to see what was happening in the world.

In a morbid way, he was hoping some catastrophe had struck somewhere that could explain the intensity of the feeling in the pit of his stomach. But the world seemed to have survived the last twelve hours without major mishap. Yet something was wrong.

At 6.30 Bahir went down to the gym to take his mind off his fear, then swam a few fast laps in the pool. Back in the villa he was about to wake Clea, but decided against it. She probably needed the sleep. He rang Jalal and suggested they breakfast together, then dialled room service and ordered up a selection of delicious food.

Clea was awake, but kept her eyes closed. Her head was pounding from too much champagne the night before and she couldn't face Bahir – not yet. She replayed Darcy's declaration of love over and over in her head, wondering if she had encouraged him in some way. The kiss had surprised her more than she liked to admit. It had felt so natural, and she knew she had responded. But it was wrong. She was with Bahir, and any new feelings she had for Darcy had to be suppressed.

Later that morning, after a quick breakfast, Clea chose from her rapidly expanding wardrobe a pale blue dress by local designer John Cavill. Both the dress and matching cropped jacket had pleated detailing and she teamed them with a navy pillbox hat and accessories. Her hair was swept up into a chignon, caught at the nape of her neck with a silver clasp. Clea stared at herself in the mirror. A few months ago, she would have laughed to think she would own an outfit like this, let alone have somewhere to wear it.

Bahir wore a smart charcoal-grey suit with a pale blue striped shirt and a floral tie. 'We match!' he exclaimed when he walked into the bathroom as she was applying her lipstick. 'Anyone would think we did it deliberately. You look beautiful.' He kissed her freshly painted mouth.

Afifah, Basmah and Khalid were already sipping tea in the Platinum Club when they arrived. Afifah jumped up and hugged her brother. 'Well, look at you! Don't you look marvellous!' Bahir made her spin around to show off her outfit, a Zac Posen fitted silk dress in sunshine yellow that perfectly highlighted her olive complexion. Her long hair cascaded down her back in soft curls, and she grabbed her yellow and black detailed hat to show him the full effect.

'Bellissima!' He kissed her forehead.

'Tell her she shouldn't show her arms off like that – you look like you belong on the streets,' Khalid sneered from the sofa. Afifah pulled a face at him and looked at Bahir hopefully.

'While I think you look enchanting, it might pay to put something more on before Father gets here,' Bahir said grudgingly.

'I'm already here,' Sheikh Faisal said. He escorted Yvonne into the room. She looked striking in a cream and black striped blazer with black pencil skirt by Ralph Lauren. 'Afifah, put something on your arms immediately,' he commanded.

'Yes, Father,' Afifah said flatly, and put on a crossover semi-sheer top in yellow and black that tied at the back.

'I think that makes the outfit even more elegant,' Bahir said warmly to diffuse the situation.

Jalal arrived looking fresh and ready for the races, and complimented Afifah on her appearance, insisting she do another half-hearted twirl for him. The moment was awkward – Sheikh Faisal had yet to speak to Jalal about his marriage, and Afifah was afraid he wouldn't.

The Sheikh's security guard appeared at exactly 11.30 and escorted the party to the private lobby, from where they were ushered into a number of cars. The procession moved off with two motorcycle policemen behind and in front.

'Is it always such a palaver when you all go to the racetrack?' Clea couldn't help asking Bahir.

'No, sometimes we're way down the list of important dignitaries – and I have to say I prefer it that way. But today we're the main act – we've got the flags flying for Dubai and Qatar,' he replied.

Moonee Valley Racecourse was an oasis of green in the thick of suburbia. From the vantage of the grandstand it was easy to appreciate the land value: there were close to forty hectares bordered by dense urban housing on three sides and a freeway that streamed cars twenty-four seven. The view of the city skyline only a few kilometres to the south was inspiring. And it was here on this hallowed amphitheatre that equine history was remade each year in the Cox Plate – a Weight for Age race won only by champions. The names of the past winners were emblazoned in the collective memory of the track – Phar Lap, Kingston Town, Sunline, Makybe Diva, all horses that had climbed to the apex of thoroughbred achievement and equine immortality.

Anticipation sat heavy in the air; like sweet jasmine on the breath of summer, it was exciting and intoxicating. The crowds streaming into the track were here to see the horses. The purists and the punters alike were waiting for the moment when the gates burst open and sent a field of Australia's best horses flying onto the track with a deafening roar. Moonee Valley was the colosseum for this time-honoured race.

All eyes watched the mounting yard, eager for a clue: a nod

from a jockey, a sign from the horse. Fitness, strength and attitude were all balanced up in the search for The Winner, an elusive horse that lurked in every race field.

The Sheikh and his group were guests of the Moonee Valley Committee and dined in the committee room, which was crowded with excited dignitaries, racing industry heads and guests. Every year, Darcy was invited by one of his friends on the committee and had brought Tom along as his partner for the day. He was exchanging tips with the club treasurer when the Sheikh's party arrived. He excused himself to speak to Clea.

'You look very beautiful today,' he said quietly, so only she could hear. But Clea smiled sadly without acknowledging his words and moved back to Bahir's side before Darcy could apologise for his behaviour the night before.

The Sheikh and Yvonne were seated with the club chairman and his elegant wife while Bahir, Clea, Jalal, Afifah and Khalid were all positioned at the vice-chairman's table.

Darcy was in agony. He had to speak to Clea, but how? In a moment of desperation he scribbled a note on the back of a race ticket and dropped it in Clea's handbag when she left it on the seat while watching a race. But on her return, she pulled the ticket out in confusion, thinking it had fallen in by mistake, and placed it on a pile of losing tickets without reading Darcy's note.

Two races later, Bahir was feeling embarrassed by the betting tickets piling up on the table and picked them up, walking towards a rubbish bin. He flicked through a few to ensure they weren't winners, and spotted Darcy's note: *I have to see you, please. I can't stop thinking about you – Darcy.*

Bahir looked across at Afifah, who was talking to Darcy over by the coffee machine. This was getting serious. They had clearly organised a meeting. Bahir's brow creased in anger. He would speak to Darcy that afternoon before Afifah was compromised.

When the Tatts Cox Plate finally came around at 4 p.m., the club chairman led the party down to the mounting yard at the back of the grandstand, surrounded by windows full of racegoers all eager to see the champions parade.

Alexander the Great wore the number one saddlecloth and emerged from the pre-parade area first, with Abdul hot on his heels. Trainer John Gallows spoke animatedly to the Sheikh about the horse's condition as they watched Alexander's chestnut coat glistening in the spring sunshine like polished copper. Jockey Derek joined them, sporting the Sheikh's racing colours with great pride. 'From barrier six I'm hoping to go with them at the start and settle midfield. This is always a truly run race and I can't let them get away from me, so I'll be up there when we enter the straight,' he assured Sheikh Faisal.

At the signal for the riders to mount up, John and Derek strolled between the horses onto the lawn in the middle of the mounting enclosure. Alexander started to dance around on his toes as Derek approached and wouldn't stand still, despite Abdul's coaxing. Regardless, John grabbed Derek's leg and expertly heaved him into the saddle. Alexander momentarily reared but Derek soon had him in check and after a few more circuits of the yard they led the field out onto the track. As soon as his hoofs touched the turf Alexander wanted to be off, but Derek had him hard held with the horse's magnificent neck arched over and muscles rippling.

'I think I need a hand,' Derek called out to one of the stewards. 'But watch out, he's entire,' he added, referring to the horse's status as a stallion.

The steward manoeuvered his grey horse alongside, then ducked out of the way when Alexander pulled his ears back in displeasure and tried to bite the older horse. But Alexander began to settle down as they trotted down the straight to the starting gates at the 2040-metre mark, the presence of the older horse keeping him calm.

A crack field of ten horses was lining up for the year's ultimate contest, each of them not only a top performer at Group One level but also top earners, thanks to prize money. One by one these experienced athletes were led into the barriers until the field was set and the lights flashed on the barriers.

The gates were flung open and the crowd roared with deafening excitement as the horses took up a position and galloped past the winning post for the first time. Alexander was against the rails travelling three back, and had his head down in a relaxed fashion. All binoculars were trained on the race.

But a Weight for Age race at Group One level was never an easy prospect, and no sooner had Alexander settled than one of the local favourites applied pressure by going to the lead and pulling away by three lengths. The local jockeys knew this game well and spurred their mounts up to the tearaway, making sure the lead was shortened. At the turn into the straight the field fanned out in spectacular fashion across the track, a row of champions storming home to catch victory. Derek looked over both shoulders quickly to gauge where his main rivals sat and took Alexander up to top pace in the mad sprint home. Three horses pulled away at breakneck speed with 200 metres to go. Alexander was in the middle, and to the cheers of the crowd he stepped up a gear and exploded to the winning post, claiming victory by a convincing one and a half lengths.

Bahir grabbed Clea and whirled her around with elation before planting a firm kiss on her lips. The chairman escorted the group down to the winning circle just as Alexander the Great entered calmly and Derek flung himself off the horse in a victory star jump.

'Look at him,' Abdul said beaming, and turned to Sheikh Faisal. 'He's so fit he wouldn't blow out a candle!' Sure enough, the horse looked like he'd just gone around in a Class Three race, his recovery was so quick.

Clea joined in the photos and celebrations, but suddenly felt out of place. Darcy's stolen kiss had disturbed her more than she'd realised. She didn't belong in this world, and when everyone was watching the race replay for the fifth time, she slipped away to sit quietly by herself. Bahir caught up with her back in the committee room, brandishing the famed Tatts Cox Plate in silver with gold mounts.

'Where did you disappear to?' he chastised.

'Bahir, I don't know if I can do this,' Clea murmured.

'Here you are, another celebratory drink and a famous Australian party pie.' Jalal interrupted them and handed Bahir a glass of mineral water and a pie with tomato sauce. 'I can get you one too, Clea, if you'd like,' he suggested politely but she shook her head, annoyed by his presence.

Bahir took a bite out of the pie, declared it was too hot but delicious, and put down his plate to wait for the pie to cool. Suddenly his face flushed and he reached out a hand to steady himself from a wave of dizziness. 'Would you please excuse me?' He walked to the bathroom with Jalal following.

'Are you all right?' his friend asked as the prince leaned on the sink gulping in air.

'Peanuts, there were peanuts . . . Get help,' he managed to stammer out as he felt in his pockets and pulled out his EpiPen, an autoinjector of adrenaline, which he needed desperately to halt the onset of anaphylactic shock. Jalal didn't move.

'Ambulance,' Bahir gasped as his airways went into bronchospasm. He pulled the pen out of its storage tube and stared in disbelief at the indicator window that showed red – it was empty. He collapsed to his knees clutching at his throat.

Darcy suddenly opened the bathroom door and almost knocked Jalal off his feet. Within seconds he had assessed the situation. 'We need an ambulance now!' he shouted to anyone who could hear. 'Khalid!'

At that moment Khalid rushed to the bathroom, took one look at his brother, who was leaning against Darcy on the floor struggling to breathe, and pulled an EpiPen from his own pocket. He jabbed it hard into Bahir's outer thigh until the indicator window showed it had done its work. All three of them held their breath as they watched Bahir's face turn from blue to red, and slowly back to normal. Within a minute Bahir was able to breath, albeit raggedly, as the adrenaline acted to open his constricted airways.

The ambulance crew arrived soon after and whisked Bahir off with sirens blazing, his father insisting on travelling with him.

Jalal and Khalid stood side by side watching the retreating ambulance. 'Thank God you were here.' Jalal patted Khalid on the back. 'I didn't realise you carried a back-up for your brother – a clever move.'

Khalid looked distressed as they climbed into one of the cars to follow Bahir to hospital. 'Don't you know I also have a severe peanut allergy? That could have just as easily been me.'

Abdul sat in the passenger seat in silence, nursing the coveted Cox Plate. He dared not turn around and look at Jalal in the back for fear his hatred would show. Where the police had failed, Abdul had finally traced the elusive Zayd Farouk. The name had rung a bell, but it had taken a long time to figure out the connection. Abdul was sure Zayd was the tough young man who had been Jalal's groomsman for his endurance horses. Abdul knew every key horseman in Dubai, and had been able to confirm it at last. Zayd must have received the stolen viruses and taken them on board the boat in France. Perhaps he had even tested hendra on the prostitute to ensure it was as lethal as promised. Abdul wondered if Jalal had also been on the boat.

The puzzle was almost complete now, and there was only one question remaining for Abdul. Was the son the product of his murderous father – had he tried to kill Bahir? One thing Abdul did know for certain: this blood feud begun in the Saudi Arabian desert village of Khadelem would end here in Melbourne.

Yvonne and Clea were still at the racetrack, as was Darcy, so Darcy contacted his driver to collect them. He escorted the two women back to the hotel in a tense silence. He desperately hoped Clea would respond to his message, even now, but Yvonne's presence prevented any intimate conversation. He dropped the women at the hotel and continued on to the hospital.

Darcy was never a big fan of hospitals – they made him acutely aware of the vulnerability of the human body. Sheikh Faisal was still sitting with Bahir, who was hooked up to an IV drip and being carefully monitored for a rebound reaction, common after anaphylactic shock.

'I'll sit with him for a while,' Darcy suggested. The Sheikh took the opportunity to go in search of a decent cup of coffee and make a few phone calls, leaving the two old friends together.

'I only remember this happening once before – do you recall? We were about twenty-two at the Kentucky yearling sales and you had a piece of chocolate that must have contained peanuts in one of the hospitality areas. That's when you told me Khalid suffered from the same allergy.' Darcy settled into the chair by the bed.

'Thank God he was there.' Bahir smiled weakly.

'I didn't realise they put peanuts in our meat pies – water buffalo, kangaroo and camel I can imagine, but not peanuts,' Darcy joked. 'I know you're normally so careful. Who would have guessed a pie would contain peanuts?'

Bahir was silent for a while, his mind turning over. 'Something isn't right, Darcy. I check my adrenaline pen regularly. It was full only a few days ago but when I suddenly needed it – empty.'

'Could you accidentally have released it somewhere along the line?'

'It's virtually impossible. It has its own case.' Bahir turned his head and looked out the window at the evening sky. 'It was the way he stood there,' he continued quietly.

Darcy knew immediately. 'Jalal?'

'He didn't call for help, he just stood there. Darcy, could it be possible this whole thing was orchestrated?' Bahir asked in a hushed tone, as though even saying the words out loud would give them more significance.

'But *why*? You've been friends all your life, why would he do that?'

'When he spoke to me about Afifah, I saw such rage in him. It was only for a fleeting moment, but it was there, Darcy. It scared me.'

Darcy was shocked. 'What could he hope to achieve by killing you? It doesn't make any sense.'

'I told him I'd give him a few weeks to change Afifah's mind before I spoke to my father about calling the wedding off. If

I were dead, there'd be no one to protect her interests and persuade Father to release her from the marriage.' Bahir gripped the white sheets of his narrow hospital bed.

'I know he's always been in love with Afifah, but murder is a rather dramatic way to solve the problem, don't you think?'

'There is one other thing,' Bahir said. 'Father has promised he will get Jalal the shipping contracts out of Qatar, once the marriage goes ahead. It's a very lucrative business.'

'I see.' Darcy hadn't realised there was a financial incentive behind the marriage.

'I want you to look into it,' Bahir pleaded. 'I might be overreacting, but . . . please keep him away from me.'

Darcy promised he would do what he could, and was about to leave his friend to rest when Bahir put a hand on his arm. 'Darcy, Jalal's jealousy of you – does it have any foundation? If you're in love with my sister I might have some influence with my father —'

'Influence with me over what?' Sheikh Faisal walked into the hospital room.

'We were just talking horses, Father. I'll fill you in later.' Bahir hastily covered the true nature of their conversation.

Unable to tell Bahir his real feelings, Darcy stood to leave. It would have to wait – there were more pressing matters.

49
Darcy's Penthouse, Melbourne

Darcy poured a single malt whisky over three ice cubes and swirled the glass, deep in thought. Darcy had never really liked Jalal, but considering him a murderer was a totally different story. Reconciling the action with the history was almost impossible, so he decided to break the mystery down into pieces. He called Abdul first and checked how much Jalal had received from the insurance on his two horses put down due to the hendra. Bismarck had been insured for twenty million pounds and Drake for ten million. Jalal's collect was fifteen million pounds in total, but it still made no sense when his family was so wealthy. It seemed that whoever was responsible for the hendra also had a plan for spreading equine influenza, and Darcy couldn't work out what Jalal stood to gain from this.

The ice in Darcy's glass cracked as the alcohol warmed. Darcy took a sip and then froze. Jalal had flown to Australia with a stopover in Hong Kong, long enough to visit the racing stables. But why Hong Kong? What could Jalal be trying to do?

He sat down and tried to think through the facts logically. There was no point sending the police in the UK on a wild-goose chase. Jalal had been present at both horse studs when the infections occurred. Additionally, he could have accessed Bahir's EpiPen easily. A tiny trace of peanut or peanut oil was enough to send the highly allergic Bahir into deadly anaphylactic shock.

The computer pinged into readiness when he switched it on. He checked his emails quickly and was about to close his inbox when a subject line caught his eye. He opened the email, which was from the Kensington jeweller he'd contacted weeks ago about his watch. *I have found the owner of Frederique Constant Tourbillon number 188, a wealthy Hong Kong gentleman who owns casinos in Macau. My sources inform me he is very unlikely to sell. So far I haven't been able to trace the number eighty-eight. Please let me know how you would like to proceed.*

Darcy considered the implications of the information for a moment. There was his answer, staring him in the face.

He typed Salah al Din's name into Google. A few newspaper articles and a Wikipedia entry turned up, and after scrolling through he found what he wanted. It was an article from the *Wall Street Journal* in early September 2008 on the collapse of Lehman Brothers Holdings. Darcy quickly scanned the article until he found the brief reference he needed: *Lehman Brothers lists amongst its major investors the Muntasir family from the UAE, whose global transport empire is now under threat.*

Darcy picked up his mobile and dialled Inspector Sutherland at Scotland Yard. He quickly explained recent events and the conclusions he and Bahir were drawing.

The officer listened carefully, taking notes. 'We can have a look into the company finances from this end and see if your suspicions are right,' he suggested. The case had been baffling Scotland Yard and the inspector was grateful for Darcy's help.

Two tense hours later Darcy leapt as the phone rang and almost upset his second glass of whisky, which was balancing precariously on the arm of the sofa. Scotland Yard had come back with the goods. Salah al Din's fortunes had sunk when Lehman Brothers became the first major casualty of the global financial crisis. His vast transport company struggled to secure any financing and was now being broken up and sold off to try and save the core shipping division. In mid-July even this crucial mainstay of the business was threatened with receivership, but two injections of cash, amounting to fifteen million pounds, had come through since to stave off the inevitable collapse. This had bought some time but nothing more.

Darcy explained his own investigation with the watch, and the link between Jalal and Hong Kong.

'I still don't see the connection,' Inspector Sutherland said.

'But there's a very strong one – you just have to understand how the gaming industry operates,' Darcy said excitedly. 'If equine influenza struck the Hong Kong horse population they'd go down like flies. Because of the way the horses are housed, it would be almost impossible to stop it spreading. Racing would be closed for at least three months, maybe more, and the Jockey Club would lose a fortune in betting.'

'I was under the impression the Jockey Club was very wealthy, so while it might affect its short-term profitability, given its large cash reserves surely it could withstand the downturn and be in a strong position to recover quickly,' the inspector countered.

'You're right,' Darcy agreed. 'But have a think about all the money that would normally be bet on the races. We all know gambling is the lifeblood of Hong Kong, so do you think the punters would just sit tight and wait for the races to resume?'

'The casinos in Macau,' Sutherland breathed.

'Exactly. Gaming went up in Australia with the EI outbreak in 2007, and yet that outbreak only affected two states once Victoria was cleared. Imagine what it would do to the casino-take in Macau if all Hong Kong racing ceased. Only problem is, I don't have a link to Jalal or his father yet.' Darcy knew it was the most crucial piece of evidence.

'That's what we're here for,' said Sutherland. 'In the meantime, I think it's time we got the local police involved, don't you?'

When the Victorian police arrived at Jalal's room with a search warrant a few hours later, he was still out. A thorough search of the room turned up nothing until the officer in charge asked the accompanying hotel representative to print out Jalal's account.

While they were waiting for him to return, the officer received a call from Scotland Yard. Their speedy investigation had uncovered the issuing of an onerous debt in the form of a convertible note. The note had the option to convert into a large ownership share of the Muntasir shipping company upon certain conditions. The convertible note was issued to the largest shareholder of a Macau casino conglomerate.

The hotel representative returned within a few minutes with Jalal's full account that included purchases from the mini-bar – a sports drink, a chocolate bar and one packet of peanuts. It wasn't much to go on, but Darcy searched through Jalal's clothing to find the suit worn to the racetrack that day. It was missing. The detective dialled housekeeping and found the suit had been sent downstairs that evening for dry cleaning.

The suit was still sitting in the laundry in a pile of clothes waiting for the morning shift. It was retrieved and quickly checked. There were traces of crushed peanuts deep in the jacket pocket, and it would only take a few crumbs to set off an allergic reaction.

Oblivious to the process instigated in his room, Jalal was at that moment sitting with Sheikh Faisal in his villa for supper at the Sheikh's request.

'I need to discuss a rather delicate matter,' the Sheikh began, and Jalal's heart sank. 'It's Afifah. I hear you two had an argument not long ago?' The Sheikh had always been fond of Jalal and it hurt him to break the engagement.

'I can explain —' Jalal began, but the Sheikh raised his hand for silence.

'I don't profess to know what goes on in the mind of my daughter, or any other woman for that matter. But I do know she's unhappy and I must do everything in my power as a father to make her happy again.'

Jalal looked so downcast the Sheikh almost changed his mind, but then remembered how earnestly Bahir had entreated him on Afifah's behalf. There would be many more suitable husbands for such a fine catch as his daughter. 'I'm very sorry, son – you know I look upon you as part of this family, but I'm afraid that I have to annul the betrothal. Perhaps you two can sort it out between yourselves, but until then, I feel compelled to back my daughter's wishes.'

Jalal was close to tears and couldn't bring himself to say anything at first. Everything he had ever hoped for was being wrenched from his grasp, and he clung to it like a drowning man to a life raft. 'Afifah will never find someone who loves her as much as I do. I've always loved her. I would die for her.'

'I know,' the Sheikh said sadly. 'But you must see that your marriage to her, such as it is now, would bring nothing but pain. You'll find another suitable woman who will return your affection, and I'll make sure I help you. It's the least I can do.' Sheikh Faisal stood up to signal that the meeting was over but Jalal sat frozen to his chair, as though his worst nightmare would become reality the moment he walked from the room. The Sheikh quietly picked up some papers and moved into the study, closing the door behind him.

Tears of shame stung Jalal's eyes. What could he tell his

father, who was already so burdened by the catastrophe unfolding with his business? This was Darcy's fault – he had seduced Afifah and turned her against him, and now he would pay the price. He reached into his pocket and touched a small glass vial. He wished the second vial was in his pocket right now too, but he had already disposed of it.

Not wishing to bump into anyone, Jalal moved through the function room floor of the hotel and out into the casino. He didn't register the police cars parked at the entrance as he strode through the cavernous room full of blinking lights and electronic music and leapt into a taxi at the opposite end of the casino.

The Ambrose-Taylor stables were at Flemington Racecourse and Jalal instructed the taxi driver to drop him at the pub on the corner of Epsom Road. He continued to the stables on foot. He listened carefully by the high brush fence and, hearing nothing more than the night-time noises of the equine occupants inside, stealthily scaled the fence and dropped onto the lawn on the other side.

He waited again, every muscle tense, until he was sure the stables were all quiet. Then keeping to the shadows, he crossed the lawn, avoiding the stable office, and disappeared into the horse complex. It only took him a moment in the moonlight that filtered through the airy building to pull out the vial and feed some of the powdery contents to three of the Ambrose-Taylor horses, sprinkling it on his hand and allowing them to lick the salty substance with their fat pink tongues. Jalal didn't even notice the security camera recording his every movement.

He was back out in the driveway, walking quickly past the other stable offices, when a familiar noise caught his attention. That fool Abdul was singing to his horses again. In a snap decision, he resolved to take his vial to the Sheikh's horses as well. It would seem like the virus had eluded the quarantine process yet again. Abdul would never know.

Jalal pushed the gate and it swung in, unlocked. A light glowed from the stable doors into the night and a horse called out to him from the first row of stables. The singing stopped suddenly.

50

Flemington Stables, Melbourne

Abdul's heightened night-time senses picked up a soft footfall and he backed into a dark corner of the stable, putting Alexander the Great's bulk between himself and the door. The light he had switched on to check the condition of Alexander's hoof gave away his presence.

'Abdul? I know you're in here somewhere, I heard you singing.' It was Jalal's voice.

Abdul's heart started to pound, and sensing his reaction Alexander pawed the ground restlessly.

'I wanted to see how Alexander pulled up after his run today, so I could report to Bahir first thing in the morning,' Jalal lied.

Abdul stepped from behind the horse and opened the stable door. 'See for yourself.' He behaved as though this meeting late at night were perfectly normal. 'I think the hoof is standing up well – he may even be able to compete in the Emirates Stakes on the final day of the carnival here at Flemington on Saturday week.'

Jalal entered the stable and peered down at the hoof in the straw. 'You've done quite well for yourself with Bismarck and Drake,' Abdul said cryptically. 'Not bad for a man born in Khadelem.'

Jalal physically recoiled at the name of his birthplace, for so long a secret that it was a shock to hear the village name spoken out loud. 'What nonsense are you talking? I was born in Riyadh and I've lived in Dubai for most of my life,' he said warily. Jalal had always questioned his father's reason for keeping the secret – was he about to find out the truth?

'Of course, you were only a baby when your parents fled, so you wouldn't remember the place, but I do,' Abdul said, almost to himself.

'I don't know what you're talking about.' Jalal went to step out of the stable but Abdul blocked his way. 'Let me pass,' Jalal insisted, but Abdul firmly shut the stable door.

'And I suppose you know nothing of the hendra virus outbreaks and a plot to spread EI? Your plan was never destined to work, Jalal. The Hong Kong horses were vaccinated weeks ago against the strain of EI you stole.'

Jalal froze. How did Abdul know so much? And if what he said were true, Jalal's business was finished. Without the money from the casino deal, there was nothing standing between his family and financial ruin. His father would be destroyed, and he, Jalal, could do nothing to save him.

Abdul's voice was full of bitterness and anger. 'Have you never questioned the secret of your birthplace? Or why you bear so little resemblance to your mother?'

'My mother? What has she got to do with this?' Jalal exclaimed, confused and angry. He would tear apart anyone who slandered his beloved mother.

'Your mother is dead. She was killed a long time ago.' Abdul spoke calmly, although every nerve in his body was on edge.

'You lie.' Jalal lunged at Abdul with a fist raised but the horse man dodged behind Alexander the Great. 'My mother is alive and well in Dubai,' Jalal said through gritted teeth.

'No, she died at the hands of your father in Khadelem – I saw it all.' Abdul moved to stroke Alexander's head as he shifted restlessly around the box, sensing the building antagonism.

'Why are you telling me these lies?' Jalal implored, the bewilderment evident in his face.

'You're just like your father, a vicious murderer. First you killed the horses who had showered you in glory for the insurance money. You learnt when you killed Bismarck that the stablemate would be sure to become infected as well. So you fed the virus to Sampson the second time, not Drake, knowing that Drake was sure to be put down as well.

'I can understand why you tried to infect Dr Reynolds when she started to piece together the facts, but why did you try to kill Bahir? What did he ever do to warrant your murderous intentions?' All Abdul's pent-up hatred shone through his eyes in that moment.

'You have no proof for your wild accusations and I refuse to listen to any more.' Jalal went to pull open the stable door but Alexander shifted and blocked his retreat.

Abdul's voice remained even, but there was an undertone of hysteria that frightened Jalal. 'You come from the blood of a murderer. I saw your father kill both my mother and father with his own hands. The woman who calls herself your mother didn't stop him. She wanted you for herself.'

Jalal was confused. 'I don't understand.'

'Your father's wife – the woman you know as your mother – was barren. *My* mother was forced to bear a son for your father. You and I are of the same blood.'

Jalal lunged for the stable door again, and this time managed to pull it open, but Abdul was upon him in a flash, grabbing his shirt. 'There's nowhere your family can run to now. Your father is a murderer and will be locked up in prison where he belongs until the day he dies,' he taunted.

Jalal was overwhelmed by rage and fear. He spun around to face his tormentor. Alexander had escaped his stable and was trotting up and down the barn in agitation. Jalal glimpsed a metal object resting on the stable ledge and lunged for it before Abdul could stop him. Abdul's knife with the carved handle fitted comfortably in Jalal's hand and he crouched, ready to lunge. He had lost everything.

'I see you have your father's instincts.' Abdul looked around for a suitable weapon to defend himself but all tools had been carefully put away by the staff.

Jalal pounced on him, and as Abdul deflected the deadly strike the knife cut deeply into his forearm. Blood seeped out and stained his clothes. Once more he searched frantically for a defensive object.

'Your knowledge will go with you to the grave, Abdul – and the grave is silent.' Jalal attacked again, and as Abdul struggled to avoid the blade it connected with his shoulder. His right arm was immobilised by the two wounds and hung at his side, dripping blood, while Jalal regained his balance for a final strike.

Abdul could hear Alexander's hoofs clattering on the pavement outside the barn as he wandered around the stable compound. It was Abdul's last chance, and he desperately called the powerful chestnut horse back into the barn, where Alexander caught the scent of blood. It triggered an instinctive reaction and Alexander reared in the air, tossing his head aggressively as Jalal moved in on Abdul again.

Sensing the danger, the horse reared again and struck out with his forelegs, knocking the knife from Jalal's hands and breaking his right wrist with the impact. Jalal howled in pain and frustration and dropped to the ground to retrieve his weapon, holding it less surely in his left hand. He hurled himself at Abdul, who twisted away from the knife only enough for the trajectory to miss his chest. The weapon plunged into his side, sending more blood flowing. Jalal pulled the knife back out, his eyes blazing with fury, but he hesitated for a moment in front of the defenceless man.

Abdul had no strength left to fight Jalal off, and staggered up against a stable door. With an effort he straightened up and carefully uttered a proverb in his mother tongue. *'The knife of the family does not cut.* Remember, you are my brother, Jalal.'

Alexander reared behind Jalal and he turned in terror, his arms no use against the stallion's mighty bulk. He was knocked to the ground and cowered as the horse lashed out with his white hoof. The sound of bone cracking rang out over Alexander's enraged roar and a stream of blood trickled down Jalal's forehead as he lay motionless on the stable floor. Abdul dropped to the ground next to him and held his head.

'Your father robbed me of my family,' he hissed. 'But in doing so he led me to a new one.' Abdul looked around the barn at all the horses watching over their stable doors. One after another the horses called out, their voices shrill with the sense of danger and the smell of blood.

Abdul collapsed next to Jalal, blood seeping from his wounds. Alexander stood quietly by Abdul's side nudging his prostrate body gently as security guards rushed into the stables to check on the commotion.

51

Derby Day, Victoria Racing Club, Melbourne

Clea tested the powder found in a vial on Jalal's body and determined it to be equine influenza. Her program of vaccinations for the Newmarket serotype of EI had proven successful. Of the forty-two horses in the Ambrose-Taylor stable, only two tested positive to the virus while the others showed signs of an immune response in their white blood cells. But with the Spring Racing Carnival in full swing, no risks were taken.

The stables were placed under full quarantine, strict protocols were observed by staff and a tight ring of security surrounded the formerly active stables. Tom and Darcy were devastated their horses would not be able to compete for the carnival riches, but they knew there was always another race to be run.

The other Flemington stables were initially quarantined as well, but rigorous blood testing failed to turn up any evidence of the virus. Although the other stables' horses missed a few mornings of track work, they were deemed fit to race in the four-day Melbourne Cup Carnival.

Abdul's wounds were deep, but he was soon out of hospital on handfuls of antibiotics to prevent any infection – a real risk given the hygiene of his knife. He spent a lot of time recuperating in the stables with Alexander the Great, who had saved his life. No one had discovered the real nature of his relationship with Jalal, and Abdul planned to keep it that way. He felt no need now to expose Salah al Din as a murderer – no prison cell could inflict more pain upon him than he was already suffering from the loss of his son. Abdul's family was finally avenged.

The blow of Jalal's betrayal devastated Prince Bahir. Jalal had been one of the few people in the world he truly trusted. That Jalal had killed the magnificent stallions for insurance money was unthinkable in itself, and his attack on Abdul beggared belief. Abdul was the cornerstone of their horse empire.

But when it came to himself, Bahir could not accept that Jalal had also attempted to murder his own blood brother. Bahir stayed in his room for most of the week after Jalal's death, barely speaking to anyone – not even Clea, who had moved out of the hotel to give him some time alone.

Finally Sheikh Faisal was able to get through to him. 'This isn't your fault, Bahir,' he admonished gently. 'You can't take responsibility for Jalal's actions. He wasn't a child, he was a man with his own agenda.'

'I should have known,' Bahir said in anguish. 'I should have been able to stop him.'

'No, a good man doesn't always recognise evil,' Sheikh Faisal consoled. 'Come, my son, you must show the world you are strong. You can't hide away in here forever.'

Darcy had tried to convince Bahir to see him, and finally Bahir responded to one of his calls and asked him to come up to the villa. Among other things, Darcy was determined that Bahir should understand the situation with Afifah.

'I wanted to talk to you about Afifah,' he said, pacing the room anxiously. 'I'm afraid you've got it all wrong. I should've come to you when I first realised Afifah had a crush on me, but I really thought it would just pass. I'm not in love with her.'

'Have you told her?' Bahir asked with obvious relief.

Darcy nodded. 'She knows, and she's accepted it. Things seem to be slowly returning to normal between us.'

Bahir was puzzled. 'But what about the note? You said you couldn't stop thinking about her – that's very misleading.'

Darcy was caught. 'What note?'

Bahir went to his bedroom and came back with the scribbled bet ticket that he'd kept since the Cox Plate. He handed it to Darcy. 'I'm sorry to say this, Darcy, but I just don't think you're telling me the truth.'

Darcy knew he couldn't lie. Bahir had gone through so much and had been so bitterly deceived by Jalal. Darcy owed him the truth. 'The note wasn't for Afifah.'

Bahir looked at him for a moment, unable to comprehend his meaning. But finally he realised what his friend was implying. 'Clea,' he said, shaking his head.

'I'm sorry, Bahir. But I think I'm in love with her.'

Bahir had every right to be angry, but instead he just looked as if Darcy had knocked the wind out of his sails.

'Does she feel the same way?' he asked, turning quickly away to hide his emotions.

'No. She's in love with you, Bahir, I'm sure of it, but . . . she can't handle the fact that you're married. You'll break her heart.'

'I know.' Bahir looked at his friend sadly. 'But I warn you, Darcy, I'm not giving up.' He paused. 'Do you really love her or is this one of your nine-day wonders?'

Darcy was more certain than ever. 'It's the real thing.'

'Then may the best man win.' Bahir's voice was heavy with resignation. In his heart he knew Clea could never accept the life he offered. Bahir wondered from which direction the next blow would come.

'I'm so sorry about Jalal,' Darcy said, as though he could read Bahir's thoughts.

'I don't know how I could have been so blind,' Bahir said quietly.

Saturday dawned in a burst of golden light to herald one of the great days on the world racing calendar, Derby Day at Flemington Racecourse, where a crowd of over 100 000 was expected. Droves of girls in flimsy dresses and men in polished shoes and smart ties flocked to the track. Those who followed Derby Day tradition were adorned in black and white, making for an elegantly monchromatic crowd, as opposed to the riotous colours and costumes on display at Flemington on Melbourne Cup Day.

Out on the front lawn, Fashions on the Field had kicked off with an eager throng of women and men of all shapes and sizes. The well-dressed group mingled in the fashion corral, anticipating their moment of glory on the catwalk. Feet already shifted uncomfortably under the strain of four-inch heels; mirrors and a myriad of lipsticks were produced for last-minute touch-ups, the sunlight reflections momentarily blinding the audience perched in the grandstand to enjoy the spectacle. Hats were swept high and jauntily tilted, hatinators perched cheekily amid well-coiffed locks and fascinators of all persuasions fluttered in the breeze. The backdrop for this throng was a multitude of roses, tended to perfection in order to bloom on these four days in spring.

A city of marquees had sprung up in an area appropriately called the Birdcage. Plumes of every variety mingled in these coveted havens, each marquee battling to outdo the others with its decor and hospitality. The privileged few milled about inside drinking champagne and eating canapés. Hopefuls strolled past the elaborate entrances, anxious to be recognised and granted access. Those with star power or the right connections relished the art of marquee-hopping, ignoring sore feet to gain best bragging rights. Nowhere was this more evident than the fabled Emirates marquee, reinvented each year with a new decadent theme.

Naturally, the Sheikh and his family were the guests of Emirates, and despite the horror of Jalal's betrayal and tragic death, the Sheikh and Bahir decided to put on a brave face and attend the races. Darcy, dressed in his morning suit, was in the committee room as a guest of one of the members.

Afifah, too, attended, but was battling her inner demons. Although she was elated to be free from her betrothal, she was shattered by what had happened to Jalal. Her black and white striped dress and dashing hatinator seemed inappropriately cheerful for her introspective thoughts. Yvonne was more suitably attired for the mood in a simple black silk dress and a wide-brimmed hat with white linen camellias.

The family converged on the mounting yard when Eclipse Stable had two runners in the Saab Quality, a Group Three race over 2500 metres. Clea greeted Darcy coolly and kept her distance, although she couldn't keep a blush from creeping over her cheeks. Over the past week she'd been consumed by the work of managing the potential EI outbreak and had avoided Darcy as much as possible.

Bahir couldn't help but notice the awkwardness between his friend and Clea. He stood next to her, watching the horses enter the mounting yard.

'I'll be gone soon, back to London, and I so want for you to join me there. I know I can't offer you everything, Clea, but I *can* take care of you, and I can offer so much love.'

Clea was silent for a moment. 'Bahir, my family and my career are here. I can't just leave everything to come and be your mistress. If only . . .' The words hung heavy between them.

'I know,' Bahir said sadly. 'Don't make up your mind yet. Think about it when I'm gone.' But in his heart he knew he had lost her.

Derek and another jockey appeared in the mounting yard decked in the Eclipse colours to ride Marengo and Sun Tzu, although to distinguish each horse they wore different-coloured caps. John gave them final instructions, then he and Abdul legged the jockeys on board.

Clea noticed Abdul taking hold of Marengo's bridle, breathing into his nostrils, and when the horse dipped his head and affectionately nuzzled him, Abdul whispered in his ear.

As the horses paraded out onto the track Darcy took the opportunity to speak to Yvonne, who was standing a little away from the group, leaning on the padded rails.

'You look very smart today, Darcy,' she said admiringly, wondering if one day her own son would look so composed in a morning suit.

'I'll be in the UK again in a few months,' Darcy said, then stared at his hands nervously. 'I was wondering if you'd allow me to meet my brother.'

'I'd be delighted.' Yvonne gave his arm a squeeze and joined the Sheikh as they moved towards the viewing seats, thankful her dark glasses hid the tears that had sprung to her eyes.

Abdul stayed in the mounting yard next to Darcy to watch the race, his binoculars dangling heavily around his neck. Clea stood by Abdul's side, marvelling at the calm of this extraordinary man in the face of all his recent troubles. She interrupted his silence to say, 'I saw you speak to the horse just before the race – can I ask what you said?'

Abdul hesitated for a moment. 'I told him to fly like the southerly wind,' he whispered.

Author's note

Although the *Riding High* story is fictional, the racing world in which it is set is very real. In naming my horses throughout the book, I may have inadvertently used the names of current or past champions. Suffice to say that my horses are strictly fictional characters and do not represent real horses, either living or dead. The same goes for my human characters.

The Eclipse Stable and Ambrose-Taylor colours are my invention and any resemblance to existing race colours is entirely unintentional.

I have been a little flexible with the Dubai racing calendar. The Dubai racing year actually begins in early November and ends with the Dubai World Cup in late March.

The equine influenza outbreak in Australia in 2007 was estimated to have cost the Australian racing industry one billion dollars. The damage was further exacerbated by a substantial reduction in the foal crop, which will undoubtedly impact race fields in the future.

The hendra virus is a deadly zoonotic disease – transmitted between or shared by animals and humans – that has infected six people in Australia and killed three, including a farmer from Mackay in 1995 and a Brisbane vet in 2008. In the initial outbreak, in 1994, a horse trainer and fourteen of his horses died. There has never been a recorded case of hendra in the Hunter Valley. For the purposes of the story, I have allowed Prince Bahir to recover more quickly than the past human infections suggest. My deepest sympathy goes out to all whose lives have been affected by hendra.

Acknowledgements

First and foremost I have to thank my support crew – my darling fiancé Neville Fielke for enriching my life and always believing in me, and my wonderful mother Dulcie Boling for her untiring support and for dragging me away from the computer for coffee when my eyes were going square.

A very special thank you and hug for my editor Belinda Byrne, who is such an inspirational joy to work with, and to Arwen Summers for her valuable work. Also my thanks to my publisher Kirsten Abbott for giving me a go, to everyone else at Penguin who has helped me with *Riding High* and my agent Selwa Anthony.

Other thanks go to my many enthusiastic friends in the racing industry and in particular, equine vet Dr Susannah Hawke, and my dear friend Jo Hutson.

I also want to acknowledge many others who have supported me along the way, including my sister Kate, dad John and close friend Krissy. The list could go on and on – my heartfelt thanks to all.